THE
SILVERBERG
BUSINESS

THE
SILVERBERG
BUSINESS

Robert
Freeman
Wexler

Small Beer Press
Easthampton, MA

Small Beer Press
150 Pleasant Street #306
Easthampton, MA 01027
smallbeerpress.com
weightlessbooks.com
bookmoonbooks.com
info@smallbeerpress.com
Distributed to the trade by Consortium.

Library of Congress Cataloging-in-Publication Data
Names: Wexler, Robert Freeman, author.
Title: The Silverberg business : a novel / Robert Wexler.
Description: First edition. | Easthampton, MA : Small Beer Press, [2022] |
    Summary: "In 1888 in Victoria, Texas, for a simple job, a Chicago
    private eye gets caught up in much darker affairs and ends up in the
    poker game to end all poker games"-- Provided by publisher.
Identifiers: LCCN 2021051418 (print) | LCCN 2021051419 (ebook) | ISBN
    9781618732019 (paperback) | ISBN 9781618732026 (ebook)
Subjects: LCGFT: Detective and mystery fiction. | Novels.
Classification: LCC PS3623.E955 S55 2022 (print) | LCC PS3623.E955
    (ebook) | DDC 813/.6--dc23/eng/20211022
LC record available at https://lccn.loc.gov/2021051418
LC ebook record available at https://lccn.loc.gov/2021051419

First edition 1 2 3 4 5 6 7 8 9

Set in Parkinson Electra Pro.
Printed on 30% PCR recycled paper by the Versa Press, East Peoria, IL.
Author photograph by Regina Brecha.
Cover illustration "The Sea Captain" © 2022 Jon Langford (yarddog.com). All rights reserved.

For Rebecca and Merida

PART I

Victoria, Texas, 1888

Everything was intertwined, with the complexity of a three-dimensional puzzle—a puzzle in which truth was not necessarily fact and fact not necessarily truth.

—Haruki Murakami,
The Wind-Up Bird Chronicle

1

The Business

I woke from another swimming on land dream, the kind where I'm walking, no hurry... until... *I can't remember how.* By the end, I'm on my stomach, unable to move. At least it hadn't been the *other* kind of dream, where I'm after someone, or someone is after me—or some Thing; it's almost on me and I can't shoot my gun. No, that's not it: shooting is complicated. The trigger, I don't know how to use it. I scream the bullets out; they either miss or have no effect. They don't stop what's after me. I always wake up yelling. Embarrassing when you're not alone.

Morning sun slashed through the window. I had gone to bed without closing the curtains. Rolling away from the glare didn't help. Sleep would not come back. I worked to recall where I was: floral wallpaper, chipped washbasin—the room I took last night in the Delmonico Hotel, Victoria, Texas.

I got out of bed, splashed my face at the washbasin, pissed in the pot, and dressed, ending with a brown cotton sack-coat to cover the Bulldog revolver in its shoulder harness. I carried my hat, a brown derby, down to the hotel's restaurant. From the doorway, I studied the room—one quick glance—as I've done in many rooms for the last ten years. Single diner, man, dressed for town, dark vest over white shirt

3

with detachable collar. The shirt looked new. He wasn't heavy and he wasn't thin.

I didn't *need* to examine him, or anyone in the hotel, but that's what I do. Studying a room is a practice I can't stop. Because there are times when doing it keeps me alive.

The waitress was small, with dark hair and a smile that told me nothing except that she was awake and doing what *she* needed to do. Which at this moment was take me to a table. As I passed the man we exchanged nods. The waitress sat me near a window; I watched the flow of pedestrians: a stout woman and two children, a grinning old man covered in soot, a young redheaded woman with a man who had the weathered face of a rancher.

A man glanced in; he wasn't old, but his eyebrows and hair were bone-white. His rusted eyes stared into mine—I froze, unable to act, unable to save myself . . . a wave crashed the shore, then another, waves that towered, that smote the sand with unknowable force. I tried to run, couldn't, tried to crawl, couldn't. The hammer of wave crushed my shell . . . millions of tiny crystal shards mixed with spray-clouded air. Daylight faded. The spent wave departed, leaving sand sculpted into fantastic spirals, and . . . a stench . . . rot . . . the kind of rot you get after a storm passes and the sun bakes whatever the waves dredged from the depths.

Another scent came to me . . . earthy, earthy and pleasing—my hand touched warmth. A mug. The blessed waitress had brought coffee. I drank. Unease receded, waves subsided to harmless foam. The dining room was clean and dry. Outside the windows, sunshine and no white-haired man.

The waitress returned to refill my coffee cup and take my order. Stupidity began to lift. My stomach reminded me that yesterday I had eaten little. I hadn't meant to drink whiskey, not so much anyway. The problem was Galveston—childhood home left long ago. I had been there for a cousin's wedding, also attended by ghosts from the past, particularly one in a green dress. Seeing her had made me wistful, made me reflect on my life in Chicago, the crime investigations and frequent travel to towns where people often resented my presence. She looked happy enough with her husband and three children. To her, my life no doubt appeared adventuresome. Which enforced her belief that she had made the correct decision—women may have romantic notions about adventure, but they choose domestic stability. I can't blame her for being sensible.

My waitress had also brought the local paper, *Victoria Advocate*, dated Saturday, October 27, 1888. Today was Monday the twenty-ninth. I perused a section called "The Outside World, An Interesting Jumble of Both Foreign and Domestic News for Victoria Readers," in which I discovered that the champion boxer John L. Sullivan, at twenty-nine years of age, has made and spent $300,000 in the last three years but is now broke and incapable of fighting; the many dog farms of frozen Manchuria provide us with splendid fur to make our coats, and:

L. Herman, a New York money changer and banker, has disappeared with $5,000 belonging to Polish Jews. The money had been entrusted to his care and was to have been sent to England.

That last item . . . I had been hired to investigate a similar crime. Sometimes, fraud is so apparent yet unrecognized that the intelligence of the whole of humanity becomes questionable. And yet, humanity somehow continues to advance, inventing and creating, as if there's a wall between intelligence and gullibility, so that no matter how educated or experienced a man might be, there's a fraud to which he will fall victim. By that logic, I would have to be included as one of the eventually gullible, but I haven't fallen yet. Unless I was so unaware that I didn't recognize it at the time and still don't.

This is the thinking that keeps a detective awake at night.

I ate my eggs and beef and flapjacks. The other man, his breakfast over, lingered to roll a smoke. A family entered, a man and woman accompanied by miniature versions of themselves.

What brought me to Victoria was a group calling themselves the

Romania-America Relocation Movement. They solicited donations from East Coast Jews to pay for moving Romanian Jewish refugees to a new colony on the Texas coast. Money accumulated in an account in New York. Nathan Silverberg—the man who presented the plan to donors—had been sent to Victoria, carrying a bank draft. On arrival, Silverberg was to open an account, look at property with local representatives and purchase land for the colony. But the settlement was a sham. My job was to find Silverberg and the money.

Silverberg was a well-known and respected member of the Jewish community in New York. Which didn't mean he wasn't part of the swindle, but it was more likely that the swindlers used him to get the money. Either way, I would have to find him. Rabbi Henry Cohen, of Galveston, had hired me. I met him at the wedding and agreed to help. I had things I wanted to get back to in Chicago, but I didn't think this Silverberg business would take me long.

My boss, Arthur Llewelyn of the Llewelyn Detective Agency in Chicago, allows me to take jobs without getting approval from him. I've been with him long enough that he knows I won't say yes to the wrong things. I sent him a telegram from the Galveston train station explaining the situation, telling him the job might take a week or so.

Breakfast over, I got up, leaving the newspaper for the next diner. I set the derby on my head and went outside. Steady rainfall had accompanied my train, and the morning sun steamed the puddled residue. I can't say I enjoy Chicago winter, but I do like a pleasant autumn. I like that there *is* an autumn. Growing up on the Gulf of Mexico, I hadn't known such a thing existed.

I crossed the street, avoiding mud and the swarm of horses and wagons. Victoria's population, I've been told, is approaching 4,000, but it still has the feel of a frontier town. Seeing the sign for a barber's, I stopped and went in for a shave and a mustache trim. Next stop was Sibley and Sons Bank, where Silverberg was to have deposited the check. I entered and approached the clerk, a thin man with gray eyes and beard, and gave him my Llewelyn Detective Agency card.

"I sent a telegram that I would be coming," I said.

"You sure don't look Irish, Mr. Shannon," he said. He went to find the manager.

I've been told I don't look Jewish either. No doubt some people can see the secret marks on my forehead, but most take me as a regular American. I don't feel like one; I doubt Jews will ever feel they belong with the regular Americans. No matter how much freedom there may be here, compared to most of Europe, someone will eventually come along to shove us back into our ghetto.

The family name was Chanun. Changed for convenience by the bilge rats in charge of immigration when my grandparents arrived in New York.

The clerk returned and led me into an office larger than an entire Chicago tenement apartment. A fleshy man in a well-made jacket stood to greet me. He was about my size (five foot eight inches). Beneath his soft exterior, roughness hinted, indicating a different occupation prior to assuming the desk. Probably railroad construction or mining boss. And the scars on his knuckles said brawler.

"Bert Wilson, what can I do for you, Mr. . . . ."—he glanced down at the card—" . . . Shannon. What brings you to Texas?" I shook Wilson's pudgy but not weak hand, then sat. He kept talking. "We don't get many detectives around here. Did have to call in the Pinkertons last June. Trade union agitators disrupted railroad construction around Stockton. I suppose you know about that kind of thing, up in Chicago. They catch all them bombers?"

"They caught some people. Maybe the right people." Two years had passed since the bombings in the Haymarket. Four men had been hung, others remained in prison.

"Make an example, I say. Don't know how *you* do things, but down here we string 'em up good." He smacked his desk, rattling the inkpot.

The problem with the kind of thinking you get from the Wilsons of the world is that it ignores the idea of uncovering truth and giving someone a fair trial. He wouldn't know anything besides bombs and anarchists. What happened was, some lunatic brought a bomb to what was supposed to be a peaceful meeting. They were radicals, sure, but that doesn't mean they can't get together in public. The mayor had even been there. After he left, the police moved in to disperse everyone. The bomb-thrower probably thought he was defending his brethren from an illegal attack by the police. That doesn't make it okay, but it also doesn't make it a conspiracy or premeditated act by the entire group.

When the bomb exploded, the police ran away, firing wildly and mostly at each other. They returned, angry and looking for revenge, shooting and clubbing as they came. Most of the wounded police were injured in a manner indicating they were fired on by other police, and the bullets dug out of them were the same caliber that the police used. Despite reports of killed and wounded agitators numbering far more than the police, no one ever discovered what happened to them. They sure weren't in morgues or hospitals. I know because I looked.

Next, hysteria, plots and counter-plots ferreted out by brave policemen, frenzied claims in the press of bombs that would never have worked being found in unlikely places. Then, arrests. The prosecution lied and didn't prove anything. They convicted some of the meeting's organizers, but they couldn't show that there had been anything illegal about the meeting. Maybe some of the people arrested were actually guilty of favoring violence, but that's not the same thing as committing violence. The whole thing stunk, and thinking about it made me angry.

Truth is always a juxtaposition of facts.

I pushed the subject back to my visit. "I need information about money that was deposited here." I gave him Silverberg's name, approximate dates, and the amount of money. Wilson bellowed for the clerk. The gray eyed man reappeared, left to retrieve the ledger that Wilson told him to find, and returned with a leather-bound book.

"Mr. Shannon . . . "—Wilson's eyes remained downcast at the ledger—"was this money to be used by legitimate interests? What I mean to say is, what can you tell me about it—who are you after?"

"Let's see what your records tell us, Mr. Wilson. I'm sure your bank did nothing unlawful." I *wasn't* sure, but didn't see a reason to say so.

The office showed me that the bank was prospering. The size (though size in Texas means less than it does in a city like Chicago), the furnishings—mahogany desk, leather-cushioned chairs, gas lighting. Sometimes prosperity comes honestly, sometimes from active unlawfulness, sometimes from allowing things to happen. Not long ago, I read about a bank in Wharton, Texas, that had recently made a profit by selling notes to railroad workers, mostly Mexican, guaranteeing them seventy-five cents for each dollar owed them by their employer. The railroad paid every ninety days, and workers needed their money sooner. It wasn't illegal—but it took advantage of the workers and made money for the bank.

"Ah, account opened September fifth, closed on the twelfth." He shut the ledger. "Anything else I can assist you with?"

"I need to talk to whoever handled the opening and closing."

Wilson made a noise in his throat, like he had things he would rather do than help me. He started humming "The Yellow Rose of Texas" and reopened the ledger, making a production of it. Ignoring him, I opened my notebook and jotted the information he had given me so far. His humming stopped.

"Here we are. Looks like it was Owens, Joshua Owens, but he's away. Gone to Goliad to see an ailing sister."

"I'll need addresses for both."

With the Wilson business ended, I found the telegraph office and sent a message to Goliad for Joshua Owens or his sister, asking Owens to let me know how much longer he would be there. I didn't want to leave for Goliad if he was on his way back. Next, I went to Levi Bank and asked to see the manager. Levi was Jewish. My client, Rabbi Cohen, had mentioned him. A *real* plan for resettling Jews would have used Levi's bank. The clerk I talked to said Mr. Levi was busy. I gave him a calling card and said I could wait. Which I did. My profession involves a fair amount of waiting. I don't mind. Waiting gives the brain a chance to work out problems. Crime solving, thief-taking, depends on the brain.

Sure, there's rough stuff, but that's a small part of it. I wouldn't recommend the job to a person who's shy about banging someone around, or getting banged around, but I prefer a thinker over a brawler.

To occupy my time, I took out a pamphlet that the rabbi had given me and glanced through the sea of words that painted a fantasy. After a while, the clerk came to get me. This banker's office was smaller, more sedate, and the man who greeted me was a lot more savory than Wilson. He said he was Abraham Levi, the owner. He shook my hand. I told him who I was working for and gave him the pamphlet. One of Rabbi Cohen's Eastern correspondents sent it to him after the rabbi had started asking questions about the settlement scam.

"I received a letter from Rabbi Cohen, with a description of this," Levi said. He spoke with an accent that I thought was French. He was in his sixties, not stout, not thin, with a neat white beard. I gave him time to read through the material.

"The situation in so much of Eastern Europe is deplorable," he said when he finished. "We all want to help. The way this pamphlet is put together, everything sounds wonderful. To someone who doesn't know the area."

"They went to all the big Eastern cities, telling audiences how bad it is for Romanian Jews. Silverberg and a man named Rafkin, who claimed to be a recent immigrant from Bucharest."

"Tell me about this man Rafkin," Levi said.

"According to the rabbi's sources, Rafkin was small, with dark hair and bad teeth. He spoke in a thick accent that might have been Eastern European. He said he had been living in St. Louis, with a cousin, after escaping from Romania."

"There was a man here last January," Levi said. "He had teeth that were quite rotten. His name wasn't Rafkin. I have a letter in my correspondence file that will show whatever he called himself. He had an accent and spoke of Romania. He said he lived in St. Louis and showed me copper pots and pans that he sold for a company in New York. He wanted to supply my store. Besides the bank, my family owns a dry-goods store. I recognized the pans but have always dealt with the manufacturer directly. I wrote to them, and they had no knowledge of this man."

"I'll send Rafkin's description to my office and see if they can contact someone in St. Louis. That might be a fake, but it's something to try. The fact that he's mentioned St. Louis twice makes me think that part is real."

"I find that no matter how many times I encounter such behavior, the capacity for man to injure his fellow always surprises me," Levi said. "The Chicago criminologist G. Frank Lydston explains it with something he calls neuro-psychic degeneracy. I don't know what I think any more."

Levi started talking about Jewish life in Victoria and other parts of Texas. I didn't give it all my attention because another thought started knocking around in my head, something that had been bothering me but hadn't coalesced into anything definite. A clerk came in and handed him a note and left. During the pause I realized I was ready to speak.

"What you said about people's desire to help," I said. "That's the thing that bothers me about this business. These people are taking advantage of that desire. Most crime of this sort, most of your complex, conniving schemes, are about tapping into greed. This mess is nastier because it's the opposite. It hurts more than just someone's bank account. Next time a legitimate organization, say, the Hebrew Immigrant Aid Society, needs help, people might hesitate, because along with the money, these gonifs have taken their basic trust in humanity."

Levi said he would talk to members of the congregation and tell me if Silverberg had met anyone while he was here. He also invited me to Sabbath services if I was still in the area Friday night. I didn't commit. I'm comfortable enough around other Jews, I feel kinship for them, but the worship part isn't for me.

I thanked him and returned to the telegraph office, where I had to wait while the clerk and a young woman bantered about something they thought was funny. The rabbi had given me the names of some of Silverberg's friends and business associates. I sent messages to them, asking if Silverberg had ever had dealings in St. Louis. On my way out of the telegraph office, I saw a glimmer of white hair ducking into a nearby building; I followed. I couldn't tell if it was the man who had looked in at me in the restaurant earlier, but I don't believe in coincidence.

The entry I thought he had gone into led to a store selling ladies' dresses. Inside, the only person there was a dark-haired woman behind the counter. I nodded at her and left. A dead fish and seaweed smell erupted. I leaned against a wall . . . waves, and more waves . . . when had a storm begun? But there was no storm. Sunlight continued to pummel the street; even the morning's mud was a distant memory.

2

The Gambler and the Laundress

Needing to stop and sit, I went into a tavern on the next block and drank a beer with a bowl of chili. Storms and their wreckage haunted me. Indianola, the town described in the brochure, had been quite the growing port until a couple of hurricanes flattened it, back in '75 and again just two years ago. The last hurricane had been so bad that no one wanted to live there anymore. The people of Galveston couldn't help gloating at the demise of a rival port. Hurricanes knocked through Galveston too, but my birthplace has continued to pick itself up and start over. People claim that the town is safe, quoting various geographic attributes. I hope they're right.

Assuming that Silverberg was innocent, someone running a scam based on Indianola's continued health would need to take the money from him before he learned what things were really like. Victoria was still recovering from *its* storm damage. Which meant that they couldn't completely hide from Silverberg the existence of hurricanes. *If* they were hiding things from him. To hell with all that. It's best not to speculate too much. Accumulating enough information will bring the facts into alignment. Some people claim to rely on the mind's tingle, as if the answer can emerge from nothing. I say, to reach that tingle, the brain needs feeding. Accumulate the facts. Without all the facts, no tingle. A watch without its escapement is a tiny pile of metal junk. With it, you have a mechanism to predict what minute will occur next.

Rabbi Cohen, my client, came to Texas from England, via Jamaica and Mississippi. Though he had only lived in Galveston a few months, he had already learned much about the city and the rest of Texas. When a friend in Philadelphia wrote of having contributed money to the new colony near Indianola, Cohen knew that something was wrong. He started asking questions and writing letters, and when he met me at the wedding and learned what I do, he talked me into helping. One thing I learned in my short time with him—the man could convince just about anyone to work for a good cause. The condition of Jews in Eastern Europe is a common enough topic; a charity to aid them wouldn't be considered unusual. To those on the East Coast, Texas is mysterious and exotic. The people running the scam could gamble that no one would know enough to challenge them.

From family history, I knew something about persecution. My father's parents got caught up in the Polish-Russian War in 1831. They fled Lithuania when my father was a child and settled in Charleston. My mother was born in Charleston, as were her parents. Her grandparents were from Germany. My parents moved to Galveston a couple of years after my older sister was born. They opened a family grocery at Church and 22nd Street and lived over it. I was born there, then my younger sister four years later. Secession and the war sent us to Houston, but after that mess ended, the island drew us back. I was ten. My parents rebuilt the business, eventually sold it and bought a hardware store, which they later expanded into a ship's outfitter. I never wanted to be a shopkeeper. I tried school, and a few years on schooners—preferring them to steamships—then worked as a customs inspector.

The customs department was where I started learning about being a detective. They had me infiltrate a gang of opium smugglers. I had been away at sea, and my story was that I was tired of being a sailor and wanted to make some money. A kid I knew was involved, the younger brother of a schoolmate. Along the way, I decided not to let him be snared when the net closed. The night the shipment came in, I met him in a saloon and told him to get himself very drunk. I said it wouldn't be a good idea to attend the event. I went to jail with the gang and spent a night in a cell with several of them. My bosses had arranged for people to be shuffled into different cells the next morning. At which point, I returned to the customs house to write my report.

After all that, they thought I should leave Galveston for a while. I ended up in Chicago, working for old Arthur Llewelyn, abolitionist unionist Chartist son of a Welsh coal miner.

Chartists were workers trying to improve their situations. Llewelyn had edited a Chartist newspaper in Newport, Wales. The 1839 Newport Rising disillusioned him. His cousin was killed. He moved to France, then America. Pinkerton had been a Chartist and abolitionist too. Maybe something about the movement made you a good detective. Llewelyn knew Pinkerton and worked with him for a time. They differed on some issues and methods, but both believed in catching criminals.

The tavern was getting crowded, and I decided to give another patron my stool. Patches of clouds now shrouded the sun, predicting an evening thunderstorm. I passed the town marshal's office; through the front window, I could see a man sitting at a desk, feet propped, hat over his eyes. I hoped that wasn't the marshal. I didn't want to work with someone who slouched at his desk like that. Dinnertime was approaching, but I stopped at the telegraph office first. My wire to Joshua Owens had produced a response. His sister said that Owens had returned to Victoria this morning.

Owens lived in a rooming house called Kreke's, on Wheeler Street. The place was run by a dark-eyed young woman with her hair wrapped in a colorless scarf. She didn't say if her name was Kreke, but did invite me to join the guests for dinner. I declined; I wanted to talk to Owens alone. We stood in the parlor. From there, we could hear the boarders arriving for their dinner. Owens was about my height, though his thinness made him look taller, with hair receded to a dark shrub that started around his ears and went all the way across the top of his head. He had joined the Rebel army near the end of the war and left for California after. Came back when his parents died. He had to have enlisted young, because he couldn't have been much more than forty. Which was common enough. Too much enthusiasm for war, in those days.

He remembered Silverberg. "He opened an account and made a large deposit. He was with two other men . . . I don't recall their names. One of them had an account with us under the name Riverside Land Agents. The Riverside man said they should add Silverberg to his account and deposit the money there. Silverberg said not until he saw the property. Silverberg seemed impatient, but relaxed after the money was deposited.

"I asked for a local address for the account. The other man answered. 'He is staying with friends for now. You can use the address on the Riverside account.'"

I said I would need that address; he said he would look it up for me at the bank tomorrow. "Tell me about Silverberg. What did he look like?"

Owens thought for a minute; he glanced toward the dining room, as if worried he would miss dinner. "Short and round. What I call a happy belly. Someone who has enough money to be comfortable. After the money was deposited and he relaxed, you could tell he was someone who liked to tell a joke or two. Only other thing, he had a watch, an elegant one, that he took out a few times. I admired it, and he let me have a look. It was gold. The inside of the cover was engraved 'To NS from CS, Love.'"

Owens's description of Silverberg, including the watch, matched what the rabbi had given me. "Wilson said Silverberg closed the account."

"Must've." Owens's face showed annoyance—at Wilson, I hoped.

"Did he withdraw as cash?"

"I wasn't there. I opened the account, that's all."

Which wasn't how Wilson told it. I thought I'd push Owens for more information. "Do you think Wilson would hide anything from me? What's his game?"

Owens walked to the front door and looked out the glass panel. I gave him time to continue. When I thought he was ready, I assured him that everything he said would be held in confidence. "And I would appreciate if you didn't tell anyone at the bank that we met. Wilson might ask. I was pretty firm about getting your sister's address to send a telegram. There are things I wouldn't mind knowing . . . like who closed Silverberg's account. Wilson said *you* did." He flinched; I pretended not to notice. "I would also like to know if the Riverside account is still there and how much money it has."

Owens turned to face me. "Sibley is a good man, but he's often away, and puts too much trust in Wilson. I've seen irregularities. Nothing big, but enough to make me think more is happening. I'm leaving the bank soon. My sister needs me, and I don't want to get caught up in whatever Wilson is doing."

I had him describe the Riverside men.

"One was big, with dark hair, nice city clothes. He smiled and laughed a lot. A real back-slapper. The other was small, some kind of foreigner. He didn't say much."

We arranged to meet at the rooming house tomorrow around the same time. Lightning decorated the eastern sky, but I managed to reach my hotel before the rain came. I ate steak and fried potatoes in the hotel restaurant. In the lounge, I looked at a shelf of books, choosing *A Texas Cowboy* by Charles A. Siringo. It had come out a few years ago. Siringo, as I learned, was born the same year as me, down the coast on Matagorda Island.

Before settling in to read, I put a report together for old Llewelyn. He demanded daily updates. That can be difficult when you're using a fake identity while buried amongst a gang of cutthroat thieves. Which meant that on this job, I didn't have any excuses not to do it. I sifted facts. Owens's story bothered me. Blaming Wilson felt too easy. His helpfulness felt too easy. And I never trust a man with small hands and small feet.

The storm grew more intense. Hurricane, Captain Bellis said; he sent me and Florkey up to reef the sails. The boat settled into the wind, but we had a sleepless and active night to look forward to before we could pull into the safety of the railway station. I stepped down from the train. There was Millicent, waiting for me. But who was that white-haired man with his arm in hers? I ran at them, screeching and waving my arms. He pointed a finger at my chest and I stopped moving. Wilson sat across his desk from me, meaty hands pummeling the mahogany. "Hang 'em good . . . cut off their balls and eat them! That'll teach those fuckers what happens if you try to cheat a man in Texas."

The clock in the room had yet to reach midnight. That was a lot of dream for a short time.

Sleep returned at some point. Daylight arrived. I went to breakfast in the hotel dining room. The family from yesterday was already eating, and a fat man with curly red hair sat at a table near theirs. Coffee helped send me back to the living. I ate and let my thoughts tumble and mingle. Owens's back-slapper would likely have shown Silverberg a property that he could pass off as a potential site for the colony. That would be the only way to convince Silverberg to release the money. Silverberg's account had been closed, therefore the inspection had been successful. But where, then, was Silverberg? And why did Owens flinch when I mentioned that Wilson said Owens was the one who closed the account?

The railroad had recently pushed the line through to Port Lavaca, running one train a day, mornings at 10:30. Back-slapper and company probably rode a train to Port Lavaca, then hired a wagon to drive to the coast. I reached the station early enough to talk to the conductor. And I got lucky first try. It happens. Not as much as I would like. Not that getting lucky is just luck. A good detective has to know how to talk to people. Railroad conductors don't like detectives. One of the Pinkerton agency's first jobs was spying on conductors to see which ones were running ticket scams. Sure, the railroads needed to do that, but you can't blame the honest conductors for being unhappy. Or the dishonest ones.

The conductor was a thin man with a thin mustache and thin black hair. I showed him my card. "We're not like Pinkertons," I said. "The boss doesn't hire us out to spy on workers. He doesn't hire us out to break strikes. We worked for the Order of Railway Conductors in the Illinois Central strike."

"I heard about that. Heard your people were fair."

He said his name was Caldwell and that maybe he could help. I told him what I was after and gave the range of dates. He said he wanted to get a cup of coffee. We went into the caboose. He filled a pot from a jug of water, put another log in the stove, and ground a handful of beans. From the temperature in the room, I thought the stove was plenty hot already. Maybe he needed the extra heat to make his memory work, because he did do some remembering.

"Funny thing happened around that time. Three men came aboard. One I recognized, gambler named Stephens. Another was a Western man. He had on nice new Eastern clothes, but you can always recognize a Western man, even in Eastern clothes. He was bigger and louder than Stephens, but Stephens was the one in charge. The nice-dressed man deferred to him on everything. The third was an Easterner. Directly, I took the Easterner's bag and helped him up the steps. While I had my back to him I heard him say something about how excited he was to see Indianola. Stephens said: 'Remember, caution.' I let on that I hadn't heard. I hear lots of things. It's best to be deaf to what you hear people say." He filled two mugs and we left to find cooler air.

"Trying to pass Lavaca off as Indianola," I said. I handed him the pamphlet and we sat on the caboose steps.

Indianola is the Seat of Calhoun County. It is situated on a Commanding bluff, averaging twenty feet high, which extends for

many miles above and below town. No Texas coast city occupies
a spot as Beautiful, and for many years it has been a Favorite place
of resort for Health and Pleasure seekers. The city is provided with
Superb means of communication, both by rail and water, and is
the natural trade center of the State.

This superb county, by far Superior to any on the Texas coast, is
located in a region that now attracts national attention on account
of Rich soil and an Equable climate and is often called the New
California. The seasons never fail, and the inhabitants have health
and comfort the year around.

The land is a series of peninsulas and islands. Every part is con-
tinually swept by the Cool and Refreshing salt breezes that destroy
malarial germs. Fever, the scourge of so many rich agricultural dis-
tricts of Southern latitude, is Unknown. The waters surrounding
the county teem with millions of fish and oysters, and easy and
cheap transportation to the markets of the world is afforded.

The farmer has something growing each month in the year,
and always finds an easy market for winter grown vegetables. Even
those from the wintery regions of Eastern Europe can labor in
open air in the hottest months and enjoy health and comfort. In
fact, the county is a Sanitarium.

Texas is a land free from persecution, with no restrictions on
business ventures or even the holding of Political Office. There
are but few Negroes in the county, and the political and Race
troubles that disturb the Black belts will never occur. Immigration
is pouring in and farming is taking the place of the cattle business.
Inquiries come from every state in the Union and all parts of the
World. You must act quickly to secure your place!

Caldwell slapped the pamphlet against the side of the caboose. "I'll
help you. I don't like cheats. My brother-in-law lost some of his people
in that last storm. That will never be a place anybody ought to live."

I told Caldwell about Rafkin but he said no one like that had been
with the group. He described Stephens: whitish hair, somewhat taller

than average, red-brown eyes, a tendency toward fancy dress. "He wears a ring, onyx, with a carving in it, Greek god or some such. He's a mean one, too. Never heard a good thing about him, though I am predisposed to dislike gamblers."

According to Caldwell, Stephens had a way of *being* threatening without saying anything. Caldwell claimed that Stephens didn't have that effect on him, but he had seen it with others. It's a trait I've encountered. For some, the line between humanity and wild creature is thin and unpredictable; the beast lurks just beneath the surface, warning off the weaker animals.

Was Stephens the man who walked past the hotel restaurant and stared in at me? White...blond...storm of white-capped waves gouged the coast...an oak that had stood for centuries screamed and gave up its life...nothing remained, nothing but naked earth twisted into shapes of the dead and dying. I cried for the land, but what use are tears?

Across from the Sibley bank, I waited for Owens to leave for lunch, then went in. Owens was likable enough, but that didn't mean he was telling the truth. Someone wasn't. And even if he was, he didn't have to know everything I did.

The clerk from yesterday was there, but Wilson was out. I told the clerk what I needed. He looked and told me that Riverside still had an account (containing $82.36). The name on the account was George Granger. The clerk said he didn't know this Granger personally. He gave me an address that led me to two-story frame building that had once been a house. A laundry occupied half the ground floor, and, no surprise, the other side was vacant. A TO LET sign said to inquire at Mrs. Farber's laundry. Through the window I could see a desk, chairs, and cabinets. I went over to the laundry. A bare-armed woman hummed "Oh Susanna" while muscling a load of sheets through the wringer. The bell on the door hadn't disturbed her any. A counter had another bell. I rapped on it a couple of times.

"In a minute," she said. Her voice had a sweeter tone than I had expected from the size of her cranking arm and the thickness of her neck. She finished running the sheet through and draped it over a line, then ambled on over. Up close, she was younger than I had thought. She had an inch or two and at least ten pounds on me. "What'll it be, mister?" She leaned across the counter and looked toward my feet. "Don't see a bag of washin'."

"Are you Mrs. Farber?"

"Guess so. Haven't seen my no-account Mr. Farber in ten years. Lawyer said I could call that abandonment and get a divorce, but I ain't bothered to yet. Well, if it ain't washing, you must be asking about the space next door."

"I don't want to rent it, but . . . I am interested in your previous tenant. What can—"

"That cocksucker?" She smacked the counter harder than Wilson had slapped his desk at the bank. "Gone and owes me six months' rent. That's what I know. Marshal didn't have no interest in my problem. He must've done something else. You wouldn't be here otherwise."

"The marshal didn't send me." I pulled out a card. She didn't say she couldn't read, but I told her what it said. "These Riverside men cheated some people out of a lot of money. I hope you can help me find them."

Her description of the tenant matched Owens and Caldwell's well-dressed Westerner. "Came to me in August. Called himself George Granger. Said he was a land agent needed a new office. I don't care who I rent to. Last tenant before that was a Mex who said he was a lawyer. Good tenant. This Granger promised he'd pay for six months rent. I had another party couldn't pay that much at once so I said yes. He moved in a few sticks of furniture, hung a sign. Was there little more'n a month, and I never saw any business going in or out. Sometimes I saw him and an even fancier-dress feller with white hair. Not an old man, but hair all white. Saw him up close later and don't ever want to again.

"Whenever I went to ask about the rent there weren't nobody around. One time I let myself in with my key and went through everything." She stopped and looked at my face.

"What I would've done," I said, trying to sound agreeable. "It's only his place if he pays for it. What did you find?"

Her gaze shifted over my shoulder; the bell on the door chimed. I turned to see a woman wearing a dark blue shawl on her head along with an equally dark dress.

"Got your things right here, Mrs. Barlow," Mrs. Farber said to the new woman. She ducked under the counter and came up with a tight-wrapped bundle of clothes. Mrs. Barlow paid and left.

"She's particular about her husband's shirts. He's a preacher. Handsome man too, not like the preacher where my mama took me." After some sentences about the preacher, she rambled back to the subject. "Nothing in there but a file drawer full of junk: newspapers stuffed in envelopes, old handbills."

"Things to make it look like a robust business," I said. "That's a pretty standard trick. If he needed to impress whoever he was talking to, he could open the drawer and a visitor would think it was filled with important documents."

"I found me a telegram on the desk. From a Nathan Silver ... Silver-something. Said which train he was coming in on, next day. I was planning on going down to the station, but had too much washing. The girl who helps me didn't come in like she was supposed to. I kept a lookout best I could. When I had a chance, I went over there. Three men were inside, that Granger feller, Whitey, and one other. Granger noticed me and tapped Whitey. Whitey got up quick and pushed through the door. His eyes were the color of dried blood. I don't know why, but that scared me the most. Once I saw those eyes, I couldn't move nothing. He said they'd pay me when they was ready to. He got really close, put his face up to mine and said to get away from their business. Said he knew I wouldn't want anything to happen to the building. He backed me down. I'm ashamed to say it. Me, strong as most men. You don't believe me?"

I assured her that I did, but she wasn't satisfied. She extended her right arm and flexed it. "You feel this muscle."

I did, and was as impressed as I had expected to be. "Strength isn't the only thing," I said. "Some people are more used to violence. You seem like a kind and gentle person, Mrs. Farber. It's hard to fight nastiness if you're not accustomed to it."

"Thanks, Mister. This building is all I have. My poor late daddy and his family built it right after they got here from Bavaria."

"Was that the last time you saw Granger, Mrs. Farber?"

"I sure don't like that Farber name. You call me Angie. My daddy said hold on to the property. He said even if I get married don't let my husband have title. He must've known I'd marry a no-account. My daddy was a good builder. I was sorry to have to rent half the bottom floor, but I need the money. Washing don't pay enough. Daddy had him a lumberyard. I was sawing wood almost before I was walking, and I sawed wood till I was fifteen and the Yanks burned everything up. Then I lit out with that no-account and prospected for silver. Swinging a pick and hammer is like sawing. Washing's easy work after that. Least I get to stay inside."

I let her talk. Sometimes, people have to say their bit. You never know what useful things you can pick up by listening, and showing an interest helps you gain someone's trust. Not that all I'm after is making someone tell me things. I *do* care about people, sometimes even the people I've shot or had arrested.

Once she got back to the subject of the renter I asked if I could go next door to look around. She handed me a key. The desk was clean. The file cabinet still held its worthless filler. The only useful thing I found in the place was a receipt from Ubder's Furniture. Maybe they hadn't been paid either. Multiple creditors would be useful with the local law. Finished there, I went back to the laundry to return the key, and went off to chase my next objective.

3

Poker

Galveston kids learn to deal poker soon after they start walking, sometimes before. All port cities are like that. If not poker, then whatever form of gambling is popular in that particular nation. Sailors came off their ships ready to blow their money on whores and gambling. If they were newcomers to our fair isle, kids lounging at the docks would show them where to go. Tavern owners hired kids to round up new business. From watching the games to dealing our own was a short ride. As a kid I played my share. I learned about spotting cheats and how to use the odds to keep from losing too much. Mostly because I had a good teacher, a Galveston tavern owner named Tarpon Bill. The Tarpon could detect his opponents' tells like he was reading their minds, and he played according to the odds and the hierarchy of the cards, playing with what he considered the best and folding on everything else.

The same patience that helps with detective work is good for poker. I have a group I play with in Chicago. Not high stakes, but high enough. There has to be sufficient money involved to make you care about what you're doing. Otherwise, it's just a game.

Wherever you go, you find crooked games and honest ones. Some towns are able to run off all the card sharps. Some sharps work for a particular saloon; those are harder to eliminate. I suppose if no one gambled with them, they would move along, but I've never heard of that happening. Too many people have trouble believing the evidence of their vanished money (and property); they keep playing, hoping to win everything back. Your occasional player doesn't understand that he is no match for a professional, whether cheat or honest.

Am I a gambler? I sift facts. I plod along. I choose a winner.

So, finding this gambler Stephens with the white hair and red eyes required visiting saloons, many saloons. I played the role of visitor from Chicago, looking for a good game. Here's how it went at the first saloon I tried, a place called Poison Alley. I found the owner, a bald man with a body so thin I had trouble finding him when he turned sideways. "I'm looking for some poker. The man at the hotel said to stay away from a sharp named Stephens. He ever play here?"

"No sharps. How do I know you ain't a sharp looking for an easy game? Cow hands, meat packers, they come here, drink, play cards, go home."

Poison Alley occupied the kind of shack that usually appears at mining camps or end-of-the-line towns that pick up and move along with the track-layers. Surprising that the hurricane hadn't sent it to Oklahoma or farther. I suppose it could have been slapped together from wreckage after the storm, but its bar showed too much grime and gouging.

Despite the owner's glares, I played a few hands with a couple of cowboys.

Part of being a detective is effective play-acting. When I first went to work for Llewelyn, he made me spend two months apprenticing with the Ronald P. Smith Theatre Company. They were a Chicago-based outfit that toured the West. Professor Smith, as he liked to be called, was a former Englishman. It was pretty well known that his name had been different in the old country, but whatever it was, and why-ever he changed it, he taught me makeup, costuming, and creating a character. I even had to perform.

One of the products of this training was Irish Shannon, based on the mistake people make about my name. He was the friendly one, the one people like to talk to. I decided to let Irish Shannon do some work.

The afternoon was going to involve drinking.

I went into Wykline's and ordered a whiskey. The proprietor cultivated a thin, gray mustache to go with his fat, gray head, but he was friendlier than the man at Poison Alley.

"Now then," I said. "This drink looks very fine, and I smell a pot of venison stew bubbling away like a Kerry brook, but it's poker I'm after. I've just arrived in your lovely town and don't know a soul. Poker is the game of the gods, you see. Played on Mount Olympus. Invented by Apollo himself, did you know? We poor mortals are allowed to partake, of that I'm glad. The gods have their Rules of Play and I am but a follower. Those who follow the rules will never be turned away. Now, as I have overcome the inertia of youth and learned these rules, here I am. What say you about this fine establishment?"

The man paused his mopping the bar with a dirty rag. "I don't chase gamblers away. They're good for trade. If you're a gambler—sharp, I mean—you do what you want. You get caught cheating, someone will shoot you. Or I will."

"That's very fine," I said. "Always best to know the house rules. And I'll not ask to see your weapon of choice because with me, there'll be no cause for your using it. I won't call myself a sharp, though I do play better than most. If I'm needing some money for my pocket, I'll take a game with simpletons. If I want to exercise my brain, I choose a game with the best of the lot.

"Most of all, I prefer an establishment that doesn't serve customers drinks made from the same formula they use in their lamps. Though if an establishment has gas lighting it becomes difficult to observe that distinction." I raised my glass and sipped.

Nine saloons later, I knew less than when I started. This Stephens was a man whom no one wanted to talk about, if they even admitted knowing him. I wasn't happy, but at least I wasn't hungry. Most places have a free pot of stew or beans going—food helps keep the customers inside. The biscuits and beef stew at Barring Saloon had been excellent, though the owner, an elephant of a man with a nose like a mushroom, didn't like my questions. Could be he just didn't like questions. Could be he liked having Stephens or another gambler run a crooked game. By day's end, I learned that Stephens sometimes played cards at Dixon's, Friedlander's, and the tent in an alley with no name, but no one could—or would—recall when they last saw him or say when they thought he might be back.

Evening came, time to meet Owens; I accepted the invitation from his landlady and sat down to cornbread, German sausage, and greens. I'd been eating and drinking all day, but the solution for excess is to keep going. Tonight, the only other diners were the landlady and her mother, a mostly silent woman of advancing years who ate nothing but well-buttered cornbread. Owens talked about California after the war. I had the impression there was more unsaid. We avoided the subject of the bank till the old lady left the table. Getting back to her knitting, she said. The landlady cleared our dishes. Owens pulled a satchel from under his chair and led me to the parlor.

"I found things," Owens said. His voice shook with suppressed excitement. He took a bank ledger from the satchel and opened it. "See here, September twelfth, Silverberg transferred everything into the Riverside account and closed his. The Riverside account is still open, but most of the money was withdrawn . . . *in cash* . . . two days after Silverberg's money was transferred into it."

He flipped to the first page and pointed—"Here's where Silverberg signed when he opened his account"—then back—"and here's when he closed the account. It isn't the same signature."

I agreed that the signatures didn't match, though I only had his word that the first signature was truly Silverberg's. "Who was the clerk?"

"Says Paxon, Mike Paxon, but I *know* it wasn't him. Paxon's writing is neat. His mama was a schoolteacher. She taught all the kids around here how to write properly. The only man in the bank who writes messy like this is Wilson."

I thanked him for the information. "Wilson told me Silverberg closed his account on the twelfth. He didn't say anything about moving the money to Riverside's. Didn't mention Riverside at all. Does he know this Riverside man?"

Owens said he wasn't sure. The address he showed me for Riverside matched what I had gotten from the clerk. He said he had to return the ledger tonight, before anyone noticed its absence. Wilson had been in the office that morning but had left to inspect out-of-town properties. Otherwise Owens wouldn't have dared take the book. I told him where I was staying, in case he needed to send me a message. We left the rooming house. I said we should avoid being seen together, and went off down an alley. Partway, I turned and went back, reaching the street in time to see him growing smaller with distance. I followed.

Blaming Wilson, finding the forged signature and the sloppy writing was too easy. I don't trust easy. Forging Silverberg's signature on the account—they only could have done that if the clerk didn't know what Silverberg looked like, or if he helped them.

The forged signature meant that Silverberg was dead.

I tugged off my reversible sack-coat and turned it inside out, transforming it from brown to gray, pulled my crushable bowler from a pocket, and dressed my head with it. A plug of tobacco in my cheek altered the shape of my face, and I affected the rolling gait of a cowhand. I was confident enough of Owens's destination to keep a lot of distance between us. He turned up the alley between the bank and the next building, and I stopped behind a stack of crates. The alley was empty of passersby. He unlocked the back door and went in. A few minutes later, he exited, minus the ledger, and walked back to where he had entered the alley, passing my hiding pace. He turned the corner; I waited another minute and followed.

His next stop was Sitterle's, one of the saloons I had visited earlier, a block down from my hotel. Sitterle's was long, narrow, and clouded with tobacco smoke. It was mostly bar, with a few tables toward the back. Owens approached a skinny man wearing a brown vest. I tilted my hat to hide more of my face and found an empty stool. The smoky atmosphere helped with my hurried disguise. Owens and the other man talked. I couldn't catch anything. The skinny man did most of the listening. Owens handed him something in an envelope. The skinny man looked down at the envelope, looked inside, then nodded. That's the universal language of accepting money. Owens went over to a table where a game of draw was in progress. The skinny man left. I considered following, but thought it more important to stick with Owens.

Owens watched the game. I had a feeling that he wanted to join, but there wasn't a chair available. I recognized one of the players, Saul Malley, from my Galveston boyhood. We had shared a piano teacher and an interest in cards.

It wouldn't have been a bad game to join. People were staying in on too many hands—an indicator of weak players. The kind of players you can win money from, but you have to be careful. Sometimes weak players are too dumb to fold when you're bluffing. Malley wasn't one of the weak players.

Owens left; I followed him back to the rooming house. He entered through the front door; I went around to the alley, in case he had noticed me and planned to leave through the back. An upstairs light came on. His silhouette appeared in the window. If he had seen me, he would go to the curtain and pull it aside to look. He didn't. I spat out the tobacco and returned to Sitterle's. When the current hand ended, I let Malley see me. His face showed no surprise, mostly—only someone who knew him well would have noticed the way he blinked twice and pushed his glasses closer to his eyes.

"Taking a break, boys," he said, and swept up his earnings.

We shook hands. Malley was nearly six feet tall, with dark hair and gold, oval glasses. His dexterous fingers had given him more success at music and poker than my stubby digits could manage.

"Has it been ten years?" he asked.

"Close," I said. "I left in '77. I've been back a few times to see the family, but never stay long. We played some cards in '80, when I was there for my sister Naomi's wedding. I'd heard you'd moved but not to where."

"I'm practicing law, and I married a fair damsel of this town. A schoolteacher. Dora Rosen, a cousin of Janice Shapiro, whom you may recall from long ago."

I did. I recalled as much of her as had been proper in that time, place, and age. Now she ran her father's shipping business. We reminisced, enjoying the sensation of talking old times with a long-separated comrade. He knew what type of work I did and knew better than to ask about my business in Victoria. I got to it, eventually.

"Did you see a man hanging around the table earlier—skinny guy, bald on top with a dark crust on the sides?"

He had. "Lousy player. Owes money to some ungenerous people. That's who you're after?"

"Not him, specifically." I told Malley about the job. He had some things to say about Stephens, but he didn't say them very loudly.

"That hombre is no mensch. He's mean, a mean and heartless bastard. I watched him stab a man, at a saloon in San Antonio. The man said Stephens was using a mirror. Stephens said, 'Come closer, is this what you saw?' and when the fool moved closer, Stephens slipped a knife up between the ribs and into his heart. Skinny razor knife, in and out with no fuss and hardly any blood. At first.

"Stephens leaned back, looked at the rest of us, and said: 'Next deal?' and that was it. The man he'd stabbed walked away, dazed-like, out the door, then fell flat on the sidewalk and bled to death. And you know what? I don't think Stephens had been cheating.

"He plays hard. He pushes, intimidates, but I doubt he cheats. One thing . . . he has this ring. On his right hand . . . onyx . . . carved face of Tykhe, goddess of chance. The Romans called her Fortuna. Sometimes he'll hold his hand up, Tykhe-face pointing at someone, and he'll wiggle the finger, just a touch. I can't explain because I don't understand. Some kind of mesmerism. He did it to me once. I didn't notice the trick till he worked it on me. I raised on a hand where I should have folded. He raised on my raise and I called. The other guy who was still in folded. I folded on the next card. Stephens was bluffing, obviously, but not a regular kind of bluff. I've seen him do the trick with others, since. I don't play with him anymore.

"But with all that, he's not someone the law is after. He's welcome in the card games of the wealthiest people. To them, he's charming. I don't see it. I guess he charms when he needs to and kills when he needs to. If your guy is mixed up with him, nisht gedacht."

It was getting late, and Malley said he needed to go home to his schoolteacher. We went out to the street. He invited me to come for dinner on Friday. I told him I was going to ride off and try to find where they had taken Silverberg. I said I would talk to him when I got back. "If you see Stephens while I'm gone, leave me a message at the Delmonico."

Next day after breakfast, I asked the desk clerk about outfitters. He recommended Wolcott's and told me how to get there. Outside, the air wasn't quite as steamy as my previous Victoria mornings. I was glad of that. If I was going to be spending the next few days on horseback, nicer weather was preferable.

Wolcott's proprietor was a keen-eyed man some few years above or below seventy, with gray shrubbery on his head, face, and eyebrows. A wad of tobacco bulged his cheek. I examined his stock of pistols, deciding on a Smith & Wesson Frontier model with a holster. I had my Bulldog, of course, but once I left town I wanted something to wear on the outside. Both guns used the same caliber of shells. I added a Greener shotgun, bedroll, folding shovel, lantern, slicker, Dutch oven, small frying pan, coffeepot, tin cup and plate, eating utensils, bowie knife for my belt, tin spoon for stirring, and foodstuffs: bag of Arbuckle's roasted coffee beans, a mill for grinding them, slab of bacon, cornmeal, powdered milk, cans of condensed milk, cans of beans, salt, pepper, hardtack. Excessive, maybe, but I'm not a fan of hunger.

Thinking my Galveston wedding trip would only last a few days, I had packed little clothing, none of which was trail-worthy. For travel, I used a leather doctor's bag with a carrying strap. That wouldn't be practical for horseback. I selected two pairs of denim pants, red-twilled wool flannel shirt, two blue cotton shirts, a brown duster, and saddlebags to put everything in.

"Who has the best horses around here?"

The proprietor spat tobacco. "Meacham's. East on Santa Rosa."

"Better than anything out Lavaca way?"

"Yup. You going that way you can take the train."

"I'll load the horse into a stock car. I'd rather get to Lavaca and have a good horse. I may buy a packhorse or mule there."

"What I'd do."

I could have rented a horse, or even a small wagon—roads being much improved, but I needed to be able to go wherever the trail dictated. Off the map, as it turned out.

I paid for my things, stuffed the clothes into the saddlebag, and took it, along with the duster; the rest I asked him to bundle up and hold till he heard from me. "You outfitted any other strangers, say early September? Somebody who claimed to be building an immigrant settlement between Lavaca and Matagorda?"

He shook his shaggy head. "I'da remembered. Nobody with any sense would be doing that."

I agreed. "Problem is, some people don't have sense, or maybe have some sense but not enough information." I showed him the pamphlet.

He read it and handed it back. "Seen things like that describing just about every place I've been. None of 'em true, none of 'em outright lies. Them people ever get here they'd be mighty surprised."

He didn't know a gambler named Stephens.

"Never gamble. Used to do. Lost too much in the war. Don't want to lose anything else, no never, no more."

Before checking the horseflesh at Meacham's, I stopped at Ubder's Furniture. The owner wasn't there, but his son was, an eager lad of eighteen. I showed him the receipt from the Riverside office. He looked up the account.

"Past due," he said. "We haven't sent anyone 'round to collect. I suppose we'll have to repossess the merchandise."

I agreed with him. He didn't know anything about Riverside but said he would ask his father. Talking to him got me thinking of my boyhood, working in one of my father's stores. I'm still not sad about having abandoned that life.

According to the pamphlet, this area had "but few Negroes." Meacham's was run by one of them, a man named Butler (he had bought the place a few years back and hadn't bothered changing the sign). "The man at Wolcott's said you have the best horses in town," I said.

"Did he? Well, whatever else he is, he's no liar." The man pointed to the rear. "Corral's this way, boss."

"Sounds like you're surprised at the recommendation," I said to the stretched fabric trying to cover his shoulders as I followed him toward the corral. He was a man of perhaps fifty, an inch or two over six feet with no gray in hair or beard.

"Man used to own me, boss."

"Was he a good owner?" I immediately regretted the question. I was thrown off by his calling me boss. I didn't know if I should tell him he didn't need to, or ignore it.

"Didn't beat me. I raised his horses for him. Losing me put him out of that business."

"I guess a lot of white people had to learn how to do their own farming and stock raising," I said.

My family hadn't owned slaves, but not because my parents were against it. In Galveston there was no need for farmhands, therefore fewer slaves. Some people had house slaves. They called them servants. Slaves were part of the landscape. Hard to believe, now, but that once felt perfectly normal. In response to questions from northern cousins, my father said that living in the slave-owning South made Jews feel less exposed, less likely to be persecuted. Whatever people thought of us, they thought even less of slaves and free Negroes. These northern cousins thought that Jews, with the persecution we've suffered, should work to free the slaves. And that's what they did, up there, while Southern Jews took on Southern attitudes.

"This rascal's called Tempest." Butler pointed to a horse in the corral, a large gray with white on his legs. "Guess you won't want him."

"Not if he's like his name."

Butler stopped and looked me over. "People come in, give me trouble, don't want to do business with a colored man, I let them try to show me how good they are. I say 'You don't want this one—' and they say 'Don't you tell me what I can ride, sambo' and I say 'Sorry, boss, I jes don' know what I be saying' and let them have a try. Sometimes they stay in the saddle for a whole minute." He laughed. I did too.

"Easy on my backside and ready to follow directions is what I'm after," I said. I'm comfortable enough on a horse, but I never worked as a cowboy, and these days I'm much more accustomed to streetcars than saddles. We settled on a dark bay gelding named Blue Swamp and a used saddle.

"Mind if I ride on down to the train station and back before I decide for sure?" The station was several blocks south of the center of town. Butler saddled the horse. I checked the cinch and mounted. Riding along neat streets past neat houses, I talked to Blue Swamp about the business, but he didn't offer any answers. At the station, I asked if Caldwell, the train conductor, was in—he wasn't—then I headed back to Meacham's. I traced an indirect route, away from the center of town, so I could let the horse run. Blue Swamp and I would get along fine.

I left Blue Swamp with Butler and stopped at the Delmonico to check for messages and drop my new saddlebags and duster. Then, Fossati's Delicatessen, where I ate a ham steak and thought some more. I didn't figure there was much chance of Stephens still being in the area. Not after getting Silverberg's money. But I needed to try to find Silverberg's body and anyone who saw him with Stephens and the back-slapper. Then I could talk to the town marshal and get help tracking those two.

While I worked on my thinking, the waitress offered a slice of peach pie and coffee, which both tasted fine.

A skinny man wearing a John Bull hat with a dent in its flat top was lounging outside; he'd been outside my hotel too. I tried to meet his gaze, but he was looking the other way. The side of his face toward me had a turned-down look, as if paralyzed. An itch told me I had seen him somewhere else, but I would have remembered a face like that. Caution is a great preserver of life and health, but I didn't think anyone would be watching for me and ignored my own rules. A block on, the door to Sitterle's popped open. Two men burst through and fell onto the boardwalk, grappling at each other. Distracted by the brawlers, I didn't realize that someone was behind me till the blow struck the side of my head. Either I had moved by instinct or he missed the spot he aimed for, because it hurt like hell but didn't knock me out. I stumbled into the wrestling pair. They left off their fighting and attacked me instead. None of them had guns in their hands, but I was too wrapped up to get to my Bulldog. A gun is a very useful friend when it's three against one. I kicked, getting a satisfactory howl from one of them. A second kick freed my left arm. I flailed at whatever was in range. Then the sky collapsed.

4

Determinism Causes a Dilemma

My eyes opened to a violent light, and I vomited whatever was left from however many years ago I had eaten. Voices rattled my ears and my head throbbed like a dying puppy. Someone washed my face with a damp cloth. Time must have passed. Sounds protruded... someone walking up and down a steep hill wearing piano keys... no, wings... strong wings of a raptor with the song of a mockingbird. The sky filled with enough blue to make a man cry... the mockingbird landed on a branch, trilling a song to heal or at least soften the hurt. Clouds dissolved, and the mockingbird became a guitar playing "Garry Owen."

I thought maybe it would be safe to open my eyes again. I lay on my side, in a narrow box of a room decorated with green wallpaper. My clothes had been removed and I had been dressed in a blue-striped nightshirt. A woman wearing a white cap and apron sat nearby; she had a round face framed by dark hair. She was sewing a sleeve onto a dress but looked up when I moved.

"Please don't try to get up," she said. "I'll go find the doctor."

The guitar switched to a slower tune. I must have dozed. What brought me back awake was a train tunneling through my head, whistle screaming, sparks flying. I jerked, and a firm voice told me to keep still, which wasn't easy with all the poking and whatever else was happening back there. "Looks good. Let's re-bandage," the voice said.

This time I realized that the speaker was female. She moved her voice around to where I could see what it attached to, which was a woman with hair pulled back and hidden by a white bonnet. She had a young face—too young to be digging into my head.

"I'm Dr. Morgan," she said, and stuck a hand toward me. I managed to lift mine to meet it. "I sewed up your scalp earlier. You'll need to spend the night here."

I shook my head—very bad idea. After the red lights had faded, I decided she might be right.

"The marshal wants to see you. I can put him off till tomorrow."

"I can talk," I said, but I didn't think my voice sounded too impressive.

The nurse who had been sitting in the chair came back. Together, they propped me with an extra pillow. I drank a little water, thinking it was the best I had ever had. Dr. Morgan sent the nurse to get the marshal. "And bring our patient a mug of beef broth."

A man came in carrying a guitar; he propped the instrument against the wall and sat by the bed. "Zach Griffin. I'm the law in this burg." He had a big voice, too big for the condition of my head, and wide shoulders that didn't like being trapped by a jacket.

The nurse handed me a mug. I inhaled the steamy broth and sipped. "You're pretty good on that," I said, pointing to his guitar.

"Thanks, that's most kind of you. Do you play anything . . . Mr. . . . ."

"Piano mostly, and some guitar." Having learned piano in my youth, I went through a period of trying other instruments, guitar, double bass, even trumpet. At home I have a guitar that I haven't touched in months, but I still practice my piano. I gave him my name, though I figured he had already examined my billfold.

"Tell me about the attack."

I decided to be direct with my answers. "I ducked into my hotel for a minute. There must have been a tip-off, because someone followed me from there to Fossati's." My voice was hoarse, my throat dry. I paused for more broth. "The man was waiting outside after I ate."

"What did he look like?"

"About my height, maybe an inch taller, skinny, dark beard, John Bull with a big dent on top, brown vest. One side of his face looked paralyzed."

"Sounds like Slack-Face Jake. Just back in town after doing six months in Huntsville Prison. We'll see if we can turn him up."

"The other men fell out of Sitterle's and flopped into the street, play-fighting till I got close. The man following cracked me in the head and the men in the street hit me some more. I hit them back as best I could till my head took another blow. Woke up here with a lady doctor poking into my brain."

"We like our Doc Morgan. Not many Texas cities would welcome a woman in that position."

"We have our lady doctors in Chicago, but you're right. This is a nice town. Except when people attack visitors."

"Well, you're not just a visitor, are you, Mr. Shannon?"

I hadn't been ready to bring in the local law, but circumstances have their way of deciding things. I explained why I was here, told him about seeing Owens give Slack-Face money. "Owens had a key to the bank. Maybe they gave it to him, maybe not."

He asked some questions about Silverberg and Stephens, but I was having trouble with articulate responses. Pretty soon the doctor came back in and made him leave.

I had a crazy dream. I *hope* it was a dream. A man's face hovered inches from mine. In the dark, his features blurred. All I saw were eyes, reddish brown eyes. Dried blood eyes. He said nothing with his mouth. Only the eyes. I fell into them. I couldn't move, but that didn't matter. I was finished. Nothing could help me. Nothing could ever help. I lay on my stomach in a bowl-like pit. The pit's surface was glassy, slick; I couldn't grip anything. I writhed, trying to flip onto my back so I could see what was above me. Were those eyes boring down? Was I inside them? My chest heaved, but no breath entered. My lungs filled with something that wasn't air. Not water, or dust. Invasive. Something that didn't belong in lungs. I thought of air. I tried to sketch air from memory, its sparkling contours and golden depths. Air has no straight lines. Air is pale blue, so pale, the palest blue imaginable, with a touch of green. Caribbean water. Air is Caribbean—it tastes, it sparkles. Beyond those terrible eyes, air waited. I could see it. I could smell it. Fingers uncurled to summon air, and the air . . . the air touched my fingers! That blue with hint of green warmed my fingertips. I brought one finger toward my mouth. Those eyes couldn't stop me. They tried, how they tried. Pain filled me, pain from fingertip to head. I brought one finger to my mouth and kissed it. The eyes released their hold. Now I was a tiny boat kicked from its mooring, suddenly adrift in an ocean so vast it would never be crossed. But I didn't care. I was free.

I woke thinking I had just heard the click of a shutting door. Night still colored the windows. I lay breathing, delighted to be breathing; I tasted each breath, smiling at the glory of breath. I didn't think I would be able to go back to sleep, but I did. In the morning, the eyes didn't seem as scary. That's the beauty of mornings. I remembered what Angie the powerful laundress had said about the white-haired man's eyes. Well, a rap on the head plus a description like that, and . . . nasty dream. Except it didn't feel like a dream. I looked around the room but nothing looked different.

The doctor came in and poked at my head; it didn't hurt as much. The nurse delivered breakfast. They made me eat. Then the doctor had me get up and walk back and forth a bit. My clothing had been folded and arranged on a chair; my holstered gun hung from the chair's back. Because I had managed to stay upright, I figured it was time to leave; I picked up my trousers and sat on the bed. I got them on okay, but when I leaned over to pull on my boots, my vision blurred into red and black rings. I sat up until things cleared.

"I'm not sure you should leave," the doctor said. "At least go back to your hotel and rest. And don't get on a horse for a couple of days."

I promised I would follow her instructions. I finished dressing. Taking off the nightshirt in front of a lady felt strange, but this lady had seen the inside of my skin. My derby was pretty well scuffed and crumpled, which was fine; I didn't feel like putting a hat over my injured scalp. I thanked her and settled the bill.

"I'll have to inform the marshal that I released you," the doctor said. "My advice is not to keep him waiting too long or try to leave town without seeing him."

Good advice, I'm sure, but I didn't let it bother me. Outside, I found a fine day, with a blue of sky that defied illness and infirmity. Blood-eyed gamblers couldn't hurt me on a day like this. But wagons and carriages . . . they clanked and rolled through the streets. Had there always been such a mad jumble? I started across, but the threat of a passing carriage forced back to the safety of the boardwalk. My ability to navigate had been much reduced. I decided to stay on this side of the street, for now. Except a wall appeared, a human wall. A congress of giants blockaded the boardwalk. Three of them, dressed in an assortment of dusty range clothes, as if they had just finished bringing their herd of elephants to town and were preparing to celebrate. Each wore a different colored and shaped hat, gray, brown, and black. The shortest of the trio might have only been six and a half feet tall. They stood in front of a hardware store, talking in voices loud enough to dent the sky. If the store was their destination, they weren't in a hurry to go in.

Seeing them . . . I didn't know what to do. My brain jangled against the back of my head. How does a body usually pilot a clogged passage? I stopped. More than stopped—I froze, locked in place, no way to move onward, no way to find another path. In the street, two riders passed, then another, followed by a wagon driven by a young woman wearing a green bonnet. Why did I need to go anywhere else? The street was a river filled with many craft. From here, I could enjoy my view of whatever flowed by.

Two of the giants had their backs to me, with one facing; he wore a brown hat with a broad brim. His beard and shoulder-length hair could have used barbering. He spoke in streams of profanity interspersed with precise and erudite phrasings. "Chance isn't the insanity you think it is. You're pig shit, man, if you think there's any place, any valid place, for determinism in modern thought. The world is inter-connected. Its parts are constantly banging up against one another. Sometimes what happens is predictable, sometimes not. That's Chance. You can't go around saying shit like, 'there's no external or objective truth.' Fucking archaic, man, archaic Puritan shit from a whale's asshole."

The largest giant, who wore a black bowler, stepped back; the wall of the hardware store stopped him. He leaned on the wall and I swear the clapboards moved. "What do you mean? You've never mentioned this before, I thought you were pious, and—"

"You *thought*? You don't fucking think, you follow dogma. Your brain slides through a soup of idiocy."

"Soup of idiocy, that's a hoot," the smallest man said. He slapped Brown-hat on the shoulder. "Or maybe it's a stew of idiocy? Stew is like soup, only thicker, right?"

"Shut it, Lonnie. We're not talking to you."

"You can't just dismiss the Plan of Determinism because you have a problem with religion," Black-hat said.

"And you can't keep bringing this cheese-hawk shit up again and again. If I thought you could learn to use your fucking brain, I might try to educate you."

Suddenly, the flesh-wall parted! At the corner appeared two women dressed in dark shawls and bonnets. Black-hat said, "Pardon us, ladies," and the smallest swept off his gray derby. Passing me, one of the women presented a glance indicating my unworthiness. But why? I thought to ask for an explanation of her reasoning but waited too long. They crossed the street. The brave detective must cope, must adapt. The knot of man-flesh refilled the boardwalk. No doubt they would again part for proper ladies. But for the detective, they were a pile of fallen rock. A rockslide blocked my trail once, up a mountain in Colorado. I was on my way to infiltrate a ring of mine guards who were stealing gold from the owners. I had a scary time, climbing across that loose rock, with nothing to stop a fall besides the bottom of the mountain.

"No more of this preordained crap. People make their own choices.

Stupid choices, mostly. Who would preordain all the stupid that people do?"

Black-hat moved closer to Brown-hat and waved a hand at him. "But how do you *know* that the choice you *think* you made freely wasn't the Preordained choice? All *you* have is the freedom to think you're free. But that's God's will too. The devil unsettles the mind. If you come back to Jesus you'll find peace and your thinking will settle."

"What a sad fucking existence, walking around as if everything you do is fixed from eternity. That's pathetic. If everything is predetermined, you can't ever have regret. Why regret what was inevitable? Fucking stupid. You have to know that your actions have consequences. You have to have a feeling of achieving something. You have to realize that failure could slap you in the fucking ass."

Gray-hat interrupted. "Hey, that's funny, slapping ass and fucking ass?"

"The only consistent way to represent a world whose parts may affect one another through their conduct being either good *or* bad is the indeterministic way. What interest, zest, or excitement can there be in achieving the right way, unless we are fucking enabled to feel that the wrong way is also a possible and natural way—a menacing and imminent way? And what sense can there be in condemning ourselves for taking the wrong-ass way, unless the right way was open to us too?

"I'm not talking about some goddamn metaphysical pestilence that you need to run from. Chance just means that no part of the world, however big, can claim to control absolutely the destinies of the entire shitbucket of humanity."

Brown-hat stopped talking and pointed toward me. "See that little fuck over there, with the bandage on his head?"—they turned to look— "He's been standing there, not going this way, not going that. You think he's waiting for the universe to tell him where to go? He *must* be waiting for a fucking signal from somewhere."

"Ask him, Maceo, ask the little fuck what he's waiting for."

"What you're saying . . . you don't believe that the HAND of God is in everything we do?" Black-hat choked on the last part of his statement and sank deeper into the wall, as if afraid he would be struck down by that hand.

"It's not fucking either-or. Think about poker. Somebody wins. Usually the fucker with the most skill. *You're* saying that the winner is chosen by the hand of God and was preordained before any of us were born. I would say, if there's a God, he's got more important things happening than a piss-ass poker game. Than each fucking piss-ass poker game happening everywhere in the world. Must be the hand of God is training the best poker players. What an arrogant and pathetic thought. Determinism is dead. Dead. Use your brain instead."

"Hey, Maceo, that's a good rhyme," Gray-hat said. "You should use it in one of your poems."

"You can't talk about poker, a game of . . . chance . . . as an example of your philosophy," Black-hat said.

"Poker is chance but it's also skill. What can be better than poker as an example? You've got skill but you can't control everything. Just like life. Life is chancy."

Brown-hat . . . Maceo . . . turned and stepped into the street. A wagon stopped to let him pass, the driver no doubt afraid that his horses would be injured by a collision. The other two followed. The boardwalk was now clear. But where should I go? I had needs, a plan; I wasn't waiting for a signal, was I? At the corner I turned right, still afraid to cross a street. The next intersection was clear enough of traffic for me to make it to the other side. I felt better. Walking clears the head, even a battered head. The street I was on ended at the train station. Praise the hand or ass of God! I had business at the station, with Caldwell the conductor.

Caldwell was away but had left me a note with the ticket agent. "I was just about to look for a boy to carry it to your hotel," the ticket agent said.

Caldwell's handwriting was neat and formal:

A porter recalls having seen Stephens. Recalls because he had a gambling debt that Stephens had forgiven in return for favors relating to passengers and their business—which I warned him against continuing. He said that Stephens and the well dressed

Westerner I described to you took a train from Port Lavaca on the 12th of September to Victoria and another later that day from Victoria to San Antonio. My man was certain that there was no third companion. He recognized the well-dressed Westerner as Dawson, or Lawson, who runs a saloon called McFarley's on Flores Street in San Antonio.

He said Stephens spends a good quantity of time around the coast but has no idea as to what business the man does there.

Sure, Silverberg could have stayed on in Port Lavaca, alive, or taken a different train back to Victoria. But the closed bank account, the signatures, the other men returning without him, all pointed to one thing, and it was a thing I didn't like.

I went to Wolcott's to have my supplies loaded on the Friday train to Port Lavaca. Then I stopped at the livery and asked Butler to take Blue Swamp to the station in the morning. After all that arranging, this little fuck was pretty beat. In the hotel lobby, I spotted a stocky redhead with a lot of beard, standing near the staircase, where he could see anyone coming in from either the main door or the restaurant, which had a separate entrance. He wasn't wearing a badge, but his demeanor said lawman. I told him I was going to bed now and would see the marshal in the morning. I asked the clerk to have food sent up to my room, and my part in the day ended.

I sank toward sleep with a blessed smoothness. Then, like the sudden irrevocable click of a bolt in a lock, the descent stopped. Sleep had been in reach, just across a little slip of creek, but now it might as well have been at the far end of the ocean. I rolled from one side to another, searching for that comfortable position, the perfect body-bed-pillow arrangement to ferry me onward to the land of sleep. My wound kept me from lying on my back, and the more I thought about *not* lying on my back, the more I knew that my back was *the only position that would allow sleep.* Eventually, I decided that I couldn't avoid lying that way, no matter how it might hurt. I fluffed the pillow and settled my head, and . . . a stab of pain propelled me onto my side. The relief from the pressure on my head was almost like being comfortable. I slept.

Unfortunately, I also dreamed. Those red-brown eyes chased me. I ran. Blind with fear, I ran. And lost myself in a maze. The walls were twice my height, white, decorated with black or sometimes red shapes . . . shapes of . . . they were cards, playing cards. After three jacks, I turned left. A light glowed from somewhere ahead. I walked toward it. The cards swayed, as if angered that I was leaving. One fell into the next, and the next, one after another, falling toward me. A gap appeared, the end of the maze! I ran and fell into space. As I fell, I tried to conjure the blue-green air. Air to breathe, air to buoy my fall, but no air came. I slammed into something hard, and woke on the floor. I climbed back into bed. Eventually, I slept again.

Morning came. I got up and washed my face. Beside the washbasin was an unopened deck of cards. It hadn't been there when I went to sleep. I carried the deck with me to the dining room and dropped it in a wastebasket. I didn't want it in my room.

At breakfast, a clerk brought me an answer from the associate of Silverberg's I had contacted. Coffee helped my head somewhat. I worked my way through a pile of ham, eggs, and toasted bread with butter. Another cup of coffee helped the food settle, then it was time for my morning visits.

First, the doctor, who did some probing and said I could survive without the bandage. And second, Marshal Griffin, who was sitting on the porch in front of his office, at it with the guitar again. I took the chair next to his. He managed to put his instrument down long enough to bother me for more information. He didn't complain about my not having come sooner. I liked that. It indicated that we might be able to work together. He said he had talked to Wilson, at the bank. Wilson said that Owens was not authorized to have a key.

"Wilson wanted to sack him right off," Griffin said. "I convinced him to wait. I want to look in at all the locksmiths first, see if he made his own copy. It's best to have as much evidence as possible. Meanwhile, Wilson is checking their books for irregularities."

"Find out about Goliad locksmiths too," I said. "He spends a lot of time at his sister's." I looked over at the buildings across the street, a line of small, false-fronted stores. There was a butcher shop called Murchison's next to a harness shop, then a jewelry store; the jewelry store had boarded-up windows. "Owens must be stealing from the bank," I said. "Maybe he helped Stephens too. But did he set Slack-Face on me because of Stephens, or because he thought I was investigating *him*?"

I handed Caldwell's note to the marshal. A wagon passed, driven by a woman in men's clothing. The marshal nodded at her and tipped his hat. A couple of riders met in the middle of the street and started chatting. A wagon loaded with timber had to veer around them, scraping against the boardwalk as it passed. The driver cursed, the riders laughed. A regular day in just about any town.

"Stephens hasn't broken any laws—that I've known of," Griffin said. "In fact, he's well-liked in some circles. If Owens lost money and owes him, that's his problem, but if he helped Stephens with something illegal, it gives us something on Stephens too. Dawson-Lawson doesn't sound familiar. Who else *is* there? Who connected these men to a bunch of rich East Coast Jews?"

I hadn't told him about Rafkin, the alleged Romanian Jewish refugee. Now I did, including what Levi had told me and the answer I had received from Silverberg's associate. "Silverberg must have met Rafkin in St. Louis. We connect Rafkin to Stephens, and we have him."

"Might be the end of that trail," Griffin said. "Last month—right around the time we're talking about—a man got his throat cut in his hotel bed. That was a mess. Description sounds like your Rafkin. Signed in as Grolph, barbed-wire salesman from St. Louis. Hotel people said he spoke with a funny accent, which could be anything, but I'll attest to the rotten teeth. He'd stayed there before, but survived the earlier visits.

Hotel people wouldn't or couldn't say whether they ever saw him with anyone else."

"Different names, but he always sticks with St. Louis," I said. We watched more wagons and riders going along. Time for me to do the same. I told him I was heading Lavaca-way in the morning. He recommended the Seaside Hotel and said he would wire me anything he unearthed.

5

Knack for Finding Bodies

I packed my new saddlebags with what I was taking and stowed the rest of my things in the doctor bag, which I left at the front desk for storage. Before leaving, I mailed a report to the boss and sent a telegram to Rabbi Cohen, letting him know that I didn't know much other than not to expect anything good about Silverberg's health. I assumed that I would get back to Victoria in a couple of weeks.

The train ride covered an hour and forty-seven minutes, through ranchland, scattered woods, coastal plain, and marsh. I didn't mind leaving Victoria. Having your head stomped on doesn't endear you to a place. Caldwell stopped to chat. He gave me a name to look up in Lavaca, a faro dealer named Dakota, who worked at a place called the Porthole Saloon. I also had a note from Griffin to the town marshal, but I preferred to reconnoiter on my own. I dozed. A smell woke me—sea rot, like what you find after a storm stirs up sludge and deposits it on the shore to fester. Then it was gone. I couldn't see anything that might have caused it.

Port Lavaca was an active and growing town, with steamships and schooners being tended to, freight wagons, carriages, and the clatter of construction. The town had nearly disappeared during the period of Indianola's ascendancy. Disaster for one leads to opportunity for another.

I left my supplies at the station and saddled Blue Swamp, figuring he needed exercise. On the way to the Seaside Hotel I passed a livery. I tied Blue Swamp to the rail in front of the hotel and went in to book a room and dump my saddlebag. The livery I had passed was run by a middle-aged Mexican named Delfino. I left Blue Swamp with him; he said he had some mules available. I chose one with a dark coat and white muzzle named Patience, a quality I display on rare occasions.

Next to the livery was a hardware store; they sold me a map of the county, which I took to the hotel dining room to study. The desk clerk said I was late for lunch, but was willing to find me some beans and cornbread.

Stephens and Dawson-Lawson must have taken Silverberg someplace remote, and left him there. Looking at the map, I figured that the area southwest of Powderhorn Lake seemed likeliest. Powderhorn—called a lake but really an oversized tidal pool—lay behind what had been Indianola. From accounts, Powderhorn is one of the reasons for Indianola's demise. The tide surged over the town, ran itself into Powderhorn, then flowed back to the gulf. Not many structures could withstand that kind of pressure.

After lunch, I talked to several hotel employees. They didn't recall the three I was after. Same with the other of the two hotels this town claimed. Like in Victoria, Stephens and company must have had an alternate place to stay, maybe a rooming house near the port, where they could be inconspicuous. The heat was an oppression. Where was that fabled offshore breeze? Where was autumn?

I made my way to the Porthole Saloon. The decorations looked more cowboy than sailor, with mounted heads of buck, bison, puma, and longhorn, but I doubted that anyone complained. I ordered a beer. The place hadn't drawn much of a crowd yet, which suited me. A man who fit Caldwell's description of Dakota the faro dealer sat at a table

working on a deck of cards and a plate of Mexican beans and corn tortillas. I carried my beer over to him.

"You Dakota?" He said yeah, without any tough-guy talk like they
have in dime novels. For which I was thankful. I told him who sent me.
"He doesn't like gamblers, but I helped him in a tight spot once."
"And he's been helping me," I said. I asked him if he knew Stephens
or Dawson-Lawson.

"Yeah. A dark man, despite the white hair. I do recall him and another
man a month or more back. Looked like that one you're asking about.
Stephens played poker. The big man played a little faro. He said he was
Frank Lawson, owner of McFarley's, in San Antone. He said I should
come work for him. I said I like it here."

"You didn't see a third man?" I described Silverberg. He shook his
head and told me about a couple of places where they might have
stayed. I sat in on a poker game with some dock workers, winning a
few hands, losing some. The only other thing I learned was that no one
wanted to play when Stephens was there.

None of the rooming houses that Dakota sent me to had signs adver-
tising their purpose. The first place wasn't bad, once I stepped past the
man sleeping on the porch, blanketed by the smell of what he had been
drinking. Inside was a small, neat bar, with a tall, neat man behind it.
According to Dakota, it was run by a woman named Mississippi Sal.

"Hello, my good man," Irish Shannon said, shaping what he (and I)
hoped was the appropriate greeting.

The neat man touched a handle of his mustache and looked me over.
Then he said I needed to check my hardware. Most people don't notice
the Bulldog under my coat. I slid it onto the bar butt-first. He put it in a
drawer and said I could retrieve it when I left.

"I was told to ask after a lady by the name of Mississippi Sal . . . would
she be available, do you think?" The neat man admitted that seeing her
might be possible and ducked through a curtain separating a back room
from the bar.

Mississippi Sal happened to be a tall Italian woman with a lot of gray hair piled on top of her head. "And how are you today, madam?" I said. "They call me Shannon, and I'm here to find a friend of mine, a card-playing gentleman, Stephens is his—"

The sound of a hammer being cocked cut off my words. I glanced at Mr. Neat, and at what he held: an old Le Mat. I thought it safe to assume he had the lever flipped to buckshot. It's a monstrous weapon, with two barrels, one for a 16-gauge shotgun shell and the other for 36-caliber bullets. Not a lot of range, but we weren't at sharp-shooting distance here.

Irish Shannon left the room. "Wait please," I said. "Mind talking to me while my head is still intact?"

"Persona non grata," the woman said. "Clean place, no gamblers, no gambler's friends."

"Not a friend. Law. Looking for him."

Sal appeared to be considering my statement, but the Le Mat didn't waver. I breathed a couple of times.

After too long a while for standing as the object of a cocked pistol, she said, "Sit, talk."

Mr. Neat released the hammer. I showed her my card and told her something of the story. I hoped her dislike for the man would equal willingness to help me catch him. I got a mountain of talk about gamblers and the criminal element. She grew up in a house like this in Palermo; she liked sailors. She didn't like the people who cheated them when they came ashore. As self-appointed waterfront mayor, she liked to know the doings of undesirables and had a company of urchins to watch and report. "My book," she said, looking to Mr. Neat. He went through the curtain.

"No use for Jews," she said. "They take your money. So maybe I don't care that a gambler takes theirs. But *this* gambler, this Stephens, worse than Jew. He cheated my cousin, then he stabbed him. Only wounded. Much better now. Stephens—something not right with him. Too strong. Malocchio. We would not object to seeing him hurt."

I didn't see a great need to tell her I was Jewish. You can't change someone's attitudes once they've lived in them. You have to educate people before their thinking gets fossilized. She would die, eventually, and as long as she didn't infect others, her attitudes would die with her. Problem is when there are so many people like her it's hard to see an end of it.

During her diatribe, Mr. Neat came back carrying a leather-bound notebook—her urchin reportage, I assumed. She opened it and flipped through some pages. It appeared that Stephens and the other two spent a night at Grundle's, a block over and closer to the water. They rented a wagon, but she didn't know from whom or where they went. She apologized for that. She also didn't know that they had taken the train back to Victoria minus one companion.

Grundle had the body of a former stoker gone soft. His dark beard covered some of the stains on his denim shirt. Behind his fat head a large poster proclaimed the wondrous sights of Indianola.

I gave him my howdy, looking for my friend routine, but received only a stare. These places probably have a password, something stupid, like "Hi, my name's Jake." Grundle wore a mantle of stupidity, the kind that becomes a mark of pride. Well, what choice would a person have, stuck in the muck with mules and oxen while the rest of humanity continues to rise? Of course acting stupid is also a good way to deter questioning. He probably didn't know anything—not likely that Stephens and the other had told anyone where they were going. But . . . that poster bothered me. A detail kept fluttering in the periphery, something from before my head was knocked in. Caldwell . . . he overheard Silverberg saying he was excited to see Indianola. Not Port Lavaca. If they . . . Stephens . . . Lawson . . . were making Silverberg think that Port Lavaca was Indianola, they would need props. Like the poster.

"Time to take down that fake poster," I said. "The Indianola game is over."

Grundle looked at the poster, then back at me. I grabbed his grimy collar with both hands and yanked him off balance.

"Hey, what's your fuss...."

His chin smacked the counter, cutting off whatever else he meant to say. I let go with one hand and reached for my gun. The barrel of the Bulldog against the folds of his neck stopped further protests.

"Let's be clear," I said. "You know some things. And I *like* to know things. That means you're going to talk. That'll make us friends. You want to be friends?" He managed a weak sound that I decided was a yes, especially after I dug a little deeper with the barrel.

He talked. They had told Silverberg that Port Lavaca was Indianola. To maintain the pretense, they recruited others. Grundle put up the fake poster. When Silverberg was there, Grundle only let in people he knew. He arranged for Silverberg to overhear a couple of men talking about someone buying land between Indianola and the gulf. All to maneuver Silverberg into transferring his money—the relief organization's money—to Stephens and Lawson.

Leaving Grundle to his wallowing, I left to check hostelries. There were two that rented wagons. I tried Delfino's first. He didn't recall hiring a wagon to anyone matching the trio's description. He actually kept a book, and nothing showed on the days I was looking for. The owner at the second place recognized Lawson from my description. He said that Lawson had rented a wagonette suitable for rough travel and returned it a week later.

That business complete, I went back to my hotel. My head reminded me that I was still recovering from the attack. I sat in the hotel restaurant and ordered a big fish dinner. Two telegrams had come, from Griffin and from Bert Wilson of Brownson and Sibley Bank. I read Griffin's first: "Owens taken. Cheating bank like you thought. Nothing yet on the other pair. Caught Slack-Face. He admits to taking money from Owens for your beating." Wilson's note was full of praise and offers of reward. Back in my room, I composed replies for a hotel boy to take to the telegraph office, telling Wilson to arrange payment with Llewelyn.

I told Griffin I was heading out in the morning to trace the route of their wagon.

The inside of my head thumped. Night approached. I lay on my side, staring at the mantle light by the door. Maybe I could stare hard enough to force the gas to turn itself on and light. Gunshots awakened me. I lit a match to check my watch, which said midnight. Another shot, from down the street. A pistol. Nothing to get too worked up over. I turned onto my other side.

Morning meant farewell to bed and comfort. At breakfast, I studied the map again. Powderhorn Lake still tugged at me, a pull that had buried itself in the back of my neck. I've always had a knack for finding bodies, or finding places where bodies had been, where someone died or was murdered. The first happened when I was thirteen. One morning, I woke and, without talking to anyone, dressed and left the house. I found myself on the beach. A body lay at the high-tide line, tangled in storm debris, with hands, feet, and other parts eaten by sea creatures. Similar things happened various times after—Galveston being a place where death visits often, from violence, accident, yellow fever, fire. It's happened other times, too, when hunting criminals. I can't explain it and I don't try.

I buckled on a gunbelt with my new Smith & Wesson and carried my things down to Delfino's. He helped me load supplies onto Patience and offered advice on camping and fishing. And sold me some fishing gear. A fresh-caught fish is a nice thing to eat. Then it was time to leave. I tied on Patience's lead rope and set off.

Up in the saddle, you could almost mistake me for a cowboy. Except for the bowler hat. I reminded Blue Swamp that we were friends, and friends are expected to treat each other with respect. With an agreeable horse, I could get along all right.

6

Solo the Eagle

Once you're on the back of a horse, away from the gaze of anything not made by nature, the pace of everything changes. Madness of city life dissipates. Not only that—madness of city life is recognized *as* madness. When you're in the madness, when it's your life, rushing around in carriages or streetcars, you don't see it. Only when you're out in the wild, on the back of a horse, can you name the madness. One day, I will return and embrace my madness, I know that, and I don't mind. But for now, this time with Blue Swamp and Patience, the sunshine and breezes, erased the city.

The coast is low and flat. It's a maze of islands, bayous, bays, and salt marsh. The rivers are sluggish and full of silt. None of them are navigable for any distance. Still wild, but not a wilderness like it used to be. People have been coming through for a long time. White people I mean. We're the ones who have to alter the landscape. I can't imagine what it was like for the first European explorers or settlers. If I had been born one hundred or more years earlier, would I have stayed in Europe? Maybe if I hadn't been Jewish. The reasons my family left would still have existed.

My ancestors were the brave ones—the ones who stayed despite the persecution and the ones who left to seek a new home someplace better. That's why a swindle like what Stephens and Lawson were doing could find willing contributors. American Jews—we know how easy our lives are compared to the people in Eastern Europe. Those with money to help give willingly. And those who prey upon that generosity need to be stopped.

A decaying scrap of road connected Port Lavaca and the ruins of Indianola. Only twelve miles separated the two, the living and the dead. Some crumbling houses still littered Indianola's streets; the best ones had been taken apart and freighted elsewhere. The scarred concrete walls of the ruined courthouse stood before now-placid waters. Disasters have a sobering effect, reminding us that despite all our civilization, we can't defeat the elements. The Chicago fire happened before I moved there, but I heard about it from people who lived through the horror. Galveston had a bad fire just three years ago. And of course I lived through hurricanes, growing up.

Galveston is a lot more exposed than Indianola had been. Indianola was on the mainland, somewhat protected by a barrier island. Galveston *is* the barrier island. But people don't think a storm will cause much damage. Because, as yet, none has. The people of Indianola thought the same thing. Twice. I've suggested to my parents that they move to Houston, but they won't.

In front of a shack without much roof, a trio of children— boys...girls...who could say?—sat in the dirt. Their faces were smeared with something dark. Blood, I realized, when one of them bit into the haunch of a skinned and raw squirrel. They watched, faces savage and unreadable. One stood and moved toward me. I could have sworn he, or maybe it, growled.

Stephens and Lawson wouldn't have wanted Silverberg to see the real Indianola, but I had to be thorough. "Morning, kids." I reached into a pocket for some nickels. The other two got up. The growler moved closer. I felt bad for them, living here on the puss-edge of nothing. I would give them food, if they asked or if I felt like they deserved it. But not if they tried to take it from me.

"Maybe you kids can help me." The growler was now only a few feet away. I held out the nickels. "I'm looking for some people who might have passed through here two months—" I yelped. The growler had lunged at my leg, teeth first.

Blue Swamp bolted, nearly tossing me. Patience followed. I held tight and let them run. We neared the old railway line. My calf throbbed. I pulled on the reins. "Whoa boy, whoa." I needed to examine my leg. Teeth marks dented the fabric of my jeans. Nothing torn, but I would have a nice bruise. A shriek, much like a fighting raccoon—but I knew it wasn't—erupted from back toward the ruins. Then another, louder and closer. Blue Swamp twitched his ears and started moving. I agreed with him.

The rails had been removed and carted off to be reused. The naked mound pointed back toward civilization. I was tempted to follow it. Instead, I chose a road of old wagon ruts mingled with tracks of deer, cattle, and coyotes. I passed a couple of homesteads, slapped-together affairs of storm wreckage not likely to survive the next big one. Hoping I was far off enough from those feral children, I stopped to look at my map. Stephens and company would have left the main road before reaching Indianola, and gone around Powderhorn Lake. That would be my path too. I knew I was headed the right way. I knew it without seeing any tracks or other signs of their passage.

For years, years of observation and interaction, I've accumulated knowledge of humanity's traits. I've learned the things that people do depending on the terrain they pass through, the people they meet, the needs of their activity. Most people follow a pattern, and most of the time, I can recognize whatever it is. That isn't always true—I was hunting a man once who sold fake shares in a mining company. Steven Parker. He defied patterns. He had an intuition, or something, that kept me off his trail. The only reason I finally caught him is that he was injured in a fight. Parker was someone who avoided fights, avoided places where fights might happen, but a crazy old horse-breeder named

Nelson didn't like the way Parker bumped against him on the street and followed, to beat and rob him.

Up a ways, I startled an old longhorn as it emerged from a thicket of yucca and mountain laurel. He snorted and moved along. I thanked him for not charging. His spread of horns could have felled Blue Swamp and Patience at the same time.

Coming upon the remains of a log house, I decided I'd had enough riding and adventuring for the day. My backside hurt like hell and my head wasn't much better. I unsaddled horse and mule and turned them out to graze. The lake shore is marshy, with few solid places. The former residents had built a pier. Some boards were missing and others wobbled, but enough structure remained to support me while I worked on catching dinner. I dropped hardtack crumbs into the water. Mullet came up to nibble. I netted a few, then cut them up for bait. It didn't take me long to catch a couple of handsome redfish. Back on land, I gathered firewood and kindling. During my fish cleaning, motion high in the trees made me look up; I saw a large bird, brown feathers and a curved beak. An immature bald eagle, I thought. The more I watched, the better I was able to see details among the leaves and branches; the eagle's condition surprised me. "How do you manage like that, fella?" I said. The eagle only had one wing. "Must be hard to get food."

I tossed one of the fish over to the trees and went back to dinner prep-aration. There followed a high-pitched whistling and a gust of winged movement down, then up. I turned. The eagle held the fish against a branch and ate. For such powerful and predatory birds, bald eagles make surprisingly sweet sounding calls.

While waiting for the fire to burn itself down to coals, I assembled branches into a spit and supports. "One fish was all I really needed," I said to the eagle. "Hey, mind if I call you Solo? Maybe you would prefer I don't bring attention to your predicament. If so, I'm sorry." Deciding that the eagle didn't mind, I continued. "How did that happen, anyway?"

I spitted the fish, salted it, and set it over the coals. A few turns later and it was as cooked as it needed to be.

Sunlight told me I should get up. I already missed my hotel bed, even the one in Port Lavaca. Coffee meant rebuilding the fire. In back of the ruined cabin, I found a well with a rusty but working pump, but what poured from the tap was brackish, probably inundated from the hurricane. I fed the horses corn and watered them and my coffeepot from the supply I had brought. When my coffee was ready, I sat on the dock to drink it. A fish jumped to snare an insect. Passing ducks called. I examined the treetops, looking for Solo the eagle. It wasn't such a bad morning for being away from city comfort, but I didn't feel I had the time to linger beyond finishing the coffee.

Toward noon, the trail passed another of the scattered homesteads; seeing a man outside at the woodpile, I stopped to talk. The man had long, gray hair tied in back; he squinted up from his log-splitting, then went back to it. He split three more and put down the axe. I told him my business.

He pulled out a packet of cigarette papers. "You got something to fill a blanket?"

I handed a bag of tobacco down to him.

"Oh yeah, I remember them." He made a careful job of rolling his cigarette and lit the end that wasn't in his mouth. "Well-dressed feller gave me a fifty-cent piece to say this here spot weren't hell's armpit to one of the other fellers. Three of 'em goin' south, and some days later two headed back the other way. They didn't stop but I saw 'em."

"Any other homesteads the way they went?"

"Ratface named Conroy and his woman. Few miles on toward Alligator Head. Runs some unsightly beeves that no rustler would ever touch."

The rest of the day didn't amount to anything. Later on, I tested my new Greener on a flock of mallards that rose from a marshy bayou, downing three. I made camp beneath oaken branches, built a fire, and set to plucking the birds. Figuring on stewing the ducks in that Dutch oven I'd packed, I set it on the fire and cut bacon into it to render. I pulled off a few leaves from a nearby redbay tree to use in the stewpot. Just like last night, I found myself spied on by Solo the eagle. "What are your thoughts on waterfowl tonight?" I asked. "I guess I can spare you one of these. Since you came calling at suppertime." I laid a bird on a log close to his tree. The bacon fat began sizzling nicely, and I added the duck pieces to brown, along with redbay and pepper. I may not be much of a frontiersman, but I do like to eat.

The evening started to act like autumn. I dug a wool flannel shirt from a saddlebag. Solo finished his duck and sat on a branch, looking mighty proud. I didn't want him becoming dependent on me—I wouldn't be out here long. But it *was* nice to have a companion. "Maybe you were here when they dealt with Silverberg. Wouldn't mind a word with your buzzard cousins. They'll know where the body lies."

I tasted the stew and proclaimed it dinner time.

Noises jarred me from sleep, a succession of noises that I eventually identified as the creak and jangle of a wagon and horses. I crawled from my covers. I was wearing moccasins; I often sleep in them, so I don't have to waste time trying to pull on boots if I'm woken suddenly. I found a sheltered spot to wait for whoever was coming. The Greener rested on a log, my finger loose on the trigger. A wagon appeared in the darkness—except the wagon wasn't dark. Afternoon sun dazzled the passengers, but between us hung a gauzy fog that blurred the shapes of the cart, horses, and people.

That same gauze muffled the passenger's voices. Words trickled toward me, as if falling from the sky, "fewfrbesilvroo . . . " and other nonsense. I kept shifting my head, trying to focus on the words, on any word. The speaker's voice was strong and musical, but what he said came at me like something mashed up in a mixing bowl and dumped into a pan of scrambled eggs. Another voice joined, less strong but equally garbled. I kept listening, and told myself that the first voice addressed the other as Silverberg and that there was an Indianola in there somewhere.

The wagon receded; I tried to follow. The gauze-mist froze to my skin, and the wagon—it was just ahead but I couldn't reach it, couldn't make any forward progress. The gauze-mist battered me with freezing tentacles. Exhausted from the struggle, I fell to my knees. The ground vibrated, as if a giant creature rumbled toward me. I knew it was only some weird amplification caused by the mist. What else could it be? And yet.... The rumble grew. I tried to get up, but the shaky ground kept sliding my feet from under me, and when I was finally able to stand, the rumbling gauze-wall receded, taking all the air with it. My lungs heaved. There was nothing to fill them. The gauze coalesced and grew. A wave, higher than the treetops. A storm surge, a wall of water that gave me no time to move before it crashed.

I woke hugging the Greener, with my ground sheet and blankets rumpled over me. I threw them off and greeted a miserable morning. Frost coated everything. Acting automatically, I squatted by the fire and blew on the coals to bring the embers back to life. I added fresh wood. The cheering dance of flames rewarded my efforts. Then I looked around, but everything looked like a normal frosty day. No freakish wave had exploded from the gulf.

Fighting the urge to rush onto the trail after Silverberg, I took the time to make coffee and reheat leftover duck stew. He wouldn't be any less dead now or later.

The road showed tracks that looked no different from other ruts and gouges, but I was positive that one set belonged to Silverberg's wagon. These veered onto a different path, one that pointed toward the coast. I took it. Toward midday I reached what must have been Ratface Conroy's land. I passed a few bony cattle. They were branded with a curvy blob that had another, much smaller curvy blob inside it. A path of beaten-down mud led toward a house.

Having rounded Powderhorn, I was finally getting back to where I could smell the gulf. If my map could be trusted, I had reached Boggy Bayou. Or maybe Broad Bayou. Both opened into Matagorda Bay, near its mouth. A mile or so on I came to the bay. Though the time wasn't much past noon, the sky had darkened. Not the dark of a storm, but as if a bloody veil hung between me and the sun. I rode toward the bay. Reddish light washed the salt-cedars and cactus. Blue Swamp stopped, and tapping with my heels couldn't get him moving again. He neighed and flipped his head back and forth. Ahead in the dimness, a shape emerged, like a haystack or a round hut, indistinct with distance and this crazy light. I turned Blue Swamp away from the shape; he liked that. A few yards back I dismounted. With nothing to tie the reins to, and the sandy soil not suited for a picket, I had to hobble him and Patience. The way they were acting, I was afraid they would bolt.

I forced myself into the red air. I didn't want to any more than Blue Swamp had. When I drew close enough to identify the shape, it turned out to be a sand hill, one sand hill, alone, looking at the bay. Off a ways, the Matagorda lighthouse flickered.

A sand hill on the bay side was unexpected. It could have formed in a distant time when storms tore through Matagorda. These barrier islands are always shifting. Sand hills are alive, attuned to wind and wave. But a sand hill alone felt wrong, and the wrongness increased as I moved around it. Sand hills form, blow apart, re-form, eventually becoming immobilized by growth of sea oats, goatweed, and other plants. This one was crusty, bare, more like sandstone than sand, and the front looked sculpted, carved into features . . . curl of lip, open mouth, deep eye holes. A rotting animal festered in the mouth.

Then I found the body.

I saw the skull first. A spar from some long-dead sailing vessel had been driven deep into the sand; it thrust upward about six feet. Someone had separated the skull from its body and fixed it on the spar's end. The bone was clean of gore, and the lower jaw had been tied in place with rawhide. The rest of the skeleton lay nearby; scraps of cloth hanging here and there. A few feet away was a depression that might have been a grave, dug poorly and with haste, the body dragged out by coyotes and dealt with by them, buzzards, ants, maggots, and Texas sun. I groped through the remnants of a coat and found an inner pocket with an envelope addressed to Martin Silverberg. I didn't find a wallet or the gold watch that Owens had described.

In unstable, sandy soil like this, holes refuse to be dug. I had learned that as a kid. The body was beyond interest to scavengers, but I couldn't leave it the way it was. I widened and deepened the depression with my camp shovel and dragged the remnants in. Meaning to lay it with the other remains, I lifted the skull from its perch; pausing, I looked into its sockets. "I've an idea, Mr. Silverberg. How about you come with me, help track down these gents who killed you?"

I filled in the hole and stood beside the mound of sand, mumbling fragments of recalled Hebrew. When I got back to my horses, I rearranged the saddlebags to make room for the skull.

The wind had picked up, bringing sleet. I put on my slicker. The beasts complained. I told them we'd stop somewhere soon. Maybe I could shelter at Ratface Conroy's. There surely wasn't anything else around here till Alligator Head, which I'd been told was no more than a collection of fisherman's shacks. I rode up the lane I had seen earlier, passing more cattle with the curvy blob brand—a shape that now reminded me of that leering sand hill. The lane took me to a small house constructed from warped, uneven boards and hunks of sod. When I got close enough I hollered a greeting. The door cracked and a face looked out, along with a rifle barrel.

"Any chance of dinner and a dry place to sleep?" I said.

"Barn's in the rear. I'll need two dollars." The rifle didn't move and neither did I.

"That's steep," I said. "But seeing as how your accommodations are so luxurious, I suppose I can manage it."

He gave me a hoarse laugh. "Let's see it then."

I dismounted, keeping Blue Swamp between me and his gun, and tossed a couple of coins toward the door.

"Okay, mister, you can set your mounts loose in the pen and come on back for a plate of beans."

Barn was an extravagant term for a lean-to strung together from broken parts of other structures. Everything was greasy and salt-ravaged; this was a climate unkind to wood. But . . . it had a hayloft for me to sleep in, which was much better than camping in the frosty dark. The pen was split into two parts, with a milk cow in the back section, and in the front, a donkey and a mare that might once have been a decent mount. I unsaddled Blue Swamp and Patience and put them in the pen. The trough held enough hay for now.

I walked to the door. From a window, man and rifle watched me. Behind him, something moved, a crablike shadow. The man who I assumed was Conroy let me in. His face did have a pronounced rat-tishness. "Name's Conroy," he said. "The missus there is loading up the table." His rifle's name was Sharps, Sharps of the large caliber and long range. He pointed to my Smith & Wesson. "You wouldn't mind hanging that up whilst you eat?"

"I'm not crazy about the idea," I said. "But I wouldn't want to be unfriendly." I unbuckled and hung. I still had my Bulldog and wasn't about to volunteer it.

The house was somewhat warmed by a fireplace that appeared to be a remnant of a previous dwelling. The Conroys had likely built their hovel from ruins of what they found. Stitched-together blankets nailed to opposite walls divided one dirt-floored room. I assumed that their bed lay on the other side. This side had a table less rough than its surroundings, chairs, butter churn, pots black from the fire. A shovel, hoe, axe, and other tools hung from nails. Conroy was wearing overalls that would need their yearly wash before I could determine color. Mrs. Conroy had thick brown hair bundled up on her head and the tired face of someone who never has time to stop working. She spooned beef and beans into three bowls and set them on the table. A plate of cornbread was already in the middle. Conroy leaned his rifle on the wall and sat. I sat. She sat. We ate. The beef and beans had an odd, fishy taste.

A watch chimed. Conroy took out a very nice piece of timekeeping and flipped it open. Letters engraved on the inside were visible. I knew where he had acquired it. The question was whether he found it on Silverberg's already-dead body, or killed him.

I didn't comment on the watch and didn't want to appear too interested. We talked about the weather, Northers and hurricanes. I volunteered that I was from Galveston. They didn't ask what I was doing out here. Conroy said they managed not to starve to death from a bit of farming and the few head of scattered cattle. With dinner and topics of conversation ended, I slung my gun belt over my shoulder and left for the dubious comfort of the barn. I laid out my bedroll in the hayloft, with my duster for a pillow and my Bulldog under it. As usual, I changed from boots to moccasins.

Somewhere in the night, a neigh from Blue Swamp mingled with a dream of that strange sand hill. In the dream, the sand hill had grown to the size of those old-time Galveston mansions that some of my classmates had lived in. I sat atop Blue Swamp. A mouthlike door opened, and a voice called, a voice that I wanted to find, but Blue Swamp refused to enter.

Awake, I opened my eyes partway. A rustle came from below. I was lying on my side, facing into the barn. Lamplight flickered, the flame set low but giving enough light for me to see someone crouched over my saddlebags and pack. I called out. A hand holding my Smith and Wesson came up, but I shot first.

The person fell into the narrow patch of light, Conroy. I jumped down. He was holding his side. Blood seeped around his fingers. A voice whispered from the darkness outside the barn: "Lyle?" Although with one ear ringing from the shot, the voice might have been a yell. Conroy produced a wordless cry. Mrs. Conroy appeared in the doorway, and I flattened myself. The crash of the Sharps filled the barn. The recoil had knocked her back, but she still held the rifle. I got up. Seeing me, she turned and ran.

Before taking off after her, I scooped up my Smith and Wesson and its holster, then checked Conroy for weapons. He had an old Navy Colt stuck in his waistband. When I pulled it out, he moaned but didn't open his eyes. Not having time to empty the cylinder, I flung his gun as far as I could into the nearby marsh grass.

Their latched door needed a couple of kicks. The blanket that divided the room flapped as if someone had just gone through. I picked up one of the chairs and hurled it at the middle of the curtain, then dove for the nearest end. I don't know what I expected would be on the other side of the curtain, but it wouldn't have been anything close to what confronted me.

7

Into Unknown Lands

A stone floor slammed my body. I rolled over and raised myself into a squat, ready to lunge for cover. The room I had landed in looked like the entry to a grand mansion. By grand I mean lots of space, carved stone pillars, dark marble floor—not packed dirt like it should have been. I've visited mansions. I've been to Wheeler's place, in Chicago. It was nice. This was nicer. The ceiling was a long way off, maybe two stories high, and vaulted. Behind me, the blanket hung. Light came from a row of candles in wall sconces. I peered through an arched opening into the next room. Where I had entered was a closet in comparison.

I eased through the archway. Like I said, the place was nice, but it was dirty. Debris studded the marble floor, dust, fragments of masonry and furniture, the desiccated body of a rat. The dust was thick enough to bury yourself in. Mezzanines flanked both sides of a long gallery. Something up there moved—I dropped to the floor. The Sharps blasted. I felt and heard the bullet crash into a pillar. Shards of marble landed on me. One hit the tender spot on the back of my head. Self-preservation had me up and shooting before she could reload. I ran to the side from which she had fired. She wouldn't be able to reach me without leaning over the railing. The sprint had me winded. I shook out the spent cartridges and pushed new shells into the cylinder.

When I started to walk, pain twisted me. I flattened to the wall as if held in place by a giant hand. My throat tightened. My head ... I reached to find ... but what ... where was my head? My hand went up, and up, finding nothing. But my eyes ... I had eyes. I could see ... therefore a head must still be connected. My cheek ground into floor grit. When did I fall? Such a nice marble floor ... its veins formed words, pictures, a map of unknown lands. I rolled onto my back. Above me fluttered gulls. Perhaps I should stand. The doctor had told me to stay off horses, but I didn't listen, disobeyed my doctor's orders. Now ... this won't do at all ... lounging about while Mrs. Conroy creeps back to find me. I tried crawling, but the gun in my hand got in the way.

Getting up took a while, then I had to wait for the dizziness to pass. The other end of the room was several miles off. I started toward it, searching for a way up. I passed a few shapely tables, decorated with crystal vases, dead and crumbling flowers piled around them. My feet stirred the dust. Sweat dripped from my face. I couldn't tell *where* the heat came from. It just was.

A grand staircase jutted into my path. I looked back—the distance I had walked surprised me. I started up the stairs, holding the bannister for support. The stairs ended at the mezzanine; I could go right or left. I chose right, the side Mrs. Conroy had shot from. A walkway extended back the way I had come, with a railing on one side and a wall on the other. Paintings decorated the wall, but time had left them murky. The opposite mezzanine was identical, except there were doors on *that* wall, spaced twenty or so feet apart. I hoped Mrs. Conroy wasn't hiding behind one.

Some ways on, my walkway turned to connect with the other side, to a stairway leading up. I was nearly to the first landing when the scrape of a boot on pavement sounded from above. My moccasins had kept my progress silent. I backed down to the mezzanine and waited near the stairway's entrance. The sound of footsteps stopped. I imagined Mrs. Conroy standing there, listening. I could outlast her, I could stay so still that no one.... She screamed, a banshee wail of attack, and ran at me with that Sharps. I fired. Red splashed her chest; that Sharps went over the rail and clattered at the bottom. I was very happy to see it go.

My head throbbed. The boom of that Sharps and my own gun hadn't helped. I squatted by her body. What does it mean to eat someone's cooking and a few hours later have to kill her? Good of her not to have poisoned my dinner.

"You fixed me a fine plate of beans, Mrs. Conroy. I'll take you back and bury you with your husband, if he's dead."

I slung her over my shoulders and set off toward the staircase, then down and across the long gallery. Spotting the Sharps, I dumped Mrs. Conroy's body. I picked the gun up by the barrel and slammed the hammer against the stone floor until I was satisfied that it would take a gunsmith to make it work again.

Echoes of clattering faded, and I heard something—the sound of many feet on stairs. Feet that weren't booted, feet that sounded like bare bones on pavement. A stench of rotting seaweed and wrecked ships descended with the sound. I ran. At the blanket-curtain, I paused to look back. In the shimmery distance, shapes moved, low and wide shapes that reminded me of crabs. I pushed through the curtain.

Conroy . . . I thought it was Conroy . . . sat in a chair by the door. A pile of sand covered his feet, and I caught more of that rotten ocean smell. His head was a nude skull, dry, yellowy-white bone. The revolver that I had flung into the marsh grass—or another like it—lay in his dead hands, dead fleshy hands. Then his skull-head turned toward me, and the gun-hand lifted. I sprayed my remaining bullets at his face. Bone fragments and smoke filled the air. He dropped his revolver.

Something fell from his mouth and struck the revolver, making a metallic clink. I picked it up. A copper disk, with a design scratched into its surface, the shape of Conroy's cattle brand, with that same gash of mouth. Like the savage face on the sand hill. I threw it into the fireplace.

I stayed long enough to do two things: take Silverberg's watch from Conroy's pocket and shatter the lit oil lamp against the wall timbers.

Night-dark still covered the sky, but the burning cabin brightened the barn enough for me to load my things onto Patience and Blue Swamp. I left the gate open for Conroy's horse, donkey, and cow to do as they pleased. And off I rode.

Some time later, the trail led up through a gap between tumbled boulders. In retrospect, the rocks should have been a clue—this wasn't a region where such things normally abound.

The boulders were twisted, misshapen things. They reminded me of the hardened sand hill where I had found Silverberg's remains. A whistling blur of feathers hurtled down. Solo. Blue Swamp bolted into the rocks, dragging Patience along. I managed to slow him, then stop. The boulders had risen to form a high and narrow cleft. I tried to back Blue Swamp, but the damn mule Patience wouldn't move. We had no choice but forward. Solo circled overhead, cried, and flapped off into darkness. Had he been trying to keep us from going through the gap?

Daylight, or something like daylight, showed me a landscape resembling churned and twisted mud that had hardened into rock. Purple sky banished the sun. Nothing lived, nothing grew. No birds passed above. If the sun still existed, no hint shone through, nothing to cheer a hopeless traveler. I've seen land after the battering of hurricane or flood. I've seen lava beds out west, but even those crack and erode and admit life. This void showed no trace of ever having looked different. If all water was removed from the lifeless bottom of the ocean, exposing whatever muck covered the seafloor, and a thousand degree sun baked it for a century, it might look something like this.

The gulf should have appeared by now. From Conroy's house to the bay couldn't have been more than a mile. But no water, nothing to interrupt the endless hardened muck. *Where have you gone, oh water of my youth?* Perhaps this dryscape would continue until we reached Florida. Desiring someone to talk to besides my horse, I twisted around to get Silverberg's skull from its saddlebag. I rested the skull on the pommel. "See where we are?" I said. "Not the nicest place for an excursion."

Onslaught of dry and cold and crippled earth... permeation of nothing, nothingness that subtracted life, drained color. What of time?... what of...? Without features to vary the monotony, without sun or even cloud... mind dulled... deadness of thought joined deadness of land. Images... can I find the images of memory? Only those will expel the nothingness: childhood... a small man with a pencil... a woman playing the piano... waves of gray-green water lashing the shore. Hold them, tumble through the choking surf, ride ivory steps upward and farther upward, into the light, the dancing light, light that smiles and sings. Hold now and breathe, breathe in light, breathe out air. Waves pass unseen. And again. Crusted land, crusted and buried. Is this the end? Life smothered and dried into this tortured crust?

I don't know how long I rode. At some point, Blue Swamp refused to continue. I dismounted. "Sorry big guy. We should stop here. One place looks like another. Nothing for you to graze on." My watch had stopped, as had Silverberg's. I looked for a smooth, or at least smoother, place to lay my bedroll. The animals followed, staying close. "I guess this will have to do," I said, dropping my bedroll. I unsaddled them. Neither showed an inclination to wander. I filled the Dutch oven with water and spread some corn on the saddle blanket. The water would only last another day at most. Before slipping into my bedroll, I opened the flaps of the saddlebag that held Silverberg's skull. I didn't remember putting it back in there. "I have your watch," I said. "But I've gotten us lost. I'll find our way back. Don't worry."

Sleep didn't come easily. I moved my bedroll several times, searching for a smoother surface. Night never appeared, though the purple sky might have darkened some. In the morning, or at least in the period that followed my lack of sleep, Patience was gone. I scouted for tracks, but nothing penetrated the iron landscape. All I found was a smear of what might have been dried blood, but it looked too old to be hers.

There wasn't much in her pack that I needed. With no fuel for fire, I left the cookware but took the bacon, hardtack, and condensed milk. I would eat the bacon cold if I needed to. With water low, I hesitated over the powdered milk and cornmeal, but brought them. Ever the optimist.

"You'll have to carry some things," I said to Blue Swamp, and led him away. I walked for a while, wanting to spare him the extra weight. Air pressed on me. My weight, weight of air, weight of time . . . time banished—buried with the concretized muck. Horizon . . . horizon moved, keeping me distant. Somewhere past the curve of earth I would find a spring, a meadow, the gentle shade of cottonwoods. Something moved . . . distant . . . a flicker . . . bird? . . . beast? Blue Swamp whickered. "You saw it too? Well, let's ride." I mounted. "Not too fast, boy, not too fast." But some force rushed us onward. Jagged air tore my cheeks. I tied a neckerchief over my mouth to spare my throat. Through slitted eyes loomed an upthrust rock wall. I yanked the reins. Blue Swamp reared and bucked. I flew.

Consciousness danced at the end of a tunnel, an opening so distant that all the steps in the world couldn't take me there. Consciousness flickered, beckoned . . . I crawled. What else could I do? Though the effort had defeated stronger men. If only a sun awaited me, a sun and a sweet breeze, but those didn't exist, had never existed . . . fantasy wrapped itself around me, dreams of a soft world, a place where laughter danced and birds flew in complex formations, changing direction in the clear, cold air . . . if only there could truly be such a world. In the nothingness, my laugh sounded brittle. I crawled toward the sound of agony, crawled until I found another, my companion, whose strength had carried me, now broken.

I put a bullet in Blue Swamp's head and collapsed against him. Were those my tears? My head filled with them, rain, the only rain this blasted land could know.

8

A *Saloon full of Skull-Heads*

The ground rose. The slope was too gradual to see, but my legs felt it. Their ache turned to a lance of pain that ground its way through my calves. I labored on, weighted by saddlebags and the Greener, inventing games and tricks to keep the feet moving. Talking to Silverberg's skull helped—I hadn't left it, I couldn't. I told it what I saw and what I wanted to see. "Just past the horizon there'll be a western sky, peaks and ridges flecked with gold, and the trees, aspens and firs . . . a warm summer sun . . . soft green grass to rest on . . . a perfumed breeze . . . her hand in mine."

But who was "her?" Never mind, there was always a her in this kind of fantasy, and the next ten steps would take me to her, the next twenty, fifty . . . and on. When I needed rest, when I knew that I couldn't go farther, I pretended that the sun was setting, and I stopped to make my bed. I even slept, but something woke me, some subtle change in the flat and heaving air.

I sat up and looked around. Lights flickered. Real lights? Or fragments drawn from my desperate imaginings.

Off I went, hopeful, but expecting the lights to vanish, or keep ever-distant, like the mirage of water that confounds desert travelers. I trudged, getting no closer. When I stopped, unable to go farther, a structure sprawled into view, a two-story frame building with a false front. A couple of pillars remained to support what used to be a porch roof. A faded and indecipherable sign hung above the second-story windows. The building reminded me of a saloon I had been to once, on the trail to somewhere west of the Mississippi, a little town I couldn't remember the name of. Except here, a strange mess jutted from the roof, rounded painted shapes, brown-and-gold checkerboards, raspberry, pink, and silver stripes, a gold hat. Closer, I could see that the shapes were connected, with more shapes beneath, like hats on a hat stand. The false front screened any view of how the hat shapes joined the roof.

The door was a simple bat-wing, like any saloon. Inside was even more dim, despite the lights that had drawn me. Instinctively, I stepped to my left, not wanting to be framed by the glow of the doorway. I held the Greener pointed down but ready to bring into action. Nothing moved in the dusky interior. My eyes adjusted. I made out tables and a bar. A man slumped over the bar, head down and unmoving.

Someone yanked the Greener away, and a pile of bricks smacked the back of my head, sending me to meet the floor.

I came back to life with a throbbing head, again. A scene emerged: someone had propped me in a chair, across a round table from a man . . . a man with a bare skull jutting from his shoulders, like Conroy's when I fled from the dead mansion. The skull-headed man was dressed like a ship's captain, double-breasted blue jacket with brass buttons, white shirt collar. The jacket showed some mends and fading, but was brushed clean. On the table between us sat two glasses and a bottle of liquor marked with a label in some Eastern European script. The skull-headed man filled the glasses and glided one toward me with his left hand, a nimble, long-fingered hand, a hand of flesh connected to a wrist of flesh that emerged from a coat sleeve. His skin was a deep bronze color. He wore a ring on one of his long fingers, a gold band set with a wine-colored, rectangular stone. An imaged was carved into it, the upper body and head of a winged woman, with one breast bared. Nike, I thought, but my knowledge of classical imagery isn't the best.

The Greener wasn't in sight, and my outside holster was empty.

The skull-head lifted his glass to his lipless mouth, tipped it back, and drank. Throat muscles worked the drink down. Grayish flesh, like exposed ligament, filled in the bottom of his lower jaw and connected it to upper jaw and neck. A ridge at the back of the jaw showed where an ear should be. The rest was bone.

I left my glass where it was.

Other skull-heads sat at a nearby table, playing cards, drinking, like a Day-of-the-Dead tableaux. I had left Victoria amidst Day-of-the-Dead preparations and now here I was, awakened to some macabre dream-version of the festival in which skeletons walk (and more than walk, as I was to discover). Past the table of skull-heads, stairs led up to a second floor. Another skull-head descended from there. This new-comer ... curvaceous body ... scant costume ... said saloon girl, and on reaching us, the newcomer flopped onto my table-companion's lap and wrapped her arms around him.

My skull-head ... Ring Hand ... pushed her off. He stood, bowed toward me, then pointed to the card-players' table.

I shook my head. "Thanks, but I'll pass if you don't mind. Not interested in cards right now."

He bowed again, made a noise at me that came from his throat, and carried the bottle to the table of card players. Not knowing the stakes, or the nature of my opponents, playing poker seemed like a bad idea. That was what part of me thought—the part that was here ... here? ... the part that didn't run screaming, the part that said if I *did* try to leave, Ring Hand, or whoever had clipped my head, might do worse to me. Though I wasn't playing poker, the same rules applied—watch, wait, calculate odds, keep the train on the tracks. The right side of my head throbbed. I ran my fingers over a lump. At least it wasn't the same place that had gotten stomped back in Victoria—Victoria ... how long ago that felt, another person had begun a journey there.

The skull-woman claimed Ring Hand's seat. She leaned toward me, throating something that sounded like a question. The table pushed her breasts up. Soft shadow of cleavage ... nipples indenting the flimsy garment, but ... in the hollow at the base of her neck, smooth, rosy skin turned to gray ligament and ended in bone nightmare. My eyes must have looked too long at the dark wonderland of her cleavage. She got up and plopped sideways onto my lap. Before I could react, she put an arm around me and squeezed my face into her breasts. I tried to push her away, but nothing I did had an effect. One arm—that was all she needed to hold me. Her other hand rubbed my groin. I responded like you would expect—that part of me acts independent of reason. My erection brought a sound from her, a lower throating, and she loosened her grip on my head. I turned my face to breathe. Then I jerked away; the chair fell, taking us with it. I was able to roll her off me. She got up, throated, and walked away—an annoyed flounce in any language.

The lump of my Bulldog pushed into my chest. I stood, leaving the chair where it had fallen. The gun's presence reassured me. I wouldn't use it, yet.

Watch and wait. There were six of the skull-heads, including the bartender and saloon girl. I walked toward the bar. And ... discovered that the slumping bartender wasn't a skull-head. Dark hair surrounded a bare spot at the crown. He wore a tan work vest with extra loops and clips hanging off of it, all empty. Scattered along the surface of the bar were a compass, sextant, and other tools. The bar was a fancy affair—especially considering where it was—with carved scrollwork, and on the back wall a mirror with a frame that matched the bar's carving.

I pushed on the man's shoulder.

"*Hauen Sie ab!* It is not the time, it cannot be the time."

That's what I thought he said, but I couldn't be sure of the exact words. The first part wasn't English and the rest had a Germanic accent that was tough to understand.

He lifted his head, noticed me, and stepped back. His mustache-lidded mouth opened, a look of what I assumed was surprise. "*Mein*

Got! You are not on of the *Dämonkreaturs*." He stared, taking in my presence. "Who *are* you and how did you come to this hell-place?"

There was a sink behind him. I asked for a glass of water. He worked the pump and filled a glass. I told him something of my story, starting with Conroy's cabin.

"Your horse," he said. "How far? I wonder, would they allow me to go to it? Meat, you see. My training is as a butcher and there is no meat here, no fresh meat. Some of my supplies . . . they allowed me to retrieve from my craft—"

"Those things"—I pointed back at the skull people—"what do they eat?"

"They drink, profuse amounts. Liquor is the only thing I have seen go into their mouths." He ducked behind the bar, emerging a moment later with a burlap sack and a collection of knives wrapped in leather. "I am sorry, I have no manners left. My name is Dellschau, Charles Dellschau. I have forgotten how it is to speak with another person. You don't mind eating your horse?"

I said horse-butchery was fine. Curious to see how Dellschau communicated with them, I followed him to Ring Hand's table. I can't say I relished the idea of eating Blue Swamp or watching Dellschau eat him, but such a faithful animal shouldn't be wasted. I'm practical, and I like to eat. There are worse things out there than horseflesh.

Dellschau stopped beside Ring Hand's chair. "This man has left his expired horse a short distance away. I would like to go and collect some of its flesh for us to eat." He pantomimed, cutting with knife, eating.

Ring Hand made no acknowledgment. I asked Dellschau if that had been yes or no.

"I won't know until I try to leave."

He walked toward the bat-wings. I didn't see the movement, but before Dellschau reached the door, Ring Hand had blocked his path. He held up a hand and throated at Dellschau. Dellschau's shoulders slumped; he trudged back to the bar, cursing in German. From his posture and expression, he appeared drained of hope.

My saddlebags were near the door. I scooped them up and followed him. "I wasn't looking forward to eating my horse anyway," I said, trying to lighten his mood. "And, I do have a good-size slab of bacon in my saddlebag. Also cornmeal and powdered milk."

"Ah . . . bacon, *schönen dank*." His eyes went dreamy.

Before my groping hand found the bacon, I touched Silverberg's skull. I considered pulling it out and waving it at our captors. Maybe it would scare them. I handed Dellschau the meat and the other foodstuff. He bowed and thanked me again, and busied himself with building a fire in the stove.

"There is a storeroom behind the bar," he said. "I have found cans and jars, dried fish, dried beef, beans, grain. The air here seems to keep mold away."

Remembering the desolation outside, I asked what he burned. He turned and smiled. "Fuel . . . why, I burn parts of this building. When I need to, I walk toward the back and pull off boards. This building is surprisingly extensive; the hall goes for quite a distance."

"That Ring Hand—he's the leader? And is this . . . the ones here . . . that's all of them?"

"The guitarist is missing—he . . . he . . . I hope he never returns. I cannot face the dance. . . . The Ring Handed one, he is always here. He killed Peter, my companion."

Dellschau stared toward the table of card players, but I don't think he was seeing them. "Lost, we landed our craft on the roof. We entered through an upper window, found the stairs, and descended. At the sight of these devils, Peter drew his pistol. His shot missed. They tore off his arm that held the gun and left him lying, blood emptying from his body. I told him I would avenge, but how can I?" He lowered his head to the bar and sobbed.

By "landed our craft on the roof," I wondered if he meant the colorful hat-rack I had seen on my way in. "Some kind of balloon?" I asked.

Bacon sizzled. "This scent restores me," he said. He raised his head and turned to check the progress.

"Our aircraft. Not a balloon, not exactly. Of a purpose, not many know of us, but I see no reason to hide from you. We set off from our mooring range, flying the *Splendid Kestrel,* as fine a craft as anyone could fashion. There were three of us. Myself, Peter, and young Haskell. Our place where we store the airborne vehicles in which we travel—I won't tell you where it is. We call ourselves the Sonora Aero Club. We set off from there. Our plan was to fly down the coast toward Mexico. We pursued Morgan, a man who had worked his way into our group for the purpose of stealing a craft. But that does not concern you."

Dellschau had been turning the bacon from time to time and, deciding that it was ready, distributed the slices onto plates. From a breadbox, he pulled out a piece of cornbread and put it in the still-sizzling grease. "We won't waste anything," he said. "This poor bread needs much improvement." He added the cornbread to our plates and we tucked in. While we ate, he resumed his tale. "South of San Diego, a storm blew at us, a hurricane if you can believe it. I had been told that such are rare. This one began like a normal storm, and we were able to gain enough altitude to avoid its worst. But the sky turned an unnatural gold, and the winds blew upward and crosswise at the same time. Haskell had been adjusting a navigational rudder, and that first gust sent him over the side. Lost." He bent his head again, sobbing.

California, the coast he spoke of was California, not Texas. Those winds had carried him far. I gazed around. Ring Hand and others were still playing cards, but one of the players, the one wearing a bowler, had moved to another table; the saloon girl straddled him. His trousers were crumpled over his ankles. I jerked my head away. Dellschau must have become inured to such things. Not that his emotions were in check. I waited till he was ready to resume.

"Alas, there was no time to mourn, for we had to keep the *Splendid Kestrel* aloft. Truly, I don't know how we managed it. And now, stranded, imprisoned, I wish I had perished in the air, the glorious air!"

More yowling commenced. The sound of it was grating on me. I thumped his shoulder ungently. "Stop wailing. Tell me something about this craft, this group of yours. I have a thought or two on how to get us away from here."

He lifted his head. "You can . . . we can . . . leave? But how?"

"That can wait. I don't like to rush things. Until it's time to rush things." The thought of leaving cheered him, but it took some coaxing to get him back to his storytelling.

"Our aero club . . . we have constructed several of the craft. My involvement was due to my cousin Elsa. Her designs and Peter's *suppe* to fuel them. I'm only a butcher, but cutting meat and cutting wood and fabric are similar enough. Our club has traveled the skies for several years, exploring, protecting the frontier from marauders. The distant lands of the north hide many things, things that are best left undisturbed. I suppose this place, the southwest, does as well.

"We had avoided tragedy until Morton arrived. When he made his theft, he stabbed Miguel, I hope not fatally."

Funny thing—Llewelyn, in one of his rare bouts of revelation about his past, told me of his interest in airships. He watched Giffard's dirigible in France in 1851. He showed me reports of strange balloons spotted over Northern California, Canada, and Alaska. He went looking for them, and got caught in a freak hurricane that knocked through San Diego. I had been surprised at Llewelyn's quest. Foolishness of youth, he said. But he still hunted stories of airship development. He went to England just a few years ago to see some flights. That hurricane was 1858. Had Dellschau been here for thirty years?

"Your airship—I think I can get us up there, to the roof. Can we use it—does your ship still fly?"

"But I have tried to go upstairs. Each instance, aside from the one trip allowed for foodstuff, the ringed one blocked the stairway. You cannot imagine the things they have forced me to do. I wish they would be done with me—please, let us be away before the next dance!"

I would have felt better about my companion's abilities if he didn't have these bouts of despair, but I hadn't been through his ordeals. Who knows how I would be acting? And—most relevant—I needed him. Sure, I could set off on foot again, hope that the wasteland ended soon, but I wasn't keen on trying. "We'll do it soon," I said. "But can you make your craft work again?"

"Yes yes, of course. It was our own human frailty that brought us down, not a defect of the *Splendid Kestrel*. Battling the storm, losing Haskell, sapped our energy. We had to moor somewhere and recuperate."

Now that I had brightened his prospects, Dellschau was ready to act, but rushing is the enemy of good detective work. Allow time to establish your quarry's behavioral quirks, tics, patterns. True even with skull-heads! I hoped.

How long had I been here? There was still some food on my plate. It felt as though I had been eating for hours. I had a thought—"Where do you sleep?"

Dellschau stopped chewing and looked at me. His mouth opened, then closed. A hand went to his forehead and rested there. "Sleep?" he finally said, voice trailing up into a question. "I . . . I don't recall when I have slept. Here? Have I slept here?"

"My watch doesn't work," I said. "We're in a place that's like a dream, that defies physical rules. Maybe we're asleep. Maybe I'm dreaming you, dreaming all this." But I knew I wasn't. I felt connections. This place, the skull-heads, they were linked to my search for Silverberg's killer and the money. Silverberg's skull, the skull-headed Conroy, Conroy's impossible house . . . and here . . . from one to another, all connected. I know. I'm someone whose job it is to see connections.

Stephens was said to wear a ring, too, a ring with a carved stone.

We continued eating. Dellschau told me more about the aero club, about the flyers and their adventures. I listened without judgment. If I accepted that he had a flying machine, then why argue with the rest? During his storytelling, I tried to keep track of what was happening around me. Mostly, I kept my back to the room, sometimes swiveling a fraction to one side, sometimes watching in the mirror. The skull-head who had humped the saloon girl returned to the card game. Ring Hand banged on the table with a whiskey bottle. Dellschau swore, then muttered: "Waiting on these creatures sickens me." He reached for a new bottle and took it to Ring Hand's table.

"What happens when the liquor runs out?" I asked when he had returned to the bar.

"Cases of it, more than you can believe, as if washed to this shore from all the seas of the earth."

"Interesting. I want to see." I lifted the gate on the bar and stepped through. The back of my neck prickled—I couldn't help wondering . . . dreading . . . the thought of being stopped by Ring Hand. A hallway went on for a few feet, then an alcove appeared on the left. There were a couple of crates, no more. I commented, and Dellschau told me to turn into the alcove. Steps led down to another hallway. Crates everywhere . . . how far did the hall go? The air grew hot and stale. If getting to the airship proved to be impossible, we might have to see if this passage led someplace better.

Crates were labeled in French, Russian, Spanish, pictographs, Oriental characters, English, Cuneiform? and some with no lettering at all. I opened an unlabeled bottle of clear liquid and sniffed. Pretty raw stuff. I rummaged bottles, putting together a crate with six of the rawest, along with an old bottle of something Irish, and carried it to the bar. I asked Dellschau for rags, but didn't tell him what I was thinking.

Another skull-head came in. He wore a tan jacket and a wide-brimmed black hat, an old style, like a bowler but with a flat top. He carried a Spanish guitar. I say "came in," but I didn't see any entering . . . only the new skull-head, standing near the others as if he'd always been there. Dellschau returned, a bundle of rags hanging from his hand. When he saw the new skull-head, he made a half-strangled noise. The rags fell from limp fingers. Ring Hand throated at us.

"He wants me again. I can't . . . not the dance."

Ring Hand started our way. He reached into a pocket and pulled out a red bandana . . . no, two of them. He flattened one on the bar and folded it into a ribbon about three inches wide, then did the same with the other. He rapped on the bar, startling me—I was far too jumpy. Dellschau's head jerked up at the sound. Ring Hand shook a bandana and throated at us some more.

"I can't," Dellschau said. "But I dare not refuse." He came from behind the bar, and Ring Hand wrapped the bandana over his eyes.

I uncorked the Irish and poured myself a shot. The saloon girl skull-head came over and led Dellschau to a clear space between tables. The skull-head guitarist began to pick out a melody. Dellschau, it appeared, was expected to dance with her!

Ring Hand picked up the other blindfold and held it toward me. I gulped down my drink. He tied the cloth and led me closer to the guitarist. Someone put my left hand against a smooth roundness of wood . . . my fingertips recognized a familiar shape . . . a double bass. Someone pushed my right hand to the strings and throated. I was expected to accompany the guitarist.

Years since I had played a bass. Such a large and bulky instrument was too impractical, however much I liked it. Despite my circumstances, plucking the thick strings sent me into a trance. Note to note to note . . . only the notes mattered. I know I wouldn't have felt so nonchalant if my position and Dellschau's had been reversed—forced to dance with death, with a skull-headed whore. I would have started firing away with my Bulldog, whatever the consequences. How long we played was as unclear as all time had been since I entered the desolation zone. Most of the guitarist's tunes were familiar: "Take Me Back to Town," "Stay the Night," "Fading Lovers." My fingers burned with the pressure of mashing string to fingerboard. I ignored the pain as best I could, but the buzzing of poorly made notes distracted me. I stopped, letting my left hand hang at my side, wriggling fingers to restore feeling. The blindfold came loose.

Ring Hand stood before me. Hard to read facial expressions when there's no flesh, but I swear he looked at me with warmth . . . friendliness even. Pleasure at the music we played? He bowed, and gestured toward the bar, releasing me from service.

I found the trail back to that bottle of Irish. Dellschau was slumped like he had been when I first saw him. His pose made me wonder if the dance had ended just prior to my arrival. I recalled his earlier words: "It is not the time, it cannot be the time."

9

The Splendid Kestrel

Time is a hill, a hill that grows as you climb, grows to mountain size. Wind and rain alter the mountain, exposing rock, minerals. Looking back the way you came gets harder. Sometimes, all you can see is the rising path ahead of you. You get to the top. Everybody does. Sometimes sooner than we expect. The journey is what matters. Here in skull-head land, time means nothing. The skull-heads are actors on a stage, doomed to perpetual repetition of the same scene. Maybe they *are* doomed; so am I if I don't get away. Since the blindfold session, I had chosen to stand on Dellschau's side of the bar, liking the solid feel of its timbers between me and the skull-heads. They went on as usual, playing poker—five-card stud exclusively—with bowler hat taking breaks to hump the saloon girl. This place challenges my methodical nature. I opened my notebook to document what had gone on, my conversation with Dellschau, our meal, the blindfold dance, and was puzzled to discover that I had already done that. When? Had these events happened . . . and repeated?

We had to escape, and soon.

Thanks to my boss Llewelyn's interest in airships, I've heard of some of the recent attempts at powered flight. None of those craft could do half of what my new friend claimed for his. I asked him to explain the process of activating his air machine.

"The *Splendid Kestrel* is powered by a special engine. The engine rotates the paddlewheels, and exhaust gases lift the balloons. Some time will be needed for the gases to build up pressure. We will be safe ... I hope we will be safe ... once we have enough lift to detach from the roof. But how do we keep the creatures away while I start the process?"

"I'll take care of that," I said, hoping it would be true. "You must have to carry a lot of wood, or kerosene, or something."

"The fuel is *suppe* ... Peter's invention. The *suppe* is a compact solid. It burns slowly yet with great heat." He spoke without looking at me, as if afraid of revealing too much.

Alcohol burns. Not with as much heat as kerosene, but it burns. Waiting time was over. I took the rags and twisted them into ropes that could squeeze into the necks of the bottles. I had Dellschau uncork them and make a row on the floor. "Gather whatever you need—these instruments," I said, and pointed to the sextant, compass, and assorted oddments. "Whatever else you have here. All I have are these saddle-bags. How do they move so fast? Can't let them see what we're doing." I surveyed the room. The poker game continued. "Can you hunt up a few strips of wood, kindling? We'll need something to light the wicks." He did as I asked and placed the ends of the sticks in the fire. "Now, switch with me. Keep yourself where they can see you, and let me know if anyone moves."

I pulled a strip of wood from the stove and lit four of the alcohol-soaked rags. Taking one bottle in each hand, I stood and tossed both at the card-players. One struck the table and shattered, exploding into flame. The second overshot, but made a nice splash of fire on the wall. Dellschau flung two bottles and ran toward the stairs. I lit another and left it on the floor, then picked up the last along with my saddlebags and followed him.

Dellschau clomped up the stairs. I reached the bottom and turned to light and throw the last bottle. Smoke and flames engulfed everything. I couldn't see any skull-heads. That didn't make me feel too good. I drew my Bulldog and continued upward. Behind me, boots thumped. The guitarist flowed toward me, burning instrument raised to strike. I shot. One slug hit his chest and the other smacked a hole in his forehead. He fell backward down the stairs.

At the second floor, I scrambled through an open window onto an overhang. Dellschau's flying machine rested on the flat roof. It was tall. When I had seen it on my way in, the lower parts had been hidden by the false front. The craft had a boat-shaped body, with paddlewheels, though not in a place where they would ever reach the water. One giant gasbag projected from the middle; a smaller one stuck out in front, with two others toward the rear, one on each side. An engine whined and rumbled. A ladder took me to a ship-like deck, about the size of a fishing smack. Dellschau was forward, hunched at a bank of panels and pressure gauges, like the controls of a railroad locomotive. He saw me.

"The lift-crown is charging," he said. "Now we wait for it to reach buoyancy. What of those—did any follow?"

"I stopped one on the stairs. I'm not ready to believe we won't see more of them. Do you have any weapons?"

He moved to an iron-banded chest secured with a combination lock and opened it. I dropped my saddlebags, and he passed me an ugly, short-barreled gun that had what looked like a cake tin hanging down in front of the trigger.

"We call it the rapid-fire pistol. It fires one hundred rounds, like a Gatling but with no crank." He pulled a lever back. "That cocks it. Pull the trigger, and it keeps firing until you release the trigger. Very powerful, but only good for short range."

The building beneath us shook. Setting fire to a structure that also served as platform for an escape vehicle has its drawbacks.

Assuming that any pursuing skull-heads would follow the way we came, I had been watching that side of the roof. Movement drew my attention back to Dellschau—the skull-headed saloon girl stood on the railing near him. I yelled for him to duck, and yanked the trigger.

My gun shrieked; Saloon-Girl sprouted holes and fell backward. Then a weight struck my back and knocked me flat. The gun flew from my hands. I pushed myself to my feet and grabbed my Bulldog.

A body sprawled a few feet away . . . no, not a body . . . the bass—that was what had knocked me over. Ring Hand appeared; I hadn't seen him coming. He opened his mouth and throated. I thought he sounded disappointed. I fired at his chest.

He fell. His body convulsed. The wound in his chest leaked a thick brown sludge. The deck tilted, righted itself. We were floating! I holstered my Bulldog and ran to the railing to look over. I shouldn't have turned my back on Ring Hand.

I had a moment to gaze at the receding roof, then a hand yanked me around. I punched Ring Hand's stomach. Which did about as much as slapping a wall with a sheet of paper. He didn't defend himself or try to hit me. I aimed my punches at where I had shot him. That appeared to bother him some. He bounced me off the railing, then put his arms around me and started to squeeze my guts. His fingers were where I could get at them. I thought I could pry up his pinky fingers and break them. They didn't move. His squeezing was cutting off my breath. I thrust my feet against the top of the railing and pushed; he fell, with me on top. His grip loosened enough for me to break free. I kicked him as I got up, then again. Seeing the rapid-shooter on the other side of the deck, I saved the last kick and ran toward it.

He grabbed an ankle to trip me. I got up. Too late. Somehow, he stood in front of me, holding the rapid-fire gun. I reached for my Bulldog, but he fired first. His gun blew up, tearing off his hands. Splatters of metal stung my face. I ran at him, knocked him against the rail, and pushed him over. Watching him fall . . . I hadn't realized how high we had gone. The dead land was a brown smudge. Ring Hand joined it. I turned toward Dellschau. He held another of the rapid-shooters.

"I feared hitting you," he said.

"Well, we're away," I said. I went up to look at saloon-girl's body. She looked pretty well killed; I picked her up and dropped her over the rail.

Dellschau was carrying the bass to the railing, but I stopped him. "I want it."

"Your face," he said. "I have a medical kit in the cabin. Come." A short flight of steps down from the main deck led to a cabin with some seating and a small kitchen. The cabin muffled the howl of wind and machine—a din that I hadn't noticed until it was absent. I sat, laying the bass at my feet. He got out the kit and looked over my various scrapes and gouges.

My injuries were bearable, but my clothes weren't. I had a clean shirt in my bag, but extra trousers were back with Blue Swamp. Dellschau rummaged through some drawers.

"Haskell was too slight and I am too stout. Peter's will be too long, but I can shorten them." He held a pair of brown dungarees against me, then cut some inches from the length. "That will serve until I have time to hem them. Now, let me see about food." He put on a pot of beans and salt pork. The fresh produce had transformed to a petrified mass. Same with the stuff that had been in the meat locker. At least the water supply was intact. Beans and salt pork could keep us going.

Dellschau pulled out his charts. I knew they wouldn't give us anything useful. I hadn't told him about my entering the cracked land via the Texas coast. He might have drifted as far as Texas, but I didn't think so. We weren't someplace that anyone could find on a map. He pointed to the Sonora Desert region, southern Arizona, northern Mexico. "A harsh and dangerous land, I have been told. But a land that ends. If only my instruments hadn't failed, so that we might know our direction. Electrical damage from the hurricane, no doubt."

The human brain is remarkable in its ability to convince itself of the familiar, whatever the evidence. Well, I wasn't going to argue with him. We had to be going somewhere . . . better to be traveling in the air than down below. A sentiment I believed even more when we reached the battlefield.

10

Above the Endless Conflict

Armies fought from lines of trenches divided by desolation. Soldiers advanced, overran the opposition, or were slaughtered. Bodies remained where they fell. Wails of the hurt or dying stabbed the air. We couldn't tell who the armies were, what nationalities. Methods of killing shifted. One moment we passed over something like the War Between the States, with muzzle-loading percussion cap rifles, then to swords and longbows, to repeating rifles. Groups covered in armor swung at each other with short swords, then an infantry charged, bayonets clamped to flintlocks. Some of the fighting was mismatched. A company of rifles decimated armored sword-wielders, repeating rifles triumphed over wheel-locks. Armored, mechanical wagons crushed a troop of infantry, grinding bodies into the dirt.

The fighters either couldn't see us or were too intent on the killing. Unable to endure the blood and din, we fled to the cabin. The cabin walls dulled the sounds of war like they did for wind and engine, but walls couldn't make us forget what was happening below. I've gotten callous, I've seen crime and death, but nothing prepared me for this slaughter. How can man be so cruel to his fellows? And not just man . . . in some of the armies, we saw women, armored women slashing with blades, women firing rifles, bows, hurling javelins.

Could those combatants not recognize the futility of their actions? No scrap of land is worth such suffering.

Fortunately, my bass hadn't been damaged when Ring Hand threw it at me. I played to distract us. Without a bow, I plucked slow tunes. Its tones helped bandage the death and blood.

Farther on, smoke obscured the endless conflict, a thick black layer that pulsed like a living thing. Screams and flashes of gunfire penetrated the murk. My playing lagged. Not even music could save us. Dellschau neglected the controls. The *Splendid Kestrel* charted its own path. I lay on the cabin's deck, eyes closed, hugging the bass. An explosion lifted our craft, then dropped it. We both slammed against the cabin wall. Our gazes met. Dellschau looked shaken. I'm sure I did too.

"I should increase our altitude," he said, but closed his eyes.

More explosions followed. Some were dull rattles, others sent us to bobbing like a dinghy in a rough sea. Leaving the comfort of my bass, I crawled to Dellschau. Crawled because I didn't yet have the will to stand. I shook him and yelled in his ear. "You, get up!" I couldn't control my voice. "Get moving! Steer us away, anywhere, just away." I heaved him to his knees. We both stood, and together we made it to the controls. The voice of war thundered at our bodies. He tugged on a brass lever but it wouldn't move. The deck tilted and the engines throbbed. The largest explosion yet tossed the ship sideways. Another followed, and another again. Dellschau strained against the lever. He called for my help. We pushed together.

Stinging brightness flashed.

I clamped my eyes tight. The greatest blast yet ripped the air. A force gathered beneath us, sucked us down, then . . . threw us up . . . and . . . up. My eyes opened to blackness, the black of sightlessness. I fell to the deck. The force of our rise pummeled me, crushed my breath . . . blackness joined blackness.

"We shall make landfall by evening," Captain Bellis said. He spoke with the reassurance of his years at sea. "Haven't seen a blow like that since '33." He called out for more sail, and the crew responded. The sea sparkled with that peculiar brilliance that follows a storm.

Captain Bellis was a tall man, with a face channeled by wind, sun, and salt spray. His skin was chestnut from the sun and, I guessed, some amount of African heritage. His age could have been anywhere from forty to eighty. He might be immortal, preserved by salt breeze and wave. Iron hands gripped the wheel, hands that no wind could pry off course.

Reassured by the placid ocean, Channing returned to his cabin. A landsman, he had slept not one second during the storm, desiring to meet death with open eyes. Ah, but now calm seas put fears aside. He dozed, awakening from a brief but disturbing dream about an endless trek across a wasteland, the arid opposite of ocean. Horrible creatures pursued him, beasts with horses' bodies and heads that were bare human skulls. Whenever they drew close, he aimed a pistol and shouted. The shout—his voice— apparently served as bullet, in that peculiar dream-logic that never makes sense outside of sleep. Having, in waking life, never fired a gun, perhaps his sleeping brain was sending a message that he should learn how.

He cast off the final vestiges of dream and splashed his face with fresh water. When he ascended to the deck, land, blessed land, smudged the horizon.

"Channing—there you are," the captain said. "I was about to send the boy to wake you for dinner. I would be pleased to have you join me in my cabin."

Channing accepted and followed the captain down the ladder. In the doorway, Channing stopped for a moment, surprised to find his one fellow passenger waiting at the captain's table. The lady had, throughout the crossing, kept to her berth. He had seen only glimpses of her since their embarkation.

She stood to greet them; the captain introduced her as Lady Patricia, daughter of the Earl of Walbright. She taller than

Channing, near the captain's height, with a vast supply of red hair. She had a squarish face that he nonetheless found appealing. Her smile revealed a missing lower tooth.

"I am Peter Channing." He was unsurprised that she had not heard of him, a mere architect. He wondered why the daughter of an earl crossed the ocean in such an insignificant vessel, a thought she soon answered. Meal conversation flowed around the vagaries of ocean travel. The storm had not bothered her—she had grown up with ships, her father having been a naval officer. Their captain had served under her father. She said that she only sailed aboard ships whose officers she knew.

Captain Bellis revealed that Lady Patricia had spent a good part of the storm hauling ropes and reefing sail with the crew. He spoke about it with great excitement (and respect, Channing thought).

"Perhaps you consider such activity to be unladylike, Mr. Channing, but sailing is as natural for me as riding horses is to country ladies."

"I don't have any notions about what is ladylike," he said. "My mother worked as hard as my father, running the inn. My sister and I performed whatever tasks were needed until we left, she for the stage and I for university. Though I do wish our mother had managed to experience more leisure before sickness overcame her."

"And what did you learn in your university?"

"Architecture. My specialty now is municipal buildings."

More conversation followed. Captain Bellis was called to duty, but he insisted that they remain and finish the wine. Which they did. Channing learned that she was bound to New Moldavia on a visit to her sister, whose husband was attached to the British Consul, and he told her about his commission.

"A synagogue?" she said. "Are you Jewish, then? Channing doesn't sound like a Jewish name, though I suppose one doesn't need to *be* Jewish to design a synagogue."

"I *am* Jewish, of Russian heritage. Our name is Chanun, but my parents encouraged me to change it when I went to university."

"That's rather disingenuous, isn't it? Hiding one's identity. Are we English so unaccepting? What about Disraeli?"

"Disraeli was only born Jewish. His family baptized him Anglican when he was twelve. I don't think he would have been prime minister otherwise. Look at what Rothschild had to go through to serve in Parliament. So, yes, England could be more accepting. Although that was some years ago." Thirsty after speaking so forcefully, he picked up his glass of wine, drank the rest, and poured himself more before continuing. "I don't hide my religion to those who know me, but having a more Anglicized name is useful. It has likely helped me gain commissions where, using my family name, I might have lost them."

"Then you should be happy to be visiting a Jewish colony."

"Yes, I am quite interested in seeing how things are run there. America has been accepting of the Jewish people, but this is the first large-scale enclave. I'm curious how these Romanians have adjusted to life on the wild frontier. I can't say I would find it enjoyable. But they had few options."

He tried to steer the conversation away from religion, but the lady was not an easy conversation partner. He felt himself babbling, trying to fill the silent spaces. If so, blame wine and lack of sleep. And the unavoidable differences in social position and religion, even if she was, say, less ladylike than expected of women from her class. When the last glasses were emptied, they separated.

That evening, the ship moored alongside the Indianola jetty, and in the hubbub of docking and disembarkation, he met her again briefly. A carriage waited for her, a handsome vehicle painted black and red. Two Negros loaded her trunks.

"Farewell, Lady Patricia," he said. "I hope you enjoy a pleasant visit." She extended a hand, and he gripped it. Her fingers were strong, from handling rope and sail.

"And you, with your architectural commission." She spoke in that kind but distant way that the aristocracy have. He was accustomed to it from his dealings with town councils, which were most often led by whichever lord or earl controlled the area.

Channing waited for instructions from his employer, using the time to amble, looking at buildings and sampling the local cuisine—seafood prepared in surprising and fascinating ways. He sketched the harbor, the churches and synagogues, the fine stonework of the aqueduct. By the third morning, having heard nothing, he ventured to the telegraph office to send a message.

The fifth day, still with no reply, he asked a clerk at his hotel to recommend a place he could go to arrange transportation. Though Indianola housed a considerable Jewish population, the colony was farther inland. The clerk assured Channing that the road was quite easy, and directed him to a man who hired carts and drivers. The following morning, Channing departed by oxcart along a wide path that soon narrowed, passing through farmland and villages. The driver, a slab-headed man with no hair, spoke little; after the first awkward hour, Channing ceased his attempts at conversation.

In one of the villages, they stopped for the night at an inn run by a tall elder gentleman with a face smooth as polished granite. Channing slept poorly. The next day, fertile fields gave way to rock and desolation, a desolation that increased the farther they went. Channing asked the driver how far these barren lands stretched, but for an answer he only stared ahead.

Has there ever been a country more bleak? The sun ceased to shine. The sky assumed the color of crumbling brick. They passed no structures and no people. Channing pulled out his watch. It had stopped at half past nine. After he knew not how many miles of this, a building appeared on the horizon. The driver turned toward it. Channing asked if it was familiar to him. The man might have nodded. They reached the building much sooner than Channing had expected, its distance having been apparently exaggerated by the dull air and blasted earth. The building was constructed from mismatched and unpainted timbers that looked as if they had been reclaimed from ruins. The front door gaped; a hingeless slab of wood leaned against the wall.

Inside, a man was sweeping dirt into an immense pile. He turned at Channing's approach. From the back, he had looked as normal as ... as a man, but ... when he turned ... his face.... his face was nothing but bone, white bone. His jaw flapped up and down, as if speaking, but without lips or tongue ... all that came out was a throaty rumble. He raised a hand, a hand of flesh, and pointed toward a desk. He picked up Channing's bag and carried it. Channing turned and fled the building. The driver blocked the doorway, his head now like the other, bare of flesh. Channing tried to crash through him. The impact was like ramming a bull. He fell. His last sight before passing out was the driver's bone-face looming over him.

Something cold pressed the back of my head. I opened my eyes. I lay on a cot, in the cabin of the *Splendid Kestrel*. My head rested on a pillow covered with a damp cloth. No shouts, no explosions broke through the walls. I stood. And immediately sat. When the room stopped jumping, I tried again. This time I made it to the door. Sun dazzled my eyes. Dellschau sat at the controls. I started toward him. The sun steadied me. He heard me and turned around.

"You're up! Here, sit." He helped me into the other chair. "Your head struck the deck quite hard. I have been alternating hot and cold compresses for several hours."

"Where are we?" The view from my seat showed ocean. Ahead was a green smear of shoreline.

"Mississippi, if my instruments are to be trusted. I don't know how we came so far, but ... "

"Mississippi is better than where we've been," I said. I shuddered, overcome by a wisp of memory, or dream, or both. "How about turning left and taking me to Texas?"

His face showed something, but I couldn't tell what.

"We need water. For food and drink, but also as a component of our engines. We will have to set down somewhere, Louisiana. The charts show locations of population centers. We must avoid being seen. My charts may not be as accurate for this area."

We passed over tiny dots of fishing vessels, a schooner, and later, a steamer. Dellschau wasn't too concerned about being seen from a distance. The issue was landing. Toward evening, we passed the Mississippi Delta's maze of swamp and bay. "Hard to find solid ground around here," I said. "You'll have to head inland."

Tonight had more moon than Dellschau was comfortable with. He brought us lower. Scattered lantern-lights oozed through the trees, but the population was fairly dispersed. Closer to the ground, the heat grew, that muggy heat I knew well from my youth. The temperature surprised me. I wouldn't expect it to be freezing, but it was November; it should be cooler, even in the Louisiana swamps. Dellschau shut off the engine. We floated down. The only sound came from wind rubbing against the lift balloons. We settled in a clearing near a dark splotch of water. He yanked open a hatch.

"Here is a hose. If you feel strong enough, I shall need you to carry the nozzle to the water while I unwind the hose. This water will be brackish, but it will serve for engine use, and that will leave the fresh for our consumption."

He gave me a lantern and heaved a roll of hose over the side. I followed it down. It's hard to explain how good it felt to have real earth touching my boots. A barred owl hee-hawed from the trees. Frogs bellowed. The dank rot of swamp filled my lungs. One thing I didn't want to run into was an alligator. It was an alligator kind of place. Nearer the water, the ground became mushy. I sat on the root of a century-old cypress and leaned the lantern against the trunk. From there, I could ease the hose into the water. The nozzle submerged, and I waved the lantern to let Dellschau know that the hose was ready. He wanted me to hang around till the tank was full so I could guide the hose through the underbrush as he retracted it. Water gurgled, and the hose started its sucking. The mosquitos started their sucking too. Despite that, I closed my eyes.

A sharp pain spiked my calf. Solo the eagle was on the ground, about three feet away. My leg had a painful spot that felt like the shape of his beak. "What was that for? And how did you find me?" Something had changed. I jumped to my feet. The pump! I must have dozed. The pump had stopped and the hose was gone. I turned and ran. A tree root sent me sprawling. I scrambled up and over it, and took more care where I put my feet. The snake of hose receded through the undergrowth. Beyond it, the *Kestrel* hovered at about fifteen feet. I reached the hose as the end left the ground. I grabbed, twining my legs around it, and rose. He had expected that. I fell. Severed hose tangled my legs.

His voice called down. "I am sorry, my friend."

I slipped out my Bulldog. I couldn't see him, but the side of the *Kestrel* made a nice target. A spotlight plastered me to the ground. In its light were my saddlebags and the bass.

"I hope that you will not try to shoot at me," Dellschau said. "I would regret killing you. As it is, you are near enough to your Texas to manage more conventional transport. You have already learned too much about the Club, but you did help me escape."

The light died. I couldn't see a thing. By the time I could, the sky was empty.

11

Teddy Wells and his Texas Players

F riday morning, Lafayette station, I waited for a train to Houston. From there I could connect to Victoria. Reaching Lafayette had taken a succession of transports: wagon ride from a man driving a load of live crawfish to Houma, stage to Franklin, another to New Iberia. I stopped for the night in New Iberia and took a morning stage to Lafayette. In New Iberia I had myself a very welcome bath, a haircut and shave, then ate an enormous pile of crawfish. After dinner, I bought a newspaper. The date bothered me. Considering the temperature, the month felt right, but getting to it was the issue.

I sent a telegram to Llewelyn. Figured he should know I was still breathing. I said I would write a proper report on the train. I also sent a note to Griffin. That one was intentionally brief: Returning to Victoria; evening train. Maybe when I saw him I would tell him more.

My head ached, a background throb that the heat and humidity didn't improve. I had been banged around a lot, with my head taking most of the abuse. But the ache didn't bother me. At the moment, nothing bothered me. You know why? Since that moment when Dellschau and his craft lifted off into swampy darkness, my world reverted to a simple and recognizable normalcy. Road, trees, horses, people with skin on their faces. I liked that normalcy and wanted more. I wouldn't mind never seeing another skull-head, airship, or that dead scratch land.

The bass was still with me. I made carrying straps from the remnant of Dellschau's hose. It was an unfamiliar type, made from tight-woven linen strands; it had worked well enough as straps, but a bass is a very heavy instrument. I don't know why I bothered with it. Maybe to prove all those things had really happened. Bass, Silverberg's skull, my dents and bruises, all formed quite a collection of souvenirs. At least my body would heal. And I still had a man to find. A cold trail, but I had followed those before.

I had a thought and then I didn't, a wisp that dispersed and trickled away, but instead of trying to catch some of the strands, I let myself drift. Spices and sunshine, thread and hope, lust and language . . . I wanted something to lead me to a path, a faint game trail cut through the underbrush, track of deer, peccary, raccoon, bobcat, all inter-mingled. Intermingled but not lost, never lost, trails into paths then roads. In the city, no one can identify what streets began as animal tracks, but the tracks remain, buried deep beneath pavement. Sleep and no-sleep, thought and not-thought, travel and not-travel, every-thing has the same meaning. There is no opposite, no antonym.

The train came, and I boarded. Ignoring scenery and my fellow pas-sengers, I scribbled a report of what I had been doing. Who knows what the boss would think of it. Maybe it would be my last report. Maybe that would be fine. The part about Dellschau would interest him. I felt pretty stupid, getting tricked like that. Makes you lose all trust in your fellows. Not that I have much. I've seen too many betrayals in my years of chasing thieves and murderers. Maybe I would come upon him again someday. For now, I would be busy enough. Stephens the gambler—that's who I needed to think about. Figure out what he had been doing all this time I was gone. I had just been getting started on my investi-gations. Maybe while I . . . was gone . . . the marshal had found him. Or found someone who knew him well enough and was willing to talk. With all that money Stephens had acquired, I didn't see any reason for him to have stayed in Victoria. Though maybe he liked the town. And he might not think anyone was hunting him. His kind always believe that they're invulnerable.

When my train reached Victoria, the day was near to ending. Fiers, another operative from Llewelyn's, was waiting for me. He was a dark-haired man with an indefinite chin that he disguised with too much beard.

"Boss wired. Said you'd reappeared," he said.

I wasn't surprised that Llewelyn had sent an operative when I neglected to report, but I would have preferred someone other than Fiers. Once upon a time, he had been unhelpful during an incident in Northern Michigan. I hadn't died, but not because of anything he did. Fiers was the kind of operative who was kept around as filler. He was usually left out of the big jobs. So I guess I was disappointed that my disappearance hadn't rated someone better, like Creek Johnson or Betsy Milton.

We walked toward the hotel. Fiers didn't offer to carry anything. The heat still bothered me. It wasn't worse than you might expect from the time of year, but I hadn't come to it in the natural way.

"Been here a couple of months. Boss told me to find your bones after the local law couldn't turn you up. Also supposed to help finish your job. Guess I won't need to do that. Followed your trail easy enough, but couldn't get anywhere after a burned-out cabin near some shacks the locals call Alligator Head. Care to tell me about it?"

I pulled out a sheaf of papers and thrust it at him. "Read that," I said. "And then mail it off to the boss. Or carry it to him yourself."

He took the bundle without looking at it. "Boss said wait around and see if you need me."

"I'll let you know tomorrow. What I need now are clean clothes, food, and sleep."

He went into the hotel. I leaned the bass against the hotel wall and lingered outside. The sun was dropping past the opposite roof. An unmistakable rattle and hoofbeats from a stage came up the street, followed by the stage itself. Its roof was jammed with people, musicians, playing on guitars, bass, clarinet, and fiddle. They were singing a song about Oklahoma. I don't know how they managed to stay in time with all the bouncing and swaying. The stage stopped in front of the hotel. The fiddle player wore a black slouch hat and plaid shirt; everyone else wore white hats. The fiddler lowered his instrument and called out "Ahhh, do it mister man, do it now ... Ah-haaaa!" and the song flew to the finish.

Onlookers clapped. The musicians started climbing down. From somewhere across the street, sunlight on metal caught my attention. I found the source and was surprised that I wasn't the target. I yelled toward the musicians. "Rifleman on the roof."

I threw myself down on the boardwalk. The rifle boomed. A bullet blasted into the hotel wall. The stage team bolted, taking the stage, which the musicians had been using for cover. They scattered; a couple of them fired toward the opposite roof. The clarinetist, his instrument in one hand and pistol in the other, ran behind a stack of empty crates. The way he ran and fired at the sharpshooter reminded me of my shots at Mrs. Conroy on the balcony. The gun had even sounded like Mrs. Conroy's Sharps. But it wouldn't be her. Aside from both her and her gun being dead, this one hadn't been pointed at me.

The fiddle-playing leader settled under cover of a nearby water trough. We waited for another shot. After a minute, he eased past the trough for a better view. "Can't pick him out in the sun," he said.

I rolled over to his trough and had my own look. The place where the shot had come from was bathed in glare. Nobody wanted to be the first to decide that the sharpshooter had left. I could squat behind this trough for hours.

Fiers called from the hotel doorway. "Shannon. Shooter looks gone."

"How about if you head upstairs and try to get a better look?" I said. Fiers's lack of response might have indicated agreement, but I didn't hear footsteps going anywhere. Meanwhile, I continued to work on my waiting.

The fiddler spoke. "Shannon—is that your name? I hope that's not your bass over there."

I turned. The bullet hadn't struck the wall. Or, rather, it shattered the neck of the bass on its way to the wall. "Somebody doesn't like musicians," I said.

The clump of boots came our way, accompanying a person whistling "The Wild Rover." The footsteps and whistling stopped, and a voice hollered toward them. "It's Marshal Griffin coming. How's about nobody shoots me?"

"That you, Zach?" the fiddler said. "Thought I recognized the whistle. Come on over."

Footsteps resumed, and the fiddler and I got up from our shelter. Marshal Griffin entered the glow of the nearest gas light. He seemed about the same, big shoulders straining his jacket, hat low on forehead. The only thing missing was his guitar. I hadn't wanted to see him yet. The train ride and report writing had given me plenty of time to think about what to say to him, but I wanted to do it on the other side of sleep.

"Hey there, Teddy," the marshal said to the fiddler. "Guess I'm not surprised you were mixed up in a shooting." He looked over at me. "Shannon! I got your wire. Guess you aren't dead."

"Almost was, a couple of times," I said.

The fiddler wanted to shake my hand. I let him. He said his name was Teddy Wells. He was about my height, with prominent cheekbones and smooth skin. His face carried a big smile, a remarkable smile, considering what had just happened. Probably he was happy he hadn't been shot.

"Shannon here gave us the warning," Teddy said. "I suppose that shooter was after me."

Marshal Griffin went over to examine the damage to the hotel, and my bass. "Nice bass, Teddy. I guess you'll be needing a replacement for the concert."

Teddy patted the body. "It *is* a good one. Has power in it. Not ours though. Jake's is just fine."

"It's mine," I said. That was as much as I felt like talking about, for now. The marshal didn't ask for more.

The other musicians joined us. Teddy introduced them. They already knew Griffin. Also, the clarinet player wasn't a man. Her name was Katherine, and she was quite a lass, tall, brown eyes, strong slim fingers. Along with her white hat, she wore tan trousers. Her long legs ended in a pair of black boots. Griffin and the musicians decided to relocate to a tavern. I preferred keeping that appointment with bathtub and bed. I told Griffin I would find him in the morning.

"Shannon, you be sure not to miss our concert at the dance hall," Teddy said. "Come in and give Jake a rest on bass. We'll be playing some good ole Texas dance tunes."

I thanked him and said I would give a thought to his proposal. The hotel clerk retrieved my bag and assigned me a room. My old doctor bag was a pleasing sight. Considering my loss of clothing from the pack I had left with Blue Swamp and the sparse amount I had brought with me for my original Galveston wedding trip, I was going to need to get some laundering done and buy a few things.

A gray morning propelled me to the hotel dining room for breakfast and coffee. After I had drunk enough to revive my eyes, I opened a long letter from Rabbi Cohen, dated November 5, 1888, his response to my letter from before I left for Port Lavaca. The clerk had given it to me last night, but I hadn't felt like reading it. The rabbi said that he warned Silverberg's family to expect the worst. I felt guilty. I should have written to the rabbi from the Lafayette train, but I was too concerned with shaping a coherent report for my boss. I composed a short note—Silverberg's body found, more to tell in letter, will post later today—and asked the waiter to have it taken to the telegraph office.

I would enclose Silverberg's watch with the letter, for the rabbi to forward to Silverberg's family. His skull—last night, before shutting off the gaslight, I took it out and told it we were in Victoria and that I was back on the trail of his killer.

Along with my food, the waiter brought a message from Fiers. He said he was carrying my report back to Chicago. I guess that meant I didn't need his help.

The newspaper at my table was the edition of Saturday, June 1, 1889. Lots of information on people selling beef. The advertisement for the N. T. Gaines drug store listed them at telephone number 1. That was a new thing for Victoria. Someday soon it will be possible to talk on the telephone from here to Galveston, or Chicago, or even all the way to London. What else had I missed? I found an article about politics—Cleveland had been defeated but was expected to run again.

Those months—I would never get them back. At least the hotel hadn't tossed my bag. Time-wise, my absence hadn't been any longer than that of a fur trapper's season in the woods. The disjoint, the feeling of having been away was similar, but a fur trapper knows how much time is passing, lives it. I had been someplace where time is a fantasy.

I read through "The Outside World" section.

The Archives Judaiques of Paris makes the number of Jews in the world at 6,300,000.

All new Russian ships of war are to be lighted exclusively by electricity, and by next year it is expected to have the whole Russian fleet so lighted.

Congressman Archie Bliss, of Brooklyn, recently remarked: "It costs money to be a member of the House. I have been a Congressman for fifteen years, and have spent $10,000 a year outside of my salary. It has cost me $150,000 therefore, to represent my constituents."

I set the paper down and tried to eat. A couple of the musicians came in. Katherine, the nice lady clarinetist, and Jake, the bass player. They asked if they could join me. We chatted for a little while, but I was having trouble focusing on them. I kept seeing Ring Hand, his expression of betrayal at the end, and Dellschau's betrayal of me. My companions were too pleased with each other's company to notice my distance. Throughout breakfast, Jake looked at Katherine like she was ice cream. And who could blame him? There was a time when I might have done the same. I finished my coffee and got up.

"I need to go talk to the marshal," I said. "I guess I'll see you folks later. I'm looking forward to your dance concert." Outside, the heat wasn't too bad yet. The sun would be burning its way through the morning clouds soon. A whistle drew my attention to the other side of the street. Solo was perched on the opposite roof. He had some white feathers on his head now; I hadn't noticed them in the Louisiana dark. He stared with great intent at the area where the bass had been. I put a finger in the bullet hole and looked back toward Solo. His perch must be where the shooter had been positioned. I tipped my hat to him and moved along.

From the doorway of the marshal's office, I could hear Griffin's guitar; I was glad he still had his instrument attached. Too many other things had changed. A dark-bearded giant of a deputy leaned back in an oak swivel chair, legs and size fourteens taking up most of the desk's surface. Near his boots was a Colt .45. He wore his hat low on his head, trying to look asleep, but I could see his gaze shifting to cover me. I stopped and gave him a moment to decide whether I was worth talking to. Apparently I wasn't, at least not in the amount of time I allowed, which, I admit, wasn't much. I could have ignored him, walked back toward the sound of the guitar. Instead, I leaned across the desk, grabbed his boots, and pushed. The chair rolled back and toppled, tumbling him to the floor. He lay for a moment, then lurched to his knees and glanced toward his gun.

"I wouldn't," I said, but he did anyway. I tapped his wrist with the barrel of my Bulldog. He howled, and his gunmetal hit the floor with a nice thud.

"That's not a good way to make friends," Griffin said. The racket had drawn him from the office. Instead of his guitar, he held a shotgun.

"He's read too many dime novels about tough deputies," I said.

The deputy got to his feet. He was clutching his bruised right wrist with his other hand, but that didn't stop him from taking a couple of steps toward me. "Lemme punch this clown, Marshal."

Did I already say he was big? How big had been hard to tell when he occupied his chair. A good twelve inches and fifty pounds more than me kind of big. His hat was off and his hair was long and wild.

"Sit yourself down Gorman. Shannon, you come on back." I followed him to his office. He closed the door. "You didn't have to do that," he said.

"Maybe not." I sat in one of the horsehide-covered armchairs opposite his desk.

"And I suppose you had a good reason to burn the Conroy place, if that was you."

"Houses like that catch fire easily." We looked at each other for some time. He tried a different subject.

"I know someone who can repair your bass," he said. "Odd thing, your disappearing and coming back carrying a bass all the way from Louisiana."

"Farther than that," I said.

I told him about stopping to spend the night at Conroy's place and waking to find him going through my things, shooting him, being shot at by Mrs. Conroy, and going into the house after her. "Lantern must have gotten knocked over in the confusion." I could tell that my story hadn't satisfied him, but he didn't ask me anything else.

He gave an account of what had happened during my absence. Stephens's partner, Frank Lawson, was dead, murdered in McFarley's, his San Antonio saloon. The alleged killer was a drunken Mexican tracklayer. Stephens had been there playing cards, but no one admitted to have seen him with the shooter. Griffin said it was outside his jurisdiction but they would tell him anything they learned. No sightings of Stephens since. Or the money.

"Long gone from here," I said. "With that much money, he can go wherever he wants. Unless there's other business here that he's working on."

"If he's vengeful he might try to do something to Owens, that man from Sibley's bank," the marshal said. "Owens is a witness for the prosecution whenever Stephens is apprehended. He was convicted for theft and got sent to the state prison in Huntsville."

"What about those musicians—Teddy the fiddler. Why did someone take a shot at them?"

"It's happened before. Teddy and his boys have helped clean up messes all over Texas. Last year they helped some people beat a land grab by a banker in Flatonia. Someone needs protection, Teddy comes. Or the band goes to a town for a dance and somebody asks them for help. So no surprise he might get shot at from time to time."

Griffin got out a couple of cigars. I clipped an end and lit it. He picked up his guitar. I was in no rush. The best way to read a cold trail is contemplation. Crooks tend to make mistakes. More likely that I could find something by relaxing and waiting. Besides, it was nice sitting here. The lost gap of time I didn't like, but sitting in a normal chair in a normal office in a normal town—that wasn't so bad.

"There is a Stephens connection," Griffin said, through a web of cigar smoke. "Seems that Leon—he plays lap steel—seems his favorite nephew was pretty well done up by gambling. This was in San Antone. At McFarley's—Lawson's place. A gambler named Rose. Teddy and Leon went in and straightened this guy out. Happened about three months ago. Lawson was killed a few weeks later. Not really that much of a connection, but still."

"Who ended up with the saloon after Lawson got himself shot?"

"Good question," Griffin said. "I imagine the law in San Antonio can tell us."

I thought about my bass, Ring Hand, and the ring that Stephens was reputed to wear. The rings weren't the same. Stephens wore the goddess of fortune. That made sense—he's a gambler. But Ring Hand's was an image of a winged woman. I didn't think that Fortuna was depicted with wings, and I refused to believe that Stephens and Ring Hand were the same person, or creature, and that I had actually been with—and killed—some alternate incarnation of Stephens. Though if I had, maybe

I had killed Stephens too. That kind of silly thinking gets a detective in trouble.

Something else was bothering me. The street by the hotel. Solo—his perch. The angle was wrong. Once the musicians came down off the roof of the stage, the sharpshooter couldn't have hit them. If he had been aiming for Teddy, or any of them, he would have shot when the stage stopped and they were finishing the song. The only thing that had been in the sharpshooter's line of sight was my bass.

The marshal was talking about the musicians, Teddy Wells and His Texas Players. Griffin demonstrated with his guitar, something about how Teddy arranged a tune, compared to the usual way. I got up. The music and cigar were nice, but I had thought of something I needed to check on. The marshal had mentioned a land-grab, which led me back to the land scam Stephens had worked. Land and money, money and land. I told Griffin I would see him later. On my way out, the big deputy wrinkled his face at me. I tipped my hat.

Victoria's courthouse was a wood structure dating from the 1840s. The town was getting ready to replace it with a new one. The land office was a dim room with too many file cabinets. A tired-looking clerk directed me to what I wanted. I had never looked in the courthouse for records of *actual* purchases by the Riverside Land Agents. I hadn't felt a need—the bank gave me an address and the office was a fake. They were stealing money, not buying land. Two hours later my search revealed that they *had* bought land. Certainly not for a colony of Jewish immigrants. There was a parcel around Garcitas Creek, where Victoria County ended at Lavaca Bay. That area had the same terrain as where I had found Silverberg's bones and that sand hill with the face. What could Stephens want there? Nothing but salt marsh and proximity to hurricanes. Nobody wanted hurricanes.

The address listed for *this* Riverside was different, De Leon Street. I went looking, and found a two-story frame Italianate with a balcony over the front door and a widow's walk over that. The pillars supporting the porch roof (and the widow's walk above it) were wood with granite bases. The pair that flanked the entry had a different look—the stone was a similar color but new-cut, not weathered like the others. I leaned on the bell till a Negress in a maid's uniform opened the door. The house belonged to a Doctor and Mrs. Calderon. Mrs. was in. She was tall, with fine features. Her black hair showed some gray, and her eyes were green like the gulf on a sunny June morning. She had me sit in the parlor and offered tea, which she said her maid was just bringing her. Her English had a very slight Spanish accent.

The interior of the house was cool, and I was happy enough to sit for a few minutes and escape the sun. I told her what I was looking for. Not surprisingly, they had no connection with Riverside or any other land agent.

"Perhaps the person thought this lot was still empty," she said. "The house has only been here two years. It was moved from Indianola, after the last storm."

"I'm sure you're right about the address," I said. "But that other thing . . . Indianola. Makes me think they knew the house was here. It was moved from Indianola, and the man I'm after has an interest in that part of the state. There could be something about this particular house, from before it was here."

An old Mexican woman with her head wrapped in a shawl brought our tea. "Thank you, Lupita," Mrs. Calderon said.

I don't drink tea often, but when I do, I like it strong, with a little cream but no sugar. She liked hers sweet. We sipped.

"A land speculator had the house moved here. That's what the agent who showed us properties said. We came from San Antonio—my husband bought a medical practice here—and the house reminded us of the one we were living in there. The familiarity attracted us. We did change something. Two stone faces. They formed the base of the front pillars, stone carved into a rounded head with no eyes and a gaping, fleshy mouth. Lupita refused to enter through the front. Maldito! she said. And in truth, they disturbed me as well. Walking past them, I always felt in the presence of cold, and of rotting fish.

"And my husband, the doctor, a scientific man—even he admitted that they bothered him! We had the stones removed and replaced with new supports. The mason we hired said he was unfamiliar with the type of stone that the heads were made from."

More sand hill faces. I wrote the name of my hotel on a card and gave it to her, made a note of the stonemason's name and the land agent they used, and left. Stephens . . . running a land swindle to raise money to buy land . . . worthless land. The reason for that eluded me, shrouded by the thickest fog the gulf can spit out, but a reason was only important if knowing it led to my finding him. Otherwise, I had little interest in the way of things.

12

Afternoon Dreams

F ollowing Griffin's recommendation, I lugged my bass to the Maggini music shop on Forrest Street. It was a two-story frame house, painted green, with a rectangular patch of front yard and a magnolia tree. A bell on the door clanged. I walked past a sampling of fiddles and guitars that hung from the wall and lifted the body of the bass and neck fragments onto a wooden counter. Past that counter was another counter, covered by a jumble of instrument parts, violin, guitar, something that looked like a crossbow. A wrinkled and hunched Italian emerged from a back room. I showed him the reason for my visit. My bass excited him. He yelled "Marinella!" and a woman I figured was his daughter came in. She was a small lady, three or four inches shorter than me, with features that added up to more beauty than if sampled as individual elements. Maybe her nose was longer than the ideal, or eyebrows too thick, but none of that meant anything. Not with her. Poise, I thought. And confidence. Her apron, decorated with sawdust and varnish rather than flour and butter, told me who would be doing the work.

They turned the body upside down and around and peered inside through the f-holes, chatting away in Italian. "Testore," he said. "Over a hundred years old."

"Rare, very rare," she said. "We have never seen one." Her English was perfect, with a hint of accent that I might not have noticed if I hadn't heard her Italian. "How did this happen?"

I told her; she scolded me. "You should not have allowed such a treasure to be damaged! You cowboys with your guns." She said something else in Italian. I recognized a couple of impolite words.

They said they would need several months, allowing time for selection of the proper stick of wood, growing it up to maturity, curing, shaping, all that. When I left the shop, the sky threatened rain, and my stomach reminded me I hadn't eaten since breakfast. This combination of facts guided me. Directly, I took a seat at Fossati's Delicatessen, a table toward the rear and facing the door. The man who ran the place brought me a menu. Like the Magginis he was Italian. A downpour began, and I was happy to view it from the comfort of my table. A large man wearing a duster with the collar up filled the door. His hat obscured his face. He came inside and shook off some water. Which is when I recognized him.

"Real Jim-Dandy out there," he said. Then he recognized *me*. I started to get up; he—faster than I would have thought possible for his size—reached my table, lifted my hundred-eighty pounds, and tossed. This I noticed in retrospect. At the time, there was only the thump of my body against the top of another table, a table that was blessedly empty of food or cutlery. I slid across the table to the floor. He appeared, his bulk occupying my entire line of sight. He was close enough for me to kick his kneecaps, but before I could, he backed out of range.

"Marshal says I'm supposed to cooperate with you," he said.

I thought that was a good idea and said so. I'm not sure he agreed.

The proprietor scurried over to make sure we weren't going to destroy any of his property. The deputy turned and walked out. "Looks like everything is fine now," I said. With the rain still plummeting outside, I was content to stay. Also, my food hadn't arrived yet.

———————————

A telegram from Rabbi Cohen awaited me at the hotel. I asked a hotel boy to get me a bottle of rye, and took the message up to my room. The rabbi was joyous about my survival, and assured me that he had said nothing to my parents when he heard I was missing. I was glad. So caught up in the job, I had forgotten the connection between the business and my family. I wasn't accustomed to that. It's not healthy having the two mix. My parents know my work is dangerous. They don't like it. And they worry. They expect months to pass between messages from me, so the gap—my missing time—wouldn't have alarmed them. But still, I felt some guilt that the rabbi had to hide things.

I wrote them a letter, saying that I was still in Victoria and would pass back through Galveston before returning to Chicago. The boy brought my bottle; I opened it and poured enough to drink. Afternoon progressed. This job was getting to me. Had gotten. The empty glass needed a refill. I paced the room. Window, Welsh pear design curtains closed against the sun, dresser, my face in the mirror, saddlebags—I laid Silverberg's skull on the dresser. Whatever I might claim about patience, you always reach a point where you want a job to end. And I was there, even past it. Not because someone shot at me. That kind of thing happens. More because the shot *wasn't* at me. "Why did someone want to destroy the bass?" I asked the skull. I knew the answer. Or, at least, knew that the answer had to do with where I had found the instrument.

I wrote yet another report to Llewelyn and a letter to Owens, all warm and nice about how he could leave prison sooner if he helped us find Stephens. Then I wrote a note to the warden at Huntsville, asking him to keep Owens uncomfortable.

Thinking that beds are nice things, very nice things, I lay down and let myself drift. I don't remember sleeping, but I had a dream, or something like a dream. Galveston, walking along the beach. Storm debris littered the sand. Dead fish, parts of ships, stained glass from a church, the bloated body of a dead horse. A man prowled through wreckage. I stopped and asked him for directions to a saloon called Grangers. He spoke with his back to me, face nuzzling the debris; his words were slurred and muffled. I tapped his shoulder and asked again. He turned. Seagull feathers erupted from his mouth; his cheeks bulged with them. He spoke again, but his words made even less sense than before. I yelled and knocked him down, then ran. Inland, it stopped being Galveston. I thought I recognized Chicago. I found the saloon and went in, asked for a rye. The bartender was a woman with the greenest eyes, greener than you could imagine a green. Once I saw those eyes, I didn't want to leave, didn't want her to leave. I can't tell you much about her other than those eyes. Did she speak to me? I held my drink glass, imagining it was her hand. She left me to take care of another customer. I couldn't believe it. I had to stop myself from assaulting the other man. He made a joke and she laughed. It was the kind of laugh that went with her eyes. Again, I wanted to attack the other man. How was he able to encourage a laugh when all I could do was stare, bereft of speech and wit? There was a mirror above the bar. The door opened, and in the mirror I could see a large man with a hat pulled low, obscuring his face. His posture looked familiar. He sat between me and the man with the humor. When he removed his hat I saw that his face was a skull.

I screamed and ran from the bar. The door led into the terminal of a train station, a vast and beautiful expanse of marble. I gaped at the ceiling, a vision of stars, stars surrounded by outline drawings of con-stellations. Scores of men and women rushed past. Some bumped me. No one stopped to apologize. I couldn't remember where I was going. My ticket showed a time but no destination. I walked over to the departure board, dodging bodies too intent on their trajectories to notice me. Impact knocked me to the marble floor. This time, someone stopped, reached to help me up. I looked into the skull-face of the man from the bar. I took his hand. He throated and pulled me to my feet. He had grown or I had shrunk . . . my head reached the top of his belt.

He patted my head and went on. Now, everyone dwarfed me. I had to work even harder to keep from being trampled. I reached a wall and flattened against it, staring at the terminal and its giant occupants.

A familiar woman stopped and looked down at me. She wore a striped vest over a puffy-sleeved white shirtwaist and a dark skirt. She lifted me, pressing me tight against her bosom. Her smell, a complex brew of stale sweat, laundry soap, and tobacco, choked me but also soothed. She murmured things and carried me, petting my back as you would a cat. We traveled down several flights of stairs illuminated by electricity. Deeper and deeper we went. The air grew colder. She set me on a counter. A pile of dirty bedding lay nearby. She lifted a cauldron onto a coal fire and submerged some sheets. While waiting for the water to boil, she removed her vest and then her blouse, retaining only a white camisole. Her arms were thick with muscle.

Despite the fire, the cold bothered me. I asked for a jacket, but she couldn't hear me over the noise of her work. I raised my voice and waved my arms. The cold increased. I stood, jumped up and down. Why didn't she see me? My feet slipped. Ice had sheeted over the counter. I fell on my rear and slid. There was nothing to grab, nothing to stop me. I flew off the edge and into starry darkness.

Pain jarred my head. I had flopped onto the floor, head first. It's always the head that takes the punishment. The ceiling looked down at me and laughed. Although the bed was within touching distance, the thought of getting myself back up there felt too complicated. Beds are nice, but floors can be nice too. Or would be if someone hadn't left a rotten fish nearby. That's what I smelled, only then I didn't. The smell winked in, and immediately out. I had met that particular stench other times, like in the crazy mansion after I shot Mrs. Conroy. My head was bothering me then, too. With those tender memories to propel me, I raised my bulk from the floor and splashed my face in the basin.

Silverberg's skull was still on the dresser. I picked it up and sat on the bed, holding it in my lap. Skulls and skull-heads. They twist and twine, twist and crawl. Hungry sockets, unsatisfied and unsatisfiable. Nothing fills your gaze, but trouble not—someday everyone will see as you see, eat as you eat. Death takes our flesh. But what does death give in return? An unfair transaction. Skull, this business tires me. Mud contracts—yes, mud—vital pungent ooze through which terrestrial life transitioned, leaving aquatic dancing to the fishes. Smoke and screams, soundless vapor and vaporless sound. Where is the secret? Uncover the secret. Perish the secret. There is no secret, no secret no more. I shoved the skull back into my saddlebag.

My report to Llewelyn, letter to Owens, and telegram note for the Huntsville warden were lying on the table. I put on a clean shirt, my last clean shirt, and bundled my dirty clothes and took them downstairs, along with the report and letters. I gave the mail and telegram to the desk clerk to take care of for me. He asked if I wanted to give him my laundry, but that dream had me wondering how Angie Farber, the mighty laundress, was getting along.

At the laundry, a Mexican woman didn't look up from her folding. A man, also Mexican, came in from the back carrying a basket of clothes. He greeted me. I knew I was in the laundry that belonged to Angie Farber, but didn't see her. I talked to the Mexicans. They were Elena and Johnny Romo, and they had never heard of Angie Farber. They said they had run the laundry for ten years, bought from a geriatric named Elijah Wilson. I thanked them and left, walked next door, to what had been Riverside Land Agents. It was the entry to the Romos' home.

13

Dancing

Adrift, I went to Malley's law office, but didn't find him. I had sent him a message to tell him I was back, but didn't say anything specific about meeting. He had given me his home address, but I was feeling averse to domesticity. I'm not *opposed* to domesticity. Sometimes, I long for it, sometimes the idea repels me. Sometimes, I'm indifferent.

The late afternoon sun submerged Constitution Square in molten gold. Brightness shattered the sidewalks and caked the streetlight poles—new since my last visit, and gas rather than electric, therefore doomed to obsolescence. A sidewalk board cracked underfoot, its surface rotted by the hard, bright air. An abyss opened. The stench of overheated air and dirt battered my face, twisted my breath into useless dust. I hurried past it, stopped at the water tower, what locals called the Standpipe. Water was pumped from the Guadalupe River into the tower, and from there gravity sent it on its way to homes and businesses. Because of the heat, the Standpipe had been allowed to overflow, and children danced in golden spray, splashed gold at one another. A redheaded woman led a boy-child to the golden crew. She released his hand, but he remained by her side, wary of entering the throng. A drenched boy noticed him.

"Edwid," the drenched boy said. The shy boy ... Edwid ... Edrid? ...
Edward? called out "Colin!" and ran, laughing and splashing, to the
drenched boy.

In a drinking alone turn of mind, I entered the nearest tavern, which
made me think of my dream—the lady bartender with the greenest eyes,
but if she existed it wasn't here, not today. A poster by the door showed
an illustration of Teddy Wells and the other musicians, reminding me
of my nighttime plans.

Later, after my part of the planet turned its back on the sun, I got
up and walked toward Casino Hall for the dance concert. I bought a
ticket and went in. Moonlight ruffled the floor. Couples passed, smiling,
laughing. The pleasing atmosphere gentled my wariness. Doors separated the foyer from the performance hall. I glanced into the hall. The
stage had a piano and several chairs. The ground floor was open for
dancing, with seating in the balcony; I've seen that arrangement in
dozens of towns. Across the room, Marshal Griffin talked to a stooped
man in a dark suit. Wanting to remain hidden, for now, I moved up to
the balcony. People drifted in, the expected types, ranchers, towns-
folk—businessmen *and* laborers. Caldwell, the railroad conductor,
passed, accompanied by two other men. I wanted to talk to him, but it
could wait.

The band walked on stage from the rear. Teddy waved to the crowd
with his violin bow. Everybody except Teddy was dressed in matching
black shirts with white hats and ties; Teddy wore a blue, black, and gray
plaid shirt with a gold tie. There were two guitars, the bass, clarinet,
and a lap-slide guitar. Marshal Griffin hopped up from the dance floor
and turned to the audience. "Evening everybody. These folks have
come a ways to entertain you, so let's give a nice warm welcome to
Teddy Wells and his Texas Players." People clapped; the marshal left
the stage, thumping Teddy on the shoulder as he went past.

"Well now, what a pretty sight," Teddy said. "Are y'all ready for
some dancing?" He turned to the band. "Boys, how about that
'Lone ... Star ... Rag.'"

...unseen notes rumble into the dancehall, into head, down arms to hands, fingertips. Strings! Strings flood the air with sound. Activated dancers heave their bodies into motion. Couples crowd the dance floor, conjoining movements, becoming super-movements, the physical manifestation of the notes pouring from the stage, from fingers plucking strings, on clarinet keys, on bow....

I watched, torn between the body—the soul's—desire to dance and my work. A tall man wearing a dark vest and white shirt danced with the redheaded woman I had seen at the Standpipe. Dr. Morgan— the woman who had sewed my head back together—danced with a bearded man in a well-cut gray suit. The band played a series of instrumentals, then Teddy said, "Oh, Tommy, sing us one about Nancy-Jane!"

Stage lights cast strange shadows, crablike forms that roamed the dance floor. The air throbbed with their passage. Music battled them; notes that bathed the room with a protective shower. A song ended. "Oh yes," Teddy said. "That was the 'Old Victoria Stomp.' After this next one we're taking ourselves a break." He lifted his fiddle and began a waltz. The rest of the band merged their instruments with his. A fancy-dressed man with white hair walked through the dancers. His appearance jolted my memory. I rushed to the stairs, but was blocked by a cloud of cigar smoke and the men attached to it. A familiar, loutish voice: "...call it luck, or tact, or fate—but some types of people are always superior to other types of people and always will be. But the main point is, if the Negro gets himself too much education, who will work in our factories and clean our stables?"

The men laughed, expelling more cigar smoke. "But we owe it to them to provide equal education," one of them said. The others laughed again.

"That sounds right to me," I said.

"Well if it isn't Mr. Shannon." The speaker was Bert Wilson, from the Brownson and Sibley Bank. "Still after your man?"

I said I was. He seemed amused by my desire to get to the stairs. "Pretty lady catch your eye?" This drew another laugh from his companions. I pushed past them. But couldn't find Stephens among the press of dancing bodies.

The song ended. "And we'll be seeing you back here later," Teddy said.

Someone started turning up the gas on the house lights. Crab-forms receded, banished by brightness, though one remained, waving its claws at the dancers till the light finally drove it scuttling through a door to the right of the stage. The light didn't show my quarry but did allow the marshal to spot me.

"There you are, Shannon. I didn't think you'd miss the show. How do you like our concert hall? Equal to those of Chicago?"

"It's very nice," I said. "And Teddy and his band sure know how to make the people dance."

A tall, gray-bearded man asked if he could talk to Griffin. I went to the bar for a beer and had just enough time to finish before the lights dimmed and brightened to call everyone back. I walked in with Dr. Morgan and her companion. Her dress had a different cut. Corsetless, I realized. I greeted her and pointed to the back of my head. "You fixed me up back in October," I said. "Healed nicely, thanks." She said she was glad to hear it. I didn't tell her that the wound was still bothersome. For me, October was last week—how could I explain that to her?

The air in the hall was warmer, with a damp tinge and an odor of sea wrack, like someone had just opened a barrel of salt cod spoiled by moisture. I had been smelling something like that for some time, in several places. Closer to the stage, the odor increased, then it was gone, cut off like a closed door. I went up the steps next to the stage and met the musicians.

"Whenever you want to come on up, you say so," Teddy said. "You really *do* know how to play?"

"Sure," I said. "Nobody's using the piano. How about 'Take Me Back to Oklahoma,' 'Osage Romp,' and maybe 'Fading Lovers.'" Songs that I had played with the skull-heads—I hadn't thought beforehand about playing them here; the idea popped into my head when Teddy spoke.

But playing them made sense. Did anything make sense? Music connected everything, Victoria, Ring Hand's crew.

Teddy said he would call me up when it was time. I returned to the balcony. Song and dance resumed. Some dancers returned in the same configurations, others with new partners. The marshal and the doctor danced a reel together. I heard a step behind me and turned. Caldwell walked down the aisle.

"Thought it was you," he said. "Been gone for some time. Funny, saw you *and* saw that gambler Stephens."

"Yeah," I said. "I lost him in the crowd."

"He comes and goes. Always see him—when I see him—as a sidelong glance. Moving from one car to the next, or stepping down to the platform. Almost like I hadn't seen him, or hadn't registered seeing him till he was already gone. Odd thing, that."

I agreed with him. "I don't imagine he's here for the music, or just to put together a card game. Whatever he's after has higher stakes." More talk like that followed. Teddy announced that they had someone new coming in to play piano and several moments passed before I realized he was talking about me. I told Caldwell I had to go. Walking through the dancers, I felt exposed and vulnerable, which was silly. No one there knew I was about to get on stage.

"And here . . . he . . . is!" Teddy said, in his stage-holler voice. I had learned that his holler was an important part of his act, part showmanship, part unrestrained joy of music. "Mr. Shannon is here to help take us all the way back to Oklahoma!"

On stage, time weaves and bubbles. A song starts, and sometimes each note is a labor to pass, but sometimes the notes burrow deep into the brain, layer after layer, layers that shine with a light that surpasses the sun, then fade, vanish, never to be seen again nor even remembered, except for the way you might recall a particular flavor in a special meal. I had thought I would play and keep part of myself detached, able to watch . . . for Stephens . . . the crab creatures, but my inexperience, and the band's level of ability, forced all my attention on the notes, on Teddy's gestures, hollers, directions. And . . . I didn't care;

the music took me in, guarded me. How many songs did I play? At the end of "Grand Junction Rag," I told Teddy I was through. I walked off the stage and through the dancers. Anonymity was destroyed, for a moment; then the next song took control.

A hand gripped my wrist, and I looked into the hazel eyes of Marinella from the Maggini violin shop. "You play well, for a man of guns," she said.

She took my hand and kissed me. There is magic in music, yes, but there is more magic in a woman's kiss, even one so brief . . . that period of contact—lip onto lip, lip lifted from lip—entire civilizations rise and fall, crumble into remnants of a long-dead culture with no recollection of its former grandeur. My lips shaped themselves into a smile, a lost smile, a smile wishful for the vanished people who created this tumbled palace. We stood, faces close.

"Now dance, dance with me," she said; she led me into the crowd. I didn't mind. I didn't mind at all. She was, as I said, lovely. And not connected to my job. The song was a waltz. Hand to fabric, fabric to flesh . . . my hand contoured to her shape . . . the glorious shape of woman. I was surprised she was wearing a corset. I said so.

"I made it," she said. "It is quite comfortable. I don't over-cinch it, like some. Women's clothing is made to go over a corset and wouldn't fit properly without. Is it vain to care about such things? I care how a violin or even a guitar looks, as well as how it sounds. Why not my own appearance?"

I assured her that I cared too. I said she looked better than any musical instrument, except one made with her own lovely hands. Sure, I can be a sap sometimes. Why not? I meant it. I needed a break from the business, from crime and filth. Too much of that and you see crime and filth in everything, in everyone. Here was a beautiful woman giving me her attention. For the rest of the night, I was going to be one of the regular people, a shopkeeper, or rancher, anything but a thief-taker. That plan worked for a couple of songs. Then, the glow of a stage light showed me a man with white hair. I stopped dancing. Stephens's dance partner was a dark-haired woman. They disappeared in the press of bodies.

"I have to find a man I just saw," I said. "The man we've been looking for."

"If you must," Marinella said.

She didn't like it. That's fine. I didn't need her to like it. I wouldn't mind if she waited—another dance with her would be nice. I said so, but didn't wait for her response. I plunged into the dancers and worked my way to the other side, but Stephens had vanished again. Having ended up near the bar, I decided to get a beer, then I stood at the edge of the crowd. The dark-haired woman who had been dancing with Stephens walked toward me, arm in arm with the redheaded Standpipe woman. I stopped them.

"Excuse me, ladies."

The redhead smiled. "Oh, you're the piano player. That was wonderful."

"Thanks." I asked the dark-haired woman about Stephens.

"I've never seen him before. He asked me to dance. I didn't really want to. His eyes, they reminded me of a copperhead."

"I've met him," the redheaded lady said. "You're right about the copperhead, Flora. He came to the ranch house to talk to Uncle Pike. Said his name was James Granger. He wanted to buy the parcel over by Gleason's cove. Uncle Pike wouldn't sell, and this Granger . . . his eyes changed, like there's murder inside them, but not very deep inside. Uncle Pike's been fighting since he was old enough to load, and even *he* was spooked. But he still wouldn't sell, spooked or not."

I thanked the ladies for their help and asked the redhead to tell Marshal Griffin if she or her uncle remembered anything else. Deciding that I could watch for Stephens and enjoy myself at the same time, I went to ask the lovely Marinella for a dance. She was with her father, but before I could reach them, a glow of white hair moved in the opposite direction. I followed. I didn't even think about an alternative. Though I yearned . . . the body beneath the corset. Not tonight, not for tonight.

Past the stage was a door of unfinished pine, leading—I assumed—to an alley between buildings. It was the door that the crab-thing had passed through. I hadn't seen Stephens go out, but there were no other options. Getting there, I had to slip through the dancers. Not easy during a reel. My back received a stinging blow from an elbow, but that was the worst of it. The knob turned easily. In the dimness I could see the shape of bricks. I sensed a sweep of motion to my left and a splash of something pale against the darkness. I set off after it. Being toward the rear of the dance hall, I should have soon reached the end of the building, but it continued, changing from brick to stone, rough blocks about the size of a door. The surface under my boots was hard and uneven.

Light increased, and I could see that the walls weren't constructed; they were stone etched with deep furrows. The air was dead and hot. My footsteps crunched on broken bits of stone. The path sloped downward, and curved into a descending series of switchbacks on the side of a steep hill. Several layers below, white hair flashed again. I walked faster. But beyond the next curve, the path ended at a cracked-off tongue of rock. In trying to stop, I slipped. There was nothing to grab. My feet slid over the edge, but something caught my collar; I hung for a moment, then was pulled back to solidity. The hand that saved me let go. It belonged to Gorman—Griffin's big deputy. And I was extremely happy to see him.

"Followed after I saw you go through a door where there hadn't never been no door," he said. "And this sure ain't Victoria. Leastwise no part I ever been too."

"It looks a lot like a place I didn't ever want to get back to," I said. "That Stephens man we're after went this way." I wasn't sure what to do. My psyche rebelled at the thought of continuing. At the same time, I calculated the difficulty of climbing down the mountainside to the next level of path.

"We ever want to go down there we'll need us some ropes," he said. "Let's go get 'em."

The path led without mishap back to the door that we had exited, but the room on the other side had changed. It was empty. No band, no dancers, no cigar smoke.

"Huh?" Gorman said. "Where'd all them people go? We sure weren't gone long enough for folks to clear out."

We went out the front door. The temperature felt like the same night, or at least the same season. Next stop was the marshal's office, where a young deputy named Nebel told us that Griffin was at a fire on Forrest Street. I recognized him as the thick-bodied redhead who had been looking for me in my hotel, after the doctor discharged me with my sewn-up head. By the time we got to where the fire was, the blaze had been contained, and only one building looked damaged. After awhile, I figured out what the building had been.

The marshal stood with the Magginis, Marinella and her father. She had an arm around her father's shoulders. A fireman with a big blond beard stood between them and the blackened building, arms stretched to block their way. The marshal saw us and walked over. "Where've you been, Gorman?" He nodded at me. "Haven't seen either of you since the dance. You two getting along?"

"We're pals," I said.

"That Stephens gent has been around," the marshal said. "You take off after him?"

"Tried to," I said. "What happened here?"

"They were asleep. Marinella woke, smelling smoke. Lucky they got out alive."

The bearded fireman steered the Magginis toward the street. When Marinella noticed me, she let go of her father and screamed my name. She rushed over. Her fist smacked my cheek. I went down. She stood over me, yelling in Italian. Gorman and Griffin kept her from doing any more damage while I got up. She calmed down enough to talk in English.

"The man with white eyebrows came in. He said you sent him to pick up the bass. I didn't believe him. He made me scared, but I wouldn't let him have it. *He* did this." She yelled some more in Italian.

The marshal took her arm and led her back to her father; without her support, he looked ready to collapse. "Now, you two get some rest. Go wake Alice Duncan and sleep there. You can sift through your things once the heat dies down."

Marinella and her father left; their steps looked pained, labored. The firemen wound their hoses back onto the wagon. Onlookers dispersed.

"What could he have wanted with that bass?" Griffin said. "Listen here, Shannon. You need to tell me where you got it."

"After you see the door at the back of the music hall."

But the door was gone.

We went to his office. "Coffee," he said. Nebel poured. We sat around the front desk. I told him about following Stephens through the door and Gorman saving me.

"It *was* peculiar, Marshal," Gorman said. "Go out a side door and there you are, different place, different smells, not our town at all, probably not even our state."

"Outside that door was a landscape like where I found the bass. Except the other time, I got there from the coast. Stephens, whoever he is, he's connected somehow to this other place, whatever it is, and he's connected to the bass because it's *from* there." I thought my statements sounded like nonsense and was glad to have had Gorman as a witness to some of it. The marshal was hard to read. I had begun to think that he already knew something about this, that he had come up against skull-heads even, but I wasn't going to say anything.

"If that's true about Stephens and the bass," he said. "Did he want it? Or want it destroyed?"

"Destroyed," I said. "I think he's the one who shot at us, aiming at the bass, not Teddy or someone in the band."

Griffin went into the office and came back with his guitar. He strummed a sad melody. "Something else about Stephens and the gulf," I said. "There were other land deals." I described the Riverside Land Agent's purchases, the house listed for Riverside's address, and what the redhead had told me.

"Why would anybody want those worthless patches of nothing-land?" Gorman said. "He swindles all that money, and then wastes it."

"Dr. Calderon and his wife haven't been here long," Griffin said. "But I've got no reason to think that they're involved."

"The town's growing so fast, it's hard to keep up with addresses," I said. "Stephens might have assumed it was vacant. But . . . I can't stop thinking about the Indianola connection . . . something about that specific house. Probably it's symbolic—he's buying land on the coast and that house is from there. He's a gambler. Gamblers are superstitious, looking for good luck symbols."

Like stone sand faces.

I hadn't told them about the sand hill with the face and Silverberg's skull mounted like a totem. Maybe Griffin had seen the sand hill when he went over my trail. And what did that hill signify? Ritual sacrifice of Silverberg to a god of sand hills? To keep the hurricanes away so the land wouldn't be worthless? I know people who believe in things like that. I know people who believe in a lot of silliness. But I don't know anyone who's met skull-heads. Not who's talked about them anyway. And I sure wasn't talking about them.

"We've got a quarry who slides in and out when he wants to," Griffin said. "From where and to where?" We said the same things back and forth till Gorman got disgusted and said he was going home to bed.

I changed the subject. "Teddy and the boys gone?" Griffin nodded. "Wish I could have said goodbye. Maybe they'll make it up to Chicago sometime." Then it was my turn to go. Sleep called.

14

Hiding Places

Investigation can be exhausting and not very exciting unless you get lucky and catch someone committing a crime. The process, the tedious, repetitive process is what *creates* the possibility of catching a thief, murderer, or anyone else. So I revisited card games. I checked rooming houses. And I spent too much time with Griffin and Gorman, and sometimes young Nebel. We burned a lot of tobacco. We tacked a map of the coast to the wall and marked where the Riverside Land Agents had purchased property. Gorman went to Port Lavaca to look in the Calhoun County court records for Riverside purchases. They had made several, including the area near Ratface Conroy's. Griffin wired the sheriffs in several of the other coastal counties and asked them to look for Riverside in the court records.

Gorman wasn't so bad. I even apologized for knocking him down.

Every day, I reported my lack of progress to Llewellyn. He sent a few notes back, but he never mentioned my account of skull-head land.

We heard from the other counties. Nothing reported in Brazoria, which was the northernmost of those Griffin had wired. Matagorda and Jackson Counties showed several, across the bay from the ones Gorman found in Calhoun. We added them to the map, but that didn't tell us anything. There had to be a reason—Stephens wasn't buying land for fun—but the answer was as elusive as the man. Gorman said reasons didn't matter. Catch the man and it's over. Which is often my view, except when it isn't. With this job, my thinking fluctuated, and fluctuated again. An amount of inhabiting your quarry's mind can help to anticipate their next move. A whole branch of detective thought follows that idea. Most of the time, everything is straightforward. Galveston waves are straightforward; they strike the shore approximately six seconds apart. What happens inside them, the swirl of sand lifted from the beach, deposited down the line, fossils and shells exposed—none of that is straightforward.

Gorman and a deputy from the county sheriff's office went looking for signs of Stephens at the places we marked. I stayed in town. I didn't want to go anywhere near that sand hill with the face or the entrance to skull-head land.

Most nights, sleep was an ordeal. I kept having nightmares of sand faces and burning violins, the death keen of my bass.

The Magginis salvaged what they could from their shop and started over. I think Marinella's father would have given up, but she wouldn't let him. This was all through Griffin—she refused to talk to me. Another regret. How many regrets can a body absorb before turning into a blind and squalid creature?

The stonemason who had repaired the Calderons' porch was a short Portuguese with thick arms and thin mustache. His yard was strewn with broken columns, statues, a chunk of limestone as big as a calf, and many smaller pieces. He showed me the stone heads, an intact one and a pile of crusty shards, piled in a back corner of his yard.

"I wanted to see what the stone looked like on the inside—I mean, what a new-chipped piece looked like, without the weathering. Just a chip I wanted. I struck with hammer and a fine chisel, not with much force. The whole thing crumbled. When it came apart, it stank of rotten fish. Made me gag. Very happy I was working in the yard. I shoveled the pieces into a bucket and dumped it here."

I hefted the remaining head. The weight of it was greater than its size indicated, more like a lump of gold than sandstone, but it wasn't gold. The face leered at me. From the darkness, claws grew; they slashed the air. A tongue of cold spread up my arms, the cold of deep black ocean depths . . . saltwater twisted my lungs, ice burned my body. I dropped the head.

"You feeling all right, mister?" The stonemason's weighty hand rested on my shoulder.

"Get rid of it," I said. "Crush it and bury the remains of both of them, bury them deep."

During all these various proceedings, I went to dinner at Saul Malley's house. His wife, Dora, was a charming and intelligent teacher at the Freedmen's School. Mathematics was her specialty, but she wasn't allowed to teach much of it. Coloreds won't want our menial jobs if they get too much education, so said Wilson from the bank, and his crowd were the ones who decided such things. For now anyway.

She was a good card player too.

"He taught me the rules, the basic concepts, the things your Tarpon Bill showed you," Dora said. "Then we practiced against each other."

"But two isn't enough to get the totality of the game," Malley said.

"We started playing with friends," Dora said. "I came up with a shorthand for calculating odds, but I didn't tell Saul. I practiced my method. Then we sat down with some of his regular poker players. They didn't take me seriously. I took all their money. Saul assumed it was just luck, till I explained my method."

"Which she taught me. Now none of our friends will play with us. Sometimes we'll go to San Antonio and clean everybody out."

Sure, the domestic life is nice.

In our Galveston poker childhood, we haunted one place in particular. The Oyster Tavern, run by Tarpon Bill. The Tarpon showed us the right way to play and he took our money—that's the only way to learn.

"There's only the three of us," I said, "but I wouldn't mind learning some of your mathematical card figuring. Improving my poker skills might help me catch this gambler." I had an idea that before this business was over, I would need to win some games, either with Stephens or to help me get to him.

News came down from San Antonio that Frank Lawson had a wife. She inherited the saloon, but sold it to the bartender, who had run the place while Lawson was off cheating people with Stephens. I took a train to San Antonio. I hadn't been in some time, but had always liked it there. The town still had enough Spanish and Mexican heritage to be a fine place.

The bartender was a thick-necked man of at least forty, with the kind of mustache that made eating and drinking a messy business. He admitted to knowing Stephens but said he hadn't seen him in months and didn't have any reason to believe that Stephens had been involved in Lawson's shooting. I asked him what he thought of Stephens. He said he didn't care for him but wouldn't elaborate. His expression had something . . . maybe fear. Fear or at least unease was a common theme among those who've dealt with Stephens.

I sent a telegram to Rabbi Cohen explaining that the group of claimants to the stolen money would need to hire a lawyer to file on money from the saloon. To collect anything, they would have to prove Lawson's involvement. Maybe there wasn't enough money to bother with, though saloons can be profitable.

Back in Victoria, I stopped by the marshal's office. Nebel was sitting, feet up on the front desk, reading the same cowboy book I had looked at when I first got to Victoria. So far, all I had seen Nebel do was make coffee and sit around. When he saw me, he snapped the book closed and dropped his feet to the floor. "I heard what you do to people with their feet up."

"I decided I'm through with that behavior. Marshal in?"

Which the marshal answered by leaving his office, towing his guitar. I told him that San Antonio hadn't helped with anything. We sat for some time, repeating useless theories. Griffin played a refrain that I thought was Mozart. Toward lunchtime, a tall and thin Negro wearing a railway porter's uniform came in from the outdoor furnace.

"Afternoon, Marshal. Might have something for you." He blinked while his eyes adjusted to the dimmer light.

Griffin leaned his guitar against the desk and got up. "Have a seat, Mr.—?"

"Name's Dupree, Angus Dupree. I'm a porter on the West Texas line." He sat.

I liked that Griffin had offered his seat to a colored man. I didn't think that would be common behavior here. I couldn't tell what Nebel thought of it.

The porter, Dupree, continued. "Found a man hiding in the baggage car. White man. He gave me a dollar if I said I wouldn't report him to the railroad. I said yessir, not a problem. He didn't say nothing about marshals. I wondered if maybe I should look at your posters. He was one shifty feller."

"Any idea where he went?" Griffin asked.

"Walked right on across the street and into Highwater's."

Griffin had Dupree describe the man and asked Nebel to get out their supply of Wanted circulars. Nebel pushed the stack toward Dupree. "Have yourself a look."

Dupree thanked him and accepted the stack. Figuring his search would take some time, I decided to go eat lunch. When I came back, the marshal, Dupree, and the stack of flyers were gone except for one. Nebel sat at the front desk. A one-armed, ancient sharpshooter they called Old Skete slouched across from him, eyes closed. Nebel slid the flyer at me.

"Here's who this nigger says he's turned up."

The flyer was from the sheriff's office of the city and county of New York, dated January 1889. A photograph at the top showed a mustached man in a checked tie and vest.

A Reward of five hundred dollars will be paid for re-capture of JOHN MURRAY, who was under sentence for MURDER of Abel McDonald, and who escaped from the Jailor of the City and County of New York, on the evening of the 28th of May 1888.

Description of Prisoner at the time of his Escape: JOHN MURRAY, 5 feet 10 inches high; stout built; dark brown hair; large gray or blue eyes, and sandy beard; 30 years old, and weight about 180lbs; broad shouldered, with short, thick neck; aquiline nose, very slightly turned up at the tip; fair complexion. It is said he has scarred his face since out of prison, to avoid detection. He is a carpenter by trade.

IF ARRESTED, TELEGRAPH WILLIAM C. CONNER, Sheriff.

"Looks like fun," I said. "Is the marshal out looking?"

"Yep. He went to watch Highwater's. Said we was to join him. He sent Old Skete to keep the peace in here." Nebel opened a drawer and slammed it shut. Old Skete opened his eyes.

"We're heading out," Nebel said. And we did. Our departure didn't appear to disturb Old Skete any.

The marshal sat on a bench outside a barber's. He was on the opposite side of the street from Highwater's, but not directly across. It was a location I approved of—a man leaving the saloon wouldn't spot him right off and likely wouldn't think he was watching the place.

Nebel walked toward him; I stopped to roll a cigarette, then approached. "Hey mister, got something I can light this with?"

Griffin handed me a match and said he hadn't seen anyone leave who looked like our man. He suggested I go in. "We could take off our badges, but chances are someone will know us. You could find things out a lot easier."

I said that sounded like a good idea and crossed to the other side. I had been to Highwater's when checking poker games for Stephens's activity, but I was sure no one had thought I was any kind of lawman. The interior was dim and smoky; I filled a bowl from a pot of beans and ordered a beer. I'd just had lunch, but beans gave me an excuse to linger. A drummer sat a couple of stools over, sample case of barbed wire open on the bar. He polished a strand, spread the cloth over the samples, and closed it.

"Lots of customers for that around here, I reckon," I said. He said that he had made out pretty well and was waiting for a train to Tulsa to see what things were like there.

"Been to Tulsa once," I said. "Not sure of anything that would take me back there."

At a table, three men played cards. None of them were John Murray or Stephens. The bartender brought my beer. He was a youngster with long blond hair and a missing front tooth. He hadn't been here on my previous visit.

"Got a minute?" I fished out two shiny new Morgan dollars and stood them between the fingers of my left hand, which I had flat on the bar.

"Sure, mister, what do you need?" He didn't look at my face. The coins were too pretty.

"Looking for a friend." I described Murray, relying more on what Dupree had said rather than the wanted flyer. "He told me about a good job, said to meet him here."

"How do I know you're his friend?"

I wanted to laugh at his would-be tough talk, but that wouldn't help get me what I needed. I slid my left hand and the coins off the bar, toward my lap. The bartender tilted his head in the direction the coins went. I cupped my palm, letting the coins make a nice clinking sound, then brought them back up to the bar and opened my palm.

The bartender was ready to tell me things. "That man was here. He said he needed a good horse. I told him to go to Meacham's. You know where that is?"

I said I did, thanked him, and slid the coins toward him. Outside Highwater's, I turned left. On the next corner, I let Griffin and Nebel catch up and told them where we were going. Griffin started to tell me about Butler, the proprietor of Meacham's.

"I know him," I said. "That's where I got Blue Swamp, the horse I rode when I was looking for Silverberg's body. I don't want to have to tell Butler what happened to him."

"What did happen to him?"

"Got spooked. Broke his leg on a rock." That was mostly true, and common enough. Nobody likes losing a horse, even a city man like me. We paused so a portly man in a dark town coat could talk to the marshal about nothing in particular. Outside Meacham's, we heard a horse snorting and hooves thumping the ground, then the sound of a body being thrown. The noises stopped. A man cursed. We went in, but stayed in the shadows near the door. From there, we could see what was happening in the corral.

"I reckon you've had enough of this one," Butler said.

"It's enough when I ride this bronco out of here, not when some nigger hostler says so." A gun cocked. We hove into view of the corral. "Now bring him back over here." The man who spoke matched Dupree's description of Murray. His clothes were encrusted from their meeting with corral dirt.

"Yessir, I'm coming," Butler said. "Poor horse is just a bit spooked is all. You don't need no gun." He was wearing a black derby and a striped, knee-length frock coat, which hadn't been his usual stable outfit the other times I saw him. He led the horse to Murray. It was the feisty one Butler had called Tempest.

Nebel started forward, but Griffin held his arm. Murray holstered his gun and remounted the horse. Butler stepped back to make room. Tempest reared, came down hard, humped, kicked up his rear legs; Murray flew over Tempest's head and landed in the dust.

"Take him now, Nebel," Griffin said.

Nebel hopped the corral fence. The marshal and I pointed our guns, keeping Nebel clear of our line of fire.

"John Murray, I reckon we're arresting you," Nebel said. He rolled Murray onto his stomach with a booted foot and manacled his wrists.

"Afternoon, Marshal," Butler said. "I was closing up for the day but this here hombre, he said he needed a horse with spirit."

"Thanks, Butler, that made arresting him easy, him being too uncomfortable to protest."

Butler looked at me. "You lost Blue Swamp. That was a very fine horse."

"He was."

Griffin climbed into the corral and walked toward Tempest. He spoke to the horse, his voice low and gentle. Tempest snorted and moved away. Griffin followed him, but stopped to keep from crowding him against the corral fence. He waited. Tempest waited. Griffin took another step and patted the horse's head, then rubbed his neck. Tempest made a friendly noise. Griffin rubbed his neck some more, and swung up into the saddle. They walked around the corral, with no argument from the horse. Butler opened the gate and they trotted into the town.

Nebel had prodded Murray to his feet. Butler spoke to him. "Marshal and my horses get along nicely."

Nebel and I escorted Murray to the county jail and left him with the sheriff's deputies. Griffin came back to the office after a while. He picked up his guitar. "Thanks for your help, Shannon. It's useful having someone who can go into places and not be recognized as a lawman. And good to know what kind of man you're working with."

Which was how I felt too.

At breakfast one day, I read a telegram from the warden of Huntsville Prison. Owens had something he wanted to tell me. Later, a boy came with a note from the marshal, asking me to come to the office. I wrote to the warden, having him take a statement from Owens, and went to see what the marshal was doing. Nebel was there but Griffin wasn't. Nebel said Griffin would be back in a minute. Which he was.

"Sorry Shannon. Had a noise complaint from an old woman on Clark Street. Said her neighbors were yelling at each other all night."

"Part of the job," I said.

"Nebel went to see Madame Blackley out in Diamond Hill Flats. You wouldn't know about her. She's a colored lady, was a slave in Virginia. No idea how she ended up here. Or when. Some say it was just a few years ago but then there's some say she helped found the Palestine Baptist Church in 1868."

"History lesson can wait," I said. "Let's get moving. You can tell me on the way. If the end of your story leads to an address."

"Oh sure, we can go. Close up, Nebel. Put out the sign to see Malone." For my benefit, he said, "Jerry Malone is a part-time deputy and barber two doors down. Helps to have someone close by when needed. Other deputies won't be in till later."

We set off south on Main Street. They said we were going all the way down to the end of the street, near the Guadalupe River.

Nebel started talking. "I know Madame Blackley's been here a whole lot longer than a few years. My daddy went to talk to her when I was a boy, just about twelve, I'd say, and I'm twenty-two now. This woman, she knows things. Everybody 'round here goes to her. Poor people, bankers. Went with my daddy when our new bull went missing. Knocked on the door and she told us the bull was in a thicket along the creek, about half a mile from our house. Sure thing, that's where we found him. He'd come out for food and water, then he'd head right back into the brush.

"We aren't making no progress finding this jasper, so the other day I got to thinking about Madame Blackley and went to find her. She said, before I even told her anything, 'I know why you're here. This man you're after lives in a rooming house on South Street, near the river.'"

I didn't believe people knew things unless they saw them happen or someone told them, but I also didn't care how we found Stephens as long as we found him.

"You know what place she means?" They didn't.

"Won't be difficult," Griffin said. "Not many houses over that way.

Besides the sawmill, there's a meat packer and a tannery. No one wants to live around those."

Aside from the industrial buildings, there were, in fact, only three places. A large, square, brick structure on the corner, a two-story frame with an empty lot between it and the brick building, and a log cabin closer to the river. Cattle crowded the pen outside the packing plant. The train tracks were just beyond. The odor of cattle pushed toward us, but that was better than what came from the tannery. And on top of those smells was that other, sea wrack and decay.

"Must be something rotting by the river," Nebel said. "Rains'll warsh it away this evening." During our walk, the sky had darkened considerably. I wasn't looking forward to a drenching.

The brick building housed construction supplies; the proprietor, a tall, thick-chested German, said that the upper floors were storage. We hadn't thought a rooming house would be there, but I've seen them in stranger places. That's mostly in big cities though, where people will live anywhere with a roof. The German thought that the frame house was what we were looking for.

"You head around back, Nebel," Griffin said. "We'll knock on the front door, but if no one answers we'll just go on in."

No one answered. The door wasn't locked. We entered the parlor, seeing furnishings neither fancy nor decrepit. A woman in a faded flower print dress came toward us from the kitchen.

She greeted the marshal. The tone of her voice reminded me of trains. I let Griffin do the talking. It was his town. He told her who we were looking for.

"Has he committed something, crime...?"

"Oh, no, we just want to talk to him about an associate who's missing. When do you expect him back?"

She didn't know, said he'd left several days ago. "Tuesday last it was." She said that was usual. He stayed for a few days, left for the same, was back for a month, and so on. He apparently never had visitors or mail, and rarely ate his meals there or interacted with other residents. I watched her face, trying to read fear, concern, or a lie. I expected something—from what I'd been told and what I'd seen in others, Stephens made people uneasy, at the very least. In all my years of tracking thieves and murderers, I've never run into someone so nebulous.

The landlady lived on the first floor. Stephens's room was upstairs. Another upstairs room was unoccupied. A consumptive veteran named Turner lived in the attic. Griffin asked the landlady to take us to Stephens's room. The fish-wrack hit us at the door. "Smells like someone let the swamp in," Griffin said. Then it was gone, passing us as we entered.

"Nothing rotten in here. I keep a clean house. It's that damn tannery. The wind brings in the stink."

I closed the door on her. I had a ridiculous thought that Stephens could turn himself invisible, but when he did, he stank like a dead ocean. I knew that wasn't possible, but the odor did seem to appear in places he had been.

His apartment had two rooms, one overlooking the street and the other facing toward the river. The front room held a card table and four chairs, but no signs of recent use. The back room had a mirrored walnut dresser, bed, armoire, and a night table with an oil lamp. He was a singularly tidy person. Neatly folded shirts were stacked in a drawer, trousers and underclothes in the others. A town coat and a blue silk vest hung in the armoire, with a Gladstone bag lying beneath. I didn't find anything in the coat or vest pockets, or in the bag. The rooms had a transient feel, as if at any time he might pack his things (or leave them) and move on. Which was about what I would expect for a gambler.

"Let's look for hiding places," I said. "But be careful not to disturb things too much." There weren't any hanging pictures to look behind—not that he would use such an obvious spot. I pushed the rug aside and slid my clasp knife into spaces between floorboards. Griffin removed all the drawers from the dresser. He peered into the empty space, then moved it away from the wall, squatted behind it, and thumped the back. I slid under the bed. "At least she keeps it clean down here," I said.

I heard a scrape and saw the legs of the armoire moving. It tilted, then—"Fucking Christ!" from Griffin—and it crashed onto the bunched-up rug. I got myself out from under the bed. Griffin was staring down at the back of the armoire, hands on hips. "It snagged on the damn carpet when I moved it," he said. We lifted it back into place.

The door opened and the landlady came in, drawn by the noise. Griffin explained what happened. I gave her two dollars. The rug appeared to have kept the piece from being damaged. That, and the money, satisfied her. She left.

"Best to put back whatever shook loose in here," I said. In rehanging the vest I chanced to look up; a board hung loose. From what I saw when the piece was on the floor, the top hadn't looked broken. I called for Griffin to light a lamp and bring it. He held it while I leaned in for a better look. Near the top of the armoire someone had attached strips of molding on both ends. Two boards rested on the molding but could be tilted to either side and removed. I pulled out the board that had a corner hanging off and reached up to feel around on the other board. My fingers touched something, a hard object. I took it out and laid it on the bed. It was an oilskin packet.

Inside the packet was a leather-bound manuscript, darkened and stained. A title page was in beautifully lettered Spanish. *Diario del Padre Gonzalo Herdez Maldonado entre los Señores de las Islas del Cristal.* Griffin translated: The Journal of Father Gonzalo Herdez Maldonado Among the Lords of the Chrystal Islands. The opposite page showed a fanciful illustration of a red-and-blue fish with wings flying over three pyramids.

Griffin turned pages. We looked at drawings: a jaguar head mask and what looked like a union suit with jaguar decorations; a pyramid with steps leading up to two gazebo-like things; men in tunics with short swords and square shields fighting in an arena; a hand holding a sheaf of grain or grass; a colorful bird perched on another of those union suits, this one solid red rather than jaguar spotted; things that looked like pieces in a crazy chess set. He flipped through some more pages.

"Wait, go back," I said. "Here." A page showed a rounded hill, or sand hill, with a sneering face. Around it danced several skull-headed figures, tiny compared to the hill. The drawing appeared to indicate wind and rain; a fountain shot from the top of the sand hill. In the periphery, huts, pyramids, pictures of grain and fruits battered by rain. The skull-heads I knew didn't live in a place where it ever rained.

He read through some more and returned to the title page. "This is crazy . . . Carancaguases . . . that's what we call Karankawa now. But they had nothing like this."

"They didn't even have a permanent home," I said.

"Maybe they once did. Maybe they had to flee wherever they were from and became what we know."

Galveston had been one of the Karankawa's main centers of life. There never were a lot of them and they didn't last long after Europeans came.

I went over and looked out the window, thinking of skull-heads. They sky had darkened further. "Rain will be here soon. Do we take this journal with us, or leave it and post someone outside to watch for when Stephens comes back?"

Griffin closed the journal. "I'm taking it. We'll leave Nebel outside to watch for when he comes back."

"Why not arrange with the landlady for Nebel to take the other room on this floor?" I said. "Otherwise you'd need someone watching the front and back."

He agreed, and rewrapped the journal in its cloth. I made sure that the shelf in the armoire and everything else in the rooms looked like they had when we arrived. After we got back to the office, Griffin sent for a couple of part-time deputies, people who could relieve Nebel and shouldn't be known to Stephens. And we resumed our waiting

15

Fire

The Huntsville warden sent back a telegram saying that Owens wouldn't talk to anyone who wasn't me. The warden asked if he should be a little more forceful. I said no. I would have to go up there. The timing wasn't good. I didn't want to leave while we were watching for Stephens. I hadn't seen Griffin since we found the journal. Visions of musical instruments in flames still occupied my nights. And Stephens eyes, the red-burning eyes, following, always near. I took to walking past the burned-out Maggini shop. They weren't going to rebuild there, but I couldn't shake the connection. The ghost of my bass haunted the site. I went to the house where they were staying and talked to Marinella's father, but she refused to see me.

One afternoon, I was sitting in the office playing around with a guitar of Griffin's (he kept three at the office). Old Skete napped at the desk. I had just wasted a couple of hours interviewing members of an all-night card game in a room at the Alamo Hotel. The door opened and Gorman came in, returned from the coast. Road grime covered his duster and beard. His cheek was scraped raw.

"You look kinda half-dead, Gorman," Old Skete said.

Ignoring him, Gorman looked at me. "Where's the marshal?"

"He hasn't been around. He's studying an old Spanish journal Stephens had. We found Stephens's room. But not Stephens."

"I need to talk to Griffin."

"Fine with me. If you know where he lives, lead on." All the way, through the stifling mugginess, he didn't talk and neither did I.

The marshal had a neat little frame house on Wheeler Street. A mimosa tree at the fence was blooming like crazy; most of the yard was taken up with tomatoes, peppers, cucumbers, and other crops. Back in Chicago, none of those would be close to ripe yet. Many tomatoes were bird-pecked and looking past time for picking. We didn't have to knock. Griffin sat on a porch bench with a guitar on his lap. He wasn't playing. His eyes were bloodshot, and he hadn't shaved since last time I saw him. He didn't move or acknowledge us when we got up on the porch.

"I'm back, Marshal," Gorman said. "And I need to talk to you real bad."

Griffin stared up for a moment, as if not recognizing him, then spoke, "Gorman. Deputy Gorman . . . what?" and his voice had a thick, scraped-out sound, as though from lack of use.

"Tell you what I found, Marshal, me and Crawford from the county sheriff's." He sat on the railing opposite Griffin. "We went all over that area, wherever this Stephens bought land. You know what we found? Nothing except sand hills. Least that's what we thought till we saw one up close."

A knot was forming in my stomach, and it was telling me I wasn't going to like the rest of Gorman's account.

"These weren't regular sand hills. They had mouths, big ones. Some of those mouths had rotten meat in 'em. We found those hills scattered on the coast, none closer than a mile to one another, and then in the biggest patch of land, we found a whole circle of 'em. Not a circle though, more of a spiral."

"Shape of a hurricane," I said; I don't know why I said it—the idea emerged without forethought.

"I don't know nothing about that," Gorman said.

The marshal's eyes remained vacant. He appeared to be listening, but without obvious interest. I didn't think that Gorman had noticed anything different about him. Maybe this behavior was common, though I hadn't seen it. Gorman continued.

"We slept over near the spiral. Woke to find Crawford yelling like a crazy man. He had his arm up to the shoulder in one of those mouths. I swear it had closed on him. I got him out, but some of his shoulder was ripped off. My face got scraped. From what, I don't know."

"You weren't drinking?" I said. He gave me a look filled with the dislike he had back when we first met.

Griffin spoke. "No drinking, no imagining. It's what those heads are made for, I think. A maw with appetite unsatiated." He lapsed back into silence.

We waited till I got impatient. "You've been busy with that journal, Marshal. Does it say something about skulls, and sand hills with big mouths? I noticed that picture when we looked through the pages in Stephens's room." Gorman and I had to wait some more, but Griffin did answer.

"There's only one picture. They believed it was inviting disaster to show them, show a picture; they surrounded that one picture with images of the sand hill's counteragents. They told Father Gonzalo about it, but not easily. He had to put it together from different people giving different parts so it wasn't one person telling the whole thing. What he got was, an enemy tried to wipe these people out. Long ago in a different place. The sand hills brought storms, stronger and stronger storms, till one destroyed everything they had. Gone. Like the legend of Atlantis, the lost city. They fled. Most died.

"The land washed away and became nothing but a chain of barren islands. They didn't realize until the end that the sand hills were the cause. They had thought the hills were a gift from their protector gods, to keep storms away. The journal was an attempt by Father Gonzalo to recreate and record their culture before all of them were gone. There were only a few left who knew the old stories, their history."

While he spoke, he repeated the same chord, a D, continuing after he stopped talking. His face had a strained and pallid look.

"We have to destroy those sand hill things," I said. "They're no good."

"Round up some boys and dynamite the suckers," Gorman said. "What'll I tell the boys, Marshal? Nobody would believe this."

"The three of us could do it, us and dynamite," I said.

Gorman looked to the marshal. He strummed his D. I thought his face looked better. "That's what we'll do," he said. "This journal, it pulls me back to a time that maybe never was—I don't know that I believe any of this, but there is something."

"There is something," I said.

I tried to get Griffin to return to the office with us, but he said he needed to translate one more section. I wish he hadn't.

Nebel was there when we got back, sprawled in a chair opposite Old Skete. His nose was bandaged and he had a knot on his cheek. There was an open bottle of rye and an empty glass near his hand.

"Somebody hit you with an anvil?" Gorman said.

"Where's the marshal?"

"We just came from his house," I said. "He'll be along directly. Now spill it—we know you weren't trampled by stampeding cattle."

"I need a drink first." He picked up the empty glass. "Another one, I mean."

Old Skete poured. Nebel swallowed. "You gave me the good stuff! I didn't notice on the first one."

"Figured it was necessary."

Nebel talked. He had made himself comfortable and waited. Along afternoon time, someone knocked on his door. He assumed it was the landlady or another deputy. He didn't think Stephens had come back. "Said I was coming, and when I put my hand on the knob, the whole damn thing fell in. Next thing I know, the landlady's cleaning blood off my face. Door was lying next to me. The codger upstairs came down and bandaged my nose. Looks like that Stephens feller cleared out. He didn't take his things, but you can tell. Don't know how he broke the door like that. Torn right off the hinges."

"And how'd he know you was there?" Gorman said. "We better go tell the marshal."

We saw the smoke from down the street and started running. When we got there, the house looked pretty well gone. Smoke flowed through the roof like it wasn't there, and the windows glowed with flames. Some neighbors stood in the yard.

"Anyone see the marshal?" Gorman said. Nobody had.

One of the watchers said, "Wasn't nothing happening, then next minute there's fire blowing out the front winders."

"Marshal must have been on his way here," I said.

"He's in there, I can feel it," Gorman said. He took off his duster and draped it over his head. Nebel tried to stop him, but Gorman pushed him away and charged into the yard. I yelled for him to go in the back way, but he either didn't hear or didn't heed.

"Find a doctor," I said to Nebel.

I ran around to the back door and pulled my sack-coat over my head. Smoke coated the kitchen ceiling, but the flames hadn't reached the room yet. I got down on hands and knees and crawled through the next doorway. I didn't know the layout, but from the outside it hadn't looked like there was much to the place. The kitchen connected to a small dining room, then into a larger sitting room. That room was a mass of fire and smoke. I'd never heard a fire from so close and hope I never will again. With Dellschau, at the skull-head's burning saloon . . . I don't remember the sounds, not like this. I thought I could see Gorman, and moved toward him. He was bent over something. Griffin. Flames erupted from Gorman's duster. He might have screamed, but the sound mingled with the cry of the fire. I tugged the coat off him. He looked toward me, then picked up Griffin. I grabbed his arm and pulled. By the time we reached the dining room, the flames had arrived. Somehow, we made it into the kitchen and through the back door.

Nebel was ready with a wagon. "I knew you wasn't coming the front way, and I knew you wasn't all going to be walking." Gorman's face was blackened and I didn't like his burnt-meat smell. We trundled him onto the back, then laid Griffin beside him.

"Doc's at the other end of this street," Nebel said. He took the reins.

Waiting on bad news from a doctor is about the hardest thing there is in this world. The doctor didn't say much when we brought them in. He told us to put them in beds and said to come back in the morning. I got there early and sat outside, a cigar unlit in my fingers. I wanted it, but I didn't want the fire, however small, that would light it. A nurse let me in and gave me a cup of coffee. She said her name was Dara. She was a round-faced young woman with slips of red hair showing from under her white hat. Nebel arrived, with an older man who looked enough like Gorman to be his father. The nurse came back out.

"The doctor says one of you can see the marshal."

I looked at Nebel; he told me to go ahead.

"What about Gorman?" I said, after we had gained some distance from his father.

"Not good. Too many burns, breathed too much smoke. The marshal should recover." She squeezed my hand, then turned the knob to let me into Griffin's room. He lay on top of white sheets. Bandages covered his right hand and other parts of that side, but his face was clear.

His eyes opened, and his lips shaped into a brief smile.

"I recall this is how we met," I said. "Only I was the patient, that time." I gripped his unbandaged hand and released.

"Have you seen Gorman yet?"

"His father's here," I said. "Best to let him have some time first."

"His father is a mean old wolf, but he dotes on his boys."

I sat. "Any idea how it started?"

"Someone hit me on the head. Next thing I know I'm here."

"Stephens wanted his journal back pretty bad. Don't know how he knew where it was."

He nodded. "Had a dream that Gorman carried me out. Doc says it's true. He said my being unconscious is probably what saved me. Kept me on the floor where the air. . . . " His voice broke into a cough, lots of coughs. He closed his eyes.

"Gorman went in the front, I went in the back. His coat was on fire, but he got you out of there."

He opened his eyes. "What about the journal?"

"Stephens must have taken it, or he let it burn. Were you holding it?"

"It was locked in my desk. After you left . . . I never got back to my translating. Never got the journal out. I stayed outside for I don't know how long. I picked some vegetables. When I went inside he hit me."

"I'll go look. I have no idea what happened to your place after we left. We were more concerned with getting you and Gorman to the doctor. I don't know where Nebel found a wagon, but there he was; you have some good deputies." I talked some more, till the nurse came in and said I had to go. Down the hall, another door stood open. A low wail came from inside. I walked faster. Gorman's father was on his knees by the bed, shoulders slumped. The doctor and Nebel were murmuring to him. He got up, turned, and walked out.

There wasn't anything left of Griffin's house. I walked through the wreckage, looking for the desk, for something that might have been a desk. I didn't want to find it. Fine with me if the journal burned up. It wouldn't help us catch Stephens.

That night was a hard one. Gorman joined the cast of burning instruments. Flame sprouted from the mouth of one of those sand faces; Gorman tossed instruments into the mouth, building the flames till they spread to the rest of its face. When he dove in, I woke. The morning sun promised more heat. On my way to the office, I met Nebel. His face looked better. The bandage was off his nose and the lump on his cheek had mostly subsided, leaving a mottled splotch of bruised flesh.

"Was just coming to get you," he said. "I want to go back to Madame Blackley. You should go with me."

"Okay," I said. I grinned at him. "I can't say I'm a believer." He started walking and I fell in alongside.

"Just don't make fun. You do that, she'll turn us away. My uncle did that once. On the ride over, he kept making jokes about her. We got there, she said: 'That man has to stay outta my house.' She knew what he'd been saying."

"She also might have seen through the window that he was smiling."

"Anyway, watch yourself and come if you're coming."

Like most of the town, she was sitting on her porch. In this heat, where else could anyone go? When we reached the top of the steps, she stood. She was taller than me and Nebel, and built like a tree, the kind that bend when they have to but never snap.

"Hello, Freddie," she said. She had a comforting, cello kind of voice. She turned to me.

"You've seen some strange, but you're still a skeptic."

I agreed with that. "It's my nature. It's what makes me good at my job." I guess she accepted that, because she started talking about Stephens.

"This man who stole from all those people has gone away, gone away to a place you can't follow. But don't worry, he'll return. When he returns, you can catch him, but only if you play that card game the right way. Otherwise, you won't ever return yourself. Mind you, the other players won't be cheats, but that doesn't mean they'll let you win. They'll test you good. Especially the one with the ring. He'll have the hand you think he has and you'll split the winnings; after that, you'll have his respect."

I thanked her. On the way back, Nebel wanted to talk about what she had said. I didn't. I knew who she was prophesying about, but I would never be seeing him again.

Griffin came back to work a couple of days later. His right side was still bandaged, but he said he was tired of lying around. His face had a tight look. He didn't talk much and he didn't pick up his guitar.

I heard again from the warden: "Owens insists. Urgent that he talk to you. Says his life is in danger. Putting extra guard on him and moving his cell."

"You go," Griffin said. "I'll round up some boys and blow those sand hills to Florida."

"Gorman would have wanted that," I said. He didn't reply. I don't know what kinds of guilt he was carrying. For now, he had a purpose. That would keep him from thinking too much.

I decided to go to Huntsville by way of Galveston. That would delay me, but I didn't think anything would happen to Owens in a guarded cell. All the death made me want to see my family, for a night anyway. I packed my leather doctor bag with Silverberg's skull and a few items of clothing, leaving my saddlebags and the rest of my things at the desk for my return. Once again, I said my farewell to the town of Victoria, expecting I would be back in a couple of days.

16

Luminescent Snakes

Galveston...youth...home...salty breeze...but the death cries of the musical instruments refused to leave. I fled along the beach, confronted at every turn: a violin stuck in the sand, its neck a torch; a blackened guitar; a mound of shapeless char, its musical identity forever lost. And behind me, no matter how far I ran, the leering sand face, its maw open to claim a sacrifice. I sat in my parents' drawing room. I know that I interacted with them, perhaps my sisters and their husbands, but... to say it was a blur would be overstating. A blur has more substance than what I was experiencing.

Some things intruded into my consciousness, changes during my lost time away. A new water system had been completed, wells bored two thousand feet down, mains, pump house. The water was to be too brackish to drink, but my parents were planning to install flush toilets.

I had planned to leave for Huntsville after one day, but the stupor froze me. One night of sleep, one decent night's sleep, then I would go; instead, a variation of the dream, this time with Gorman's face imprinted on the sand hills. Oblivion laughed and stayed far away. I shouldn't have come here. *I shouldn't have come here.* I forced myself to walk on the shore before bed, hoping that the simplicity of daylight and sand would improve my night. Dense clouds hid the setting sun. A storm would be due by nightfall. I welcomed it. Perhaps it would blow my dreams to another country. And the winds did soothe my slumber—I slept better during the storm than any night since arriving. The next day, my internal fog lifted enough for me to call on Rabbi Cohen.

He was a small man with a surprisingly large presence and persuasive manner. The cuffs of his white shirts were perpetually inscribed with reminders of appointments or people to contact. He had married in March, during my lost time. A local girl named Mollie Levy. I remembered her as the younger cousin of a classmate. She was out for the morning; he said she would be disappointed to have missed me. Meanwhile, we had our business to discuss. Within a few minutes of being with him, all my lost energy had returned, and I was ready to do anything to find Stephens.

"Mr. Silverberg's family is content to leave his remains where you buried them," the rabbi said. "They have his watch, and they know that he is dead. Not knowing is what is difficult."

I hadn't told him—or anyone—about keeping the skull. I don't know why I still had it except that the Silverberg business wasn't over.

"More money could be recovered eventually," I said. "And once it's proved that Stephens's land company bought property with money donated for the fraudulent colony, that property can be sold. In which case, it would be wise to set up a real land company and issue shares based on the donations. That land will have to be worth more some day."

"Why would this Stephens steal money and then buy land? Land speculation is a long-term investment, unless you have inside knowledge of something that's about to happen, such as plans for a new hotel on Broadway in New York City."

What began as a simple job involving a swindle transformed into a complex and (in the rational sense) inexplicable affair. Or presently inexplicable. My ancient Israelite ancestors would have had trouble explaining gunpowder or steam engines. Which meant that the explanation only needed more information. Information builds a structure that reveals itself upon accumulation. To help with that accumulation, I decided to tell the rabbi everything, what lay beyond the Conroys' blanket, Stephens's dead eyes, skull-head land, sand hills with faces. Why not? He believes in a shapeless unnamable supernatural being.

The rabbi was curious about the metal disk that fell out of Conroy's mouth. "There are accounts in the Talmud about the creation of lifelike beings, and of course legends, like the Golem of Chelm, the Golem of Prague. Rabbi Loew of Prague is reputed to have created a man-shape of clay which he brought to life by placing a slip of paper in its mouth inscribed with a holy name. Or as some accounts say, around its neck. So it's conceivable that this Stephens is a servant of another force and has been given the ability to make a similar creation. Although these creatures are more of an after-death existence forced upon a living being. How frightening for you to have encountered such a horror!"

Very true, I thought, and the likelihood of encountering more before I finished this business was not a comforting thought. I said my goodbye to the rabbi and expressed my regret on missing his wife.

Huntsville prison was about 70 miles north of Houston. I caught a train to Houston and waited for my connection. As I was boarding the Huntsville train, I thought a man with white hair left the opposite end of my car. I hurried to the next car, but found nothing, not even a fish rot smell.

Owens had been right about being in danger. The warden informed me that yesterday morning, the guard found him dead in his cell. Hung himself. In his fist they found a scrap of cowhide branded with the curvy blob mouth. The warden thought the cowhide was a threat or warning from someone, and Owens hadn't wanted to wait for whatever it signified. I knew it was, and from whom.

The warden and I chatted about crime and its vagaries. He started telling me a story about some Piney Woods cousins and their crimes. Figuring that he didn't get much of a chance to talk to someone who wasn't a prisoner or a guard, I let his words flow into the room unimpeded. The job was getting to me, had been getting to me. The futility of...everywhere I turned...setback and death. I didn't care about Owens. He involved himself. But this Stephens, always ahead of me, ahead of everyone. Maybe Owens wouldn't have had anything useful to tell, but it hurt, not having the chance to determine that myself, to have been blocked, again. I don't like revenge—it distracts the detective from proper methodology—but I was going to enjoy catching and punishing this man.

I left the warden's office and walked toward the stairs. The gaslights had been turned low. There were no windows. The stairwell was dim, the stairs worn slick. My footfalls echoed off the stone. I kept thinking there was somebody behind me, but each time I stopped all I heard was nothing. Nerves. Everybody gets them sometimes. Prisons aren't the nicest places. Nerves or not ... I drew my gun and promptly slipped on the smooth steps. The stumble saved me. A shot burned past. The landing—four hard steps down—stopped my fall. The impact pushed the strap of my doctor bag off of my shoulder; the bag fell into the dark well. Stephens appeared on the landing above, white hair bright in the dimness. His gun hand moved to cover me. I brought mine up, but knew I wouldn't be in time. A squeal echoed through the stairwell; then a fury landed on Stephens's gun arm. Solo the eagle dug in with beak and talons. Stephens screamed; his gun clattered down the stairs toward me.

Now, I couldn't shoot, couldn't risk hitting Solo. I started back up the stairs, but before I could get to them, Stephens drew another gun, a Colt Cloverleaf four-shot, and put a bullet through Solo's head. He threw off the eagle. I pointed my gun at his head and screamed. Nothing happened. I looked at my gun. Stephens should be dead. I screamed again. His gun hand wavered, then he swung it toward me. Confused, I ran. My fingers still gripped the useless gun. Why useless? My dreams, my chasing dreams ... in my chasing dreams the only way to fire a gun was by screaming. I stopped to listen, heard nothing. I raised my gun hand toward the empty space I had fled and pulled the trigger. The roar of the shot echoed from the stone steps. I knew it was a waste of a bullet, but I needed to know that I could pull the trigger and fire.

Down, farther down. How many floors were there? I only remembered having climbed to the third. I looked over the railing. The ordinary stone staircase had become an endless spiral that descended into darkness. The stairway narrowed. Above, it had been a wide oval around an airshaft. These steps were like a Gothic bell tower, with short risers and no landings, no resting places. I slipped on the worn stone and careened downward. A hard floor smacked me. Somehow I didn't lose my grip on the revolver.

The air was as tight and dead as the guts of a coal mine. My ear, flush with the gritty floor, sensed motion. A faint glow moved toward me, undulating along the floor, growing brighter. I sat up and laid my gun on the bottom step so I could strike a match. The light revealed two snakes, only a few feet long but with bodies as thick as my arm. My doctor bag was near one of them. The snakes glowed, from the tops of their heads and all the way down their backs to their tails. The match and the snakes' advance brought detail to the cavern: rough, scraped-out walls of rock and hard-packed earth. The nearest snake reared like a cobra. Its burning eyes lanced me with a cold flame. Reflexes took over. I grabbed my gun and pulled the trigger. The impact slammed the snake into the wall. The snake's glow remained bright. I shot the other one. Now I had a lantern. I pulled out a strip of rawhide cord from a pocket and tied the snakes to the handle of my doctor bag so I could hold them in one hand and my gun in the other.

Straight went the passage, dim in the dead snake glow. My feet stirred fine dust. There were no footprints; no one had been this way, not for a long time. After uncountable footsteps, the floor began a gradual upward slope. Just enough slope to improve my mood and make me think I was headed somewhere. An upward slope is a fine thing.

Along the base of a wall were wooden crates, old dry wood, with Greek lettering. I holstered my gun and used my clasp knife to pry off a lid. Inside were ceramic bottles, separated by burlap sacking. Wax sealed their tops. I scraped off a seal and sniffed the contents. Alcohol,

pure enough to have survived the centuries. The line of crates continued. There was light now, from ahead. No longer needing the snakes,
I cut off their harness and left them. The light increased, showing more
crates, newer ones, some with labels in English. A short flight of stairs
led up. The stairs ended in a small room, an alcove off of another hall
running perpendicular. I had been here before.

I walked toward brightness and soon reached the back of the bar.
Dellschau slumped, face in hands. Like me, he had been drawn back.
This time, I had no bacon to offer him. Beyond the bar, skull-heads
played cards at their usual table. Ring Hand stood and gestured me to
an empty seat.

PART II

Skull-Heads

Never stay in a poker game unless there are at least three suckers.

> —Herbert O. Yardley,
> *The Education of a Poker Player*

17

Five Card Stud

F our skull-heads sat at a round table, playing stud poker. The hole
card and first up card had been dealt. Stacks of chips stood before
each player. I wondered what I could buy in with. Did money mean
anything here? I set my doctor bag on the table. Ring Hand pointed to
the bag and throated, as if he could sense what was inside. I presented
the skull. He clapped and reached toward it. "Sure, take him," I said.
"But I want to buy him back later."

The inevitability of the table awaited. Fighting might work again,
but escaping with bullets didn't mean I would stay free. Ring Hand's
invitation to play cards meant—had to mean—that winning was the way
out. If I had accepted his previous invitation, if I had won my way free
then, I wouldn't be back here now. Gorman might be alive, Marinella
and her father's shop wouldn't have burned. I may talk about patience,
waiting, accumulating facts, but I'm also the one who kicks down doors
and shoots people I might have caught without violence. We're full of
contradictions, we people. Maybe skull-heads are too.

Ring Hand came back with a wooden box and a new, sealed deck.
This box, its contents—is that what a man's skull is worth?

The spot that Ring Hand pointed me to faced a window. I slid my
bag under the chair. I didn't like playing with my back to a room, but

having a view to rest and refocus my eyes was good. Even a view of dried up scratch land to the horizon and beyond. And somewhere, Blue Swamp's mummified carcass.

Inside the box were stacks of chips in various colors. I picked up a yellow. On both sides, a ring of small circles surrounded a spiral shape. I had seen it somewhere; I've seen a lot of poker chips. These were heavy, comfortable in my hand, like something that would help me. They didn't have numbers to mark denominations. I arrayed mine the same as Ring Hand's, which matched the usual color order of value: white (five cents), yellow (twenty-five cents), red (fifty cents), green (one dollar), and blue (five dollars). The chips gave me about $1,000 to work with. My detective wage was $700 a year. I silently thanked Silverberg for the use of his skull.

"Well, isn't this is a very nice stake you've given me," I said. "I hope you gentlemen are ready for some serious card playing." Ring Hand nodded and clapped softly. Realizing that I had used my Irish Shannon voice, I decided to keep him with me.

Ring Hand swept the dealt cards back together and dropped them into the empty chip box. He slid the new deck toward me. A sealed deck proved nothing. Marking cards and resealing them in official-looking wrappers is as old as the game. You can even order them premarked, although good card sharps mark their own. I tore off the wrapper and fanned the cards. The pattern on the cards' backs didn't move. If there had been any marks or alterations, they should have jumped as the card flipped past them. The deck could have been altered in some other way, but marking backs was the most common.

Ring Hand sat on my left, with another to my right, and the last two across. I hadn't given much attention to these others, my previous visit. The one on my right wore stained Rebel grays, holed in several places, holes like what a rifle ball would have made. The bowler-hatted one who humped saloon girl sat on Ring Hand's left. The skull-head between him and the Rebel wore a Spanish friar's brown tunic. The fabric was faded and torn, patched with denim. His lower jaw was quite impressive, full of horselike teeth. Their visible skin: hands and parts of arms, were differing shades; Ring Hand's skin was coppery dark, the Rebel's pale, the others somewhere between. Teeth varied. Bowler-hatted Fornicator was missing an upper incisor and canine on his right side. The Rebel's remaining few were black and jagged. Ring Hand appeared to have all of his. He was dressed in the same nautical clothes as my first visit, and his bearing, his command, reminded me of the captains I had sailed under as a youth.

The guitarist and saloon girl were absent. They had their roles in the play, and this wasn't their scene.

My opponents—had they bumbled in like me? If so, they had been here for some time. Assuming that their appearance meant anything. Were they, too, playing for their freedom? Did they even remember being free, being elsewhere, in the light, the lovely light of the sun?

Five card stud begins with a deal of two cards. The first is a hole card, dealt face down; all other cards are face up. Betting begins at the first deal, and continues with each new card. If you know what you're doing, it's sometimes possible to figure out your opponents' hole cards. Smart players watch faces during the deals, to judge if an opponent's expression changes when they see their new cards and what that expression means. Sometimes it's as simple as a small eyebrow movement or twitch of a lip. Well, these players don't have lips or eyebrows!

The player showing the highest card or combination of cards starts the round of betting, and it proceeds clockwise around the table. In stud, winning hands tend to be low. Many are won with a medium pair, say, nines, tens, or jacks. Three-of-a-kind is a very big hand. I like stud. I like the strategy. Part of the fun involves keeping track of your opponents' cards and trying to push out strong players while keeping the weaker ones in. The fewer players there are in a hand, the easier it is to work on a particular attack.

Before playing in this game, I planned to sit out a few hands—put in my ante but fold after the deal. I needed to understand how these skull-heads conducted themselves. A hand of stud doesn't take much time, but . . . what meaning does time have here? Time measured in count of cards, clank of chips, flap of pasteboard on table. Comforting and familiar rhythms, but my chips . . . if I lost everything . . . if I lost this game, would I become a skull-head, trapped in eternal play? Thinking like that *makes* you lose. In any game. Time to forget where I was, and not speculate on meanings.

"Thank you, Dora Malley," I said, and thought back through her tables for calculating odds. Her new insights, plus my Tarpon training and the ensuing years of practice would have to sustain me.

Everyone put in a white chip. Ring Hand dealt the first two cards. Mine were a king down with a ten up, cards I would normally play; I folded. Letting the hand go hurt, but I had to follow the plan, the patient plan that would free me. Father Jaw, the Spaniard friar, started the betting with two whites—presumably the minimum. A game normally has a set amount for the ante and the minimum opening bet. Sometimes there's a limit—a maximum amount on each hand. Sometimes there's no limit.

Ring Hand and I were the only ones to fold. It soon became apparent that the skull-heads played a reckless, aggressive game. They carried on as if unaware of odds, or of the upturned cards. They studied their own cards. If they liked them, they stayed in; if they didn't, they folded. But they didn't fold often. There had to be quirks, individualities. Figuring those out was going to be difficult. Bluffing is an important part of the game, but I didn't think it would work with the way these skull-heads played, except possibly with Ring Hand.

Their deals varied. Father Jaw floated the cards like butterflies. The Rebel was slow and clumsy. Fornicator hurled his, sometimes flipping someone's hole card face up, sometimes overshooting the table. On one extremely sloppy deal, Ring Hand's loud throating caused Fornicator to gather up the cards and begin again. He was more careful, for a while.

Sitting across from them, watching, I noticed that they had tongues, or at least tonguelets. Though small, they weren't stubs. They looked complete, not the remains of a larger, once-organ that had been severed. More like the tongue of a creature that no longer needed one, like a snake's vestigial feet. They had eyes too, a darkness deep in the socket ringed with a thin band of white, so thin I only noticed it when one of them turned his head a certain angle. I started to recognize variations in the sounds they made, throatings as distinctive as a person's voice. The Rebel's were deeper, with a twangy quality that reminded me of East Texas. Father Jaw's were longer and pitched higher, with what I thought was a Spanish accent. Fornicator honked like a seal. Ring Hand throated with authority and also a certain magnanimity— the voice of a host.

The Rebel's poker playing was especially childlike; he behaved as if the card combinations were magical, something to be accepted, treated as a marvel beyond his control. One time, Ring Hand, Father Jaw, and I were out. The Rebel had a king and nothing else good in sight; he played as though the king was paired with his down card. I thought he had. He lost to Fornicator's ace high. He had seen fornicator's ace, had to have known that without at least a pair of something, the ace beat his king, yet, at the showdown, his twang and shaking head showed surprise and bafflement.

Ring Hand was my true opponent. He was the one who played, who really played. He was the one in control, of the game and my fate. I had to be careful of the others, play more conservatively than usual, but still pounce when I found an opportunity. I would also have to fold late in a hand, even if folding meant losing significant chips, if I suspected that someone's illogical play was going to bury me.

A few hands later, I was high with a jack and had to open the betting. I put in my two whites. I could have folded, but figured I might learn something if I sacrificed a small number of chips and folded on the third card. Ring Hand folded then too. The Rebel was the eventual winner, with two small pairs. On another, I lost a close one to Ring Hand. On purpose. Learning things that I hoped would help my education. Because of his betting, I had suspected (rightly) that the third deal had given him a second jack.

The winning pile of chips was worth three dollars and seventy-five cents. At this rate of play, gaining their money and my freedom would take too long.

"Well that was a fine round, gentlemen." I nodded toward Ring Hand. "And well played, sir." I had been silent since the beginning. Normally, I don't talk much during a game, and I don't like playing with people who do. But this wasn't a normal game. Partly to help my nerves, partly to keep myself company amongst the muteness of my opponents, I loosened Irish Shannon.

"I can see that you gentlemen have a long-established game here, and I'm thankful that you have allowed me to join your illustrious company. How long have you been playing here, Father Jaw?" I nodded to him to indicate my attention and he throated back. "I'm getting myself acclimated. Watching, you see, but I think this is a hand for me."

Except then I drew a bust and had to fold. Fornicator won with a queen high. I was getting used to these skull-heads winning without even having a pair. I could modify my strategy, forge on with a small pair and see what resulted. Carefully, and not with Ring Hand in.

Another hand, I drew a king for my hole with a nine showing. Betting was low. My third card was another nine. Ring Hand folded. I didn't try to push the betting till the next card. The Rebel folded. I bet the limit; Fornicator honked at me, but called. Father Jaw raised, I called his raise and raised again. Fornicator honked (he often protest honked when someone raised), but added his chips. Same with Father Jaw, minus the honking. The last deal paired my king, and the final round of betting went in a similar manner. We showed our cards. The Rebel held paired fours and sevens—not enough to beat my nines and kings. But the pot was too small.

Deciding to press for higher stakes, I picked up two whites and one yellow. "The betting here, if I understand correctly . . . minimum"—I held up the whites—"and maximum."—I indicated the yellow. "These are fine to start with, but they're far too low for interesting poker. Shall we raise them?"

Ring Hand throated and looked down at his chips. Fornicator reached across to pick up the whiskey bottle that was between me and

Ring Hand. I realized I hadn't talked to Dellschau yet. I wasn't in a hurry to.

Fornicator passed the bottle around. I declined.

Ring Hand picked up four whites and one yellow. He put them in the middle, two stacks: one of three whites, one a yellow and a white. He pointed to the three whites and throated, two short sounds, like the cough-roar of a mountain lion (minimum), then at the thirty-cent stack and gave a longer purr-cough (maximum).

Not much of a limit raise, but it was progress.

Hand melted into hand, and I continued to analyze their styles. When Ring Hand was high on the opening bet, he often started with the limit. I assumed that he was trying to chase out whichever of the skull-heads was more cautious, most often Father Jaw. I kept Irish Shannon talking. I reacted to the sounds the skull-heads made as though they were part of the conversation.

The Rebel, after losing to Ring Hand, twanged his surprise, and I said, "Yes, I suppose you're right. Betting against a potential three of a kind when one has but a small pair could be seen as reckless and foolhardy. You should remember that if you again find yourself in a similar situation."

Gradually, my chips increased. My lips felt wooden and my shoulders ached. I'd had nothing to eat or drink. "I need some water," I said to Ring Hand; I motioned with cupped fingers. He clapped twice. Dellschau brought one of those ancient ceramic bottles, and Ring Hand pushed it toward me.

"Not alcohol," I said. "Water."

"*Mein Got*—you're a Man!"

"Thirsty man."

"But when ... how ... did you come to be here?"

"I went down a stairway that started someplace else."

Dellschau didn't know me.

How long had he been back, and how could he have forgotten

everything that had happened? He offered to bring me water and a plate of beans. I hadn't noticed hunger. Now the need for food overtook me. I got up and stretched my arms up over my head, relieving the tired muscles.

"He's getting me food," I said, and mimed eating. "You gents keep your game rolling along without me for a few hands if you must." Not wanting to spill food where I played, I moved to the next table. Dellschau set the plate down, but he didn't go away.

"These fiends—how can you play cards with them? Do you know—?"

"No choice. Neither of us has a choice." I didn't care to talk to him. I knew I was being rude, and for no reason—from his way of looking at it. He talked about his journey, his air wagon. He couldn't manage the idea that I had descended a stairway to get here, while he endured storm and loss of friends. He only remembered his first arrival, remembered as if it had just happened.

"Listen," I said. "I know that this place and these people—if you want to call them people—don't make any sense, but here we are. And here I am, deep in a card game that I have to win. You're not much—"

A banging interrupted. Fornicator waved the ceramic bottle at Dellschau.

"Yes-yes, I will serve you," Dellschau said. Then, to me, more quietly. "These fiends run me back and around with their whiskey needs." He made no move to get the new bottle. I ate more beans.

"You don't remember me," I said. "I was here before. You and me, we escaped in your flying machine. Then you abandoned me in the Louisiana bayous. Because of that, I can't say I have much use for you. Once we get back to playing—"

Fornicator banged the table again. "Christ help me, I must serve the *Dämonkreaturs*," Dellschau said. He took them a refill and fetched back the empty. I don't know if he had understood what I said to him about having been here before and escaping. Human brains can't fathom the unfathomable.

Cards, chips, betting. Lose one, win two, fold, lose, fold, fold, win, lose, fold. . . . Was there life, was there a world outside the game, beyond this table? The cards were a window, a tunnel, a path, a gate, a pool of water so clear it made me cry. . . . One hand, feeling good with my first three cards and what I could see on the table, I opened with thirty cents. When I raised Father Jaw another thirty cents on the fourth card, Ring Hand folded. On another hand, I bet twenty-five cents and Ring Hand folded. Then there was a lull where it seemed like every hand either he or I raised from twenty-five to thirty cents on the third card and the other folded. Or we both folded and the other skull-heads battled. That season ended. In the next, we played back and forth, bet-win, bet-lose, but we both won more than we lost. At the expense of our opponents.

"And that," I said, as I swept up my earnings from a particularly satisfying win, "reminds me of a game I played in Dakota Territory. Which I *had* thought would be the one place I would never desire to see again. Till I came here. No offense, gentlemen."

But—twenty-five, thirty cents—I needed more. This time, Irish Shannon handled the negotiations. "As I see it, moving along at this level of betting our lovely game can continue forever. But I do have appointments to keep elsewhere. Might we have another wee bit of raise at this juncture?" I pushed out a red fifty cent chip and a green one dollar. "How would you feel about this, Master Ring Hand?"

He throated and tapped the table. Fornicator honked and pointed to a white chip; he picked it up and wagged it at the rest of us. I waved my hands as if pushing him away. He honked, a short, yappy kind of honk. I talked over it. "That's very nice for your Sunday social club, but this is a real game that we have here. Real poker demands high stakes."

Ring Hand nodded toward the chips I had selected and tapped the table again.

"Thank you, my good sir. And now, to the cards."

Dellschau brought the skull-heads a new whiskey bottle, and, for me, a pitcher of water with a plate of beans and cornbread. I thanked him. Had I eaten recently? The beans stirred my hunger.

Ring Hand clapped, three times. At the sound of the clapping,

Dellschau sank to his knees, wailing. A clump of boots sounded from the stairs—the remaining skull-heads entered the scene. The guitarist waved his instrument and hooted at the card players. The saloon girl didn't wave or hoot. She descended the stairs with graceful movements, wearing a dark brown dress with sleeves down to her wrists. The guitarist wore a coat and trousers of a similar color.

Ring Hand pulled a blue bandana from a pocket. Dellschau wailed louder and put his hands on top of his head, as if he could hold himself down. Ring Hand thrust fingers into Dellschau's thick hair and lifted him. Dellschau screamed. Ring Hand wrapped the blindfold around Dellschau's head and pushed him toward his dancing partner.

This time, I didn't have to play bass or wear a blindfold. That meant I had to see. I took my food and water to a table on the other side of the room. Father Jaw and the Rebel moved tables aside to make space for a dance floor. The guitarist began with a waltz, and the other skull-heads clapped the rhythm. Saloon Girl put her right hand in Dellschau's left and her other on his right shoulder. His right hung at his side. Ring Hand stamped his foot. Dellschau moaned, but moved his right hand to Saloon Girl's waist. Dance followed dance. The progression of songs—where had I heard them? The guitarist began "Rosetta's Stomp" and I remembered . . . Victoria, Teddy Wells. The skull-head guitarist was playing the same songs.

For group dances, the Rebel paired with Father Jaw, then switched with Dellschau and Saloon Girl. Dellschau moved like a clockwork toy. His face had gone blank. I pitied him. I even forgave him for what he had done, and while I was doing that, I ate my beans and cornbread. Looking at my plate allowed me to escape from the expression on Dellschau's face. When the beans were gone, Dellschau had passed out. Saloon Girl, hands thrust into his armpits, held him upright, dancing him as if he was a puppet.

Their shocking strength . . . what if they? They were treating me well, but what happened if that changed? They hadn't taken my Bulldog, but I wouldn't be able to shoot my way out of this mess. Unless I viewed suicide as the best option. Though, considering the bullet holes in the Rebel's clothes, death might not provide an escape either.

The song ended, and the guitarist bowed, apparently finished. Ring Hand gave him a bottle of whiskey; he warbled a goodbye. Saloon Girl carried Dellschau to the bar and lifted him onto a stool. She walked up the stairs. The game resumed. My turn to deal.

To help prepare myself for more poker, with a higher limit, I thought back to games I had played with Malley and the other boys at Tarpon Bill's joint. Not just boys—there was a young lady a few years older than me. Suzanna. She played better than any of us. I never knew her outside the game and hadn't thought of her since. The Tarpon's voice in my head helped steady me, wisdom like: *"Don't be dumb and try to go all the way with a small pair. If you don't make your third, you're fucked."*

My stacks of chips grew. Then came a hand where I thought I had a sure win with a pair of queens from the opening deal; I bet high and raised when I could, figuring that the never-folding Fornicator would always call. On the fourth card, Ring Hand raised my bet. The hand had gotten expensive. I wavered . . . I overthought . . . I didn't fold. By the end, I had an incidental pair of fours to go with my queens, but Ring Hand showed a full house, jacks and three eights. *"Watch out for open pairs,"* the Tarpon said.

Now came a series of frustrating hands where Ring Hand and I both drew busts and folded. The other skull-heads battled. Fornicator never raised. He also hadn't folded since our play began, regardless of his cards. Of the three, Father Jaw folded the most, but he also tended to bet more than he should. Fornicator or Father Jaw would be the most likely ones for me to lure into a larger pot.

During a whiskey break, I picked up a blue chip and stared at the design. I remembered where I had seen it—the Spanish journal. On one page, a skull-head carried a shield with the same design, in blue and orange. Another page had a border along its bottom of spirals inside circles. Circle surrounds the spiral, traps the hurricane. The marshal should be out dynamiting those sand faces. How would Stephens react to their destruction?

Eventually, the cards moved along a little better. I recovered most of what I had lost, but I played more cautiously when Ring Hand stayed in. For my confidence, I had to win a hand from him.

And a few hands later, with the right combination of cards and betting strategy (plus an interruption), I was able to finesse a nice pot with three nines to Ring Hand's jacks and eights and Fornicator's two kings.

About the interruption: during the fourth card betting, Saloon Girl came down the stairs. She had changed to a sleeveless cream-and-maroon dress with a low neckline; the hem had a lot of ruffles that ended above her knees in front and lower in back. She wore black lace-up boots. Her body was nice, but that didn't change how the top part looked. Fornicator hopped from his chair and spread his arms. Ring Hand slapped the table. Fornicator sat, staying there until we finished. He didn't seem bothered about losing. Well, now it was fun-time for him. He hooted and started unbuttoning his pants.

I was happy enough about the break. My eyes were burning and my back ached. Then I realized I had to piss. I got up. Bodily functions happen all at once here. Sudden thirst, hunger, now this. An outhouse wasn't necessary, but I preferred not to be attacked if they didn't like me walking out the front door. I turned to Ring Hand. "Assuming we're taking a little time to allow for his fun"—I pointed to Fornicator and Saloon Girl—"I need to use the toilet. Relieve myself." I mimed the action. Ring Hand warbled and gestured toward the back.

Dellschau had returned to his side of the bar. I told him what I was looking for.

"Yes . . . I think . . . out . . . past the hallway of the liquor crates."

He had an expression that I interpreted as puzzlement, and I recalled my other time here—he had been confused when I asked about sleep.

"Do these skull-heads ever need to piss? They drink like crazy."

"I . . . I have no idea. I only see them drink. They eat nothing, and they never leave this room, except the guitarist and that . . . *hure*."

Passing where I had come in, I had an urge to flee back down that dark corridor. But there is no flight, only the game.

The hallway had a rough pine floor and equally rough timber walls and ceiling. No plaster, no paint. A wall sconce held a few candles, some lit. I stopped to open a door and look in. Like a hotel room: bed, washstand, bedside table, dresser, all covered with dust thick enough to see from the door. Dust caked the floor as well. I passed areas where wall boards had been pried off, revealing the building's empty husk. I remembered—my first visit, Dellschau said he stripped the building for firewood. Another room had similar furniture, plus a landscape of glass bottles, most shattered, some whole. The mound was higher in the back, but no part of the floor was clean. Even the bed had its layer of glass. Now I knew where Dellschau put the empties.

Farther along, a haze dimmed the light. Wind had extinguished the remaining candles. A humming noise increased. Walls vibrated. The hallway continued on, with no visible end, and grit thickened the air. I pulled my coat collar over my mouth and squinted. Wall timbers shook, as if from the approach of a massive locomotive. What would I find when I reached the outside? I wasn't going to reach the outside. The wind increased to a hurricane. The saloon stood in its eye. Grit banged into me, stinging exposed skin. I stopped. From the pattern of blowing dust, I could figure out the way the air moved. This was important. I couldn't wait. Bodily functions. I unbuttoned my fly and let loose, then fled the windy zone. I didn't want my piss blowing back on me.

Through the thinning haze, I could see a figure near the door of the bedroom I had passed. I assumed it was Dellschau, looking for more firewood to pry from the building. It wasn't.

The dress she had been wearing earlier was gone. The only thing covering her were black stockings, boots, and an insignificant dark blue camisole. A lot of freckled skin showed—up to the neck, where the nightmare began. I walked right up to her. What else could I do? There was only one way to go.

"Pardon me, ma'am, I need to get back to my card game."

She was a few inches taller than me. That put my eyes a lot closer to her bare jaws than I was comfortable with. A bottom incisor was missing. She put her hands on my shoulders and pulled me closer, held me, swaying as if to one the guitarist's waltzes. I kept my arms at my sides, but she took my right arm and brought it around her. Her grip hurt. I yelled into her face—"None of that! I have to play cards. Ring Hand doesn't want me hurt!"

I hoped that was true. I hoped she understood. Maybe she smiled. Skull-faces are stuck in a smile, but I thought the sound of her trill resembled tenderness. I put my free hand on her waist. She tightened our embrace, but gently. My cheek brushed her shoulder. The softness and warmth of her skin surprised me. Her scent was thick, not unpleasant, but tangible. Breasts rubbed my chest, and . . . I reacted. Bodily functions again. She noticed. She trilled and rubbed her pelvis into mine. Then, like she had with Dellschau, she slid her hands into my armpits and carried me.

I'm not proud of what happened next. Not proud, no, but not ashamed either. I can't deny that my body enjoyed it. She stood me on the floor by the bed and pulled back the covers. Dust clouded the air.

I've consumed hashish, twice, paste dissolved in a cup of coffee. The drug gave me an uncomfortable disorientation. I knew where I was, who I was with, but I watched from outside myself. I talked, I interacted, but it also wasn't me. Time distorted. I would reach to pick up a glass of water and observe my fingers moving closer . . . closer . . . closer . . . across a distance so vast I couldn't believe that my hand would ever touch the glass. Here, in this abandoned bedroom, through the dusty air, I watched myself. . . . She trilled. One of my hands moved to her belly, feeling softness there, under my palm, under the fabric. She sat and opened my buttons. Trousers fell. My Bulldog, in its shoulder holster, lay on top of my coat. I didn't remember removing it or the coat. I sat beside her and kicked off my boots. Stockings covered her feet. Her boots lay nearby. Someone . . . I think it was me . . . unbuttoned my shirt and pulled it off; my undershirt followed. I watched my hands work the buttons of her camisole and slide it down her arms.

Forgetting her bone-face, I stared at her breasts. She moved one of my hands between them. We lay down. Sanity returned . . . I tried to get up. Her arms locked around me. I passed beyond caring. Even when my lips pressed to her fleshless mouth, when my tongue met the gap in her teeth, her vestige of tongue.

I dozed, then woke to find her head on my chest, my arm over her back. I stroked her cheek; the bone was smooth, like carved and polished ivory. She stirred, murmured, and reached between my legs. My body responded, but this time I had to resist.

"The boys must be holding up the game for me," I said. Our clothes lay where we had dropped them. She allowed me to dress. I hung the holster in its place but moved the Bulldog to a coat pocket. I wanted to be able to take my coat off during the game without showing everyone the gun. An empty holster wouldn't matter.

"That was a truly fine experience," I said, and I meant it. "But I need to apologize for something. I don't know if you remember . . . we were on Dellschau's flying machine . . . I shot you. I'm real sorry about that." I kissed her toothy face, then each breast, and left.

18

Maze of Cards

Dellschau's head rested on the bar. Father Jaw drank from a tall, skinny bottle with a Cyrillic script label. I couldn't tell if they had resumed play during my absence, or remained suspended, like Dellschau. I filled a glass with water from the pump and drank it down. Ring Hand stood and bowed a greeting. Visions of everyday life in skull-head saloon. Maze of cards... hearts and clubs... maze of suits... diamonds swam in a dark pool of alcohol scented with oak... rearranged themselves into a flush that spread from my face and down my arms... my fingers separated two fifty-cent chips and pushed them into the middle. My hand was a bust. I had nothing. I would *never* play with that. I folded, but I couldn't take back my bet. Regaining control of the game was going to be harder than I thought.

The Rebel took that one, with a pair of kings. Irish Shannon congratulated him. "Draw to a high card, Mr. Rebel, and you won't go wrong. Draw to a low one, you'll sing a sad song."

Before the next deal, Ring Hand moved a green and blue to the middle and tapped the table. That was the first use of the five-dollar blue chips. I wasn't ready for higher stakes, but I had to be ready. I once knew a man named Reddy. A cowboy. Black hair—must not have been a nickname. Knew another man named Reddy. Robbed banks and

anything else he could find. Had red hair. Nickname, clearly. After too
many Wanted circulars, he shaved his head. I found him anyway. I was
patient and recognized him. I was ready. My cards, they were ready too.
I raised a blue. Ring Hand called. Fourth card, he folded. I raised on the
remaining skull-heads and beat them all.

Footsteps sounded on the stairs; I smelled lavender. She had put on
a scent. Fingers touched my ears and moved from there down to my
chest. Her breasts kissed my shoulders. I got up and put my arms
around her. "It's lovely to see you again, darling, but I'm working.
Let's have a nice bit of adventure later." I put my lips to her ear and
whispered, "Then I want to lay you out on the bed and see what's
under your stockings."

She trilled and turned to walk back up the stairs. I sat. Fornicator
honked like an annoyed seal and curled fingers into a fist. Ring Hand
looked at me, as if asking for an explanation. "Sorry about that, gents.
I believe the damsel has taken an interest in me. Well, no matter, let's
return to our cards."

Maybe I could use the interruption as an opportunity for changing
tactics. Aside from Fornicator, the skull-heads' play was emotionless,
win or lose. Fornicator honked when he had a decent hand but still lost.
When he won, he slapped the table and hooted, an eerie thing that
startled me the first time I heard it. Fornicator was the one I could bait.
Dangerous, considering his strength, but I needed to agitate. A couple
of hands later, I had a chance. Father Jaw held a likely bust, nothing
high, nothing consecutive, nothing the same suit, but the fourth card
came and he was still in. Ring Hand was out. I had a jack down and
another showing.

"As I was saying earlier, well, a man needs a damsel, does he not?
Working the cards, one develops some appetites, let's say. Appetites
that need release. You know what I'm talking of, Master Fornicator."—I
nodded at him—"I hope you're of a mind to share, though really, it is the

lady's decision. No forcing her into any dalliance she doesn't want, right gents?"

I still didn't know how much they understood, but I kept looking at Fornicator while I talked.

My fourth card was a second three. With his pair of fives high, Fornicator opened the betting. Father Jaw called. I gathered chips into a stack without seeming to look at the amount (yellows, reds, and a green, totaling five dollars—I was seeking drama), and—THWACK!—slammed the stack down in the middle of the table. Fornicator honked, a short, loud burst. He called my raise. Father Jaw should have folded, but didn't.

"This one is looking mighty bleak, Master Fornicator. Even a skull-headed man must choose with care. I've been in a similar place, it's true. I suppose all we can do is keep moving along to the last card and see what it bring us."

It brought me a queen. "Ah, diamonds," I said in a satisfied way, as if it meant something. The Rebel had paired his six, making him high; he bet a blue. I assembled a stack and slid it to the middle, slowly-slowly-slowly, and let go. I waved my fingers over the pot as if indicating that the chips were mine. Fornicator honked again, but called my raise. Dumb, because he should be able to see that the rebel's sixes beat his fives. The Rebel called. We turned over our hole cards. My jacks and threes took the pot. I exclaimed, "Oh, my, yes, come to me lads!" and claimed the winnings.

Fornicator howled. He jumped up and raised his fists. Ring Hand looked at him and throated. Not loud, but commanding. Fornicator honked back. Ring Hand pointed to the chair. Fornicator honked. Ring Hand slapped the table, his ring clanging his authority. Fornicator whined, but sat. I took my hand out of my coat pocket, glad I hadn't automatically drawn the Bulldog.

"Well boys, I'm glad that's settled." I had to keep my voice light. I didn't feel light, even though I was the instigator. "How about we play another hand, then?"

The stacks of chips belonging to the Rebel, Fornicator, and Father Jaw shrank; mine and Ring Hand's grew. On a hand that Father Jaw won, Fornicator lost the rest of his chips. He throated and reached a cupped palm toward Ring Hand. I hadn't expected the next thing. Ring Hand pulled out a pencil and a calfskin notebook. He flipped open the notebook. All I could see was a page with several columns of numbers. Ring Hand hummed and ran his finger down the column to the last line. He wrote something below it, closed the book, and rapped on the table three times. Fornicator rapped back. Ring Hand throated and pulled chips, bills, and coins from a pocket and dropped them on the table. Fornicator snatched them. Some of the currency was familiar, some wasn't.

Determining the right number of chips to use against his bets was going to be tricky. I decided it didn't matter. I bet what I wanted, and no one objected. But the other point about the money—while it wasn't uncommon to allow other players to raise more capital to meet a bet, at some point the game has to end. Someone wins. If Ring Hand subsidized the other skull-heads for infinity, how could I win and escape?

Along came a hand where I drew two tens on the deal and thought I might bluff Ring Hand if cards aligned. He drew a jack on the third card and didn't fold; I assumed that meant he now had a pair. Fourth card, I drew a king; I shifted in my seat a little, trying to look more relaxed. Subtle, but I knew that Ring Hand would notice. My cards were now high. I checked. Ring Hand checked. Fornicator bet. Father Jaw had just drawn a jack; the Rebel was showing a jack, and Ring Hand probably had the other two. If Father Jaw had paired something, it was lower than my tens. Same with Fornicator. My pair should be good enough to beat everything but Ring Hand's jacks. Father Jaw called Fornicator's bet. The Rebel folded. I raised to the limit; Ring

Hand folded. On the last round, I bet the limit. When I turned over my down card, Ring Hand clanked the table with his ring. I didn't look at him. Irish Shannon said something mild and inoffensive. Ring Hand called for whiskey.

Would the scene now repeat—food, dance, fornication? Dellschau brought their bottle. I asked him for a plate of beans. He stared at me, blank, as if he had already forgotten I was there, then without his expression changing, he said the beans would take a few minutes to heat. I pulled off my coat and draped it over the back of my chair.

The guitarist and Saloon Girl returned. She had changed back into her modesty outfit.

I didn't mind stopping. I wanted to think. The Tarpon could detect his opponents' tells like he was reading their minds. Sometimes I thought he *was* reading minds. He had trained himself to observe, to hear and see and detect. I've done that too. I was getting more comfortable here, more attuned, and I had noticed something about Ring Hand, something I would explore when the game resumed.

Dellschau didn't fight the blindfold. I went to the stove. Dellschau wouldn't be able to serve me. I spooned beans into a bowl and stayed at the bar to eat. I was tired of Dellschau's beans. What would I eat first, when I returned to the land of sunshine and real food? But getting there . . . the game was the key, or the lock, depending on the result. I wasn't sure I would be able to clean out Ring Hand. I wasn't sure I had the skill or the endurance. I would need sleep, wouldn't I? I had to push for a no-limit game. And risk a larger pot against him. My earlier bluff had worked. Did I dare try it again?

Knowing his hole card would help. The thing I had noticed . . . I was out . . . third card . . . Fornicator dealt Ring Hand a king. Ring Hand made a click-cluck in his throat, so faint I only heard because I sat next to him and had been concentrating ears and eyes on my opponents during the deal. He won the hand with two pairs, kings and fives. His hole card was a king. Another hand, fourth-card deal, he click-clucked on a queen. By the fifth card, Fornicator had a seven showing. He was dealt another seven and picked up his hole card to look at it again, an obvious indication that he had made three with his sevens, beating Ring Hand's probable pairs of queens and nines. Ring Hand folded.

His folding meant I didn't get to see if he had two queens, but I was sure enough. When my cards were right, I would strike.

This time, the dance didn't bother me. Maybe I was too jaded to care. Or too corrupted. I wasn't jealous—I didn't want to switch places with Dellschau, but . . . watching them . . . I began to look forward to another private visit with Saloon Girl. The problem was, I wanted to end the game before that part of the cycle. But if I rushed, I would make a mistake, and Ring Hand would devour me. I had to play like the Tarpon and know my moment. *"Late in a hand, raise hard if you can beat what you see. Know the percentages, and figure out their hole cards. Simple, huh boys?"*

Saloon Girl carried Dellschau back to the bar. She held him like he was an incidental sack of beans, but when she set him on his stool she took care that he was comfortable. I grinned at her and she cracked her jaw open to give me a trill.

Wanting to start this round with higher limits, I slid three greens and two blues toward Ring Hand, but before I could say anything, he pushed them back and held up a hand, palm facing me. I knew better than to complain. He had a plan, I supposed.

The Rebel's deal. He sent me opening cards I thought I could do something with. Same with Ring Hand, apparently. Fornicator had a ten showing and opened with his usual minimum. Third card—Ring click-clucked on a king. Meaning a pair of them. I paired my hole card, a jack, but the kings beat me. Ring Hand opened with the limit. Goodbye Father Jaw. I called. Two cards to go. The world can always benefit from optimism. Not nonsense, like the way the Rebel and Fornicator stayed in with what couldn't have been better than a small pair, but the measured optimism of the experienced player.

Fornicator's fourth card was a king, making it less likely for Ring Hand to make a third with his. And if he did, I would see it. More relevant, I paired my eight, boosting my hand nicely. Bold Tarpon play said go for a kill.

Ring Hand raised. That worried me, but . . . I knew I had him.

Last card, the Rebel gained a jack. The jack must have comforted Ring Hand; let's say he had guessed that my hole card was a jack but was now sure enough that I wouldn't get a third and was playing for a higher second pair than my eights . . . but, if that was the case, he would have folded when he didn't make a second pair. So he must *not* have guessed my hole card, and figured that his kings took the hand. "Eights bets three dollars," Irish Shannon said, and slid the chips forward.

We showed our cards. As I had assumed, my jacks and eights beat Ring Hand's pair of kings, and everyone else. Fornicator howled and shoved the table into my belly.

Ring Hand pushed the table back into place. He stood and throated at Fornicator.

I had my gun out. "Keep your man off me," I said. I had meant to yell, but didn't have the breath. I sucked in some air. Ring Hand uttered a long series of throats and gestured around the table. He touched my gun hand and shook his head. I put in the holster—no point trying to hide it anymore, but I didn't give it up.

Now would have been a nice time for Irish Shannon to say something calming, but he was taking a siesta. Fornicator . . . I hadn't even baited him. I had been too busy concentrating on how to play Ring Hand.

Time . . . cards . . . chips—I played hard and won more than I lost. Looking down at my chips, I noticed that I had nearly doubled my initial stake. And for the detective, two Silverberg skulls worth of chips! I had acquired some of the mixed currency too.

Ring Hand didn't click-cluck on a jack, just queen, king, ace, but I wasn't able to try another sure hand against him. The cards have to align. In poker and detective work, patience determines everything.

Another win, then exhaustion slammed me; I needed to stop, at least long enough to dunk my head in a bucket of water. "I'm calling for a break," I said. "I'd like to drink some coffee, wash up." I mimed rubbing my face with a towel. Father Jaw throated what I assumed was a laugh. I grinned at him and got up. I hoped Dellschau *had* coffee. More than hope—I was suddenly desperate for the stuff. Odd that I hadn't thought of coffee before.

"Coffee," Dellschau said, stupidly, as if the word was new to him. Despairing, I looked for a towel. I found one, along with a bucket, and set to bathing my head. Then I smelled roasting beans ... that scent was enough to begin my renewal. Dellschau burbled with excitement. "Coffee! How could I have forgotten coffee? How lovely it smells!"

I carried a dented blue enamel coffeepot back to the game. "Gentlemen, you can have your gin and whiskey, your ancient spirits. Coffee ... now there's *my* elixir. Nurtured on coffee, I was, and can never drink enough of it. Now, we shall see some card playing! Carry on. Your deal, Mr. Rebel, if I'm not misremembering."

Some hands later, Saloon Girl came down the stairs, again wearing her sleeveless dress with the low neckline. Fornicator sprang to his feet and pushed past Ring Hand's chair to reach the outside of the table. I got up and put on my coat. "Need to piss," I said.

But Saloon Girl changed the script. When Fornicator tried to embrace her, she shoved him and throated something final. He honked and waved his hands as if asking why. I started toward the back. Saloon Girl caught up and put an arm through one of mine. I patted her hand. That hadn't been part of my plan, but I could adapt.

Dellschau watched us pass. His face twisted into an expression that could only mean disgust and horror.

Saloon Girl was as much of this place, this situation, as the poker. Her attachment I accepted as part of the game. We went down the windy hall to our room. I squeezed her bottom, then slapped it. She squealed and tightened her grip on my arm. Her bony head rubbed against my scalp. She bit an earlobe. My turn to squeal.

The bed was still ruffled from our last visit. She let go of my arm and looked down at me from those dark sockets, then trilled, picked me up, and carried me toward the bed. Resting my hands on the polished bone of her skull, I rubbed her ear ridges. She moaned. When she set me down, I kissed her freckled shoulders, one, then the other. I kissed her right arm, down to the hand, kneeling as my lips descended. She pushed me. I sprawled onto the floor; she trilled like it was funny, and began unbuttoning her dress. She sat on the bed to unlace her boots. She slid them off, then her stockings, leaving the camisole as her only covering. I stroked her feet, moving my hands up to ankles, calves, thighs. The hair between her legs was burgundy.

During my training with the Ronald P. Smith Theatre Company, I had learned more than how to create Irish Shannon and other characters useful in the art of detection. The rest of my education happened off stage. An actress named Cecily Crawford taught me about a woman's pleasure. Specifically, her pleasure. Before Cecily, my method had always been stick it in and get the business done. I learned how it wasn't much fun for the woman that way.

My first visit with this skull-lady, I hadn't thought about anything but keeping myself unharmed. This time, I worked on her pleasure for a while. Which got me excited too; then it was time for my own buttons.

"I'll get right back to you, darling," I said. I shed my clothing and resumed my stimulation exercise. After, I lay beside her and worked on a button of her camisole. I didn't get very far. She rolled on top and guided me inside. Then I drifted. That hashish body-separation feeling descended. Pleasant respite from the cards ... not something one finds in your usual saloon card game. Yes, nothing like a trip to skull-head land. If only the food was better ... otherwise. ... A crash jerked me back to life. We both sat up.

Fornicator. He had rammed through the closed but unlocked door. The hasp had splintered into jagged strips of wood. He honked and moaned, louder than when he had threatened me earlier. And no Ring Hand to stop him.

My gal wasn't too happy. She jumped up and went at him, trilling and throating.

He waved his arms and pointed at me. She waved hers back. He tried to bull past her, but she blocked him. He put his hands on her shoulders. She knocked them away and pinned him against the wall. She held him there, throating at his face. His honking faded to a whine. She kept at him, emphasizing with shakes of his body. Finally, he slumped, defeated. She pushed him out the door.

After all that, my heart was thumping around like crazy.

She walked back to the bed. During her tussle, a breast had escaped from her camisole. I reached up and held it with both hands. She sat next to me. My heart-rate slowed, though in another couple of minutes, she got it speeded up again. Sometime later, we dressed.

"You must have a name," I said. "What should I call you?" Judging from the evidence—the bullet holes in the Rebel's clothing, the age of Father Jaw's habit, and from the way that Rat-Face Conroy had changed after I shot him—these skull-heads were the remains of people who had lived in the outer world. Did their current appearance reflect who they had been? Had my companion been a whore and was still a whore? It might be that this scenario . . . saloon . . . card game . . . required a whore, and she assumed that role.

Her body coloring and freckles reminded me of someone from Chicago, the redheaded wife of a lawyer I knew. The wife's face was pale and freckled, I mean. I haven't seen the rest of her body.

"How 'bout I call you Patricia?" She trilled. I figured that meant she liked it. "Lady Patricia." Why did I say that? She had bearing, whatever that means. She had been something, wherever is was that she came from.

Walking back, we held hands. I thought about Fornicator. If he had been upset enough to blast into our room, how would he react when I returned to the game? I don't mind admitting I felt a lot safer with my skull-headed Patricia beside me. We hugged near the stairs. She walked off, leaving me with a trace of lavender.

Ring Hand bowed and gestured toward my seat.

"And here we are again, boys," I said. "Time to play, is it? I believe the deal has returned to me."

I felt no need to wait out any hands. Recklessness . . . overconfidence, perhaps, but I won a hand with three jacks over Ring Hand's nines and click-cluck-betrayed aces. He could see two of my jacks. I played as if I thought they would beat everything. I guess I fooled him. He displayed emotion—a lot, for him—a cough-throat and a slap of cards against the table when he passed the deck to the next dealer.

That hand cleaned out Father Jaw. As he had with Fornicator, Ring Hand consulted his notebook and handed Father Jaw a pile of chips, coins, and bills. Continuing on, I lost a small pot to the Rebel, won it back, and so on, until Ring Hand called a whiskey break. Scents of cornbread and simmering food carried me over to see what Dellschau had made.

"I found a can of lard!" he said, practically shivering with excitement. "The lard makes the cornbread so much better, and that inspired me to cook the salt cod I had been saving."

His enthusiasm surprised me. We hadn't talked since I walked past him, arm in arm with Patricia, Lady Patricia. Most likely he had forgotten. I sat at the bar to eat. He took the skull-heads their whiskey. When he returned, I asked him more about how he came to be here. Actually, how he came to be back here. "Is your craft on the roof?"

His facial muscles slackened; for some minutes he stared at nothing, oblivious to my presence, to everything. I examined his face but found no clue in its topography. He still held the spoon he had served me with. It dripped sauce into the pan. I ate.

"What do you think, did I rinse the cod enough to remove the salt?" His mind reemerged, my question forgotten. I wasn't going to be able to get him to remember leaving *or* returning. Just being.

"It's very fine," I said.

I assumed that his return, like mine, had been by a different path. To the building that I . . . we . . . had burned. It—along with its inhabitants— had regenerated to receive us.

What did these skull-heads recall of *their* past?

19

What Madame Blackley Predicted

Sometimes, even strong players make mistakes. Sometimes, you play the right way and lose to some fool with that perfect combination of luck and stupidity. Never forget your opponent's lack of intelligence, because a smarter player would have folded long ago and therefore wouldn't have gotten that lucky card. That's happened before and likely will again. This time, it was Fornicator. Fitting, I suppose.

First, the limits. Ring Hand initiated a change. A big one. He throated us to attention, then pointed at each player's stake, going around in betting order. He clasped his hands over the middle of the table, just off the surface, held them there for a moment, and raised them. When his arms were fully extended, he separated his hands, throated, and pointed at the ceiling with both thumbs.

Fornicator turned *his* thumbs down. Ring Hand pointed up again. Fornicator shook his head. He picked up two white chips and waved them at us. Ring Hand thumped the table with both hands, keeping thumbs pointed up. He kept thumping till Fornicator put down the white chips and pointed up. The Rebel and Father Jaw thumb-pointed. Ring Hand looked at me.

"Are you saying that the betting is now to be no-limit?" Irish Shannon asked, for both of us. I put up my thumbs. Ring Hand tapped the table five times.

My next hand started well. The pot grew. I thought I was in control. Last card, the Rebel raised Fornicator's opening bet. I reached for my chips . . . picked up my glass of water instead. It was empty. The one remaining drop moistened my lips. Could the Rebel have three fours? Father Jaw had folded a four. The odds said not likely. I called his raise. We showed. The Rebel *did* have three fours, but that wasn't even relevant. Fornicator's full house beat everything. He jumped to his feet, raised his hands high, and hooted. The Rebel expelled a whine of disappointment.

I got up. "Need to piss," I said. And I did, I realized, after saying so, but mostly, I had to get away from the table.

First no limit hand . . . Fornicator . . . the Rebel . . . well, the Rebel had what I was worried he might have. That's poker. But I hadn't given Fornicator any attention. I couldn't afford that kind of mistake.

The wind wasn't blowing as much this time, but I still couldn't make it all the way to the end. I ducked into a room gutted by Dellschau's lumber scavenging and watered the dust. Walking back, I passed the frolic room. Having been too preoccupied with poker and my bladder, I hadn't noticed Lady Patricia lying on the bed. She wore her modesty outfit, feet bare, head propped on pillows, and . . . she was reading a book.

I had thought that nothing else here could surprise me. The idea that skull-heads might read books. . . . They have eyes, so why not? Ring Hand kept his accounts ledger. But their actions had been so limited. The card players played cards, recklessly, as though unable to learn a better way. Patricia danced with Dellschau and had sex with Fornicator (and now, me). Ring Hand was captain; seeing *him* with a book wouldn't have been surprising.

She glanced up, then resumed her reading. Closer, I read the title. *Unitarian Review*—that was even more baffling. Not that I had a particular expectation, but a dime novel would have thrown me less. I knelt by the bed and looked at the pages:

> ... in spite of all my explanations, the word "chance" will still be giving trouble. Though you may yourselves be adverse to the deterministic doctrine, you wish a pleasanter word than "chance" to name the opposite doctrine by; and you very likely consider my preference for such a word. ...

An open notebook lay on the bed—or, not a notebook: the right-hand side was a ledger, pale yellow paper with ink-faded words and figures ... onions, ten bushels, salt beef, 20 barrels ... probably from a ship's purser; the left side was filled with neat, compact handwriting in pencil. The pencil was in Lady Patricia's right hand. I read:

> But if we are not victims of a pre-determined world, what are we? What determines our actions? Can it truly be ourselves?

"You understand my voice, my words?" I said.

She looked at me, then back to the book. She turned the page. I took out my notebook and wrote: Do you understand my words, my speech?

She read it, and wrote: No. I feel your words. I hear mood and intent.

I wrote more: You know I want to leave this place?

—No. Why leave?

—I have a life elsewhere.

—Then leave.

—First, I have to win the card game.

—Then win.

—I will. But it isn't easy. Can you leave with me?

—I don't know. Why would I want to?

—Maybe you have a life elsewhere too.

—This is what I know.

My question—asking if she wanted to leave with me—had popped out, unexpected. Could she? What would happen if she, or any of them, left this place? Would they remain skull-heads, or transform back into whatever they had once been? If they had been corpses, would they be corpses again? I didn't want that for her. Life here is better than no life, isn't it?

She returned to her book, but I interrupted.

—I'm curious what you're reading. Do you mind if I look at it?

I leafed to the beginning of the chapter she was reading. A title, "The Dilemma of Determinism," but no author listed. I turned to the table of contents and found an unfamiliar name—that didn't surprise me; I've never read studies of Unitarianism, or any religion. I read the beginning, which appeared to be an introduction to a lecture: "I have the right to assume...."

After a blank line, the main text began:

A common opinion prevails that the juice has ages ago been pressed out of the free-will controversy, and that no new champion can do more than warm up stale arguments.... This is a radical mistake. I know of no subject less worn...

Strange, but the text was familiar. Somewhere, recently, I had heard similar words. I flipped through, stopping at whatever word or phrase drew my attention.

... for the deterministic philosophy the murder, the sentence, and the prisoner's optimism were all necessary from eternity...

And:

... brings us right back, after such a long detour, to the question of indeterminism and to the conclusion of all I came here to say tonight. For the only consistent way of representing a pluralism and a world whose parts may affect one another through their conduct being either good or bad is the indeterministic way...

That congress of giants who had blocked the boardwalk the morning I staggered out of that doctor's office dragging my dented head. The loud one—this was the philosophy he had been ranting about.

I returned the book to her and wrote: Have you read this before?

Her answer took some time. I watched her shape the words, admiring the neatness of her letterforms.

—I believe I have. I saw the book, picked it up, and turned to this. When I began to read, I experienced a sensation of the familiar. I don't remember specifics, but the sensation tells me that I must have read it another time. I write my thoughts, my responses, to help me remember. Do I make myself understood?

—Yes. It echoes my experience. We are part of a cycle that keeps repeating. Though it can vary. *You* made it vary, rejecting the one I call Fornicator.

—Your meaning is unclear. Are you referring to the one who disturbed us? Have I previously engaged in sexual intercourse with him?

—The cycle. You dance with Dellschau, wearing what you're wearing now. Later, you come back, wearing what you wear when we come in here, and you have sex with Fornicator.

—I think I understand. It repeats. I believe there are answers in what I read. Please let me finish. We can meet later.

I wasn't sure what to do next except get back to the game. I wrote that to her and leaned over to kiss her hand.

I asked for a new deck. Ring Hand looked annoyed, maybe. He fetched one from his alcove. I tore off the wrapper, examined the cards, and passed them to Fornicator. "Your deal, good Sir Fornicator. Please take care with this lovely new deck that our host has provided."

And now . . . to restore what I lost. I had to play with care, avoid traps (especially the trap of overconfidence). I had to avoid *thinking* that I had something. I had to *know*. Play smart, play the Tarpon way. I put the Tarpon in my head and kept him there. The skull-heads played as usual, and chip by chip, hand by hand, I rebuilt my fortune. The game . . . this period of play . . . felt longer than usual. Between hands, I kept expecting a pause; the dance should be coming along soon. I had to keep my focus on the table. Distraction is dangerous.

The Rebel's deal, and cards flowed my way. Ring Hand folded. The Rebel raised Fornicator's bet. I raised on his raise—fifty dollars—hoping to chase out the Rebel, or Father Jaw, or both. The Rebel stayed in. He shouldn't have, but then Fornicator shouldn't have either. The win gave me my largest pot of the game. "Sorry boys, but that's poker for you. Odds and chance and bravado. But there's always another hand."

Indistinguishable hands, one after another. I didn't win, I didn't lose. Ring Hand looked bored. Father Jaw looked constipated. Then this happened: The Rebel—I hadn't noticed how low his stack of chips had become. He was in, and high, but on the fourth card he didn't have enough to make the bet. Ring Hand opened his ledger. He tapped four times. The Rebel jumped to his feet and twanged at him. Ring Hand tap-tap-tap-tapped. The Rebel pointed to his cards and to the pot. Ring Hand marked something in his book and gave him money, but less, I thought, than what he had given the others. By the fifth card, the Rebel had put in everything he had. Fornicator won.

The Rebel stood and raised his cupped palm for more. Ring Hand pointed to the ledger; the Rebel twanged louder. Ring Hand shook his head and tapped five times. The Rebel's shoulders slumped liked he had been drained of everything. He walked toward the stairs. At the bottom, he looked back at us and waved. A couple of steps up, he collapsed, prostrating himself on the stairs. His muffled twangs sounded like sobs. He crawled up a step, then another, slowly passing from sight.

Ring Hand clapped for whiskey. Dellschau brought a clear bottle with a Greek label. This time, I wanted the bottle. I held it up in toast. "There goes our brave companion. Veteran of war and poker, may he live to fight another day." I drank and passed the bottle over the Rebel's empty seat to Father Jaw.

Figuring on fixing something to eat, I got up and walked to the bar.

Dellschau was still in that animated mood. He told me that he had rehydrated a pile of dried beef and boiled it for broth, then cooked corn-meal in the broth to make porridge. I said that sounded fine and sat on a stool. He served me. "And this ... how could I forget!" He picked up a leather pouch and two pipes, which he filled with tobacco. "I don't understand how I find new things in the storeroom after so much poring into its contents, but there it is." He lit his with a burning stick, then handed the stick to me.

I picked up the other pipe and lit it. "Thanks. Good find."

He gazed past me and stiffened. "What is *diese Kreatur* doing now?"

I looked in the mirror. Ring Hand was standing. He clapped three times.

"The dance ... no ... not the dance." An agony of sound tore from his throat, rising and falling like haggard breath.

The guitarist descended the stairs, followed by Lady Patricia in her modesty clothes. I hadn't seen her go up. Ring Hand clapped again; Dellschau didn't move. The mirror image of Ring Hand started toward us, carrying the blue bandana. I figured Dellschau would give in now. He had to—but he didn't. Ring Hand reached the bar. Dellschau backed away. Ring Hand tapped on the bar with his other hand, the hand with the ring, each tap more insistent. Dellschau's lips quivered. He was scared—pushed beyond scared, too much despair, too much humiliation.

Ring Hand grunted and walked toward the bar gate.

Dellschau bumped against the stove. It wobbled. He looked at it and smiled. The stove was plain cast-iron, about waist-high. Ring Hand opened the gate. Dellschau slid around the side of the stove, knocking over an ax handle that I suppose he'd been planning to burn. It landed by a smaller piece of timber. He showed that smile again and stuck an end of the ax handle into the gap between the floor and the base of the stove and pushed the smaller chunk of wood underneath the handle. He put all his weight on the handle and levered the stove.

The chimney pipe tore loose and the pan of cornmeal mush clanged to the floor. The stove landed on Ring Hand, pinning him. He throated, a loud and frantic throat. I glanced back; the card players hadn't noticed. The guitarist was drinking from the bottle of clear liquor. Lady Patricia sat on a chair, guitar in her lap. Smoke oozed from the broken pipe, but not a lot of it—the fire was down to coals, keeping the mush warm. Dellschau picked up his big cleaver.

That priest's journal—I had an insight about the drawing that showed skull-heads and the sand hill face.

I vaulted onto the bar and dove feet first into Dellschau. He went down, with me on top. I grabbed the wrist that held the cleaver and dug my fingers in. He dropped it but put his hands around my throat. I knocked them away and dug a knee into his belly. The cleaver was nearby. I rolled off him, picked it up, and flung it over the bar.

My earlier assumption had been wrong. The skull-heads weren't dancing around the sand face—they were fighting it. The sand face was their enemy too.

Ring Hand pushed the stove with his free hand, but couldn't get leverage. I thought I could roll it off, over his pinned arm, but that would hurt. "Need some help here," I yelled to the skull-heads and waved my arms. Lady Patricia dropped the guitar and ran toward me. Dellschau had meanwhile gotten up, but he didn't have any fight left. Lady Patricia helped me lift the stove. She did most of the lifting. The job would have taken at least three regular people.

Ring Hand stood. He dipped his head in thanks. I bowed back. "Hurt bad?" I asked, and touched his shoulder.

He throated and wiggled his fingers, then swayed; Lady Patricia put an arm around to steady him. The blue bandana had landed on the floor. I picked it up and set it atop the bar. Ring Hand looked at it, then grabbed it and lunged toward Dellschau. But he didn't cover Dellschau's eyes. He shoved it into his mouth.

"Wait . . . stop," I said.

Ring Hand looked at me and let go of Dellschau. Who fell onto his back and made gurgling noises. His legs spasmed.

I didn't like him, but I didn't want him killed. The bandana was deep in his throat; I yanked it out. He coughed and vomited. I filled a mug with water and made him drink. That was about all the help I felt like giving him. Back with Ring Hand, I said, "I don't like what he tried to do to you, but you need someone to bring your drinks. Let's get back to the game."

Why did I help Ring Hand? Not just because I connected him to Griffin's journal translation. We had been playing cards together a long time. Cards are important. He was a tough opponent. I wanted to get away, but that didn't mean I needed to hurt him. Besides, that's how it went the other time.

Ring Hand pulled a red bandana from a pocket and flattened it on the bar. Time for the next act, delayed but not forgotten. I wondered whether the Rebel would come back for the dance. He didn't. What did that signify?

I picked up the corn mush pot and set it back on the stove. Some had spilled, but there was plenty to eat. I filled a plate. In the mirror, Lady Patricia held Dellschau upright and danced him.

Father Jaw's deal. He shot a down card to the Rebel's vacant seat. We all looked at it for a moment; Father Jaw shrugged, put it back into the deck, and dealt again. Blur of shapes and colors, chips and cards. I won a three-hundred-dollar pot, lost a hundred to Father Jaw . . . swing up, swing down, around and around the spiral of the chips . . . whirlpool . . . maelstrom . . . drowning. . . . Between hands, I looked out the window at scratch land. What a nice place to build a house, maybe run some longhorns. They can live anywhere, eat dust, whatever they find.

On a hand with Fornicator dealing, my opening cards were queen down, nine up. Queen up for Ring Hand. He opened the betting with five dollars. Next card, I drew a second queen, Ring Hand a nine. Father Jaw pushed in ten dollars. The bet made me think his hole card was an ace. I raised him. Fornicator honked. Ring Hand gave me a sharp, quick look, called my raise, and raised another ten. Fornicator and Father Jaw followed.

Fourth card, I drew a king; I drummed the table with my fingers. Maybe they would think I had made a pair. Ring Hand drew a second queen and stayed in. He would only do that if he had paired his down card, probably a nine. Fornicator called Ring Hand's bet, with chips, bills, and coins. Father Jaw put in a mix too, then raised with a second handful. Fornicator honked a protest and hit Father Jaw in the arm. Father Jaw barked back at him. They did that for some time. Ring Hand let them.

I got up. "Water," I said. My glass was empty. I walked behind the bar, past Dellschau's still-slumped body, filled my glass and drank it down, refilled. Then, back to the table. I was all in. I had to be. I said goodbye to some chips, hoping to see them again soon.

Final card . . . second nine for me, king for Ring Hand. My two pairs would beat Father Jaw's aces and any kind of pair Fornicator had. Ring Hand couldn't have a full house because I had the other nines and queens. The only way he could beat me was with a king in the hole instead of the suspected nine.

That seer-woman, Madame Blackley, she predicted the outcome.

Ring Hand opened the betting. He pushed in a tremendous stack. Fornicator called. Father Jaw called. I pushed in a match for Ring Hand's bet, then picked up another stack and slammed it down. Fornicator honked and lunged across the table. I jumped back. I wasn't exactly surprised. Ring Hand shoved Fornicator back into his seat. He leaned close and throated at Fornicator, pointed to the middle, throated some more. He sat, and bowed toward me. I bowed back. Ring Hand didn't hesitate calling my raise. Fornicator honked again, but added all of his money except for a few coins. Father Jaw apparently didn't have enough. He pushed in what he had and throated at Ring Hand, pointing to the middle. Asking for more. Ring Hand ignored him.

We were finished. Ring Hand and I held identical cards, nines, queens, and a king. I didn't take the time to try to calculate the odds for that one. He bowed to me and throated. I let him split the pot, including the oddments of coin. He pushed my half over.

I breathed. I wasn't sure I had done that in the last day or so. Father Jaw got up to leave. "What a game that was, my good Father! The cards giveth and also taketh."

He exchanged throatings with Ring Hand. I thought of something. That Spanish priest who wrote the journal. What was his name? Fornicator passed the bottle to Father Jaw. Burned. Fire shot from Stephens's fingers and enclosed us in a burning cage. The father drank and turned to go. Gonzalo, that was the name. "My good father, are you by chance Gonzalo Herdez Maldonado, author of the journal describing the lords of the Chrystal Islands?" The father gave a throaty yelp and stared at me. Ring Hand tapped the table. He touched my arm. Excited, I thought.

"I'm pretty sure we're working together," I said. "Working for the same things, I mean." Father Jaw took my extended right hand in both of his, then walked to the stairs and went up.

Now, what of Fornicator? Crazy that he was the last to leave. He should have lost everything long ago. His stake wasn't enough to buy into the next hand. He honked and pointed at his chips. Ring Hand opened his book. He ran a finger down the column, looked up, and waved his hand at Fornicator, a chopping motion that said all it needed to say. Fornicator honked louder. He stood, waving his arms.

Thinking this would be a good time for a break, I picked up my empty water glass. "While you boys are settling this matter, I'll get myself another drink of water and maybe a bite of food." Dellschau stood at his post, seeing nothing. "I could use some stomach-filler," I said. He was oblivious. A package of crackers lay on the counter. I reached for a handful. They weren't stale.

Lady Patricia came downstairs, dressed as saloon girl. The dance, then poker, and now . . . Fornicator's turn with her, or mine? He waved at her, whined, and pointed to the table. She warbled back. He picked up his few coins in cupped hands and pointed them toward her. He was asking her for money! She shook her head and joined me. Fornicator gave a choking wail.

I readied my notebook, planning to explain the poker situation, but she tugged at my elbow. We walked down to our room. We didn't strip and do our usual. She indicated writing. We sat on the bed and passed the notebook back and forth. I described the last hand and what it meant.

—Must you continue?

—I assume so. That's how it works. Someone has to win.

—You have played the game well, and you saved the captain from the man I dance with. Tell him that you must leave. What you have done is enough.

That was certainly worth trying. We were well-matched opponents. Knocking out the other skull-heads and splitting the huge pot was a good way to go.

She slipped fingers into mine; I kissed her shoulder and got up to leave, but she started working on my trouser buttons. That caused some excitement. By the time she had my pants down, I was amazed I had ever fit inside all that confining fabric. Erections are splendid. In the proper setting, of course. I removed the rest of my fabric with speed; she eliminated hers too. Her naked body was a marvel. I crouched in front of her to repeat my previous accomplishment. That suited her just fine, then she lifted me onto the bed and curled herself over my exposed lap. Those teeth in her lipless face were unnerving, but when she started working on me with her tonguelet, I forgot about them.

Fornicator was gone when we got back. I don't know if he went easily, but he went. Ring Hand bowed and waved me to the table. Lady Patricia went with me. "Let's talk," I said. "We've battled for a while and are pretty well off. I want to cash out and go home. I've got a job to finish."

That job—Stephens, the sand faces—wasn't just *my* job. I opened my notebook and sketched a sand face. I added a picture of Stephens, long hair flowing, big ring on his finger. "I'm after him. And if I understand things, he's with your enemies."

The game, the chips, the journal, all pointed to the same story, a story that must have been happening for centuries, millennia. The saloon and the game were part of the engine that preserved, that fought to preserve the land from . . . what? . . . the hurricanes, the crab creatures? I drew another picture of Stephens and surrounded him with a ring of small circles. Ring Hand throated and nodded, two sharp jerks of his head. Lady Patricia and he throated at each other.

My hat and bag were under my chair. I picked up the hat and swept in my chips, leaving the coins and paper. "Cash me out, and I'll be on my way."

Ring Hand grunted and carried my hat to his alcove. While he was gone, I examined the various bits of money. Some bills I could use, some were interesting . . . old, I guessed . . . though the paper didn't look old. Chinese-looking images of figures and a building, and other oddities. There was a rough disk with a lion on one side and indentations on the other, as if from the block that held the coin when the design was stamped. Ring Hand came back, holding Silverberg's skull with my hat perched on top; his other hand carried a leather sack. It clanked when he set it on the table. Inside, gold ingots—a lot of them, say fifteen pounds worth.

"Good to see you again," I said to Silverberg's skull. I switched the hat to my head and transferred the sack to the doctor bag, along with all the other money. Carrying that weight wasn't going to be easy. "All right, now what? Walk out the front door?"

I hoped there was another way; even the passage of luminous snakes was preferable to the wasteland.

Ring Hand clapped a rhythm: 1-2-3-4 . . . 5-6, 1-2-3-4 . . . 5-6. The echo of his clapping faded. A bleating sound came from down the hallway, a goatish bleat followed by a white goat, a female. She pushed open the bar gate and trotted toward us. Ring Hand squatted, patted her head, and throated into her ear. She bleated in response. Ring Hand stood and throated at me, then pointed to the goat and throated some more. The goat trotted back to the bar.

"Follow her?" I pointed.

Ring Hand nodded.

"Good playing with you."

He dug into a pocket and pulled out something on a leather cord and put it in my hand, nodding. The nod conveyed something . . . importance? . . . reverence? It was a beat-up red poker chip with a hole for the cord. One side was the loop of small circles surrounding a spiral shape, and on the other, a figure like the one on Ring Hand's ring.

"Thanks." I put it in a coat pocket. He patted my shoulder.

I stopped opposite Dellschau. His eyes were still dull.

"I don't know how to help you. You can't fight them. You'll have to find your own way." I couldn't tell if he heard me. Lady Patricia put her arms around me and I did the same to her. Holding her body was a pleasure I would miss.

"Coming with?" I said into her ear hole. She shook her head. I kissed her teeth. "Maybe we'll meet somewhere else some day."

Dellschau croaked some words. He raised his hands like he was trying to hold me, pleading, face all twisted up. I looked at him, then at Ring Hand. "Can I take him?" I pointed at Dellschau, then waved toward the goat. "You'll need a new bartender and dance partner for Lady Patricia, but you can do whatever you did before he came here." Ring Hand bowed, and motioned for us to leave.

The goat had gone through the bar gate and into the back hall. I didn't think I should allow her to leave my sight. I went through the bar gate and grabbed Dellschau's arm. "Let's go. No time to gather your things."

"Bye all," I said from the other side. That's when I remembered I had left Silverberg's skull. I stopped. The goat said, "Maaaa." She turned to face me, shook her small white beard, and resumed her trotting.

I would have to leave it. I waved at Lady Patricia. "Please take care of Silverberg for me."

20

Zlateh the Goat

I assumed that the goat would veer into the luminous snake passage, but she kept trotting straight down the hall. We passed the frolic room, the broken bottle room, the wood-stripped rooms. The wind strengthened. "Hey, goat, will we be able to get through the storm?"

She answered with another "Maaaa."

The wind fought me, though the goat acted as if it wasn't blowing. "Faster," I said to Dellschau. "We have to stay near that goat." I was sure that if she got too far ahead, the wind would send us back into the building. Those skull-heads don't make it easy. I ran like I've never run before. The effort of running, I mean—a lot of effort—but it felt like my feet were stuck in a bucket of oatmeal. Somehow, I got within a body-length of the goat, and closer to her, the impact of the wind decreased.

Without slowing, I turned to look at Dellschau. He had stopped. I didn't. Maybe if it had been Lady Patricia, but Dellschau was no Eurydice. He would have to find his own way. With me gone, would the game resume among its original players, with Dellschau as server? I wasn't going to go back to find out.

We went through the blown-open rear door. Past the door ... the landscape ... converse of the dried and blasted earth outside the building's front. The colors: reds, blues, greens, yellows—but saying their names described nothing. There were colors I had never seen and couldn't even try to name. Colors that felt soft, or crisp, or icy-hot. They flowed and flittered, alive, glistening. My footsteps stirred a soft magenta dust that swirled into the air. The wind still pushed, but it felt different, more of an all-over pressure. A path—a goat trail—sloped upward, through leafless shrubs the color of overripe tomatoes. Thick, spongy-white worms as large as my arm crawled over them. There were tall grasses here and there, and other things that looked like cactus, but blue, the dark blue of midnight.

Walking up the goat trail, I remembered a folktale from my youth. "Mind if I call you Zlateh? It's a good name for a goat." She didn't maaaa to the contrary.

The story was about a family that had to sell their old she-goat to raise money for Hanukah presents and food. The eldest daughter was to take the goat to the butcher in a nearby town, but they became lost in a crazy blizzard. The goat found a haystack and showed the girl how they could hollow it out for shelter. The haystack gave the goat plenty of food, and the girl could drink the goat's milk. They were stuck until the storm ended, for days or what seemed like days. In some versions, they went straight home; in others, they wandered into an enchanted forest and met a giant giraffe, which carried them on her back to various adventures before returning them to the haystack so they could set off for home. And in other versions, one or more of the family's cats went with them.

There was a time when I made my mother tell me the story every night.

Something amongst the colors moved toward us. The colors and the dust made it hard to see more than a few feet. Whatever the shape was, it was large, a wagon maybe. I reached into my coat. The butt of my gun was a comfort to find.

What I thought was the canvas top of a freight wagon flapped in the wind. Except it was orange.

Then I screamed.

A shark, a purple shark with a red underbelly, flew over us and off into the burgundy haze. I stopped, watching it go. I became aware of other things flying. Fish, lots of them. They were drab compared to the colors around us. The wind that pushed at me was pressure from the water. And . . . I screamed again—past the fish were shadowy things that might have been giant crabs.

Another "maaaa" came from the goat, Zlateh. She hadn't stopped. I had to keep pace with her. She was my only protection, from the giant crabs, from everything.

The force of a wave tumbled me; not the water itself, but pressure *from* the water. This time, Zlateh came back. She bleated a more urgent sounding bleat and prodded me with her head. There were creatures on both sides now; giant crabs, though not really crabs. Crabwise in their general appearance. The brain assigns the closest available association. Instead of claws, more like palm leaves, flapping and grasping, and faces like those sand hills . . . I screamed, again. No one could view those creatures without fear.

Zlateh bumped me into motion. Though the dust clouded and thickened, it didn't touch us. A clear space surrounded and protected us, a bubble of air, air solid enough to repel attack.

We climbed, leaving the crab creatures and dust billows. The bag's strap dug into my shoulder. I cradled the bottom in my arms to take some of the gold's weight. Light increased. An orange tarpon swam past—seeing it—my old poker guide's namesake—helped keep panic away. My grip had frozen on my gun. I released it, and thrust my hand into a coat pocket. I didn't want anything exposed, where some random fish might bite. Which probably couldn't happen; we were safe in our bubble, but . . . how could we be safe? We were under water, under deep ocean water. Fingers touched a smooth disk—Ring Hand's poker chip. I took it out, slipped off my hat, and hung the chip around my neck. My good luck charm.

New shapes appeared, motionless, pillars. They were broken remnants of statues. I didn't dare stop to examine them. The shapes were those from the priest's manuscript, feathery serpents and snub-nosed beasts. Their bright colors were gone, washed off by centuries of ocean currents—colors released into the ocean, to flow and writhe but never be reunited with their former hosts. Fragments of statues stretched far off into the shimmery murk. The destroyed city of the Karankawas, or whoever they had been. Were there answers here, buried, covered by the colorful sediment?

The path wound through the scattered ruins. I didn't see anything that looked like buildings, no houses or temples. Maybe they had reserved stone for monuments, with dwellings made from wood or some other less permanent material. Another—or the same—shark swam near. I had seen many sharks, washed onto Galveston beaches or caught by fishermen, but none so large or colorful. I was glad that we occupied separate spaces.

Off to one side, the land dropped into the darkness of deep ocean. When on board a ship, I had never considered, or feared, the limitless depths I traveled above. I hoped that would still be true. Zlateh didn't take us near the edge. I was fine with that. There were fewer sculptures now, and the path made a slow descent.

Another shark appeared. It swam down and stopped, hovered near Zlateh. Not a shark—a dolphin with dark green coloring. It squeaked and chittered. Zlateh answered with a "maaaa." Just two land creatures strolling along the ocean bottom. The dolphin swam closer. One eye was level with mine. That eye—I had never seen anything like it. Deep and dark, with a brain behind it. A brain that knew things, knew me. That eye conducted a long examination, then the dolphin flicked its tail and off it went.

I wanted out. I wanted air and sunlight. "How much farther do we have to walk down here?" My voice sounded scared, and that scared me more. Zlateh stopped to look back at me.

"Maaaa," she said.

At last, we moved uphill. The colors faded to greenish gray and brown. Now they were just colors, no more flowing, no more song. I wanted to be in the air and sun, but the colors ... I would never feel such colors again. The path steepened, winding through rocks as big as cows. I bent forward, using hands to help me climb. Zlateh hopped from one rock to another, never slowing. My legs screamed at me to stop, but I couldn't stop. The light grew brighter. That helped. Days later, the steep rock-path smoothed into a sandy incline. The sand was harder to walk on, but sand meant we were close to shore. That was a good thought. I hoped it was true.

My head broke the surface, then Zlateh's. She trotted up onto a sandbar. I followed. And, holy fuck, there was the ruined Indianola courthouse, twenty yards of water separating it from my sandbar. We crossed to the other side of the sandbar; Zlateh kept going. I hesitated at the water's edge—I didn't want to get wet!

But I didn't get wet. Zlateh's bubble still protected me. At its deepest, the water came to my waist. I stepped ashore. The sun burned into the sand. I felt the heat through my boots. I hadn't felt it when we were on the sand bar, when I was still inside the bubble. Zlateh nibbled on salt grass. Her job was done.

I dropped my bag of gold in the grass and sat beside it. The breeze off the water rusted the underbrush. I think I dozed. Birds that had been disturbed by our appearance returned. Is this what the world feels like? "This must be where we say goodbye," I said. "I can manage from here."

She said "maaaa," the sound muffled by the grass in her mouth.

"Thanks, be seeing you then." I switched the bag to my other shoulder and set off walking. I was starting to develop an appetite. There hadn't been time to pack anything from Dellschau's hoard. I took out my watch, wound it, and set the hour from the sun, guessing eleven a.m. The heat told me it was still summer. I hoped it was the same summer. A decent road should put me in Lavaca by four o'clock. Last time I was here, the only people were those feral children. With all I had just survived . . . the idea of having to fight off a pack of rabid, biting children . . . that scared me more than anything in skull-head land. I jogged up the road toward Port Lavaca and didn't slow for some minutes.

At a quarter to twelve, a blunt shape appeared down the road; I kept walking, and the shape became a horse-drawn wagon with a couple of people on the seat and a cow tied to the back. I stood aside to give them room. The occupants . . . their appearance . . . I stared. That was all I could do. The people, they had skin, skin all over their faces, and one had a beard growing through its skin. Their heads were covered, one by a bonnet and one by a black derby. They stopped, and the bearded one, its lips moved and noises slithered out. The sounds were familiar, but what did they mean?

They weren't skull-heads. They were a man and a woman.

A laugh spat from my mouth, then another. The man said something else, and the woman too. Laughter possessed my body, laughter that lived outside my will, emerging from some deep and hidden zone. I tried to cover my mouth, but the laughs burned through my feeble hands. Knees met dirt, and I howled. The feral children—did they answer my howl? The wagon began to move. I laughed it away from me and lay by the roadside, hoarse and gasping.

Evening came, stars, a quarter-moon. Drained of laughter, I got up and walked. Walking brought me to a barbed-wire fence, then a gate. I opened it and fell in a dirt lane. The dirt held comfort, but for too short a time. Something lifted me and draped me over a saddle, filling my head with horse-smell. In darkness, I woke. Someone had removed my boots. A bed embraced me and led me back to the land of sleep.

Next time I awoke, the room had lightened. A woman wearing a dark skirt down to her ankles, white long-sleeved shirt, and a shawl over her head brought me a washbasin. She motioned toward it. "*Para lavar*," she said. "*Es la hora del desayuno.*"

I thanked her in Spanish and got up to wash myself.

The house belonged to a mountain-sized rancher named Japhet Amador. He was the one who had slung me onto a horse. He must have felt the heft of my bag and known what it meant, but nothing was missing. His face had skin, skin and a dark beard. Spoken words became familiar again, and I responded with words of my own. Amador didn't ask questions, but I assumed he had gone through my bag. There was a lot of money in it, but no skull. All I said was I was hunting a man, had lost my horse, and needed to get back to Victoria. I asked Amador the date; he said it was the fifth of August. It was common enough for someone to want the date after being in the wilds without a calendar. I had left Galveston for Huntsville prison on July 23. The poker game had used up less than two weeks of my life.

The house was a combination of adobe and timber; the kitchen was adobe, which made cooking inside a lot more bearable in the heat. Amador put me to work on breakfast preparation. "*Mi esposa* . . . wife . . . and her *madre*, they are the cooks, but they have gone to visit *familia* in Refugio. Tulia, the housekeeper makes tortillas. I can cook, but I wouldn't have let both of them leave if it meant no tortillas. You can help make *tortillas enchilades.*"

On top of the stove, a pot of water was moving along toward boiling. Next to the stove was a bowl of dried red chile peppers. My first task was chopping garlic and onion.

Amador talked of the joys of ranching. "*Me encanton las vacas.* I love to sit in the fields with them. I love to pat them. I love to sell them to people who appreciate the love, and love to eat them. And I love to eat them too." He dropped a handful of peppers into the boiling water.

The front door opened and the clump-clank of boots and spurs flowed our way. A skinny Anglo cowboy poked his head in and asked in Spanish why they hadn't been fed yet. Amador tossed a garlic clove toward him; the cowboy laughed. "*El fuego está listo,*" he said, and left.

"The men are spoiled by the women's cooking," Amador said. "On a gringo ranch all they would eat is beef and beans every day." He skimmed peppers from the boil and dropped them into a food mill. He left me to add the onion-garlic mix and grind everything into the onion bowl, along with a ladle of pepper-cooking water, and went outside to check the beef that had been cooking in the outdoor oven.

The woman who had brought my wash water (Tulia the house-keeper, I supposed) came in and started mixing a batch of corn tortillas, then cooked them on a griddle. Amador returned to blend flour and lard in a pan for roux. When he was sure that I knew what to do, he went back outside. Tulia brought me a baking pan. When the roux was ready I stirred in the sauce, salt, pepper, and dried oregano. Next step was for me to ladle a coating of thickened sauce onto the baking pan, top that with as many tortillas as would fit, sauce the tops of the tortillas, sprinkle onions and cheese, then repeat. The whole process was a lot like dealing cards.

After adding the third tortilla and its topping to each stack, the pan went into the oven. I started a second pan. Tulia fried eggs. Amador brought in a charred burlap sack and plopped it onto the counter. The scent told me it was the beef he had been roasting, and I thought I might faint with desire. He inspected my work. "Nicely done, for a gringo," he said. "Time to ring the bell."

What sounded like a cathedral bell blasted from the front porch, followed by the clump-clang of ranch hands. I carried hot trays to the dining room and Tulia followed with eggs. An egg went onto everyone's tortilla stack, with beef on the side and coffee into mugs. All the cowboys had skin on their faces, and they spoke to me. Eating happened. I thought about moving in.

The energy infusion caused by rest and real food cannot be denied. I could have run to Lavaca. Amador loaned me a creamy-maned horse named Felix. I was to leave it at the livery owned by Delfino, the man who had sold me Patience, long long ago. I arrived there in time to send a telegram to let my parents know I wasn't dead yet, and to the rabbi, and one to Llewellyn promising a longer report to follow. I wasn't sure I still had a job, but figured I would keep acting as if I did.

The 1:20 train took me to Victoria. On the way, I read the *Victoria Advocate* that had come out on the third. Under the heading "Items of State News:"

A Negro living in Cass county is hanged by a posse of men for poisoning the water in the well of his employer, Mr. Shaw.

The posse didn't consider that a poisoned well would also have poisoned the man himself and everyone else who used it. And, in the "Outside World:"

Mrs. Elizabeth Cady Stanton retains a wonderful amount of vitality after a long life of activity as the leading champion of women's suffrage in the United States. Mrs. Stanton is in the seventy-fourth year of her age, and it is just about half a century since she first became an advocate of "women's rights." She and Miss. Susan B. Anthony have worked together for the greater part of that time. Up to this period of life she keeps the countenance that has become familiar to millions of people all over the country, but she is not now to be seen on the platform as in former years.

I had met the very impressive Mrs. Stanton some years ago, soon after I went to work for Llewellyn. He had assigned me to hire some young toughs as protection for her when she was in Chicago. There had been the usual death threats and other sorts of ugliness from people who don't think that women have rights.

The train pulled into Victoria. I returned to the Delmonico Hotel and claimed a room, where I unpacked everything but the gold and took the bag downstairs to be put in the hotel safe.

I still didn't feel quite human, but a shave and a bath helped, and I followed that with clean clothes and a fried chicken dinner with onion soup, cornbread, and peach pie. It was nice having food that hadn't been scraped together by Dellschau. I didn't see anyone I knew and had minimal conversation with those I had to interact with. Something didn't feel right about people. I knew that whatever wasn't right was more likely inside *me*, but I couldn't stop thinking that all these people with skin on their faces were the freakish ones.

I went up to my room to get ready for sleep, but lost myself staring out the window. People walked the streets, doing whatever it is that people do, committing crimes, falling in love. Mundane life. I was a bird, hovering, winging the breeze, able to observe but not participate.

Empty. Was I empty, an empty shell? If so, I vowed not to stay empty. I would fill my shell, with light, with lust, with the mundane. To settle my thoughts, I took out my gun-cleaning kit. Mundane tasks at bedtime are calming. I hadn't fired the gun since killing the luminous snakes, but I had been through a lot of dust. And had walked underwater. The job steered my brain toward relaxation, then I lay on the bed, a regular bed in a regular town, with a regular sun to wake me in the morning.

I didn't recall returning to the ship. The bow and its winged Nike figure-head pointed into glorious blues of sky and ocean. Diving seabirds shrieked; some settled onto the bowsprit and rigging to eat their prey. Off the starboard side, an approaching green of land. Somebody spoke, a woman's voice, a familiar upper-class accent.

"The island of Saint Lucia," she said. "My home was once there."

I turned to look at her. She was a few inches taller than me. Her squarish face . . . Lady Patricia, from my earlier voyage. Yet, I knew her more deeply. How? Her green bonnet matched her eyes. She smiled, showing a glimpse of a dark gap in her bottom teeth. When she moved to stand with me at the railing, a sense of relief, of answered expectation shook my body, but the shake became chills. I couldn't get warm. My teeth banged together. The pinky toe on my right foot went numb, the way it always does at the beginning of winter. Lady Patricia pulled a shawl from her bag and spread it across my shoulders. She held the ends together with a hand on my chest. Warmth spread from her hand. My chills eased. I shook, a heavy shake like the release of one final sob.

"Thank you," I said. I gazed at birds diving to catch their meals. The ship had tacked, removing the island from view. The vastness frightened me. I turned away. "There's no horizon," I said. "Distance, nothing but distance, distance without border." My former shake became a sob, a series of sobs that traveled out of me and on, beyond the edge of sight. The sailors ignored my sobs; Lady Patricia kept her hand in its comforting place.

Again the ship tacked, bringing the island back into view. Was this land our goal, the place my architectural commission was taking me? But that was long ago, a different voyage.

"Something I've meant to talk about," Lady Patricia said. "Your perceptions. They are built, assembled, by your own consciousness, painted by your experience. If you see a tree, it's because you expect to see a tree. There are things or places that appear familiar because your perceptions won't allow you to see them as unfamiliar."

We sat on a sofa in the captain's cabin, which he had generously vacated for our use. Lady Patricia slept, her head resting on my shoulder. I eased my left arm around her and laid my hand on her thigh. The chills and sobbing had left me spent. I dozed, but soon it was time for the ceremony. I shook her and we got up. She removed her bonnet and unpinned her hair, releasing a luxurious dark red fountain. I tilted my face up to kiss her cheek.

"Are you happy?" I said.

"Very much so. Joy has been absent for so long that I forgot its taste. You know so little about me, my past. I come from a rather old and titled family. My father was a naval officer and later owned a fleet of merchant ships. He built a vast seaside mansion in Saint Lucia, where we spent our winters. The house was my playland, but the harbor was my school. The family's servants were aging or crippled members of his crews. With them, I sailed the seas around the island. I was as good a sailor as any boy. Better. I hated returning to the more constricting life of a lady in England.

"Then tragedy. A terrible storm struck. Waves overran the shore, higher and higher, driven by the gale. But it was more than a storm. Creatures came, creatures too horrible to describe. Wind and wave destroyed the house, taking off the roof and battering the walls until they could no longer stand. I survived. I lived in foam and air until the ocean cast me upon another land. The water fled. Without its sustaining liquid, the earth became rock, a landscape of nothing. In this nothing, I found others, other victims, others who defend against the storm. I joined them. Their fight is mine. Is yours as well. Now we can fight together, stronger, smarter."

On deck, Rabbi Cohen waited; beside him was Captain Bellis. His ancient face could have been Aksumite . . . Etruscan . . . Sumerian. He reminded me of Felipe, a man I knew long ago. Felipe wasn't his real name, but no one could pronounce the one he told us. That was from back when I was working on the *White Arrow*, schooner of Galveston. We picked Felipe up off the Yucatán, floating on a piece of wrecked fishing boat. We were surprised that he recovered; after he was up and active, he adapted pretty well to work on the ship, and served with us till we made it back to the Campeche area. He didn't speak much Spanish for a Mexican. Mine was better. The Mexicans in the our crew said he was Mayan, but they used that name to mean ancient, one from beyond.

A sail had been stretched over the deck to block the fearsome sun, with chairs arranged for guests. The rabbi held out his right hand and we shook. "This is his event," the rabbi said, indicating the captain.

Captain Bellis took off his ring and held it up, stone facing toward us. It was an amethyst with an image of a winged woman. "We have come to the next waystation," he said. He spoke in a loud, pure tone. Maybe there was an accent but I had no idea of what kind.

"My ring represents Victory of Accomplishment. All stages of life are waystations leading on to the next, though most people fail in the journey. The odds for your success are deep, but you will prevail."

Lady Patricia and I linked arms.

"Go, now," the captain said.

We turned and walked down the aisle, past the rabbi and the other passengers. Gorman sat in the last row. He got up and threw his long arms around both of us in a firm embrace. We continued to the stern and looked at the vessel's wake. Above floated Dellschau's *Splendid Kestrel*. From it came the sound of a steamboat's calliope. We waved in acknowledgment. Holding hands, we jumped.

Moonlight gave a dim shape to the hotel room window. I had been dreaming—I knew that, but I had lately endured so many things that *should* have been dreams, or nightmares, that I wasn't sure I could still tell the difference. I lay awake for a while but ended up sleeping enough to have a long series of dreams, the kind that feel as if they must have taken an entire night but are probably compressed into a twenty-minute chunk of sleep. Some were vague, some intensely detailed, details that I wouldn't mind forgetting. But in the morning, I woke with a sense of rightness. Rightness that I had abandoned Dellschau to find his own way home, rightness in determining that Ring Hand wasn't Stephens.

In one of the dreams, Ring Hand spoke: "Victory must prevail against Chance." Which didn't make a lot of sense, but I think I understood it anyway. And in another, the voice of the woman from the ship, Lady Patricia: "I have written some of my thoughts for you to read."

The Saint Lucia mansion that Lady Patricia told me about in the dream—it was the same place I had chased Mrs. Conroy into, now, like the ruined and sunken city I passed through with Zlateh, the domain of the crab creatures.

When I was getting dressed for breakfast, I found folded sheets of paper sticking from a coat pocket. Pages from the purser's book that Lady Patricia wrote in, pages filled with her handwriting.

I have been thinking about our place. Whether we determine the trail of our lives. It occurs to me that our experience encompasses multiple levels. There is the now, in which I dance with the creature you call Dellschau and appease the needs of the one you call Fornicator. There is the past, where I came from—or, where I may have come from, because I have no memory of another place. And, also, there is the purpose of the repeating play, which I believe is a mechanism of service to others, to other beings, perhaps. Our actions in the play accomplish; the activity translates, as a steam engine moves a paddle and then a boat. This is our work, though much is obscure and much is unexplainable, because you would be unable to understand the explanation.

You were here, and wished to be elsewhere. You worked to

engineer your departure. Dellschau does not want to be here, but is not equipped to engineer his departure. Why? It cannot be preordained, so it must be inherent, some trait within him. This is unfortunate—his desire to be elsewhere is blocked by his lack of ability to make elsewhere a possibility. I don't think I can help him. I think that he would reject me, but even if he accepted my help, I believe he must act on his own, as you did. Why is it that you embrace me and he rejects? Something inherent. This is always the mystery.

I folded the pages and put them back in my pocket.

21

Detective Work Begins Anew

The waiter gave me a telegram from Llewellyn, granting permission to keep doing what I was doing. Silverberg's family wanted his killer found. And I still wanted to take him. That much I knew. My resolve, or whatever it is that keeps me on a job, was still intact. But the dream, or dreams, had disturbed me. Parts were as real as anything else that I had experienced lately, perhaps more real. I needed to incorporate the messages into my consciousness. After breakfast, I walked. Aimless. I tried to let myself enjoy being back in the world. It was a nice day for living. Hot, but the kind of heat that nourishes. People were out there, living, as people do. I could join them, couldn't I?

My wanderings led me past the marshal's office. I went in to let him know I was back. Nebel sat at the desk up front, reading the Victoria paper. He seemed pleased to see me.

"Didn't know if we'd be seeing your face again. Marshal's out recuperating. Got himself shot in the leg breaking up a little altercation."

He told me where to find the marshal. The answer surprised me, but I guess it shouldn't have. Marinella opened the door. She and her father had moved to a house on William Street, a two-story with a wide front porch. She didn't want to let me in but was willing to acknowledge the god of official business.

"Zachary is resting. I will ask if he wants me to bring you to his room."

She didn't offer a seat. After what happened to her shop, her home, her life, I couldn't blame her for being mad at me. Stephens's need to destroy an artifact of the skull-heads made sense now.

The parlor where she left me was more alcove than room, with just enough space for a coat rack. I could see into a sitting room with green wallpaper and a comfortable-looking sofa and a couple of chairs. Maybe I could accept why she was mad at me, but I didn't like being left to stand in a doorway. I started toward a chair but stopped when I heard footsteps. Griffin hobbled into view. He saw me in the alcove.

"Come in here and sit, Shannon. I don't feel like walking all the way to the door." He landed in the closest arm chair and set his crutches down. I sat in the one across from him.

"Marinella shouldn't have left you standing like that."

"She doesn't like me much."

"I'm not sure I like you much either." He let that hang for a minute. "Now, you going to tell me where you've been?"

"Same place Gorman found me after the dance, or same kind of place."

His face turned sour at the mention of Gorman and stayed that way as I kept talking. "I discovered some things about Stephens. Mainly that he isn't who or what I thought, but he's something else. Which may or may not help me find him."

After all my time in skull-head land, and after my night of dreams, the world ... my place in it ... everything was different somehow. I didn't know how to convey that to the marshal. Plus, he didn't like me. And I was getting to the point where I didn't like him either. I wasn't the one who started this mess, but I was the only one who knew how to fix things. I kept talking. "Listen ... the things that have been happening— these are events that have always *been* happening. You know some of this from the journal. Two opposing forces. Neither are our friends, but one is less of a friend.

"Those sand hill faces—whatever they are isn't good for us. Good for people, I mean. They probably don't care about people either way—they're not trying to hurt us, but what they cause hurts us. Hurricanes, for example. Hurricanes are a natural force, but the sand faces manipulate them, make them stronger. Does it matter why? They do what they need to do and we're incidental. But we have to protect the public, like arresting Stephens and destroying sand hills."

He finally responded. "I did that. I blew them up. Boys I had with me think I'm crazy. I probably am. But I did it."

I asked if he had heard any sightings of new ones, but he was through talking about it. He looked at me for a while and I looked back at him. Meanwhile, the sun came and went a few times and the cotton grew chest high. A couple of months later he said something about being back at work in the morning. "I can't stop you from doing the job you were hired for," he said. "But when you're in my town you follow my rules. I hear anything I don't like, I'm putting you on a train back to Chicago."

Taking that as a dismissal, I got up to go. His attitude bothered me. I wanted Stephens, and I would get him, but I didn't feel any need to tell the marshal how I was planning to do it.

I went back to my room and started a report to Llewellyn, but couldn't concentrate. Instead, I sent him a telegram saying I was back in Victoria and working. Then I wandered the streets again. Next to the Bear Tavern, which had stale biscuits but decent beans, back when I was searching the saloon poker games for Stephens, I paused in front of a house with velvet curtains opened to the afternoon light. Inside, a young woman sat on a sofa that matched the curtains. She looked up, and, seeing me, waved. I nodded and moved along. Although there wasn't a sign, I knew that it was a whorehouse called Sweetie's.

Evening came. I wasn't hungry but wasn't ready for bed. I sat looking out the window; Griffin's unhappy face kept getting in the way, then Gorman's burned face. I drank, watching the stars traverse the sky.

The morning sun couldn't make me leave the bed. Detective work begins anew, but I lay there, not asleep and not awake, for days or what seemed like days. The bed felt nice; I thought my mattress was something I could get to know better. But at the same time, I wanted to be elsewhere. Chicago. I'd been gone from there a long time, and it was home. People need a home. I rolled this way and that, and each new position needed time to be explored in its fullness. Some positions are better than others. It's a shame that people don't slow their lives enough to experience a simple pleasure like mornings in bed. And why just mornings? A bed is always a welcome companion.

What finally got me up was the emptiness in my belly and an urgent need to piss. With one of those items accomplished via chamber pot, I set off on the long journey to the dining room. As usual, I paused in the doorway to examine whoever was there. I kept expecting to see skull-heads. I should have felt happy to be back in Victoria. Not that Victoria is a place in which I want to spend much more of my life, but it has become a familiar place. A place where people's heads have all of their skin, muscle, hair, and blood. But I couldn't get . . . acclimated. The poker game had been so all-consuming that its absence left a jagged void. I stared at the street, surrounded by the commonplace, luxuriating in the commonplace. . . . And yet. A lack.

The feeling wasn't unfamiliar. After my masquerade as an opium smuggler, once the smugglers were locked up and my job was finished, the letdown was similar. And it happened again, other jobs when I had to infiltrate a group and throw myself into a role. This time . . . I missed them. Ring Hand, the Rebel, Father Jaw, Lady Patricia—I really missed Patricia, all over my body. I even missed Fornicator, a little.

Now, the commonplace was my world. I wasn't sure that I liked it. But whatever I felt about being back, I did know that I wanted to get Stephens. For now, that would have to be enough. I took out and reread Lady Patricia's letter and imagined the faintest trace of lavender.

After a lot of breakfast, I went back to my room to finish my report, telling Llewellyn about the adventures in skull-head land (excluding my personal dalliance, if you want to call it that). I gave it to the desk clerk to post and went looking for Malley. People who I thought were deputies had been loitering in the hotel lobby. Maybe they were watching for someone else, but a portly young man wearing a white hat with an absurdly wide brim trailed after me, his boot steps echoing mine. I turned a corner and ducked into the first doorway. The boot steps accelerated. They and their owner passed. I stepped onto the boardwalk and followed him. He glanced in windows and across to the other side of the street. I stomped my boots on the boardwalk, making him turn. He stopped. I kept moving. He crept a hand toward his gun. I walked closer, closer. His hand reached the holster but shook too much to do anything about it. I stopped a nose-length from him. He'd managed to get his gun partway out. I squeezed his wrist, forcing his hand limp. The gun slid back into the holster, but I tightened my grip. He bit his upper lip to keep from whimpering. A vision of Ring Hand shoving the bandana down Dellschau's throat made me laugh.

"Tell your boss I don't like being watched." I released his wrist. He pulled it to his chest for comfort and tried to deny who he was; I didn't stay to listen.

Malley had an office on Forest Street, next to a hardware store. A note tacked to the doorjamb said he was at the courthouse. I found him there, managing a case of cow thievery. A deputy from the county sheriff's office was testifying for the prosecution. Although I had only recently finished a large breakfast, when the brief affair was over, we went to Fossati's for a sandwich. Malley wasn't bothered by his client's conviction. "Man was guilty as a blind prospector, and stupid too, but he deserved defending as much as anyone."

"In less enlightened times, they'd have hung him when they caught him," I said.

He gave me a report on Stephens sightings. They were few, all involving high-stakes games. Figuring I liked that kind of thing, he told me about a recent murder or suicide. A man named Gregson was found dead in his bedroom. He was a new citizen of Victoria, having come to start a steamship line, refrigerated beef transport from Port Lavaca to

New Orleans and Mobile. He bought a mansion on Bridge Street and joined society. He had been a card player—that interested me.

His body had deteriorated . . . decomposed in a way that baffled the medical examiner. It crumbled, desiccated and crumbled into coarse sand. His head was a bare skull. That part interested me too.

"The marshal didn't tell me about it, but he wasn't really in the mood to talk. Not to me anyway."

Malley laughed, but I could tell he didn't think it was funny. "There's been discussions toward replacing him. People saying he can't handle the job."

"He's a tough one, but he might not want to be marshal anymore. Somebody you care about gets killed, it's hard not to let some of yourself die too. Sometimes you stop caring about other people. Sometimes all the death makes it so you can't do the work." I didn't want to talk about that subject any more. I told Malley what I needed from him.

"If I was to pick a card game . . . what place would be most likely to attract Stephens's attention? Not necessarily somewhere he would play, but a money game, a game that would make him want to play with whoever was taking everyone's money."

Malley thought for a moment. "Sparrow's Saloon . . . no, Branlat's. It's a classy place, run by a Frenchman. Attracts money people. Stephens hasn't played there that I know of. He's played at Sparrow's. Not sure how welcome he is, but no one ever tried to ban him. I'll take you to Branlat's Friday night. We'll try Sparrow's too, then maybe the week after go to some other, lesser places. If you want to be seen in several games."

Which I did.

I paid a hotel boy to send for Nebel without giving away who wanted him. The lobby was empty of deputies, but I took a roundabout walk to the saloon I had designated for the meeting place. Nebel didn't appear surprised to see me. I told him what I was after.

"I don't think the marshal wants me to help you, but if you think it's important I don't see no harm in taking you there."

"Thanks. I might have been overly forceful in suggesting that he not post deputies in my hotel."

"I don't know anything about that, but he don't have much to say about you that's nice."

Gregson's house was a massive, two-story Greek Revival, fitting residence for a refrigeration tycoon. The door was in the middle of the wide porch, with two windows on each side. "Nephew in New Orleans inherits the place," Nebel said. "He's given word that he'll be selling after the legalities are settled."

We opened the front door and entered a sizable parlor. The leather and horsehair furnishings said bachelor. A dead-fish odor came toward us. "What about staff? He didn't take care of all this on his own."

"Bedroom where he died is on the second floor." We started up the stairs. "He had a cook, maid . . . two maids, actually. They all gave statements. Which didn't amount to nothing. Nephew wanted them to come back and clean Gregson's room, but they refused. I don't think *anyone's* cleaned it yet."

There were two large front bedrooms and several smaller rooms toward the back. Up here, the dead-fish smell was more like ocean rot. A familiar ocean rot. It poured from Gregson's bedroom. We went in.

"You should've smelt it the day we got here. Kind of like a dead whale that's been roasting on the sand. Was something, getting what was left of the body out of here."

There were windows on two sides, all of them open. On the bed, clumps of grit remained. That was where the smell was strongest. I didn't feel a need to get any closer to them. I tied a handkerchief over my face and went through all the drawers and closets. I had to duck out a few times to breathe. From a window in the back, a warm breeze carried fresh air.

"Did the servants live up here?"

"Cook lived in a little room at the back of the kitchen. She's the one found him. Smell found her, more like. She didn't usually go upstairs.

She said she hadn't seen him in at least a week and hadn't known he was home. She didn't see him that often. He usually communicated by note. He would get in late, after a card game, and write a note saying when he would be down for breakfast and what he wanted, whether he'd be having dinner at home. Things like that."

I walked to the other front bedroom. More dark wood furniture. "Anyone using this one?"

"Wasn't supposed to be."

The bed didn't show any obvious evidence of having been slept in, but I didn't examine it closely enough for hairs and such. Instead, I pulled on some dresser drawers. They contained a selection of shirts and trousers. The closet held a couple of silk vests, one dark red, one green, and some jackets that you would expect someone to wear with vests like that.

"You see these?" I said. "The marshal and I found clothes like this when we searched Stephens's room. This is the kind of thing he wears. I'd like to talk to the maids. They'd have to have known if someone else was staying here."

The maids were a colored mother and daughter who lived out where the town got scarce. We spent some time getting from the road to the house. We had to find our way through the craziest and most densely planted vegetable patch you could imagine, if you have a good imagination, and even then you wouldn't expect some of the things they were growing. I know that I wouldn't, but I'm more familiar with vegetables on a plate than the ones outside. And then, once we reached the house, we had to go out again because the kids playing on the porch told us the ladies were picking squash or maybe berries.

Berries it was. They had filled a couple of buckets with blackberries and it looked like they could fill a dozen more before they finished. They got up when they heard us coming. They were shorter than me, thin but strong looking.

"Howdy ladies," Nebel said. "You selling these at the market? My momma sure could make a nice pie out of some of that. I wouldn't mind buying a bucketful off you."

They haggled a bit and settled on a price. "Now then, we come here to ask some questions about whoever was living in Mr. Gregson's other bedroom."

During the haggling they had been smiling, but by the end of Nebel's last statement their faces shut the door. They denied that anyone else lived there, said they had never seen anyone, and more variations on that theme. Nebel started to talk at them like they were slaves. I didn't like that, but I didn't think he meant to do it. Things are changing in Texas, but not very quickly. I touched his arm. "Let's not be so demanding, Nebel." He didn't look happy about my interruption. I turned to the women. "This man we're after is frightening and powerful, I'll grant you that. So I don't blame you for not wanting to say anything. I expect he would find out if you did. We'll be going now."

The younger one spoke. "Thank you, sir. You best be careful chasing after that one."

We wound our way back through the vegetables to the road. "This is the damnedest manhunt I've ever happened on," Nebel said. "You get ones like this up there in Chicago?"

I agreed it was the damnedest.

We took turns carrying his bucket of berries. At a Mexican café, we stopped for dinner. I ordered a pile of food. Since my return, I couldn't stop eating. The food in skull-head land had sustained me, but I needed more, needed to recover whatever I had missed while I was there. I had acquired a particular liking for the baked tortillas that Amador had prepared. I described them to the waiter, and he said they could make them the way they made them in the place where the cook came from.

Nebel wasn't sure about spicy food but was willing to try. I was developing a liking for the young cowboy deputy, had been since before, when he took me to see Madame Blackley. At first I had thought him too much a cowboy to be a detective. He was young, but willing to learn. He asked questions and listened to the answers.

The waiter brought us beers. I wanted to talk to him about skull-heads, but first I needed to know if Gorman had described the place he had trailed me into, the not-Victoria outside the concert hall. He had. Nebel had also helped the marshal with the sand face dynamiting. I told him about the land of skull-heads. How I got there the two times.

"Prison warden told the marshal about your visit. And about how you'd vanished out of the building. Left his office and nobody saw you again."

I found that information interesting but also infuriating. I guess I thought that the marshal could have been a little friendlier or at least more cooperative. I didn't say any of that to Nebel—he worked for Griffin and would still be working for Griffin when I was back in Chicago. No sense disrupting his job by sowing mistrust or displeasure.

"All that poker stuff," Nebel said. "But why? And why hurricanes and why does Stephens want to help the hurricane creatures?"

Why indeed and why ask why. Lady Patricia asked a lot of why in her letter.

"In detective work, sometimes the Why is important and sometimes it isn't," I said. "Or, looking too much into the Why can become a distraction from catching the criminal. If you catch someone doing something, maybe it's nice to know why they did it, but the important part is catching them. That's with your normal crimes, like murder or horse thievery. With Stephens, we may never know the Why. How can we? His actions don't make sense to our brains. What or who makes the sand faces and why? And why do they seem to want hurricanes? Finding that information is for philosophers."

Which got me remembering that essay Lady Patricia was reading, and got me longing. What was it I wanted, exactly? I wasn't lonely. Or I hadn't felt lonely previous to my meeting her. I still don't know if she could have left skull-head land.

Griffin was sitting on my hotel room bed, accompanied by a ten-gauge.

"Afternoon, Marshal," I said. He swung the gun barrel at my leg, but I moved out of range. In retrospect, I wasn't surprised he attacked me, but my reaction—I saw the barrel coming at me *before* he moved. I took another step back and put a hand on my gun. I'd wait to see what else he might do before deciding whether to shoot him.

His swing and miss had thrown him off balance, but he used the motion to lurch to his feet. "I said I'd send you back to Chicago if you did anything in my town."

His shotgun pointed at the floor but it would be easy to move higher. I was fairly sure that he wouldn't shoot me.

"I'll leave when I'm ready," I said. "There's a killer loose in your town and I'm the only person who knows how to catch him. The best thing you can do is leave me to my job."

He said a few more things, but the crisis was over. He left. I wouldn't mind seeing the last of this place.

I woke from another burning instrument dream and got up for a drink of water. My watch showed midnight. I didn't try to get back to sleep. Instead, I walked to Sweetie's. A group sang cowboy songs around a piano played by a woman wearing a blue bonnet. I would have preferred a less boisterous crowd but stayed anyway. Sweetie, a tall woman with a gray streak in her dark hair, served me a cup of peppermint tea and said I could join the singers or sit and wait for an unoccupied lady. I sat on the sofa. A silver-haired man came in and joined the singers. The piano player smiled at him, and when the song ended they went upstairs, thus ending the revels. Two men left: one stayed and sat opposite me with his singing partner but he didn't appear to be interested in going upstairs with her. He was a cowboy with ears like salad plates; she was older, with the face of someone who's seen and experienced too many nights like this. A lady with piled-up dark red hair, like Lady Patricia from my dream, came down the stairs holding the arm of a skinny young man. Salad-plate ears saw them and hopped up from the sofa. The young men left together.

I moved over to the piano bench and plunked the opening keys for "Fading Lovers." The tired woman and the redhead came over and stood by the piano. The redhead looked nothing like Lady Patricia, but I decided I liked her anyway. I smiled at her and she smiled back, which is what they're supposed to do. I'm too cynical to pretend she actually cared, but not too cynical to recognize that I needed comfort tonight and would have to pay to get it. I reached the end of the song and asked her if she would be kind enough to take me upstairs.

This redhead wasn't as young as I had first thought, which was fine with me. I'm not fond of young whores. I would rather young women try something else before turning to prostitution, though most of them probably have. Women *do* have somewhat better lives now, but not all women. You don't get into this business because you like it. Sweetie's is a high-class brothel, and if it's like other high-class brothels, you can only work there when you're young and fresh-looking. Age and disease happens, and you get kicked out. Then you have to work your way down the chain.

Her name was Bessie. She hooked her arm in mine and walked me up to her room. I said I would like to pay for the rest of the night. "No sex," I said. "Tonight I just want to sleep next to a beautiful warm body." I stripped to my underclothes and climbed into the tall four-poster. In the morning when I woke, she was sitting up, reading a Dickens novel. That, and the freckles on her bare arms, made me think of Lady Patricia with her reading and questions.

Hearing me stir, Bessie looked over and said good morning. "I hope you slept well," she said. "You looked nice and relaxed."

She directed me to a bathroom down the hall, which had a flush-toilet and running water, and I did my business. Back in the room, she had removed her nightgown and lay on top of the covers. "I know you said no sex, but if you know how to pleasure a woman, that would be a nice way for me to start *my* day."

I stripped and climbed up with her.

———————

Friday evening, I set off to meet Malley, and we went to Branlat's. I won big. It wasn't that I didn't or couldn't lose a hand here and there, but I didn't lose many. And it wasn't luck, no run of unbelievable, perfect cards. Insight. I could read everybody. I knew when a man was bluffing, or when someone held a winner. I didn't feel like taking their money, but that's how it had to be. Word needed to get around.

After the game, I went to Sweetie's to find redheaded Bessie. I paid for the rest of the night, and for every night after. It cost a lot but didn't make much of a dent in my poker earnings. I admit it, we had sex that night, after Branlat's, and I enjoyed it, but most nights, I just wanted companionship, wanted something, someone, to help fill the lack. Bessie was smart and thoughtful. I knew that she didn't actually care about me, but talking was nice. I didn't spend any time trying to convince her to leave the business she was in. Any encouragement might just reinforce the futility of her situation. If it was futile. Who was I to judge?

Over the course of the week, I had smaller but still substantial winnings at the other places Malley took me, then another Friday conquering Branlat's. Middle of the next week, the hotel waiter brought a note with my breakfast, written in a clean, precise hand.

> If you care to, please consider this invitation to join an
> exclusive card game at Anderson's, in the rear of Hall's Hotel on
> Forrest Street, 3 o'clock Friday, August 16.

The note was signed R. Stephens. I was surprised he used his real name, if Stephens was his real name. Regardless, that was the name we knew him by. Criminals never believe they can get caught. In his case, the belief appeared to reflect the truth. Up to now.

Thursday night I told Bessie that it might be our last. I didn't know what would happen when I met Stephens, but I didn't think we would both walk away from the encounter. I couldn't tell her what I was doing, but she wasn't all that curious anyway. Maybe she liked me for more than the money, but she knew our relationship wasn't permanent. It's not just that way with whores. Real estate brokers, clothing salespeople, even doctors—everyone likes you while you're a customer or if they think you'll be a customer again, but at some point it's over. Everything ends.

22

Zlateh Again

I entered Hall's Hotel at 2:30, wanting to arrive before the other players. A man like a buffalo, minus the horns, stood at the bar. He didn't make mirror eye contact. A man sat at a back table, facing the door. He dealt cards to an empty table. His red vest was like the ones at Gregson's house. That and his unmistakable hair made me too eager. I reached into my duster. He glanced up, but he didn't act like he knew me. I avoided looking straight-on at his eyes.

"Are you the man who has been winning money from Victoria's prominent citizens?" Stephens's voice sounded like a turtle shell, but louder, like someone who shouts orders in a stamping mill or some other clangorous place. I don't know why, but I had thought he would have a mellow, persuasive kind of tone.

"Keep your hands on the table," I said. But as I was drawing my gun, something stopped my arm. A hunk of meat in the shape of fingers squeezed my wrist. The gun slipped back into its holster. What felt like another hunk of meat landed on the collar of my duster and yanked, pulling the fabric down to trap my arms. I struggled, but the only thing that happened was some of my shirt tore.

"I don't know why you're threatening me, but as you see, I have protection." He got up and walked toward me. His eyes tried to gouge a hole in me but were having trouble sticking. When he was close enough, he reached to take my gun. Smart guy, but I knew that. The tearing of my shirt had exposed Ring Hand's poker chip. On the way to my gun, Stephens's hand passed over the chip. He yelped and pulled back like something had stung him. I stomped one of the buffalo's insteps. He howled and let go. I stomped the other one.

The rest wasn't so easy. I aimed some punches into his belly. That was like hitting a sandbag. I was faster but couldn't get close enough to hit him while worrying about staying away from the meat at the end of his big arms. I also had to keep Stephens from getting behind me. I went in for another punch. No matter how hard someone's middle is, you have to keep working on it. He grunted, but the meat took hold of me. My feet left the floor. If he was going to crush me, I wanted him to finish quickly. Dangling there, I kicked as much as my legs could kick. Next thing, he toppled over me and we hit the floor.

A pair of boots stood a few feet away. A hammer clicked into business. "I wouldn't move," the owner of the boots said. It was Nebel. I dug my way from under the buffalo. Nebel had a shotgun pointed at Stephens. Grit stuck to my shirt where the buffalo-man had landed. The saloon smelled like someone had been cleaning fish. I brushed off the grit. More sandy grit lay around the buffalo's body. His head had a big red dent. From the butt of Nebel's shotgun, I assumed.

"I'm very glad to see you," I said.

"Marshal had the hotel copy any notes you got so we knew where you'd be. What's the play?"

"We take him in." I jerked a hand toward Stephens.

Nebel looked at Stephens; the eyes trapped him. Stephens started yelling at Nebel, at that stamping-mill volume. "Deputy! Get this goddam thief out of my sight. Him and his partner tried to bushwhack me. Me! You know who I am, deputy? Get moving!"

Nebel's gun wavered. I had to stop Stephens's mouth and close those eyes. I put a fist to his jaw. He went down; I yanked out my gun and pointed it at him. "I'm arresting you for the murder of Nathan Silverberg and the theft of monies entrusted to him. Also suspicion of arson, the house of Marshal Griffin and the Maggini music shop. Let's take him in, Nebel."

Something on my periphery moved. Nebel yelled and went down. His shotgun fired; pellets clanged into ceiling tin. The buffalo-man had his arms around Nebel's legs. The flesh had peeled away from his skull. I emptied my gun into his head. He released Nebel. A door slammed shut. Nebel was having trouble getting to his feet. I holstered my empty Bulldog, scooped the buffalo's gun from its holster, and lunged for the knob of the door Stephens had just gone through.

When you're chasing someone, you never go straight through a door. Or, let's say, it's rare that someone lives to do it twice. The back door opened inward. I turned the handle and pulled, keeping out of the opening. Then I ducked and rolled through. The idea is to give someone a small, moving target. I landed on a dull green, spongy carpet, rough, like the hide of a pig. Stephens hadn't stayed to shoot at me.

I checked the buffalo's gun, a Colt Army single-action .45 with no bullet under the hammer and the other five chambers filled. My .44s wouldn't fit, but it would be useful till I emptied it. I stuck it in my waistband and reloaded my Bulldog.

Stephens's flight surprised me. I hadn't seen him as the running type. Either his coming into contact with Ring Hand's charm had spooked him, or he was going toward a place he knew, a place that would give him an advantage. Ridged lines spread, fan like, across the carpet. I stumbled over a low wall that flexed like a tree branch. Careful of the bumpy lines, I took off again. But found that I couldn't run, couldn't even walk fast. Like when I was trying to catch up to Zlateh, except here, there was no wind pushing me. Stephens didn't appear to be having the same problem, but he was still in range. I pointed the buffalo's gun and screamed a booming sound. Nothing happened. I yelled it louder, twice. I must have missed. He didn't flinch or falter in his stride. Was that how I normally fire a gun? I spun the cylinder to check the loads. Still five, and none dented from the firing pin. I slipped it back into my waistband and tried with the Bulldog. I could trust my own gun. I yelled. Again, nothing. Stephens moved out of range.

I holstered it and followed, but I still couldn't run. Weights sucked at my feet. I moved slower and slower, dragging against the current. My lungs were heaving with the effort. I dropped to my knees. I crawled. Crawling was easier, but the rough carpet bothered my hands. I lay flat and pushed with my legs, sliding along the green carpet like I was swimming. Land-swimming . . . push-slide . . . push-slide, but I had to stop and breathe. My lungs couldn't burst, could they? That was just something people said. Filled to bursting, or some such phrase. I forced myself up to a kneeling position. Hadn't something like this happened to Moses on the way up Mount Sinai? But that was a desert.

Stephens had vanished over a green ridge. I stood and tried walking, a few steps, then more. Everything seemed to be working again. I scrambled up and over the ridge. A walkway led to a wider path. The walkway was springy, like the ridge, like the floor.

Not a floor. I wasn't inside a building. Above, darkness, the darkness of evening. The ridged carpeting, the slope, were leaves, huge leaves; the first walkway was a stem, the larger one, a branch. The branch-walkway was rough, covered with stiff fronds. It was wide enough for two people side-by-side. Silence surrounded us, the kind of silence that means life has stopped, that whatever else might be here has hidden itself or fled. Was everything running from us, or from something else?

A thicket of fronds slowed me. Stephens stopped. I couldn't see his arm, but I knew what he was doing. His shot didn't hit anywhere close. In this light and distance, shooting is a waste of bullets. I saved mine and kept moving. The gunshot echo faded, and another sound emerged, a dull, marching sound, many feet on a spongy carpet. A sound I've heard before.

He arrived at another branch, or maybe it was the trunk of what-ever plant this was. The darkness doubled, making it harder to judge distance, but I thought I had gotten closer to him. I drew the buffalo's gun and tried a chance shot, pulling the trigger like I always did. The bullet startled him. It passed close enough to remind him about me and slowed him enough for me to gain another foot or two. The trunk was steep, but not so steep that I had to put the buffalo's gun away and use both hands to climb. Something slowed Stephens. His body convulsed, leg twitching as if caught. That last jerk freed him. He started moving again, but I had shortened the distance. I spent some time aiming, and shot. I couldn't tell if I hit him, but he stumbled and slid, stopped himself, and lunged forward.

He was definitely moving slower. Maybe he had twisted an ankle. I thought that more likely than damage from my shot. His part of the branch leveled, giving him a chance to increase speed. I fired. He stumbled again.

The marching sound grew louder, but different, like the marchers had left the carpet and started up the leaf-slope. Whatever it was, however many there were, they couldn't all cross the stem together. Stephens's right arm swung around, and I flattened myself. Two shots, neither close, I'm happy to say. I saved my bullets and got up when I heard him moving. The branch ended at a wall, a wall of tree so wide it was hard to see the curve of its trunk. Clusters of fronds protruded from the trunk wall. Stephens climbed, using fronds for hands and feet. He moved at a diagonal, trying to get higher and put the trunk between himself and my gun. I fired. His leg jerked, then hung limp, but he made it around the curve. I stepped onto the trunk and moved laterally, thinking I would get below him. The fronds were stiff enough to walk on, but I had return the buffalo's gun to my waistband and use both hands.

Stephens wasn't where I had figured he would be.

A shot skimmed past my head, from below. Using the darkness and my expectation, he had tricked me. I drew the buffalo's gun and fired at what I thought was the white of his shirt collar. The slug hit him—he cried out, slipped, caught himself, then slipped again.

That last shot finished off the buffalo's gun. I tossed it into the void.

There was a branch to my left. I slipped down to it and flopped onto my belly. The branches were long ovals, wide enough for me to get comfortable. A bullet thudded into the surface under me. That was five.

From the sound, I thought he had a Smith and Wesson .44. It would be a six-shooter, but I couldn't assume that he kept a chamber empty. He had shot Solo with a hidden Colt Cloverleaf; I would have to be wary of that if I got close to him.

I risked a downward glance. He lay on a branch about ten feet below mine and offset by an arm's length. I pointed the Bulldog at the area below his white collar. His body jerked. I waited. He could be waiting too. He might be reloading.

The marching had become a shuffle. Sea rot rose ahead of it. Stephens hadn't moved. I expected he wouldn't until I reached him. Keeping my gun pointed at him, I descended. While I was occupied with stepping from the trunk to his branch, he rolled onto his side and lifted that Colt Cloverleaf. I shot it from his hand. I'd been meaning to hit his shoulder, but that was fine. The bullet went where I looked. He flopped onto his back. Blood stained his right side. It looked like I had hit him in the torso and both legs. One leg wound was just a graze; the other was deep. The body shot would have broken some ribs and messed up his insides. Maybe enough to kill him. That didn't make me any less cautious. His branch was wider than the one I had just left. I squatted beside him and checked for other weapons, found a billfold. He didn't open his eyes, and his breathing was bubbly sounding. A groan oozed from his mouth. I transferred his billfold to a pocket of my coat. In another of his pockets, I found a plain iron key, and put that with his billfold.

I prodded him. "I wouldn't mind if you told me where to find the money you stole, if there's anything left, and what this key goes to."

Pain burned into my lower back. I yelled and rolled over him, to his other side. One of my feet slipped, dangled for a moment. After getting all of me back onto stability, I realized that some wobbling thing was stuck to my backside. I felt around and yanked out a clasp knife. I stared at it. The blade was about the length of my pinky. It hadn't gone all the way in. Blood—my blood—smeared the blade.

My rear hurt like hell, but he hadn't had the strength to damage much. I jammed the knife into his shoulder and twisted. He screamed.

"Tell me about the key." I gave him a minute, then twisted the knife some more. His scream turned into words, but they didn't make any sense.

"Smoke flies from a crack in the pavement . . . crack in city street. Any city. Every city. Smoke flies . . . not smoke, insects, thick as smoke, waves of insects, many kinds, so many kinds. Numbers blacken the sky. They eat everything. Devour . . . they devour." His eyes closed, opened again, staring up as if seeing insects. And maybe he was. I fought the urge to look up.

"They collide with each other, collide with buildings. They shatter—some of them . . . shatter. Others burn. Ash falls, ash and insect fragments, there, a wing, there, an antenna, shards of carapace, broken heads with burning eyes. No one can breathe insect air. People collapse, gasping, choking on burnt and shattered insects, blind in the insect dark. A policeman fires his revolver into the air, again and again, then presses it to his skull for one final pull of the trigger."

He turned away from his insects and stared into my face. "They're everywhere. You know that."

It was time to get myself away. Taking him back for trial wasn't going to be possible. I couldn't carry him down the tree and fight my way past whatever was coming up.

Which had gotten closer.

Sound and smell increased. Stephens knew what it was, but he didn't live long enough to welcome it. I didn't feel for a pulse. Sometimes, you can see the life fizzle out of a person. I rolled his body into the void and listened to it flop and whoosh through the lower branches. Maybe that's disrespectful of the dead, even someone who tried to make *me* dead, but I was curious what effect his death would have on his allies. Assuming they were his allies.

I peered down the giant tree trunk, listening for any change. The darkness wavered, darkness within darkness, sounds so dark they penetrated my flesh, wrapped my spine from the inside. Whatever was coming . . . it froze me. My feet stuck to the branch. I became part of the branch. I was a frond, a frond on a giant branch. Insects buzzed my head, my frond-tip... I feared them, feared their devouring maws. They chewed on the branch, on me, on my arms, my face.... From above, a different sound, a not-insect sound, a sound that awakened me.

"Maaaa."

Ring Hand's goat—Zlateh, my rescuer—stood on a nearby branch. Her white fur glowed in the stifling blackness. She repeated her call. I didn't need a third one. I holstered my gun and climbed. The knife wound stung, and the back of my trousers was sticky-wet, but my blood wasn't pouring out fast enough to scare me. And Zlateh didn't wait. She leapt to the trunk and climbed like she was walking on a road. The other sounds climbed too. I didn't look down. Zlateh reached another branch and stepped onto it. We walked a good distance. The branch became smaller. It bent beneath our weight.

"Hey... Zlateh, are you sure about this?" I said.

She jumped. When I reached the spot she had left, she was waiting on another branch... the branch of a different tree? No hesitating— I jumped, grabbing stem and leaf, whatever I could hold. Leaves and fronds scraped my face. My legs swung into space, pulling at the rest of me. Something clamped onto my coat collar. Zlateh. She pulled me up. I lay on the branch, gasping, but not for very long. Zlateh nudged me to my feet. We moved off. I didn't want to know whether our followers could cross after us.

More of this went on, days of it, up a trunk, onto a branch, down a trunk. Some branches intersected with those of another tree, others required jumping. I paused from time to time, to listen for the marching sounds. For now, we had eluded them.

One final leap ended at a mesa of brown and red stone. We crossed it to a trail that led along the rim, a knee-straining series of switchbacks. The trail leveled, and ended at a door. The door to the music hall that I had followed Stephens through after Teddy's performance. I was glad to see *that* door. That door and I were old friends, comrades. A door to be treasured. It was unlocked. I thanked Zlateh and went in.

23

Goodbye, Victoria

I stepped onto the boardwalk in front of the concert hall and spent a minute or two orienting myself. The sun had been up a couple of hours. When I was ready, I walked toward the office of Dr. Morgan, who had stitched my head back together. My backside was stiff and throbbing. Not finding my wound exciting enough to put me in bed, she cleaned, bandaged, and sent me out, advising rest. Agreeing with her prescription, I went back to the Delmonico. I heaped my bloody clothes and got in bed. I had just enough energy to look through the contents of Stephens's billfold before drifting off.

Rapping on the door woke me. I changed into clean clothes and let Nebel in. He said the hotel people had let the marshal know I was back. It was the morning of the eighteenth; I had gone through that door the afternoon of Friday, August 16. Nebel and I had a drink from the bottle in my room and I described my chase after Stephens—the crazy terrain and the action but not the goat or marching crab creatures. I could have said more. I had told him about Zlateh and all that, from before, but I didn't want him repeating everything to Griffin and it wouldn't have been right to ask him to withhold things from his boss.

I gave him the billfold but kept the key. I had an idea of what it went to, and it was outside of Griffin's jurisdiction.

Nebel said that when he fell, when the buffalo-man grabbed him, he wrenched his knee. It took some time for him to get to his feet and hobble to the door. He saw the spongy carpet and distant branches, even took a step onto it, but didn't think he could follow with his knee paining him. He sent the bartender for Griffin. By the time the marshal arrived, the door showed a normal back alley. The scene had changed during the few minutes that Nebel took dragging a chair over so he could rest his knee.

"Remember that house I took you to, feller had rotted up his bed-room?" Nebel said. "Well, yesterday the dead man's nephew came to dispose of the property. I went through with him. Those vests and things that you said belonged to Stephens, well, none of them was there. Don't know when, but he musta come back and got 'em. Could've, anyway. Weren't no one watching the place. Guess he won't need them no more."

I agreed that was true.

"Well, time you went to see the marshal."

He didn't seem to want to take me, but I assumed there wasn't a choice. I had hoped to leave town without having to see Griffin again. Nebel's wrenched knee was still bothering him. With my sore and patched backside, I had no problem matching my walking speed to his. A dark-haired man of thirty or more, with a thick, oft-broken nose, sat at the front desk. "Marshal in?" Nebel asked; the man said sure is.

"That's Rowe," Nebel said, keeping his voice quiet. "Marshal finally hired someone to replace Gorman. He worked for the county sheriff in Goliad." Griffin's door was closed. Nebel rapped on it. "Shannon's here." We went in. Nebel put Stephens's billfold on the desk. Griffin glanced at it, then sat back and stared at me. His stare always made me feel like he knew what I was thinking.

"Heard you've become quite a card player. Must be a lot more profit-able than the detective business. It's nice not to have the constraints of being a public servant."

"I had to play, and I had to win, to attract Stephens's attention." Winning had been my tool. I hadn't thought much about the money.

However ... I had gathered a nice sum (minus what I'd been giving to Sweetie and Bessie), and ... I had liked getting it, liked it quite a bit.

I told Griffin the story I'd told Nebel. He always knew when I was leaving things out, but I don't think he cared anymore. "I wish you'd brought the body back for official identification," he said. He opened the billfold. It held $4,025 cash and some trade cards. One for a shipping insurance company, and five for a James R. Ross & Company Real Estate, James R. Ross, agent, with a Galveston address.

"Odd that there wasn't an office key, if that's his office," Griffin said.

"Maybe in his room, wherever that is. He wouldn't need his key unless he went to Galveston. I guess I'm headed there to find out."

My train was due to leave at 1:55. I divided the gold into two packages, putting one in each side of my saddlebags to make carrying easier, and checked out of the hotel—permanently this time. I went to Malley's office to say goodbye. As I plod along, I tend to discard my earlier life; seeing him again, talking about our past, had been a treat and a needed anchor to life outside the business.

"I'm tempted to go with you," he said. "It's been a while since I saw the old town. Less to draw me back with my parents dead."

We shook hands and parted. I sent a telegram to Rabbi Cohen: "Stephens dead, looking into affairs in other location." And a similar one to Llewellyn, except I told him where I would be and why. Nebel was waiting when I returned to the station.

"Supposed to report back that you took the train you said you was taking." He looked at his boots, then toward the tracks. Avoiding my eyes, I thought.

"Hope your knee is back to feeling good soon," I said.

"Thanks. I reckon it's been mighty interesting working with you. I'm sorry the marshal is so sore." He looked at me then.

I told him you can't be everybody's friend, but that I thought the marshal was a fine lawman. He agreed with that. Boarding time came. Nebel stood on the platform and watched the train depart. Not liking the idea of people knowing my itinerary, I got off in Rosenberg and found a stage to Houston. From Houston, I boarded a steamship traveling down the bayou to Galveston Bay and across to the island. Being on detective business, I went to a hotel rather than to my parents' house. I thought about sending a messenger to them with a note, but it was best if no one knew I was here. Same with the rabbi. I would see him when it was over.

The thermometer at the hotel had said ninety degrees. I didn't mind. The gulf breeze made it bearable. My eventual goal was to locate the office of James R. Ross & Company Real Estate and see who came and went. For now, I just walked. I needed to adjust, mentally and physically. Galveston was birth home. Part of me was always here. Being back helped fill that jagged hole from skull-head land. The island had shaped me, as it shaped everyone. Hurricanes, war, yellow fever. Islanders survive everything. So far, I had survived everything.

I passed what had been the Oyster Tavern and tipped my hat. The Tarpon would be close to eighty, wherever he was. I had lost his trail long ago. I hoped that my recent cardplay would please him.

The address was on Market, near 25th, a neighborhood where I could loiter without drawing attention. The area was busy enough and derelict enough to hide anyone. Dark curtains covered the James R. Ross & Company office windows. The door was solid. I watched for parts of two days, seeing no one. The first night, I watched to see if a light showed. I also spent some time in the courthouse, looking for any real estate transactions. I hadn't wanted to attract attention, but it became necessary to talk to people at neighboring businesses. The butcher, the store selling workingman's clothes, the bartender in the nearby saloon, the woman in the corner grocery. Nobody remembered Stephens. That shouldn't have surprised me. And now it would stay that way.

After dinner the second night, I went to try my key in the lock; it worked. I entered, shut the door, and locked it from the inside. Nothing stirred. I had brought a bulls-eye lantern. I lit it and lowered the flame.

The interior was bare.

No desk, or chairs, nothing on the walls. A back door opened to an alley, an ordinary alley. No back doors leading to other places, at least not at the present time. The key worked on the back door too. I slid the cover over the lens of my lantern to darken it, but I wanted *some* light. I eased a curtain over a couple of inches and sat on the floor to wait.

Outside, life passed the way it always did. I heard bits of it. Youths being youthful, a drunk singing "Carrie Anne," a street preacher looking for business, and others, unidentifiable in their silence. None of that outside life came in. Morning arrived. I left by the back door for a piss and a bite of eggs and sausage. I wouldn't have minded someone to share the watching with me. After breakfast, I risked going back in, through the rear, gun in hand, but no one had entered during my absence. I thought I would give it another night. This office must be something that Stephens had set up but not put into use. In other words, a waste of my time.

The next night, street life was much the same as the previous. I'm usually able to stay awake, but I think I dozed. The moonlight had changed. The shadow on the opposite wall . . . sand hill, growing . . . ocean rot smell. . . . My gun was out. I stopped myself from firing. Instead, I pulled the curtain over another inch; the shadow changed into nothing. Keeping my gun in my lap, I resumed the waiting.

The knob of the alley door turned. I had been dozing again; the sound caused my hand to tighten on the Bulldog. I gathered myself into a crouch and raised the gun to point at whoever was entering. The lantern sat on the floor. My other hand rested on the lens cover, ready to flip it open. The door swung in. Scant moonlight framed a man-shape. A dead-fish smell entered with the moonlight. I opened the lens cover. Its beam found a face. A bare skull. A skull-head wearing Stephens's red vest. The clasp knife was still lodged in his shoulder. I shot twice into his body. He fell. I moved closer and loosed two more bullets, then holstered the gun, picked up the lantern, and swung it down on the skull, again and again. Bones crunched. The flame went out. At some point, I dropped the lantern and fled through the open door.

Partway around the corner, I stopped. Someone would investigate the shots. I didn't want them to find Stephens's body. I went back and dragged the body down the alley. It was heavier than it should have been. On reaching a pile of broken-up timber, I decided to stash the body underneath. I made a space and left to find a wagon for hire and a can of kerosene. When I returned with a buckboard pulled by two horses, a couple of policemen were patrolling the block. I parked and waited for them to leave. Gunfire in this part of town wasn't something that would require a long search.

When I felt it was safe, I got the horses moving again and returned to the alley. The body was still there. I lifted it into the back, along with a pile of the wood. Foul-smelling grit rubbed off on my hands. Down island, at a swath of deserted beach, I stopped and gathered driftwood to add to what I had taken from the woodpile. I built a pyre, doused the body with kerosene, and watched from a dune until nothing remained but ash and embers. Then I went back to my room and slept.

We live our lives, most of us. We go from thing to thing and place to place, sometimes without moving. We acquire layers, for protection, for disguise, layers that sometimes sing like a rainbow on a sunny day. We lose some things and gain others, but sometimes the loss—no, not loss, loss sounds like an error. Sometimes a thing, a person, a part of us, is taken, stolen, despite vigilance, despite protection spells. But we still live our lives. Blood moves along the tracks, through depots, across rivers and valleys, making connections until the machinery runs down. Which it does, always.

The following day, I went to see Rabbi Cohen and told him most of what had happened after our last meeting. I showed him Lady Patricia's letter—I needed to be sure that he believed me. He said he knew the essay that Lady Patricia had been reading and was very impressed with its author.

"I had assumed that the sand faces were idols made to repel hurricanes," I said. "But the journal and my experience indicates the opposite. Those sand faces brought storms powerful enough to sink a civilization." I had decided that there were two kinds of skull-heads, from the different tribes, if you wanted to call them that. Ring Hand and the others in the saloon, and the dead kind that smelled like rotten fish—Ratface Conroy and the buffalo man. And Stephens.

"I think he's finally dead. I killed him over there, and I killed him here. That ought to be enough."

He agreed that it ought to be.

"I have been considering what we discussed before," he said. "The question of why Stephens would buy land if he was stealing money. Certainly not for investment. You weren't particularly interested in discovering his reasons. Has your thinking changed since then?"

I said that it had. He continued.

"My thoughts keep returning to the idea of home. A home in the United States for Jewish refugees, or a home for them in Palestine. A home for refugees of war or famine. All living things require a home. Why not these crab creatures, as you call them? Though their home is incompatible with ours, their desire for it is no less valid. Surely there are lands they can inhabit where we can coexist?"

I said I doubted that would be possible. "I don't think they live in the same world as us. Whatever that means—somehow a different realm, like something Jules Verne would imagine for one of his adventures. The storms are a bridge to connect their world to ours. To transform our world into what *they* need. I don't think the storms are powerful enough for that. If they were, we would already be gone. Maybe they succeed by doing a little bit at a time."

The rabbi needed to leave for one of his numerous appointments. Happy to be out in the sun and sea breeze, I accompanied him, to the synagogue, the jail, offices of various Galveston businesses. Between stops, we continued our conversation.

"The crab creatures aren't necessarily crab creatures," I said. "They're an approximation. Lady Patricia said my perceptions are formed by my experience and expectations. Our minds convert what we *see* into what we can *comprehend*. Maybe we could coexist with giant crabs, but that isn't what these things truly are. They're something else, something beyond our understanding."

Stephens must have been a regular person once, must have begun his life the same way we all do. At what point did he change, if he changed, to become an instrument of the crab creatures and sand faces? A card game? It's always a card game. Perhaps he lost to some sand face equivalent of Ring Hand, and had to spend the rest of his life and beyond servicing their plans. Which made me even happier that my game happened to be with the side that I wanted to support. I don't know that I could have beaten a malevolent Ring Hand.

PART III

Galveston and Chicago

Last night I almost dreamed it
But it dreamed me instead

—Jon Dee Graham,
"Home"

24

Business Over

With my Silverberg business ended, I returned to Chicago and ordinary detective work. The next jobs were reasonable—jewel thievery, murder, arson, international intrigue—and I dealt with them reasonably. Llewelyn wanted to find the aero club, as Dellschau had called it. From time to time he would ask me to go back through everything Dellschau said, to see if there was some other detail that might help him. Eventually, he retired to northern California. He said he was tired of winter. He's still looking for aeronauts, I suppose. I took over the agency, which means I don't have to run around the country anymore.

The work is good, but I don't need the money. Aside from my gold, I had all that cash, the odd bills and coins that I won from the skull-heads. I showed them to an expert at the University of Chicago. Well, most of them were quite rare. The man wanted to know where I had acquired them. I told him a Texas poker game. That was mostly true. I knew that the game hadn't been in Texas, but I started off there and it *was* a poker game. A certain amount of disbelief was involved—some of the currency was too pristine for its age—but the primary thing was that he wanted them. And to Chicago professors, Texas was still the wild west, and that could account for most anything. He made the university buy everything for its antiquities collection. They offered a lump sum and a monthly payment for thirty years.

I thanked Ring Hand for my good fortune, and I still wear that poker chip he gave me.

Sometimes, I wake in darkness and think I smell rotten fish and sea wrack—a moment of intrusion, then nothing. Sleep doesn't return easily. I fix a pot of coffee and sit at a window, seeing nothing. Or I go walking. Streets are different at night. A city street is never fully deserted. I always see someone, somewhere along my journey, but we never speak. The late night and early morning walker is a solitary beast. Memories of the Silverberg business flip through my head—the humid streets of Victoria, Gorman's burned face, Griffin and Marinella. On occasion I hear from Malley. He wrote when Marinella became Mrs. Griffin. I hope they live a life free from the kinds of nastiness I brought them.

Burning instruments eventually stopped invading my dreams. I don't know when the dreams ended, just that during one of my walks, the thought occurred to me that they had. The business was now an empty room, an empty house, a land once inhabited but now a scene of ruins, like the drowned city I walked through with Zlateh.

High-stakes poker games interested me more than they had prior to that business. Sometimes I played for fun. Chicago was a city with a lot of money, and I won a fair amount. Also, gambling houses hired me to force out the professionals, especially the cheats. It gave me great pleasure to join their games and take their money.

But life contained a lack, a small creature that shared my body. Sometimes it slept. For months I might even almost forget it existed. Then something would happen, some small thing that would cause the lack to awaken.

World's Columbian Exposition, 1893. They hired the agency to monitor gambling at the casino. I checked on my operatives who were doing the work, and afterwards I wandered the exhibits. The exposition was a crazy-huge thing, occupying nearly seven hundred acres, with scores of temporary buildings, canals, replicas of Christopher Columbus's ships, a moving sidewalk. A lot of electricity was involved. For weeks, I had been considering whether the exposition was something to visit or avoid. The job finally dictated the answer.

While riding in a Venetian gondola toward the horticulture exhibition hall, I saw a man walk across a bridge. It was Ring Hand. Or Captain Bellis, the man with the ancient face. His clothing was different—robes of some cultural or historical significance—but I recognized his walk. His carriage. I hopped off the boat as soon as I could and hurried back. Nothing. I wandered through the press of humanity. Then, in the horticulture exhibit, I turned away from a dazzling rainbow of orchids and collided with him. Close, the resemblance ended. Apologies and an offer of refreshment repaired the damage. He was a visitor from Salonika, Avram Modiano, a Jewish doctor who had learned English in Manchester.

He wanted to try American whiskey. The bars at the exposition were more expensive than the usual, but saved us from having to leave the grounds. We spent some time talking about Salonika and the Ottoman Empire. He called Salonika the pearl of the Mediterranean and the Jerusalem of the Balkans. I told him my family originally came from Vilna, the Jerusalem of Lithuania. I had visited Salonika on my last voyage as a sailor. My memories were of a crowded port inhabited by merchants and their customers from all over the Mediterranean and Turkey. I said I wished I had been able to stay there longer.

"The Ottoman Empire is doomed," he said. "Though all empires are doomed, even your American one."

"I wouldn't call it an empire, yet. Some want it to be, some don't. But sure, it will fall apart eventually. For now, it's an infant."

"Infant mortality is high."

We followed our whiskey with a beer. He was curious about the Jewish communities around the U.S. I told him something about

Galveston, describing it as an infant Salonika. "Though infant New York is more accurate. New York has the largest number of Jews. Recent immigrants from Eastern Europe live mostly on the Lower East Side. Those who's families arrived earlier, from Germany, live in other parts of the city. They don't mix."

Although he no longer reminded me of Captain Ring Hand Bellis, memories and imaginings suffused my thoughts, leaving me unsure whether I had truly visited Salonika or dreamt a voyage there with Captain Bellis. With Ferris's massive wheel as backdrop to a parade of elephants, I couldn't even be confident I was in Chicago. We made our goodbyes. I told him I would try to get back to Salonika someday.

The lack. What I have found, since my return to Chicago, is a distance from humanity. Not a disinterest—I care about people, about suffering, and joy, but I don't belong any more. That's an approximation, but it works. Ring Hand and Lady Patricia, she called them defenders against the storm. And said I was too. Was I somehow abandoning that duty, by returning to my former life? But I had completed my job, eliminating Stephens, in both places. I was free. I needed to be free.

Music has helped. I started playing again, first getting back into shape with piano, then I bought a cello. I took lessons and practiced a lot. Music introduced me to new people. I'm part of a fluid group who get together for fun. And, because the world has progressed, there are women who play with us, or rather, who let me play with them, because they have a lot more talent and experience than I do. Sometimes they indulge my whims, and we play the skull-head's dance music, and at night I try to dream of Lady Patricia.

Our viola player reminded me of Lady Patricia. I had grown accustomed to finding pieces of her in various women. That didn't bother me. Whatever I saw was my imagination, or mostly my imagination. I might have attempted to explore the viola player's resemblance further, but she was in a committed yet necessarily secret relationship with the wife of our clarinet player, a marriage of convenience; his interests also favored his own sex. Everyone got along nicely, and I was glad to be part of their lives.

One other thing, or rather, person, took me back to the exposition, also renewing my Victoria remembrances. A telegram came from Nebel. He was visiting Chicago for his job. I met him at the train station. He still had a young face, but had gained some weight in the four years since Victoria. He had left the deputy business. The owner of a meat packing plant had hired him as a bodyguard and assistant, and the job kept growing. They sent a lot of refrigerated beef through Chicago. Things had slowed since the stock market panic early in the year, but Nebel thought they would manage well enough.

"Everybody has to eat," he said. "And shipping rates have dropped considerably."

We took a streetcar to the Exhibition. The crowds impressed him. He had been to San Antonio and New Orleans, but Chicago was like another country, especially the exposition. The day was sunny, with a cool wind off the water. He marveled at the lake.

"All of that is fresh? I could swear I'm looking at the gulf."

I suggested that we could find a boat to take us out later, if he had time.

"How's the marshal?" I said. I told him I had heard about his marriage.

"Doing pretty well I guess. Got himself elected to the state legislature. Never could figure why he disliked you so."

"Just the way of things, sometimes. It was his town, but I had to do the job my way. He didn't like my way. Gorman died. And Marinella blamed me for the fire. Which did happen as a result of my way of doing things."

I described my final encounter with Stephens. I didn't want to ask, but I did it anyway—"Have those sand hills with faces appeared again?"

He hadn't heard about any, and there hadn't been bad storms in his part of the world. Maybe we had stopped their plan of destruction. Or reconstruction, as the rabbi might have said, looking at it from their viewpoint.

Nebel returned to Victoria, along with a check from me so he could buy a large share of the meat packing business he worked for.

That night, on one of my late night/early morning Chicago walks I passed a figure sitting on a stoop, hunched, head in lap. A nearby street-light illuminated the scene. The figure wore a red wool hat with a blue tassel. I couldn't see the face or determine sex. Normal walk etiquette dictated that I keep going. But I stopped.

"Do you need help?" I said.

The figure didn't respond. I moved closer. A moan pushed its way out. Closer, I smelled sea rot. The figure lifted its face, skull-head now visible in the streetlight's glare. It leapt from the stoop and knocked me to the pavement. Howling, I fought it off, my blows wild and panicked. At some point, I was running. I didn't look back. Block after block, and none of them familiar. The architecture had a twisted look, windblown, or half dissolved by acid. Fog clung to the buildings and writhed over the street. A tendril brushed my face and I wailed at a burning pain. More fog tentacles appeared. I pulled my jacket over my head and kept running. My head and shoulders felt warmer—was my jacket smoldering? I kept it tight over me.

Then, the buildings were gone. My feet slapped the boards of a pier. I reached the end and flew into dark water. I floated on a swinging cot; light stung my eyes. I closed them. Fingers stroked my forehead, gentle despite the roughness of their calluses. Some cooling jelly had been plastered to the skin of my face and shoulders. I found it hard to stay awake.

"He should come 'round soon," a booming male voice said, loud against my stinging eyes.

"Softer, Captain, please," a woman said. "You're not on the maintop."

Her voice was a familiar soothe. My eyes opened to meet the square face and piled red hair of Lady Patricia. I smiled up at her.

"We found you in the wreckage, on a section of roof," she said. "Parts of broken houses floating everywhere, and bodies. You were the only living one we found. You're sunburned, too." She helped me stand. Beyond the stern windows, the Galveston shoreline glistened in the morning light.

"No time to put back," the captain said. "Unless we meet a returning ship, you'll be with us for a while."

I said I didn't mind. Life on shore had grown constraining. And I was to share Lady Patricia's cabin.

"I'm serving as first mate, this voyage, so I have many duties. But there will still be time for leisure." She smiled.

"I can work my passage," I said. "When I've recovered."

"Good. We'll have storms, and clear sailing. With stops as needed for food, water, and trade." She took my face in her strong hands and kissed me, then went back on deck, leaving me to rest.

I woke, somewhat convinced that I had been dreaming. I was in my Chicago bed and my skin wasn't burnt, but I wouldn't call that definitive. I also woke feeling contented, thinking that soon I would find my lack diminishing the way those burning instrument dreams had. But there was something in the dream that I should have considered—floating wreckage of houses, bodies.

The exposition ended with the assassination of Carter Harrison, Chicago's popular mayor; soon after came the discovery of a mass murderer in our midst, killings so terrible they shocked even this imperturbable detective.

Ensuing years brought war, national expansion across the Pacific Ocean, motor vehicles, more electricity and telephones, new presidents, some birthdays. I went back to Galveston twice: for my father's funeral in '94 and my mother's four years later.

After the death of our father, my younger sister, Leah, along with her husband, Isaac, and their daughters, Miriam and Anna, had moved in with our mother. For my mother's funeral, I stayed with them, sleeping in the house of my childhood. My other sister, Naomi, lived two blocks away, with Morty and their three boys, Abe, Harry, and Jacob. Leah was the smartest of us. She ran our father's business but was in the process of selling it.

Malley came to my mother's funeral. It was good to see him. I wasn't planning any visits to Victoria. Some places . . . though not the place, or not the fault of the place . . . but an aversion existed. I hadn't told him anything beyond the fake immigrant colony scam. I suppose I could have, but I'm secretive about whatever business I'm working on. The fewer people who know, the less likely someone will talk to the wrong person. Probably true of any business.

"The Tarpon ended up moving in with a sister in Nevada," Malley said. "Though he must be long dead by now. I heard about it from a man who used to tend bar at the Oyster. I defended him on a charge of drunken fighting in a public place."

"Let's find a card game," I said. We visited a few taverns to make money off of sailors and drink to the Tarpon's memory.

I stayed in Galveston for a week. The kids all wanted to hear about the detective business, and I entertained them with adventures. Anna was eleven, Miriam thirteen. The boys climbed from fourteen to eighteen. I had seen them all so infrequently that their existence was always surprising. Children were mysterious. I suppose you have to have them to understand them.

Rabbi Cohen was still in Galveston. I expect he had no desire to leave. He and I took a long walk down the beach. We talked about skull-heads and sand faces, him being the only person besides Nebel with whom I could discuss that subject.

"Seeing my family," I said. "I shouldn't worry but I do. It's easy to live far away and not think about how exposed to storms Galveston is. If there's anyone you can enlist, people who will watch the island for signs, I would appreciate it."

He said he would do that.

25

Galveston, 1900

Nineteen hundred arrived, end of the old century or beginning of the new one, depending on your preference. I reached forty-five, which I'm told is the age of contemplation. My lack troubled me less. I survived, like people do. A group of employees offered to buy the agency, and I accepted. Forty-five is also the age of retirement, it seems. I still work a few jobs for them, squeezing out card sharps, various frauds. Nothing that sends me away from Chicago.

My musicians have tried to get me married, or at least paired with someone for dinners and parties. They introduced me to Mary Glaser, a sculptor. Nothing about her reminded me of Lady Patricia. I considered that a good development. Comes a time when you have to embrace the life around you. In the summer, she and I rented a Wisconsin lake house. Mornings, I fished. I practiced cello. She shaped her clay and sketched. Mary's work with clay had made her hands strong—so there *was* something she shared with Lady Patricia, those rough sailor hands.

Other people were in and out, to play music and frolic in the lake. Victorian modesty was not observed. We were back in town by September. The papers talked of a powerful hurricane striking Cuba, but I didn't foresee anything ominous from that.

I heard from the rabbi on Saturday, September 8, a long letter dated a few days previous. The part at the end scared me.

Something very Odd has appeared on the Bay side of Galveston. I have not gone to see them, but the newspaper described them thusly: "Sand hills have been found in Several locations, all places along the Bay where such Hills do not Naturally occur. The Sand has been treated with something to harden it, and Shaped into crude Faces. Rotting meat and parts of Animals were found in the mouths, recalling some form of Ritual sacrifice."

Now I Find myself Perturbed. I feel helpless yet possessed by the need to do Something. Please advise!

I tried telephoning from the agency. The operator couldn't connect me. I went to Western Union and sent a telegram, telling the rabbi to warn as many people as he could and take his family off the island. I sent the same message to my sisters. Later in the day, people in bars and restaurants were saying that a ferocious hurricane had struck the gulf coast. Islanders were accustomed to flooding from storms. We called them overflows. Water came, water went. But the lack of contact worried me. Overflows don't destroy telegraph and telephone lines. I needed more details.

A reporter I knew had gone to work for Hearst's new paper, the *Chicago American*. I called on him. Baker—the reporter—showed me proofs of the evening edition: "Island City Swept by Waves, Bridges Destroyed . . . Wires to Main-Land Gone . . . steamer driven two miles inland."

I kept reading. "The bridges are four in number, three for railroad uses and one the Galveston County public wagon and pedestrian bridge. It seems hardly credible that all those bridges could be swept away without the city suffering tremendously in the loss of buildings, general property, and lives."

It chanced that a vacationing Texas doctor named William

Crosthwait had come into the *American* building hunting news of Galveston. Hearst wanted to send a train filled with doctors and medical supplies, and asked Crosthwait to organize the job. Baker took me to Hearst's office while all this planning was happening. Hearst asked questions about Galveston and what I did. He wasn't familiar with the agency but thought my skills might be valuable.

"You can make a plan but think fast, decide what to do if the plan isn't workable and act as needed?"

I said that described me pretty well.

"He can handle it, Chief," Baker said.

Hearst had Crosthwait tell his secretary what sorts of supplies they would need, and while that was happening, Hearst telephoned the Santa Fe railway office and asked them to prepare a fast train. He wrote a check for $50,000 and told his secretary to cash it for incidental expenses. The secretary and Crosthwait went off to recruit doctors and purchase supplies. I left to find a federal judge to deputize me, figuring that with whatever chaos we would find, an official designation would be useful.

On the eleventh, the *Tribune* printed a long list of victims. I recognized some names. The paper said there were more than 1,000 dead. The city was now under martial law.

These ongoing reports made me anxious to be off. By the twelfth, the rains from the hurricane were hitting Chicago. What a storm! Our train left early on the thirteenth. I brought all the papers with me and tried to comprehend the enormity. My sisters? Their husbands and children? Hearst said that a lot of what had gotten printed was extrapolation and exaggeration. They just hadn't been able to put enough people on the island to document the true situation. One of his people, Winifred Black, was the first newsman—newswoman—in there. Everyone else based their stories on talking to whatever survivors filtered into Houston. But still, even if half was exaggeration, the remaining half was a very serious calamity.

The train reached Houston around midnight. Winifred Black met us at the station. Hearst's aid train was a result of the news she had sent back from her infiltration of Galveston, and afterward, he put her in charge of setting up a hospital in Houston. She seemed tough enough to handle the job.

She told us about her adventures getting into Galveston. "I put my hair up under a hat and dressed as a boy. I snuck in with a crew of workmen. Two of them were in on it. They shielded me. Sentries everywhere, with bayonets! To keep out looters. Once I was there, I went around talking to people. What I saw, well, you'll see it yourselves. People are numb. But they're working, clearing wreckage and burning the dead. No choice. Too many to bury! The stench is awful. They're saying three thousand to ten thousand people killed and from what *I* saw, it's *a lot* closer to the higher number."

One of the Hearst people gave Crosthwait a thick roll of twenties and told us to go on to Galveston. An hour later, we caught a train to Texas City, getting there about three in the morning. Texas City is the last stop on the mainland, across the bay from Galveston. Normally the train would keep going, over one of the railroad bridges, but all of them were gone.

We were seeing a lot of downed trees, collapsed buildings, but nothing like what we would find on the island. A steamer was stranded in shallow water. I bellowed over to them. They lowered a boat and rowed across to see what we wanted. The ship was the *Kendall Castle*, of England. We hired sailors to take us to the island, for $20. I rode with Crosthwait in the first boat. We jolted through debris. Here and there bodies floated, adults, children, cattle. We became aware of a glow over the Galveston beach front, across the island from our destination on the bay side.

"Burning bodies," one of the sailors said. "Hundreds and hundreds. They ferried corpses out into the gulf and dumped them overboard. Next day those bodies started washing up on shore, even the ones they weighted. The ocean didn't want them. Now they're burning every corpse they find."

A weird compression, more numbness than pain, filled my head. Bodies. I've said before—I have a knack for discovering them. Finding a body here or there, when I'm looking, that's a feeling that guides me. Here . . . in this bay of death . . . too many bodies were calling. I couldn't think yet about who might be among them. The stench increased. Galveston's odor—it would sicken anyone, but to me, that bottom of the ocean rot . . . Silverberg, Victoria, Stephens. I wasn't sure I would be able to function . . . I . . . Stephens, looming gigantic, his red eyes roasted my flesh. Shriveled strips floated on the waves, adhered to the sides of the boat, and the ocean, all its weight above, squeezing me into nothingness. I swam into a cave, a cavern so vast it held the world, and beyond, the sparkling Mediterranean of Salonika's harbor. Captain Bellis gave the order "Moor ship!" and our boat thumped into the remnants of a Galveston pier.

Someone led us to the Tremont Hotel. With my dazed head plus the ruins making the city unrecognizable, I don't think I could have found the way without help. Hotel people said that the water in the lobby had been four feet deep. The hotel stood at the highest point on the island. Receding water had left a coating of slimy crud that they were still cleaning. Scores of people had sheltered in the upper floors. A clerk found us beds; I would be sharing a room with Crosthwait and another doctor. Not that we had time for more than a nap. Sunrise meant that our work would begin.

What the night had hidden, daylight showed. I don't have the words. Maybe you've seen the photographs, even the moving pictures made by a man from the Thomas Edison company. Magnify that and add color, sound, smell. Corpses of cows, horses, dogs, people. Every structure close to the gulf, gone. Homes had been lifted from their supports and carried elsewhere, some lowered intact, some shattered. Wind and waves sculpted a wall of debris thirty feet high that helped save parts of the Eastern side of the island, though elsewhere it had acted as a dam, collecting the water that came in. And underneath all that . . . people buried, a few still alive. Some wanted to burn the entirety, but first the living, if any, needed to be freed.

The relief committee people had assigned Ball High School as our headquarters. Like everywhere else, the building stood amidst piles of wreckage, and the structure had suffered, though it fared better than many. The doctors got to work, patching the patchable. I found the rabbi there. He was on the relief committee, running the hospitals. His clothes were torn and dirty. Seeing him . . . well, if he was here, the situation was well taken care of.

His family had survived. His house was damaged but livable.

"The water kept rising. Mollie played piano and I sang Gilbert and Sullivan till we decided to leave. We went next door, to the Lees' house because it was more strongly built. We had to carry the children. Roof slates flying everywhere, water up to our shoulders. Mr. Lee and I cut holes in the floor to let the water in, to keep the rising flood from pushing the house off its foundation."

He stopped and looked at me. "Your sisters . . . have you heard . . . ?"

I hadn't.

"Leah and Isaac, Naomi and Morty, the three boys—neighbors found their bodies. They were all at Naomi and Morty's house. It collapsed on them. Miriam and Anna, we don't know. . . . Please forgive me for not telling you sooner."

I could grieve later. For now, there was work. The rabbi estimated that forty to fifty of Galveston's Jewish community of nearly one thousand had died in the storm. I thought about people I used to know, the former sweetheart I had last seen at my cousin's wedding, at the commencement of that Silverberg business. She turned up alive, though her eldest child died, swept out into the darkness. One of many.

"Isaac Cline from the weather office survived; he lost his wife but saved his children. He said the storm contradicted all experience. After passing Cuba, hurricanes never move into the gulf, strengthen, and strike Texas as this one did. And the day of the storm, the waves were terrifyingly high despite moving against the wind, which was blowing from the bay side. He knew that if the wind changed, the island would be covered, or worse."

Like something was holding back the full force of the waves, letting it build up for a smashing blow.

We were in a classroom that the rabbi was using as an office. People came and went, taking towels, bandages, whatever was in there, and we didn't try to hide our conversation, until a moment of silence, then, after someone left, Rabbi Cohen closed the door. "Listen: I saw the crab creatures! I might have been asleep, but I saw them. They were out in the worst of the high water, breaking houses apart, piling debris, building the wall. If not for your accounts, I would think I had been addled by the storm."

He looked at me with . . . relief? . . . expectation? "Well," I said. "It's . . . we knew that wasn't a natural storm, or . . . was *more* than a natural storm. Honestly, I don't know if you should keep living here."

Someone knocked, and the rabbi got up.

"I don't know if *anyone* should keep living here," I said.

"But it's my home," he said.

He opened the door. A nurse came in with a cart of bandages. I unloaded them onto a shelf. After she left I said, "Likely that others saw or dreamt the same thing. They just didn't know what they were seeing. They didn't have the context."

We left the door open, and the flow of people needing things kept us from talking any more about that subject. For the rest of the day, I helped in the clinic. After dinner I rested, watching children play with bits of cloth and wood. Children can always play. One was using a crab-like twist of cloth to build a wall of splinters, echoing Rabbi Cohen's dream-tale of crab creatures. Had these children experienced the dream too? They say that children are more perceptive than adults.

I slept on a cot at the school. The next morning, I walked across masses of slime and detritus that had replaced the wide and once-lovely streets. Piles of wreckage hid bodies and parts of bodies. The horror of lifting a shattered wall fragment to find a child's amputated foot. The clinging awful stench was a living beast, but it was different from that ocean rot of Stephens and the crab creatures. This was the essence of death *and* life. Survival. The smell of humanity dying and simultaneously birthing itself. The other rot was only death, no, far beyond death and into the stale realm of the afterdeath.

Seeing a flaming pile of wreckage and bodies near the beach, I recalled my burning of Stephens. Eventually the sight of these pyres occurred so often it became inconsequential.

These piles of sodden plaster, roof slates, bricks, wood, ocean sludge—the terrain of skull-head land in its pre-hardened state. That barren landscape originated as something like this, chopped and blended and spat out to dry and die, land where life can never form again. I remembered my Lady Patricia dream from long ago, her tale of destruction. Had anyone been flung from here into skull-head land to join Ring Hand's fight?

Naomi and Morty's house didn't look like it had ever been a house. Everything was a heap, a heap that included debris from elsewhere, other houses, other bodies. The house next door was upside down. I discovered later that it was actually from across the street. For a time, I stood silent. My older sister and I had never been close, and I wasn't fond of her husband, an accountant for the Kempner businesses who liked to criticize me for leaving the family.

I mouthed the same prayer fragments I had used for Silverberg and went to see what was left of Leah's house—my childhood home. Which had survived. Damaged, like everything. Windows broken, but the roof looked intact. The sight of it, standing . . . nothing prepares you . . . the salt, everywhere the brackish water, cisterns spoiled by ocean, my own drip wetting my cheek to dry in the sun, leaving crusts, leaving the deep and unbidden emptiness where slivers of gold entwined with smoke and lavender attempt to weave survival. The gulf after a storm laughs at us, sparkles and laughs while dolphins play.

Within the house, something clattered. I took out my gun and went inside. Two young women stood in the kitchen. I put my gun away.

"Uncle," the taller one said. "How did you get here?" We embraced. They were my nieces.

When the storm began, they had been at a friend's house; they survived in a stranger's attic, packed in with a dozen others. They didn't want to talk about it and neither did I.

Survival makes little sense. Sometimes our plans save us, sometimes we need luck. Choices. We make them even when we think we don't. Even folding a bad hand doesn't guarantee a better hand in the future. What saved the house was the tin roof staying on.

"Mama had some men replace all the roof nails just over a month ago," Anna said. "Bang bang, bang bang, going on for days."

"Maybe she knew this might happen," Miriam said.

One choice saved the house, but another meant she wasn't here to see the success. I fetched my bag, and we started the job of cleaning the crusty layers of gunk.

Clara Barton soon arrived on the island, leading the Red Cross. She organized the distribution of clothing and construction of temporary housing. In order to recover, people need shelter. They need to feel safe.

With travel from the island having gotten easier, I decided it was time to take my nieces to Chicago. I gave the rabbi permission to use the house as temporary shelter for families who needed it. I wasn't ready to let the place go. We boarded a steamer for New Orleans, and from there a train to Chicago.

Chicago worked for a while. The girls went to school. My sculptor lady liked to have them visit her studio. She took them to drawing classes. They resumed piano lessons. I lived mostly as I had, adapting where necessary. Changing after a life alone wasn't easy. What did they think of me, these orphan girls?

Turned out they were curious, and worried.

"Uncle, where do you go, when you're sitting here but not here?" Anna asked. "Your body is in the chair, you're holding a book or a newspaper, sometimes you're even speaking with us, but you're also somewhere else."

They had obviously been talking about me. I was glad they cared. I told them about my lack, about Silverberg, everything. They understood lack and loss better than I did. After that conversation, I was hoping for a dream visit with Lady Patricia, but you can't always summon what you want.

Winter was difficult. They had to learn a new language of dressing and acting. In Galveston, even if the temperature was low in the morning, by lunchtime it had usually risen to a comfortable place. A Norther might blast you with freezing weather, but it never remained long. Here, if a day started cold, it stayed that way or got even colder.

We lasted till the end of the school year, then moved back to the island.

Galveston was renewed. After the disaster, people from everywhere gave to the relief of the city, rich people, poor people, foreign governments. The contributions reminded me of Silverberg, the funding for the colony that never was. There were still people willing to give, to help. And people who had sworn they were leaving Galveston either stayed to rebuild, or returned, like us.

The crab creatures and the sand faces didn't succeed, this time. They would need to find a home elsewhere.

As terrible as the Great Storm had been, as massive the destruction, the city remained. A more powerful storm might wash it away, like Indianola or the Chrystal Islands. Maybe our technology will save us. There's a plan to build a sea wall that will deflect the force of the waves, and another plan to raise the island's grade. Galveston will still be a big pile of sand, but at a higher elevation and sloped to conduct water away from the center of town.

I've said before, the island draws you back. A pile of sand twenty-five miles long, but it's a permanent attraction, a home that won't grant release. It was my nieces' home. It was my home too. I even joined the congregation of Rabbi Cohen's synagogue. I still don't care much for religion, but the companionship, the community, is necessary. With my nieces—my adopted daughters—I'm part of that community. I have to be. Someone has to watch for a return of those sand faces. I'm still here.

Acknowledgements

Thanks to: Gavin J. Grant and Kelly Link of Small Beer—your edits improved and enlightened, and Small Beer's proofreader, Rebecca Maines; Jon Langford—looking at his art (especially the skull-headed cowboys) in his book *Nashville Radio* helped my ideas coalesce. The Greene County Library (as usual) for inter-library loans and other assistance finding things, especially Amy Margolin, Karl Colón, and Tamar Kreke. Catherine Best at the Briscoe Center for American History at the University of Texas, for looking up resources for me to pull when I visited, and for the librarians there who loaned me a camera to take pictures of maps, and later, Marisa Jefferson and Aryn Glazier for finding, digitizing a tape of Rabbi Henry Cohen speaking, and sending me the file. The Texas State Historical Association online resources provided much information on the history of Victoria and the Gulf Coast area.

For indispensable help with poker, Derek Barker and Rich Malley.

Readers who looked at various drafts, Rebecca Kuder (always), Steve Connell, Daryl Gregory, Susan Jett, Nancy Jane Moore, Paul Witcover. For help with Spanish, Ruth Hoff, and for German, Gudrun Eberhardt, Anne Eberhardt, and Pascal Hitzler. For advice on historical research and writing, Matthew Goodman, Howard Waldrop, and Marley Youmans.

For music, Steven R. Smith and his solo guitar album *Old Skete*. When I didn't feel like writing, or only had a few minutes during a lunch break from my job, I would start the album and immediately be there. Also, Tim Kerr and Jerry Hagins, for *Up Around the Sun*, which formed a soundtrack to writing the poker scenes.

Writing happens in various places, restaurants, cafés, libraries, hotel rooms, my desk, the dining room table. One of my favorite places is Emporium Wines & the Underdog Café in Yellow Springs. It's the soul of the town. If I'm stuck on something I can look up and spy on people. Sometimes I get there late and can't find a table, but most days it's fine and I get a lot done.

I read too many books to list them all. Particulars: *A Pecos Pioneer* by Mary Hudson Brothers; *Kindler of Souls: Rabbi Henry Cohen of Texas* by Rabbi Henry Cohen II; *Crossing the Rio Grande: An Immigrant's Life in the 1880s* by Luis G. Gomez; *African Americans in South Texas History* edited by Bruce A Glasrud; *The Tejano Community, 1836-1900* by Arnoldo DeLeón; *Galveston, A History* by David G. McComb; *Storm of the Century* by Al Roker; *Through a Night of Horrors: Voices from the 1900 Galveston Storm*, edited by Casey Edward Greene and Shelly Henley Kelly; *The Last Stitch* by William L. Crosthwait, M.D. and Ernest G. Fischer; *The History and Heritage of Victoria County* (3 Vols.) by Victoria County Genealogical Society; *History of Victoria County* by Victor M. Rose; *The Diseases of Society: The Vice and Crime Problem* by G. Frank Lydston; *The Education of a Poker Player: Including Where and How One Learns to Win* by Herbert O. Yardley.

I mangled parts of William James' lecture/essay, "The Dilemma Of Determinism," giving them to a character as his speech and quoting from its original publication in the *Unitarian Review* September 1884. Text for the settlement brochure was adapted from an 1893 map of the Port Lavaca Development Company's Fruit Farm and Garden Lands in Calhoun County, Texas. The item about L. Herman and Polish Jews attributed to the *Victoria Advocate*, Saturday, October 27, actually came from *The Canadian Crescent* (Canadian, Texas), Vol. 2, No. 2, Ed. 1, Thursday, November 8, 1888.

Some historical figures were abused in the making of this novel. Charles A. A. Dellschau was a butcher and folk artist from the late 19th and early 20th century. He created paintings and narrative about the Sonora Aero Club and its flying machines. Singer/fiddler/bandleader Teddy Wells is based on Bob Wills (born in 1905, after the time of the novel), but less the real Bob Wills and more the character in the 1941 film, *Take Me Back To Oklahoma*, in which Wills and his Texas Playboys arrive in Peco, Dakota Territory, playing and singing on the top of a stagecoach.

Henry Cohen was born in London in 1863. He was the rabbi of Galveston's Congregation B'nai Israel from 1888 to 1949, and died in 1952. As an organizer of the Galveston Movement, from 1907 to 1914, he helped approximately ten thousand Jewish immigrants from Eastern Europe enter and settle in the U.S.

Madame Annie Blackley, clairvoyant and philanthropist, was born into enslavement in Falmouth, Virginia. She came to Victoria in 1882 at the age of 42 (though some accounts put her arrival around 1868). Blackley was widely known as the Seer of South Texas because of her clairvoyant abilities.

The goat is borrowed from the Isaac Bashevis Singer short story, "Zlateh the Goat."

Robert Freeman Wexler's novel *The Painting and the City* has recently been released in paperback by the Visible Spectrum and his short story collection *Undiscovered Territories: Stories* came out in late 2021 from PS Publishing. He was born in Houston, Texas, and currently lives in Yellow Springs, Ohio, with the writer Rebecca Kuder and their child. His website and blog are at robertfreemanwexler.com

SHIRLEY JACKSON AWARD WINNER
ADAPTED INTO THE TV SERIES, MONSTERLAND, ON HULU

"A bleak and uncompromising examination of 21st century masculinity through lenses of dark fantasy, noir, and horror." — Laird Barron"

"Profoundly human, deeply flawed characters. What sets this collection of short stories apart is the way the supernatural, magical and horrific are utilized like a light source, illuminating dark places while casting even deeper shadows. Ballingrud's writing is piercing and merciless, holding the lens steady through fear, rage and disgust, showing a weird kind of love to his subjects, in refusing to turn away, as well as an uncompromising pitilessness."
—*Toronto Globe and Mail*

paper · $16 · 9781618730602 | ebook · 9781618730619

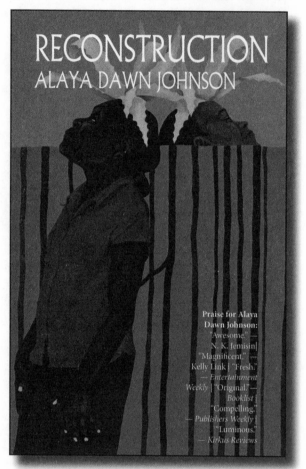

"In the title story 'Reconstruction'—one of two stories original to the collection—Sally uses her grandmother's spells to help protect a Black Civil War regiment while meditating on anger. These ten immersive stories embrace multiple speculative genres and take place in worlds both real and unreal. Much like *Lovecraft Country,* the stories combine horror and fantastical elements with anti-racist themes." — Margaret Kingsbury, *Buzzfeed*

"Johnson is one of the few writers in the genre who handles high emotion without preciousness, and she brings an almost unbearable pathos to many of these stories." — Simon Ings, *The Times of London*

"Vivid, imaginative, and often brutal prose." — *Chicago Review of Books*

paper · $17 · 9781618731777 | ebook · 9781618731784

"Each and every story in *Big Dark Hole* stands distinct in my memory. . . . Ford employs the tools of fantastic fiction to explore the strangeness of twenty-first-century American life." — Matthew Keeley, Tor.com

"One can encounter a myriad of strange and otherworldly things in a big dark hole; sometimes, we discover these holes in the most unexpected places. This new short story collection explores the extraordinary that lurks just behind everyday life. . . . Seamlessly blending the surreal with the mundane, Ford gives readers an innocuous ride to places they never knew they wanted to go." — *Library Journal*

paper · $17 · 9781618731845 | ebook · 9781618731852

"A synthesizer of the domestic & the fantastic, of soaring myth & the grittiest realities, of lewd dialect & high lyricism."
— KAREN RUSSELL

DANCE ON SATURDAY

ELWIN COTMAN

"Inventive, incandescent stories, rich in strangeness. Elwin Cotman's writing is a tonic to ward off drabness and despair."
— KELLY LINK

NPR BEST BOOKS OF THE YEAR · PHILIP K. DICK AWARD FINALIST

"Cotman wields a compelling literary voice packing both a wallop and a deft touch." — *Pittsburgh Post-Gazette*

"The core of the book is a cleareyed survey of the complexities of Black American experience, distilled in a few lines from the title story: 'I hated the powers for what they had done. But I learned the pride. That I was of a people who could take all the hate and poison of this world, and laugh, and go dance on Saturday.'" — Amal El-Mohtar, *New York Times Book Review*

paper · $17 · 9781618731722 | ebook · 9781618731739